The Secret Life of Shirley Sullivan

Also by Lisa Ireland

Breaking the Drought
Feels Like Home
Honey Hill House
The Shape of Us
The Art of Friendship

The Secret Life of Shirley Sullivan

LISA
IRELAND

MICHAEL JOSEPH
an imprint of
PENGUIN BOOKS

MICHAEL JOSEPH

UK | USA | Canada | Ireland | Australia
India | New Zealand | South Africa | China

Michael Joseph is part of the Penguin Random House group of companies whose addresses can be found at global.penguinrandomhouse.com.

Penguin Random House Australia

First published by Michael Joseph in 2020

Cover photography and illustrations by Miguel Sobreira/Trevillion Images, Macduff Everton/Getty Images, Valeri Hadeev/Shutterstock, Tarapynia/Shutterstock
Cover design by Louisa Maggio © Penguin Random House Australia Pty Ltd
Author photograph © Nikita Cherry
Typeset in 12/16.5 pt Minion Pro / Adobe Caslon Pro by Midland Typesetters, Australia
Printed and bound in Australia by Griffin Press, part of Ovato, an accredited ISO AS/NZS 14001 Environmental Management Systems printer

NATIONAL LIBRARY OF AUSTRALIA

A catalogue record for this book is available from the National Library of Australia

ISBN 978 1 76089 559 4

penguin.com.au

FSC www.fsc.org MIX Paper from responsible sources FSC® C009448

For all the women who paved the way,
most especially my mother, Lorraine

Chapter 1

Saturday

Tina, the receptionist, smiles as the automatic glass doors close behind me. 'Good afternoon, Mrs Sullivan. Lovely weather we're having.'

I make my way across the carpeted foyer to the imposing marble-topped reception desk and sign the visitors' book. 'It *is* a beautiful day. Looks like summer is getting ready to make an appearance.'

She nods enthusiastically and prattles on about her plans for the weekend while I cluck and nod, feigning interest in her social life like a benevolent grandmother. She talks about camping or hiking; I'm not sure which, because after a minute or two I tune out and start thinking about my own weekend. I create a mental checklist of all the tasks I have ahead of me to make sure tomorrow will go off without a hitch. I feel a bit like a secret agent.

When Tina runs out of steam about her weekend plans I force myself to engage by asking her how things are going with the new boyfriend. She blushes before launching into a fresh round of chatter. Obviously I make all the right noises, because when she pauses she's looking at me with affection. 'Where's your daughter today, Mrs Sullivan?'

'Oh, one of the grandchildren had something on so I caught the bus. Didn't want to let Frank down. He'll be expecting me.'

She pats my hand. 'You two are so sweet. You give me hope, you know? My mum and dad got divorced when I was eight years old, but when I see you and Mr Sullivan, well, it reminds me that true love really does exist. He'll be pleased to see you.'

Maybe he will. It depends what kind of day he's having. On a good day Frank's eyes light up the second he sees me. 'There's my girl, my bride,' he says proudly. He sweeps me into his arms and twirls me around. For a moment the years melt away and we're two young lovers dancing at the Palais Royal. But on a bad day he calls to the nurse to complain about the silly old woman who's wandered into his room.

Lately there have been more bad days than good.

Of course I don't say this to Tina. Instead I say, 'Thank you, sweetheart.'

'You'll find him in the courtyard, getting some sun,' she says, and I smile in thanks as I head off to another set of glass doors.

I make my way along the wide central corridor, passing a number of bedrooms with engraved numbers on their doors. The carpet in here is utilitarian – flat in pile and beige in colour – but the walls are painted in a soft blue hue and there's a mural, a tableau of clouds and trees and flowers and birds, on the wall outside the main lounge area. Once I pass the dining room I turn right and make my way down a narrow corridor, stopping at the entrance to the dementia ward to punch in the code that allows me access.

My gut clenches every time I walk through these doors. Here all pretence that Sunset Lodge is some type of holiday resort for 'seniors' is gone. There's no carpet – the floors are covered in mottled grey linoleum – and even the heavy scent of disinfectant doesn't mask the ever-present odour of urine. No one's bothered to paint a mural in here. It's so depressing I don't know how Frank stands it.

I make a quick detour to Frank's room on my way outside. One of the carers, Glenda, sees me and sticks her head in the door. 'He's in the courtyard, Mrs Sullivan.'

'Thanks, Glenda. Just thought I'd do a wardrobe check while he's not here. Fiona's taking me shopping next week so I'll get Frank a few bits and pieces for summer. I might get rid of some of these old things and pack them up now. You know how sensitive he can be about people touching his things. No sense in upsetting him unnecessarily.'

Glenda smiles and nods. 'Good thinking. Let me know if you need a hand taking anything to the car, won't you?'

I nod, not bothering to repeat the story about the bus. I pull a folded-up shopping bag out of my handbag. 'I'll just pop a few things in here. I'm sure Frank will never notice.'

She leaves me to it and I quickly scan the contents of Frank's wardrobe, deciding what can stay and what needs to go. I grab a few sets of underwear and socks, a pair of trousers, some T-shirts and the green woollen jumper I knitted for his eightieth birthday.

I leave the overstuffed shopping bag by the bedroom door and pause to use the mirror in Frank's ensuite to check my appearance. My hair is still looking good after yesterday's weekly trip to the salon, and the pink tones in my favourite silk scarf give my complexion a pleasing colour. Satisfied with what I see, I touch up my lipstick and make my way to the courtyard.

Frank is sitting in a wicker chair under the shade of the jacaranda tree. His legs are stretched out in front of him and his trouser legs are rolled up so his skin catches the dappled sunlight. He's always been a sunworshipper.

My pink-coated lips form a wide smile as I wave to him, but he continues to stare into the middle distance. There's not a flicker of recognition on his face.

Today is not a good day.

One of the male carers – a new one whose name I can't recall – places a garden chair next to Frank and beckons for me to sit. I thank him, and he nods and moves away to give us a modicum of privacy. Not that there's really any such thing in this place.

I sit and turn my head to Frank, resisting the urge to touch him. 'It's lovely out here today.'

He looks at me and I see the confusion in his eyes. I think it's my voice that does it. The sound is familiar but he can't quite place me. 'It is indeed.'

I try not to let my disappointment show on my face. I'm grateful for the days that he still recognises me, although they're happening less and less. It's been months since he recognised Fiona. I think that's the reason she keeps finding excuses not to visit. The pain of seeing her beloved daddy like this is more than she can bear. Most of the time I have little patience for her discomfort. 'Do you think *I* like seeing him the way he is?' I've said on more than one occasion. 'This isn't about us, it's about your father.' But on days like today, when Frank's eyes glaze over and he treats me like a friendly stranger, I resolve to be more sympathetic towards my daughter.

I point to the exposed skin of his legs. 'I hope you have sunscreen on. Easy to get burned in beautiful weather like this.'

He screws up his nose. 'Pfft. Sunscreen. Can't stand the stuff. Makes the sand stick to your skin.' He smiles indulgently. 'You sound like my wife. She's always trying to get me to put on suncream when I'm on patrol. She's fair-skinned, you see. Only has to look at the sun and she gets burned. But not me. My skin's tough as old boots. Even if I go a bit pink at first, I end up tanned. My Shirley can't seem to understand that.'

I bite my tongue and refrain from talking about skin cancer. He's had half-a-dozen basal cell carcinomas cut out over the past decade, but of course the Frank sitting next to me doesn't know that. He's back in his youth.

Instead I say, 'So you like the beach, then?'

He nods. 'It's my second home. I'm a lifesaver, you know, at Bancoora. Lovely little beach. Best spot in the world, if you ask me.'

He closes his eyes for a moment. When he opens them again they're brighter, as though he's just had a wonderful idea. 'Look, you couldn't do me a favour, could you? You couldn't give a bloke a lift? I need to get back home to Shirl. She's probably worried sick by now. I got lost somehow and ended up in this place. I keep telling them that I need to get home, but no one's listening.'

'I'm listening.'

He breaks into a heartwarming smile. 'So you'll take me home?'

I want to take him in my arms and promise him everything will be all right, but today I'm a stranger to him and I don't want to cause him further distress by crossing any boundaries. The staff tell me when he's like this it's best to play along as much as possible. 'I can't today,' I say carefully. 'I don't have my car.'

His face falls momentarily before he regains his composure. 'Tomorrow, then?' It pains me to hear the desperation in his voice.

'Yes, love,' I say, and it's a blessed relief that this time I don't have to lie. 'Tomorrow.'

Chapter 2

December 1961
Bancoora Beach, Victoria

'Come on, Shirl, don't be a chicken. The water's lovely once you get used to it.'

Shirley Miller squinted into the sunshine at her friends splashing their way through the glittering shore breakers. It wasn't the cold she was afraid of; it was the water itself. 'You know I can't swim,' she called over the sound of the breaking waves.

'It's not deep,' June replied.

Mary joined in the cajoling. 'Come on. We'll look after you.'

There was nothing Shirley hated more than a spoilsport, and besides, she'd never hear the end of it if she didn't go in. She could hear June now telling the other girls at work what a wet blanket she'd been, and there was no way Shirley was having that. She sucked in a breath and gingerly waded out, gasping as the cold water lapped at her thighs and then her waist. She clasped June's shoulder. 'No further.'

June laughed. 'You're fine. Honestly.'

Shirley grimaced and dug her toes into the sand as a small wave rocked them.

'Face the shore,' Mary suggested. 'That way your back takes the brunt of the waves.'

Shirley shook her head. 'I don't want to be taken by surprise. If I get knocked off my feet I don't know what will happen.'

June laughed again. 'Don't be silly. Nothing's going to happen. The surf's not rough today. And if you get knocked over, you can just stand back up again.'

'Here, hold on to me.' Mary thrust out her hand and Shirley grasped it gratefully. After a few minutes she found her feet and settled into the rhythm of the gently breaking waves. She followed Mary's advice and turned her back on the oncoming waves, and, once she knew what to expect, discovered that she was actually enjoying the thrill of almost being lifted off her feet for a moment each time a wave broke. Once Shirley relaxed in the water her thoughts turned to other things. Well, one thing really: dancing at the Palais Royal that evening. She tugged Mary's hand. 'What are you wearing tonight?'

Mary shrugged. 'I couldn't afford anything new this week so I'm just going to wear my yellow dress. You know, the one I wore to Carol Baxter's twenty-first birthday party. I'm not wearing the stole though, just my white cardigan, and maybe I'll do something different with my hair.' She dropped Shirley's hand and twisted her hair into a loose knot. 'What do you think?'

Shirley nodded. 'If you tease the front to give it a bit of height that will look lovely, don't you think so, June?' But June was wading out where the water was deeper and didn't hear.

'What about you then, Shirl? Do you have something new?'

She visualised the new blue shantung dress she'd pressed that morning and smiled with satisfaction. 'Yes. I made a new dress out of that fabric Mum bought for me when she went to Melbourne with Aunty Mae.'

Mary's eyes widened. 'Ooh, fancy. You're going to knock Robby's socks off tonight.'

Robby Ferguson was the handsomest boy in their circle. All the girls were sweet on him. It had taken Shirley two months of careful manipulation – flirting sometimes, being standoffish at others – for him to take notice of her, but in the end her hard work had been rewarded. They'd been out together five times already and she hoped he was getting serious about her. After all, she'd turned twenty-one months ago and there wasn't time to waste. Most of the girls she'd gone to school with already had an engagement ring on their finger and quite a few had walked down the aisle at St Mary's. Jeanette O'Connor was married and had a baby girl. (Of course, rumour was she *had* to get married, but that was beside the point.)

If Robby didn't start to look like he had serious intentions towards her then she'd have to move on to another boy who was ready to get serious. Les Harrison, for instance, who had made no secret of the fact that he fancied her. Les wasn't as good-looking as Robby. His nose had been broken playing football a few years back and it showed, and he was shorter than the boys Shirley normally dated. On the other hand, he was kind and decent and looking to settle down – all qualities that went in his favour. Les would certainly be a fair choice, but Robby was a catch. He was a good dancer as well as handsome, and she loved the way people looked at them when they twirled around the dance floor together. Several boys had told her she was beautiful, and while she didn't like to skite, she couldn't help but think she and Robby made a perfect pair. What gorgeous babies they would have.

Without warning, Shirley was hit in the back by a wall of water. She lost her footing and tumbled face first into the sea. She scrambled to stand, but her feet couldn't find the bottom and she was sucked under the wave. Panicked, she reached out, hoping to be pulled to safety by Mary, but the gesture was in vain. She thought of her poor mother, who'd implored her not to go too deep and now was going to have to bear the news of her disobedient daughter's death by drowning. She began to recite the Lord's Prayer in her head while simultaneously wishing she'd been more pious.

As another wave crashed over her, she thought about all the times she'd disobeyed her parents and fought with her sister. God was never going to take pity on a sinner like her. She flailed in a desperate attempt to save herself, but her efforts were useless. Death was certain.

Maybe He was more forgiving than she imagined, because just as she got to *forgive us our trespasses* two hands – strong, reassuring hands – caught her under her armpits and dragged her back to the shallows. The hands continued to support her as she found her feet and steadied herself, all the time coughing and spluttering.

'Are you okay, Miss?'

She pushed her hair – which had escaped from her headband and was now plastered to her face – out of her eyes and looked at her rescuer. A tanned, broad-shouldered boy with thick black hair returned her gaze. 'Yes, I think so,' she managed to get out.

'Are you sure?'

She nodded. 'I'm okay.' A small medallion hanging from his neck caught her attention as it glinted in the sunlight. *St Christopher.* Her rescuer was a Catholic boy.

'Miss? Are you here alone?'

Shirley quickly averted her eyes, lest her rescuer think she was staring at his muscular chest. Instead she looked around to see where Mary and June had got to. Being knocked off her feet had disorientated her and it took a moment to find the pair among the dozens of other bathers. Eventually she spied Mary's striped swimsuit. The girls were wading through the waves towards her. She pointed to them. 'My friends are coming now.'

The tanned Adonis nodded. 'Good. Maybe you should take a rest on the sand for a while, take some time to recover. You've had a bit of a shock.'

Shirley raked a hand through her sopping hair in an attempt to look less pathetic than she felt. She realised with dismay that the hairband she'd made to match her swimming costume was missing. 'Yes. I will. Thank you . . . I'm sorry, I didn't catch your name.'

'Frank Sullivan, at your service.' He grinned, revealing a set of ever-so-slightly-crooked teeth.

She held out her hand. 'Shirley Miller. I'm pleased to meet you, Frank. Thank you so much for your help.'

'It was my pleasure entirely. I hope you don't mind me saying this, but maybe you and your friends should stick to paddling in the shallows if you're not confident swimmers. There's a decent rip out there today.' He pointed to a calm section of water off to their left. 'That sort of thing can often take inexperienced swimmers by surprise, and as much as I've enjoyed making your acquaintance, I'd hate to have to swim out to rescue you from a properly dangerous situation.'

What a fool he must think she was. She should never have let the others talk her into going so far out. She struggled to think of something to say that might redeem her in his eyes. In her limited experience, flattery seemed to go down well with boys. 'Goodness, I had no idea. You seem to know the beach well. Do you come here often?' Heat rushed to her cheeks. What a stupid thing to say. Now he would think she was a complete idiot. Or, worse still, he'd think she was flirting with him. Which she wasn't.

He shook his head and laughed. 'I'm not a local. I'm just in town visiting my cousin. I've been to a few beaches down this way for surf carnivals – I'm a lifesaver, you see – but this is my first time here.'

'Oh, wow!' she said. 'I certainly picked the right person to almost drown in front of, didn't I?'

He chuckled and looked as if he was about to say something else, but suddenly June and Mary were upon them, fussing and tutting, saying how they feared she'd drowned. Once they'd been assured Shirley was absolutely fine, June cast an approving eye over Frank and turned her attention to him. She batted her lashes and started telling Frank how she'd warned Shirley to be careful and not to go out too far. 'Shirl's not a strong swimmer like me,' she said breathily. 'In fact she can't really swim at all.'

Shirley repressed the impulse to push her friend under the water. As if she wasn't embarrassed enough.

But Frank barely gave June a glance. 'I'm just glad you're all right, Shirley. It was lovely to meet you. I'll leave you to your friends now.'

She watched him stride out into the waves. Once the water reached his chest he began to swim, using leisurely but strong strokes, and ducking under the breaking waves with confidence. She held her breath each time he disappeared, releasing it again when he reappeared.

'Come on, Shirl,' June said. 'We'd better start making tracks. I want to set my hair so it's perfect for the dance tonight.'

Shirley took one last look at her saviour and reluctantly followed her friends onto the soft sand.

Chapter 3

Saturday

It takes me a few minutes longer than usual to walk to the bus stop this afternoon, maybe because of the extra bag I'm carrying, and I arrive just in time to see my bus disappearing around the corner. It's thirty minutes before the next one arrives, so it's starting to get dark by the time my tired feet make their way up the fancy concrete path – *exposed aggregate*, apparently – to Fiona's front door.

'It's your home too, Mum,' she keeps telling me, but it doesn't feel that way. It's been a year since I moved from the house in Geelong that Frank and I brought our baby daughter home to. We had more than fifty years in that house, good years most of them, but it's gone now.

Even though I know I'm welcome here, my heart can't accept the permanence of the situation. I lie to myself, saying I'm only here for a few days. For the sake of my sanity, I've made myself believe I'll be going home. Fiona says I'll get used to living here eventually, but I know I won't.

Not having a car hasn't helped. Fiona sold my little hatchback when we moved up here. Her husband, Gary, said I needed something newer – with airbags and whatnot – if I was going to keep driving, but no such car has eventuated. At first I was too shell-shocked by the move to even think about driving – Geelong traffic isn't anywhere near as crazy as it is around Sydney – and by the time I felt up to tackling it, Gary had moved out. He needed some space to 'think about the relationship'. Fiona's still struggling to cope with this arrangement, so I don't feel I can burden her further by nagging her about a new car.

I've tried to make the best of things. As I used to say to Fiona when she was little, there's no point in sulking. I fill my days with classes at the community centre in the mornings – they have such a lot on offer – and then a bus ride across town to visit Frank. Fiona often picks me up on her way home from work, unless she's working extra late, in which case I catch the bus. Weekends are different. Sundays I go to Mass at St Joseph's and straight to the nursing home afterwards. Usually my friend Sandra drops me there. It's nice for Fiona to have one day to herself, so the church organised a roster of people to bring me home after visiting Frank, which is pretty decent of them considering I'm such a new member of the parish. That's one of the things I love about church. They look after their own. Occasionally one of the other parishioners will visit Frank of their own accord, which I think is a lovely gesture. If Frank was in a home in Geelong he'd have no shortage of visitors – people from church, from the bowls club and Frank's old workmates – but here there's only me, Fiona and the grandchildren to make up the numbers.

Saturday is the one day Fiona visits with me, bringing whichever of the grandchildren she can persuade to join us. More often than not it's my middle granddaughter, Lou (Eloise to her parents but Lou to me). Frances is overseas right now, and Lila's usually too busy with her friends. Lately Fiona's been finding excuses to cut her visits short. Today's excuse was Lila's end-of-year play rehearsal. I'm sure Lila could have got a lift with any number of her friends but Fiona insisted on taking her, casually mentioning that she might be 'a little late' as she breezed out the door this morning. Another day this would have annoyed me but today I seized the opportunity to go alone.

As I search for my keys in my handbag the front door swings open and Fiona is standing before me. Her face is like thunder. 'Mum! I told you I'd be home in time to take you.'

'I had no idea how long you'd be. I can't have your father sitting on his own for hours in that place.'

She looks dismayed as she opens the door wider and steps back so I can enter. 'Mum,' she says. 'Sunset Lodge is a beautiful facility. The care there is first rate and half the time Dad doesn't even—'

'Doesn't even what?' I close the door with more force than I intended.

Fiona's face softens. 'He doesn't always know who we are, Mum. And even when he does, sometimes he's forgotten we've visited him before we've left the car park.'

I shake my head. 'That's hardly the point, is it? *We* haven't forgotten who he is. That man made plenty of sacrifices for us over the years and I'll be damned if I'm just going to lock him up in a home and forget about him now.'

She has the good grace to look ashamed of herself. 'Of course we're not going to forget about him. I was worried about you, that's all. I had no idea where you were.'

'I left a note on the fridge.'

'But you were so late and I couldn't get hold of you. I called your mobile half-a-dozen times at least.'

'Oh,' I say. 'Sorry. Maybe the battery's flat. You know I'm hopeless with that thing.' No part of this statement is true, but sometimes a fib makes life easier.

'If you're going to be out and about on your own, the least you could do is keep your phone charged,' she says with a note of exasperation in her voice.

'I'll try to remember that.' But this is a lie too. I never forget to charge my phone. I deliberately turn the blasted thing off when I don't want to be contacted.

I pick up the bag of clothes I've placed on the floor and head to my room.

'Dinner's just about ready,' Fiona calls after me, but I don't answer.

Once I'm safely in my room I drag out the suitcase I have stashed under my bed and throw Frank's clothes in it. I sit on my single bed and allow myself a moment. I know Fiona loves Frank, just like she loves me. But she's only fifty-three. She simply doesn't understand the indignities of old age, the humiliation of having to rely on others for things you once did with ease. I hate that we are so often at loggerheads these days, but I can't see that changing any time soon.

Before I close the suitcase I slide my hand into the zippered compartment and feel around to reassure myself that the letter I've hidden there is still safe. For a second it eludes me, but then my fingers feel the square of roughly folded paper. One might expect such an important letter to be written on pretty notepaper, but between my fingers is a sheet torn from an old exercise book. I don't need to risk taking the letter out to read it; I know the words by heart. They've sustained me these past few months.

A knock at my door startles me and I withdraw my hand a moment before Lila pokes her head in. 'Dinner's ready, Nan.'

The suitcase is still open. I have an explanation ready but she doesn't question me about it. Knowing Lila she probably hasn't noticed it, dreamy soul that she is.

'Okay, sweet pea. I'm coming.

I try to help out by cooking dinner for the family a few nights a week, but Fiona insists on taking responsibility for weekend meals. This usually means takeaway, and tonight's no exception. She's pulled apart a barbecue chicken and plonked it on a platter, and there's a bowl of greasy-looking roast potatoes as a side dish. At least there's a salad of sorts tonight – a bag of pre-washed baby spinach leaves, and chopped up cherry tomatoes. Thankfully I'm not terribly hungry.

Domesticity's never been Fiona's thing. Her career has always come first. When Gary was here he did his fair share, cooking a few nights a week and ironing the kids' uniforms, but since he's been gone Fiona relies on me to do the lion's share of the housework. Oh, she protests of course. 'Mum, how many times have I told you there's no need for you to vacuum the house? You shouldn't be pushing yourself so hard. Don't forget about your heart.'

My heart is broken, she's right about that, but I don't see how a little bit of housework will make it any worse. Besides, I have no desire to live in a pigsty.

We eat in silence for a few minutes before Lou speaks. 'How was Papa today, Nan?'

I scrape the skin and fat away from a piece of chicken before pushing it onto my fork. 'Not too bad, love. He was out in the garden when I got there.'

'Sorry I couldn't come, I got an extra shift. I didn't expect them to give me more hours so soon after my exams finished.'

'That's okay, Lou. You've got to take all the shifts you can get while you can. Once uni starts you'll be busy studying again.'

Lou's eyes drop. '*If* I get into uni, that is.'

'Well,' Fiona interjects, 'if you don't you'll just have to go back and repeat the HSC. You're perfectly capable of getting an excellent ATAR if you apply yourself. Your problem is you spend too much time on that damned computer of yours and not enough studying.'

Lou bristles. 'Mum, I want to study animation and interactive media. Being on the computer *is* studying. I studied my butt off, I'm just not good at exams.'

'I'm not an idiot, Eloise. I know the difference between studying and playing video games. You wasted countless hours on those stupid things. Makes me wonder if you were trying to fail.'

Lou lets her fork drop. 'Sorry I'm not perfect like you.' She pushes her chair out to leave the table, but I reach across and clasp her hand.

'Sit down and eat your dinner, love. Your mother's just tired. She didn't mean it.' I shoot a chiding look at Fiona. 'She knows that a high ATAR isn't the be-all and end-all. Once you get into the workforce no one will care what your score was. It's all about talent and hard work, so I know you'll be fine no matter what happens. Look at your dad. He didn't even finish Year Twelve, and he's done so well for himself.' It's a narrative Fiona's been spouting for years, so she can hardly contradict me now.

Frank was none too thrilled when she let it be known that she and Gary were talking about marriage. Thankfully she had the good sense to break the news to Frank in Gary's absence.

'Gary might not have finished school but that's only because he didn't need to,' she said, folding her arms across her chest. 'He was offered an apprenticeship at the end of Year Eleven so he took it. And he's a hard worker, Dad. He's essentially got two jobs.'

Frank was unmoved. 'Hmph. I hardly think playing bass guitar in some second-rate band qualifies as a second job.'

'Your father and I just want to make sure you'll be looked after, that's all.'

'I'm not you,' Fiona said, her lip curled in obvious derision. 'I have no intention of being "looked after", thanks very much. Get with the times, Mum. Gary and I have an equal relationship.'

I remember feeling a twinge of sympathy for my soon-to-be son-in-law in that moment, but it wasn't until the girls came along that Frank's frostiness towards Gary thawed. Once he saw what a wonderful father Gary was, he conceded that maybe

Fiona hadn't made such a terrible choice after all. It was clear by then that Gary was more than prepared to make sacrifices for their relationship. He packed up and moved to Sydney so Fiona could take a prestigious job, and when the kids came along, he was the one to reduce his hours so the kids didn't have to go into full-time childcare.

We were proud of Fiona's achievements, of course, and it was what I'd wanted for her – a life on her own terms, one in which she didn't need a man to support her. The pity of it all was that no matter how successful she was, Fiona never seemed satisfied. She was driven to be the best at everything she did – including mothering – but she was only human, and there are only so many hours in a day. For all her 'freedom', she seemed to be caught in a trap of her own making.

'Nan's right,' Fiona says, looking contrite. 'I didn't mean it to come out like that, sweetheart. It's just that I know how incredibly smart you are and I want you to make the most of your opportunities.'

Begrudgingly, Lou sits back down and the silence returns for a moment until Fiona makes an attempt to get things back on track. 'So Dad was good today?'

I know it's in my best interests to keep the peace but I can't let her off the hook entirely. It's not just her insensitivity to Lou that has me riled. 'As good as he can be while he's locked up in that place. You'd know, if you'd visited him.'

She breathes out a heavy sigh. 'I do visit, Mum, when I can. And you make it sound like a prison.'

'Well, it's not like he can leave of his own accord.'

'You know that's for his safety,' she says. 'Or have you forgotten what happened when he was left to his own devices? Honestly, Mum, the way you're talking, anyone would think that I was deliberately trying to punish Dad. All I want is what's best for him.' Her voice rises in clear irritation. 'And whether you like it or not, I have medical guardianship over Dad, which means I'm the one who gets to choose his care.'

As if I didn't know that. Such a ridiculous situation. I was out of action for only a short time, but Fiona charged in and took control without missing a beat. Now she won't relinquish the reins, even though I'm perfectly capable of managing Frank's care. I open my mouth to say so but Lou cuts in before I can speak.

'I saw something on the news the other night about old people being abused in nursing homes. Do you think Papa's being abused?'

'Of course he's not,' Fiona says. 'Your grandfather is receiving the best care available.'

'The people on the TV didn't know their dad was being abused until they put a hidden camera in the room,' Lou replies. 'How can you be sure?'

'Oh, for heaven's sake, Eloise, your grandfather is fine. Stop being so melodramatic.'

Lou stares at her evenly. 'So is the government being melodramatic by establishing a royal commission to look into the *widespread* abuse of people in nursing homes?'

Fiona huffs out another sigh. 'I'm sure there are some rogue operators out there, but Sunset Lodge is not one of them. Papa is in the best possible place for him and that's that. Now can we talk about something else, please?'

Chapter 4

December 1961
The Palais Royal dance hall, Geelong

The blue shantung had done the trick. Robby Ferguson had barely taken his eyes off her all night and, in fact, she could feel his eyes on her now as she twirled around the floor in Les Harrison's arms. Robby had already asked if he could take her home. He staked his claim after the first dance of the evening, begging her to save the last dance for him. When she'd agreed he'd winked at her and told her not to go getting ideas about any other fellows, because she was 'his girl' now. This was it, she was sure of it. Tonight was the night they'd talk about taking things to the next level. June would be beside herself with jealousy, but she knew Mary would be pleased for her. Mary had her own serious beau and an engagement was definitely on the cards. If Robby worked fast then maybe she and Mary would be walking down the aisle within weeks of each other – or, better still, maybe they could even have a double wedding! It would be such fun planning a wedding with her best friend. She and Mary had always done everything together, so sharing their wedding day made perfect sense.

'Ouch!' Shirley's foot smarted under Les's weight. He was a nice enough boy, but there was no hiding the fact he was a terrible dancer. Thank goodness that after tonight she'd be taken and she wouldn't have to waste her time with 'nice enough' fellows anymore.

'Awfully sorry, Shirl. Are you okay?'

She was, but really she'd had enough. She winced in response. 'Actually, Les, would you mind terribly if we sat out the rest of this one? My foot's a wee bit tender.'

'Of course not.' He led her off the dance floor towards an empty group of chairs near the entrance to the hall. As she went to take a seat she noticed a group of clean-cut lads coming through the door. Unless her eyes deceived her, one of them was the boy from the beach.

'Shall I get you a drink? Lemonade okay?' She realised Les was talking to her.

'Oh, yes. Lovely. Thank you,' she replied, without taking her eyes off Frank Sullivan.

Her tall, dark and handsome saviour had seen her too and was making a beeline for her.

'Well, I don't believe it. It's the bathing beauty herself.' He held out his hand to her and she took it, pulling herself up to her feet at the same time.

Now that they were so close she couldn't help but notice his ill-fitting suit. The trousers were about an inch too short. His shoes at least were clean and polished, so that was something.

'Gentlemen, it's my pleasure to present Miss Shirley Miller. Shirley, this is my cousin, Brian Sullivan, and my friend, Alan Preston.'

Shirley shook hands with the others and smiled. 'Fancy seeing you here tonight.'

'Yes, you sly old dog, Sullivan,' Alan said, swatting Frank on the arm. 'I thought you said you didn't know anyone in

Geelong. Were you trying to keep this lovely young lady all to yourself?'

Brian let out a low whistle. 'Can't say I blame you, mate. She's a looker, all right.'

Shirley felt herself blushing.

Frank gave his cousin a clip over the ear. 'Don't take any notice of these two mugs, Miss Miller. They're just a pair of country bumpkins who don't know how to talk to sophisticated ladies such as yourself.' He turned to the others. 'You two need to get a hold of yourselves and stop gawping like that. You're embarrassing me.'

Brian laughed. 'Sorry, Frankie boy. I just think our Miss Miller can do better than the likes of you.'

Frank's tanned skin was turning pink. 'Go on, get out of here, the pair of you. See if some poor girl will take pity on you and let you take her for a spin around the floor.'

Alan bowed his head to her then as he started to drag Brian away. 'Nice to meet you, Shirley. Hope to see you again before the night's out.'

She smiled and nodded. It was clear the boys meant no harm and were used to ribbing each other.

'Well, this is a happy coincidence indeed. It appears you have recovered from your fright this morning.'

She dropped her gaze, momentarily embarrassed as she relived her near-drowning, if you could call it that. 'Oh, yes. I'm fine now. Thank you again for your help. I'm not sure what I would have done if you hadn't come along. I'm indebted to you, truly.'

His face took on a serious expression. 'Well, I know a way you could repay that debt.'

She raised her eyebrows, slightly taken aback at his words. 'Oh? How's that?'

'Dance with me, and we'll call it even.'

She laughed. 'Oh. I'd love to, but . . .'

'What?'

'Well, I was dancing with my friend Les just now and he's gone to get us some drinks, so I can't really disappear on him.'

'Next dance then.'

She shook her head. 'I'm afraid that's taken too.'

'Hmm.' He rubbed his chin as if deep in thought. 'Actually, that's fine. I reckon I can wait for the last dance of the evening. How about you save that one for me?'

'I'm sorry, I'm already spoken for.'

'Oh, so you have a steady fellow then?'

'Not exactly. But I have already promised the last dance to another boy and he's the one taking me home.'

'Surely if you explain to him that you owe me a favour – seeing as how I saved your life this morning – he won't object? It's just one little dance.'

She looked into his intense blue eyes and weighed up her options. It was a risky thing he was asking her to do – Robby would probably be put out – but Frank did have a point. He *had* rescued her. One dance surely wasn't too much to ask? 'All right, Frank Sullivan, you've talked me into it. But I'll need to talk to Robby and make sure he's not too upset first.'

'Fair enough.'

'Shirley?' Les's voice came from behind her. 'I have your lemonade.'

She turned and smiled, even though Les Harrison had been the last person on her mind at that moment. 'Thanks so much, Les. May I introduce Frank Sullivan? Frank's a friend of mine from out of town.'

Les held out his hand – somewhat begrudgingly, she thought – for Frank to shake. 'Pleased to meet you, Frank. From out of town, eh? Where's home then?'

'Little place called Lindenow.'

'Can't say that I've heard of it.'

Frank smiled. 'That doesn't surprise me. It's a hamlet outside Bairnsdale, in Gippsland.'

'Ah, that I've heard of. Never been out that way myself.'

'It's a beautiful part of the world, you should come visit some time.'

Les gave a noncommittal nod as the emcee announced the next dance of the night. He turned to Shirley. 'Well, that's my cue, I'm afraid. I need to find my partner. It was a pleasure dancing with you, Shirley. I hope your foot is okay now.'

She felt a twinge of sympathy for Les, who looked roundly defeated. 'It's absolutely fine. Don't think another thing of it. I'll see you soon, Les. In fact, there's a big group of us going to the flicks on Wednesday night. Maybe I'll see you there?'

Hope once again glimmered in his eyes. 'I'll be there.' Les nodded his farewells before disappearing into the crowd.

Frank looked at her. 'I can see I've got plenty of competition here. You're certainly a popular lady. But I think you'll find I don't give up easily. I feel it's my duty to inform you, Miss Miller, that I plan to win you over.'

Shirley laughed. 'Is that a fact?'

'Take my word for it.'

She could feel the heat rising in her cheeks and lowered her gaze. 'I'm sorry, but I'm sure my next dance partner is looking for me, if you'll excuse me.'

He took her hand and raised it to his lips, brushing her knuckles with the lightest of kisses. 'Until the last dance, then.'

She couldn't help but smile at his confidence. 'We'll see.' She turned on her heel and fortunately spied Andy Baxter, her next partner, walking towards her. She greeted Andy and let him take her in his arms for the foxtrot. He chatted to her as they danced their way around the hall, and she answered with as much enthusiasm as she could muster, but her heart wasn't in it. The whole time she was thinking about Frank Sullivan.

There was something about him she just couldn't put her finger on. Perhaps it was his confidence. She had to admit she found his audacity quite attractive. If it weren't for Robby she might suggest that he make it his business to visit Geelong more often.

Perish the thought. She was in love with Robby. Wasn't she?

Mary and June were always going on about how the boys they dated made their skin tingle and their stomachs flip. No boy had ever made Shirley feel that way. Of course she'd told the other girls she was falling in love with Robby – she didn't want to be the only one of her group to admit she wasn't experiencing butterflies in her stomach every time she saw her beau – but the truth was she was more in love with the thought of wearing a beautiful white gown as she walked down the aisle at St Mary's than she'd ever been with any boy. She figured it didn't really matter. So long as she found someone suitable to have a family with, they'd have a nice life. After all, her parents hadn't exactly had a romantic courtship. They'd been neighbours and friends before deciding to get married. 'We just sort of got used to having each other around,' her mum was fond of saying. Her parents were perfectly happy and she always thought she would be too. 'Find someone who works hard and can take care of you,' was her father's advice.

Frank Sullivan didn't give her butterflies – in fact, quite the opposite. She felt calm and comfortable in his presence. It occurred to her that maybe she felt love differently to other people. Often being with a handsome boy made her nervous, and the thought of him kissing her or touching her anywhere *private* was cause for anxiety rather than anticipation. But maybe kissing Frank would be different. She'd felt safe and at ease in his arms this morning. Maybe fate had thrown them together for a reason.

Why on earth was she still thinking about Frank? Tonight was supposed to be about Robby.

After the foxtrot there was a brief break in the music. She thanked Andy and set off to find Robby in the hope he'd agree to pass on the last dance of the evening. Surely he'd understand. Frank *had* saved her life, and dancing with him in return seemed like such a small favour.

Robby was walking towards her with a huge smile on his face. He grabbed her by the hand and twirled her around, pulling her close to him before releasing her. 'How's your night been so far? I saw you sit down before. Did that klutz Harrison tread on your toes again?'

She laughed. 'How did you know?'

He shrugged. 'Lucky guess. I was watching you from the other side of the hall and I figured it was something like that. Never mind. Only a few more dances and it'll be my turn again.'

'Oh, Robby, I really want to talk to you about that. Would you mind terribly if I gave the last dance to another boy? I wouldn't ask usually but the boy in question saved my life this morning and he's asked for the last dance.'

Robby frowned. 'Surely you told him you were already booked?'

'Yes, of course I did, but he was so disappointed and he's only in town for one night. I'd really love to show my appreciation to him for what he did.'

An expression of doubt crept into his eyes. 'What do you mean, he saved your life? First I've heard of it.'

'Mary, June and I went to the beach this morning and I was knocked over by a wave. I lost my bearings and was getting dragged out into deeper water when Frank grabbed me and pulled me to safety.'

'Look, I'm glad you're all right, but it doesn't sound like a big deal to me. Any decent bloke would have done the same thing. You don't owe him anything.'

Shirley bit her lip. Clearly Robby was annoyed, but his lack of concern over her earlier plight grated on her. He seemed completely indifferent to the fact she'd had a traumatic experience. In fact, it seemed that he was only worried about his own feelings. 'It was a big deal to me, Robby. I was really frightened. Frank was wonderful. A true gentleman.'

Robby's lip curled in a most unattractive manner. 'Well, if he's such a gentleman he'll understand that it's not good manners to cut another man's lunch.'

Shirley's blood began to heat. She hated that expression with a passion. She was not any man's 'lunch'. 'He's not trying to race me off. I told him about you and said that you would be taking me home. He respected that.'

'Pffft,' Robby huffed. 'If he was being respectful, he wouldn't have asked at all. There's still a couple more before the last dance of the evening. Why don't you see if one of your other partners will make way for this joker.'

Perhaps one of the other fellows would be more understanding. She was almost certain that amiable Barry Chapman wouldn't object too strongly at all, but Frank had specifically asked for the last dance and, more to the point, Robby's attitude irked her. She dug in her heels. 'I'm asking *you*.'

'And I'm saying no, you can't give him the last dance. I won't allow it.'

Shirley saw red. 'Excuse me? I don't need your *permission* to dance with another boy. I was asking for your understanding, that's all.'

'You're right. You can do whatever you want, but here's the thing, Shirley. If you choose that bloke over me I'll know where

I stand. Don't expect me to be taking you home if you don't save the last dance for me. Understood?'

'Clear as a bell,' she said. She turned away so he wouldn't see her eyes filling with tears of rage. All these months she'd desperately wanted Robby to call her his girl, but now that he was staking his claim it felt wrong. Of course she wanted him to want her, and even to be protective of her, but the look on his face back there was downright possessive. She wasn't a chattel to be owned. She had more self-respect than that.

Barry Chapman sidled up beside her. 'Ready to jive, Shirl?'

'Sorry?'

'Jive. I believe the next dance is mine. Unless I'm mistaken?'

'No, no, you're not mistaken at all. Sorry, Barry, my mind was elsewhere for a minute.'

He smiled and held out his hand. 'Shall we?'

They took their places on the floor. Barry wasn't a half-bad dancer and the jive was a lively dance, but Shirley's heart just wasn't in it. She forced a smile and went through the motions, hoping Barry wouldn't notice her lack of genuine enthusiasm. Michael Galvin was her next partner, and he tapped Barry on the shoulder the second the jive was finished. Luckily Michael was a quiet one, and the quickstep seemed to take all of his concentration, so Shirley had time to gather her thoughts. Hopefully Robby wouldn't make a fuss when he realised she was choosing Frank. *Was* she really going to choose Frank? Because if that was the case, Robby had made himself clear. Not only would he not be taking her home tonight, but it would be over between them. She had no doubt he'd have another girl in his sights by the end of the evening. There were enough of them waiting in the wings, just dying to have a chance with him.

Was she crazy? Was she really going to give up her chance to be Mrs Robby Ferguson because of a little wounded pride? It wasn't as if there was any future for her with Frank. He didn't even live in Geelong; his home was more than two hundred miles away. She doubted she'd ever see him again once the evening was over. And yet, the idea of *not* dancing with Frank seemed unthinkable.

She knew it couldn't last, that any romance that transpired between them would be a one-night affair, but somehow that seemed better than the alternative – turning Frank down. It wasn't just because she owed him her life, although that was reason enough. But there was more to it than that. When he spoke to her, in his quiet yet confident manner, she felt completely at ease. This morning she'd felt safe in his arms from the moment he'd touched her. Frank Sullivan made her feel special in a way that Robby never had.

If she was being honest with herself, she hadn't been able to get Frank out of her thoughts since that morning. All day, while she'd been getting ready, she'd talked to June and Mary about Robby, but in her mind's eye she'd pictured herself dancing with Frank. Of course, she'd dismissed the idea as a flight of fancy, but now he was here at the Palais, the place where she came to dance almost every Saturday night. What were the odds of her meeting this boy, who'd been a stranger to her yesterday, twice in one day? It seemed like divine intervention of some sort.

Maybe, just maybe, there was such a thing as love at first sight.

Chapter 5

Sunday

I take a deep breath and decide I'm as ready as I'll ever be. I sit my suitcase next to the bench seat near the entrance, hoping that it won't be noticed or moved. Often new residents leave luggage here when they're moving in, so I figure visitors won't think anything of it. Members of staff don't come out here much as there's a separate staff entrance. But, if the worst comes to the worst I can leave it behind. It will make life easier but it's not essential. There's not much in there that can't be replaced. I've already removed the one precious item – the letter from my beloved – and placed it in my handbag, just in case.

Once I'm inside I smile at the receptionist, who nods at me vaguely as I sign the visitors' book. This girl – Karen, if I remember rightly – has been here just a few months and she only works on Sundays, so she's still coming to grips with all the residents and their families. This is part of the reason I chose a Sunday to carry out The Plan.

'Hello, dear,' I say, using my best little-old-lady voice. 'I'm taking my husband out to a family party today. I filled in the paperwork last weekend.'

She looks at me blankly. 'And your husband is?'

'Frank. Frank Sullivan.'

'Ah, yes of course, I remember now. Bear with me for a moment while I check to see that all the paperwork is in order.'

I smile again, trying to look unconcerned. There's no reason for her to be suspicious. Frank's records will show that we've taken him out on excursions before. Of course, usually Fiona is with me, but the past few times I've made a point of filling out the form myself so that when this day arrived no one would question the documentation.

Karen clicks away on her keyboard for a moment, stares at the screen and frowns. 'It says here your nephew is transporting you. Is that correct?'

'Yes, well, actually, not exactly.' I laugh. 'Ollie is technically my great-nephew – or is it grand-nephew? I've never really understood the difference.'

'So where is he?' she asks flatly.

'Ollie? Oh, he'll be along soon enough.' I look at my watch. 'I asked him to meet us in the car park at one o'clock. Don't worry, he'll be here.'

She nods. 'Excellent. But he'll need to come in to collect Mr Sullivan from the foyer. There's a note on here to say Mr Sullivan is easily upset in unfamiliar surroundings. We can't risk having him run off on you, Mrs Sullivan.'

'Frank won't run off on me, I'm sure. But I'll text Ollie and ask him to meet us in the foyer. That won't be a problem.' At least I hope it won't be.

Karen nods. 'So, it says here you'll have Mr Sullivan back by eight pm. We really do need him in the door by quarter to, if possible. There's a change of shift at eight and it would be easier for the staff if we could have Mr Sullivan in his room by then.'

'I'll do my very best.'

'And please see a staff member in the dementia unit before you leave. They'll ensure you have all Mr Sullivan's medications, and instructions for his care for the day.'

I bite my tongue and resist the very great urge I have to roll my eyes at her. As if I don't know how to take care of my own husband. Instead I nod and say, 'Of course.'

She smiles and finally says, 'Right then. Everything seems to be in order. I hope you and Mr Sullivan enjoy the party.'

'Thank you, Karen. I'm sure we will.'

I walk away, trying not to appear too hurried. I'm at the keypad outside the dementia unit before my heart rate returns to any semblance of normal. So far so good. Maybe I am really going to get away with this. Before I enter the unit, I send Ollie a text.

> Hi Ollie. When you get here can you please come into the foyer and text me? And, if anyone asks, just say you're my nephew. I'll explain later, if that's OK?
> Shirley

I add a kiss, then delete it. Young people these days seem to be overly affectionate – hugging and kissing each other all the time and so on – but he's not family, so the kiss feels too familiar. He *is* a friend, though, maybe the best one I have here in Sydney. I put the kiss back and press send.

I suck in a steadying breath and punch the code into the keypad and enter this god-awful place for (*please, God*) the last time. I'm hoping the weekend staff will have Frank all ready to go. I don't want to keep Ollie waiting for too long because I don't want him inconvenienced or, worse, talking to the staff. As I near Frank's room I'm startled to see Glenda walking down the corridor towards me. My heart thumps a little harder at the sight of her. She doesn't usually work on Sundays. I start to panic.

What if she suspects something's up? But when she gets close enough she smiles benignly. 'Hello, Mrs Sullivan. Frank's waiting for you in the sunroom. He's all ready for his big day out.'

I'm being irrational. Seeing problems where there are none. I return the smile. 'Thanks, Glenda. What are you doing here today?'

She sighs. 'Maureen's off sick. Late-season flu, she reckons, so goodness knows how long she'll be off. Could be weeks. We can't risk her spreading her germs to the residents. A dose of the flu could be fatal to some of the frailer people here, so we need to be vigilant about keeping them apart from anyone who might be infected.'

I nod my understanding. Losing Frank to an illness like pneumonia is a fear that has plagued me ever since he moved here.

'And the new girl, Amber, up and quit last week,' Glenda continues. 'Reckons aged care isn't for her. She was only in the job five minutes. Young people, eh? Seems they never want to stick anything out. So we're seriously short-staffed at the moment. I told them in the office I'd work today as a favour, but not to expect me to do this every weekend. I've got a family too, you know?'

I make sympathetic noises, but this is very good news. The already-reduced weekend staff will be under extra pressure today, and Glenda, the most experienced of them, is preoccupied with the injustice of having to work when she wasn't officially rostered on. I can't believe my luck. This should make getting out of here a breeze.

'Karen at reception said to check in with you about Frank's medication.' I am, of course, intimately acquainted with the drugs my husband takes. We won't be needing them – most are doing Frank more harm than good, in my opinion – but there's no need to mention this.

'Yes, they've been dispensed and packaged up already. I've just got to sort out a bedpan situation and I'll be right with you. Head on over to the sunroom and I'll be there as soon as I can.'

'Thanks, Glenda. I really appreciate it.'

She scuttles off down the hall and I make my way to the sunroom, where I'm greeted by a smiling Frank. 'Hello there,' he says.

'Hello, my darling. How are you?'

His eyes flicker with surprise. I wonder if he knows me today. What if he kicks up a fuss and refuses to come with me? But I needn't worry. Whether he remembers me or not, his demeanour is amiable. 'Good, good. You're looking lovely today, my dear.'

'Thank you.' I smile at the compliment. I'm not ashamed to admit I take pride in my appearance. I always have. I'll never understand women who reach a certain age and decide that they just don't care anymore. Today I've gone to even more trouble than usual. I've used Lila's straightening iron to freshen up my blow-wave and I have more make-up on than normal. I'm dressed in my cream linen slacks and a green silk blouse, and the pearl pendant Frank gave me years ago adorns my neck. I've even got a small pair of nude block heels on. We're supposed to be going to a party, after all.

I bend to kiss his clean-shaven cheek. He smells faintly of aftershave and is dressed in a pair of smart-looking navy trousers and the pale-blue short-sleeved shirt that Fiona gave him last Christmas. The girls here have done a terrific job of getting him ready. I feel a pang of regret for the way I've demonised this place in my head over the past few months. Fiona's right, it *is* a lovely facility, and by and large the carers are good, decent people who are dedicated to their jobs. Honestly, if you have to end up in a nursing home, Sunset Lodge is the place to be. Most of the residents here seem happy in their own way. It's just not the place for my Frank.

He's gone downhill at a rapid rate since he became a resident here. When he was at home he had one-on-one care. In fact, a lot of the time it was two-on-one, because my friend, Rita, was there to help. Between the two of us we made sure Frank was able to enjoy many of the things he loved. He tinkered with his car and pottered in the garden. Friends came over to have a cuppa or watch the footy with him. In the winter we'd go for walks along the beach, and in the summer Rita would take him swimming. Yes, he forgot things and repeated himself, and he was often frustrated by the tasks he could no longer do, like reading the paper or driving a car, but he still had a full life.

He might have Alzheimer's disease, but he doesn't need to be shut away from the world. He needs to live in it.

In here it seems as if he's just sitting around waiting to die. He has no stimulation – no wonder he's deteriorating so quickly. And I'm sure half the medications he's on make him worse. The nurses say he needs them to keep him calm, but have they ever thought that maybe he'd be less agitated if he had something meaningful to do with his time?

Fiona often talks about the long list of activities they have on offer here. *'I'd love to spend a week or two as a resident of Sunset Lodge. It'd be like going on a cruise ship.'*

But the activities she's so impressed by – crafts, card games, bingo, tai chi and the like – are useless for Frank. He's an outdoors type who likes to make himself useful. He's bored witless here most of the time. Is it any wonder he has the odd angry outburst? And it doesn't help that this place is strange to him. There's nothing familiar here. Nothing from our past to jog his memory, or to soothe him.

I blame myself, of course. I should never, ever, have let this happen. But I wasn't myself for a while there. I let life get on top of me and that's when Fiona swooped in and took over our affairs. Oh, she had the best of intentions, and at the time I was grateful not to have to make any big decisions, to let someone look after me for a change.

'I just want what's best for Dad . . . and for you. You know that don't you, Mum?' Fiona reached across the hospital bed and squeezed my hand.

'Yes, darling, I know. I'm just worried that moving all the way to Sydney will be difficult for your father.'

'Well, you can't stay in Geelong. You have nowhere to live.'

'We have insurance and they're sorting things out. I'm sure we'll be able to find short-term accommodation in the meantime.'

'I think it's best if you and Dad come home with me, just until things are more settled. It will be good for you to have someone to care for you for a while, Mum. You heard what the doctor said, you need to start looking after yourself. Come back to Sydney with me, at least until you're feeling a bit better. Look at it as respite. It doesn't have to be permanent.'

And so it went on. In the end she wore me down. If I hadn't had that funny turn after the shock I got when I saw the house, maybe I might have had the confidence to stand my ground. But I didn't, and now here we are . . .

I give Frank an appreciative glance. 'You're looking pretty spiffy yourself.'

'Well, they tell me I'm going to some sort of shindig.' He grins. 'Do you know anything about that?'

'I do, in fact. We're off to a party.'

'A party? Hope there's going to be cake. Whose party is it?'

I need to be careful here. I've lied to the staff and so I need to be consistent in what I say. On the other hand, Frank seems reasonably lucid right now and I don't want to upset or confuse him unnecessarily. I've told the staff we are going to an anniversary party for my sister and her husband, but Wendy died of breast cancer two years ago now. I doubt that Frank remembers that, but I don't want to take the risk. 'It's a surprise,' I say, touching a finger to my nose.

Frank rubs his hands together. 'I love surprises.'

This statement is patently untrue – the Frank I know dislikes anything out of the ordinary – but I'm happy to go along with him. 'Well, I really think you're going to like this one.'

'Can't you give me a hint?'

'Hmm, I can tell you one tiny thing. It might take us a while to get there, but I think you'll like where the party is being held.'

'Come on! Tell me where it is. You can whisper it in my ear if you like.'

I grin and oblige by cupping my hand and whispering our end destination to him.

His eyes light up. 'For real? You're not kidding?'

'No, I'm not kidding.'

'Whacko!'

My phone pings. It's Ollie texting to say he's arrived. I quickly reply, telling him about the suitcase and asking him to retrieve it and put it in the boot of the car before making his way into the foyer. I say we'll meet him there asap.

My stomach's churning. I'm anxious for Glenda to get here with Frank's medications and for this next part of The Plan to be over.

I'm tempted to forget about the drugs and just make a run for it now. It's not like I intend to keep Frank on any of that junk anyway. Ever since that unfortunate incident that got him locked up in the dementia unit he's been fed risperidone to keep him under control. The stuff has robbed him of his personality and I'm confident he'll be fine without it. I understand why the carers need to resort to these measures to keep their charges calm, but Frank is going to have one-on-one care with me again now and drugging him regularly won't be necessary. I've done my research and I have a few over-the-counter things I can use in an emergency. I weigh up the pros and cons of leaving without the pharmacy bag – if anyone questions us on the way out I could just pretend I forgot about it. I am an old woman, after all. But the risk of Glenda being suspicious is too high. Plus, if we leave without the drugs they might try to chase us down to give them to us. Now that would be a problem. I need to be patient and hope that Ollie can be too.

Luckily we don't have to wait much longer. After a couple of minutes Glenda hurries into the room carrying a large brown paper bag.

I'm bemused. Frank takes relatively few medications and we're supposed to only be going out for the day, but the sack Glenda's carrying is big enough to hold a month's supply. My confusion must show on my face, because Glenda smiles. 'I've packed a few items that I thought might come in handy,' she says, handing the bag to me. I open it and glance inside. There's a tiny bag with a pharmacy label on it, as well as a change of clothes and . . . a couple of pairs of disposable incontinence underwear. I flinch at the sight of them.

Once again Glenda interprets my expression. 'We've had a few accidents lately,' she says softly. 'It's not all the time, but I thought perhaps a family party might not be the best occasion for that to happen. I've dressed Frank accordingly and placed spare items in the bag in case they're required.'

Glenda gives my shoulder a squeeze and I nod tightly, forcing a smile. 'Thanks for everything, Glenda. You really are a gem.'

Glenda doesn't have time to indulge in sentimentality. 'I'll walk you out.' She takes Frank by the arm and the three of us make our way back out to the foyer.

Ollie's there, sitting on one of the overstuffed couches, fiddling with his phone. I wave to him. 'Here we are, Ollie.'

He looks up, waves at me and finishes texting or whatever it is he's doing before getting up and wandering over to us. Ollie's not the type to rush.

Glenda pats Frank on the shoulder. 'Well, Frank, I'll leave you to your family.'

A look of confusion crosses Frank's face when he sees Ollie. 'Who are you?'

'This is Ollie, Frank. You know, Kelly's youngest. Wendy's grandson.' I silently ask God and Wendy to forgive me this little lie – the invention of a third grandchild for my sister.

Frank looks at Ollie suspiciously.

'Ollie's been living overseas for a few years, Frank. He's probably changed a bit since you last saw him.' I make sure my explanation is loud enough to be overheard by anyone else in the foyer area, but Glenda has already disappeared and Karen is busy talking to a visitor. It seems no one is taking any notice of us at all. Ollie, bless him, is just going along with whatever I say. 'Good to see you, Uncle Frank,' he says without a trace of irony.

Frank shakes his head. 'I don't remember any Ollie. It's not the sort of name I'd forget.' He looks at me. 'And who are you again?'

'I'm Shirley. Your wife. Now, enough of all this fuss. We need to get going. We don't want to be late for the party.'

The smile returns to Frank's face. 'Oh. I love parties.'

Ollie puts his hand on Frank's elbow to support him and, miraculously, Frank lets him. And then the three of us are walking out the door and no one is stopping us. We make our way through the car park to a white Hyundai hatchback and Ollie hands me the keys.

'The suitcase is in the boot,' he says. He opens the front passenger door and tries to help Frank into his seat, but Frank insists on doing it himself and somehow manages. Ollie closes the door and drums his fingers on the car's roof as he looks at me. 'Maybe I'm way off base here, but I'm guessing this car isn't really a surprise for your granddaughter's birthday.'

I shrug.

'What's going on, Shirley?'

A mix of shame and anxiety heats my cheeks. Ollie knows he's been duped and I can only hope for his understanding. 'It's better you don't know.'

He gives me a slow nod. 'Fair enough. Tell me this, though – are you okay?'

I lift my chin. 'Never better.'

'All right then. But promise me, if you need anything – anything at all – you'll get in touch.'

'I promise.'

'I mean it, Shirl. You've been like a mother to me these past few months.'

I laugh. 'I think you mean *grandmother*.'

He grins. 'Either way, we're family now. You can count on me.'

My eyes mist with tears. I move towards him and give him a brusque kiss on the cheek. 'I need to get going, Ollie.' It suddenly occurs to me I'm leaving him here without transport. 'Can we drop you somewhere on our way?'

He shakes his head. 'No, thanks.' He nods towards a red sedan with a young woman sitting behind the steering wheel. 'I've got a lift.'

I look at the pretty brunette waiting for him and raise an eyebrow. He laughs in response. 'You're not the only one with secrets, Shirl.'

Chapter 6

April 1962
Geelong

Monday, April 9th
Bairnsdale

My darling Shirley,

How are you? Did you sleep well? I can't believe our weekend together is over already and I am back here at work. I'm scribbling this while I eat lunch. The boss has gone off to the bank so I have a few minutes.

I had a good trip back last night. I got in around midnight, but I was so keyed up with missing you and thinking about the beaut time we had this weekend that I couldn't sleep. Geez I was tired this morning. It was hard to get out of bed. It's starting to get pretty chilly here now and I couldn't be bothered to light the fire this morning, so I just stayed in bed thinking about you until I absolutely had to get up.

I'm hoping to have a bit of good news when I see you this weekend. A bloke from the footy club knows someone who works for the tramways in Melbourne. He reckons they're looking for people and that I wouldn't have any trouble getting a job. Joe, my friend from the club, is going to give me the bloke's number at training tonight and I'll give him a bell tomorrow. Darling, I know a job in Melbourne won't be the same as a job in Geelong – I'll still be further away from you than I would like – but it will be much easier for us to see each other and I think it will be easier to look for a decent job in Geelong once I'm in Melbourne. I'll take anything to be near you, as you know, but I would like to get something that pays decent money so we can get closer to our dream of buying a house. It won't be long now, darling, I promise you. Soon we can be together properly as man and wife.

Anyway, I must sign off before the boss gets back. I'll be down Saturday evening, hopefully with good news. If the job comes through, you never know, I might just have an extra surprise for you.

All my love,
Frank x

'Miss Miller, would it be too much trouble to expect those figures sometime *today*?' Mr Mason's voice boomed from behind Shirley, making her jump. She jammed Frank's letter into her pocket.

'No, sir, of course not. I'm almost finished.'

Mr Mason responded by slamming his office door shut. Shirley didn't dare get the letter out again. Not that she really needed to. She'd read it at least fifty times since it arrived in last night's post. Her heart soared every time she read the last line. *If the job comes through, you never know, I might just have an extra surprise for you.* Dare she hope that Frank was bringing her an engagement ring?

They'd been dating steadily for months now, Frank travelling from Lindenow most weekends. It had been fine over the summer, but now football season had arrived it was getting trickier. Of course she didn't want to ask Frank to give up playing, but it meant they had so little time together. He couldn't leave until after the game on Saturday, which meant the earliest he would arrive in Geelong was seven pm. Then he had to leave again on Sunday night. Twenty-four hours together a week was nowhere near enough. He'd suggested she come visit him – she could watch him play, and finally get to meet his sister – but there was no way her parents would approve of an unchaperoned visit. Maybe if she had an engagement ring on her finger they might think differently. She could see if June was up for a weekend away.

Her stomach flipped at the thought of wearing Frank's ring on her finger. *Please, God, let it be soon.* They hadn't done *it* yet, but she knew Frank wanted to. He was lovely about it, of course. He knew she wasn't the type of girl to give away her virginity before marriage. In any case, it was a sin. Frank's desire for her was obvious, but his faith would never allow him to act on it – not without a wedding band on her finger.

Truth be told, she was more than happy to wait. The idea of sex left her cold. Lots of the girls in the office talked about how the thought of making love made them feel all hot and gooey inside. No matter how hard she tried to feel otherwise, the thought of actually doing *it* was terrifying. She'd never let Frank go any further than kissing her. If he was beginning to feel frustrated by her insistence on him keeping his hands to himself, he didn't show it. He'd always been a perfect gentleman. Mary once admitted to her that she'd let Graham touch her under her dress and that the feeling was so delicious she couldn't even describe it. Shirley couldn't imagine feeling that way herself, although she was confident that when the time came her experience would be every bit as wonderful as Mary described. And if not, well, what did it matter? She loved Frank, and wanted to have his babies. Having sex was a means to an end. Once they were married she'd be happy to do her wifely duty, whether she enjoyed it or not.

She simply couldn't wait to be Frank's wife. She could picture it now. They'd have a lovely modern home in one of the newer suburbs. Frank would have a good job and she wouldn't work forever, of course; she'd be too busy raising their children. She smiled at the thought of 'the tribe', as Frank called them. He was keen on a big family – at least three, he said. Personally she thought four was a nice, round number. She let her hand momentarily drift from the typewriter keys to her flat stomach. How wonderful it must feel to have a child grow beneath your very own skin. She pictured herself in their kitchen, her belly swollen with child and a sweet pink-cheeked toddler at her feet.

Across the room, June coughed. Shirley looked up to see her friend shooting her a warning look. She put her hand back on the keys and began to type furiously. She needed to stop daydreaming before she lost her job. If things went to plan she'd be leaving here soon enough, but in the meantime she needed every cent she could earn to put towards her future as Mrs Frank Sullivan.

Chapter 7

Sunday

I look across at Frank in the passenger seat and try to ignore the trickle of drool glistening on his chin. It's not exactly dignified, and nor is the fact that I laced his McDonald's tea with a decent dose of Phenergan in the hope that he'll sleep until we get to our accommodation. It feels hypocritical to be doping him when the whole point of this exercise was for him to experience life more fully, but it's only temporary.

Yesterday, I booked a motel in Yass, about three hours' drive south-west of Sydney, under my maiden name. It's a cheapie, a little way out of town, and I'm hoping they'll be so happy for the business that they'll accept my little-old-lady story of not trusting credit cards and allow me to pay by cash. Staying overnight while we still have this car is a risk, I know, but it's one I'll have to take. I don't dare drive at night; my eyes simply aren't good enough. And besides, I'm starting to feel the effects of driving all afternoon. I didn't go to all this trouble to kidnap Frank to end up running off the road and killing us both.

This trip has been six months in the making. Once they put Frank into that locked dementia unit I knew I had to do something. Frank's a man who yearns for the endless ocean. How on earth could anyone expect him to survive, let alone be happy, in the confines of what was essentially a prison? I couldn't bear the thought of it.

I'd taken a few classes – Italian for Beginners, Tai Chi for Seniors, and Art Appreciation – at the community centre, gaining knowledge I had no use for. My main objective had been to keep Fiona happy.

'You'll meet people who share your interests, Mum. Make a few new friends.'

It was only when I started thinking about The Plan that I realised some of the classes on offer at the community centre might be of use to me. I enrolled in two short courses – *An Introduction to Mobile Phones and Tablets* and *The Internet for Beginners*. That's where I first met Ollie. He was a volunteer instructor in both classes. Well, not exactly a *volunteer* – he was there as part of a community corrections order – but I didn't know that when we first met. I did know that I liked him. Despite the vast difference in our ages, we clicked immediately.

It wasn't long before I started to enlist Ollie's help with The Plan. Not that I was ever completely honest with him about my intentions. I told him I was looking for a car for my granddaughter and he was only too happy to help me in my search. When we found the right car online, it was Ollie who negotiated a better price for me. He even agreed to store it at his place until the big day.

Today.

I hope he doesn't feel betrayed by my dishonesty. It was to protect him, really. I'll explain all that to him sometime, and hopefully he'll understand. Right now I have bigger things to worry about.

I figure no one will be looking for us yet. I keep going over The Plan in my head to look for cracks, and of course I know it could all go wrong at any moment, but I think I've covered all the bases so far. I've told Fiona that I've been invited to Sandra's birthday dinner and that Sandra's son will drop me home around nine o'clock. So she won't be concerned about my whereabouts before then.

As for Sunset Lodge, I think the best plan is to call the home at eight and tell them we're running a little late and might not be back for an hour or so. That should buy me another ninety minutes before they get suspicious. By the time they realise something's up and call Fiona, who's the other listed contact, I estimate it'll be ten o'clock. I can't see them involving the police until about midnight. I just have to hope it will take them a while to work out what's happened. I know they'll track down Ollie eventually. If they put our faces on the news he might even come forward of his own accord, but I'm counting on it being tomorrow afternoon before they get that information. By then we will have ditched this car and (God willing) slipped under the radar.

Frank snorts loudly and I glance at him to make sure he's okay. I'm a little concerned that I might have over-medicated him. I spent a lot of time researching on the internet about what a safe dosage would be, but I'm not a medical professional. In the end I'm taking an educated guess. I feel guilty about sedating him, but these first few hours are crucial. I can't risk his distress slowing us down.

So far so good, although the roadside stop near Marulan was more challenging than I'd imagined it would be. I knew we'd need to change clothes as soon as possible – we'd both been wearing distinctive clothing when we left Sunset Lodge and they always describe the clothes missing people were last seen in. It might have been overkill, but I decided to cut my hair short too. I've worn it in a smooth shoulder-length bob for goodness knows how many years. I know it's vain of me to even think this, but I have beautiful hair. It's greyed nicely – to an attractive shade of silver. I get a wash, condition and blow-wave every Friday at the salon up the road from Fiona's house, so it always looks glossy and styled. My hair sets me apart, if I do say so myself. Which is why it had to go.

I'm no hairdresser, and I was working under pressure in those public toilets at the roadside stop. Luckily the place was totally deserted when we got there. I was worried Frank would run off on me if I left him to his own devices so I took him into the ladies' with me. I had to work fast and I have to say I did a bit of hack job. Never mind. I'll try to fix it tonight at the motel. For now I've tied a silk scarf around my head to hide the mess I've made.

Cutting my hair was a piece of cake compared to getting Frank changed. Lord knows he wasn't happy about that turn of events. I had to really coax him to take his shirt off, but then he seemed to get the wrong idea completely when I suggested he remove his trousers. He couldn't take them off fast enough. He grinned as he undid his belt buckle and suggested I start disrobing too, but then his trousers dropped and he saw the incontinence pants. That's when he started to cry.

At that moment I wondered what on earth I was thinking. What if this trip makes Frank's life worse? For half a second I thought about turning around and taking him back. Forgetting the whole foolhardy scheme. But, the thing is, I can't. I made Frank a promise and I can't go back on that. Lord knows I've let him down enough times in the past.

Frank snorts again and gives a little cough. Seems like he's starting to rouse. Just as well, really. We're not far out of Yass now and I need him to be alert enough to get out of the car when we get there. He might be old and frail but he's still bigger than me, and I'm not sure my arthritic bones are up to supporting his full weight.

He continues to stir for the next fifteen minutes or so and fully opens his eyes just as I see the sign for the Yass turn-off.

It's more luck than skill, but my amateur pharmacy work has panned out perfectly. He sits up straight in his seat and roughly wipes the drool from his chin. 'Where the hell am I?' He eyes me suspiciously. 'And who are you?'

'I'm Peggy,' I say, using the alias I've decided upon for the trip. I hate to deceive Frank this way, but I think it will make things easier if I'm consistent. 'I'm from the nursing home, Frank.'

'Oh, yes, that's right. I thought you looked familiar. I forget people's names sometimes, you know. So where are we going?'

'I'm taking you home,' I say, hoping this will placate him. 'But it's a bit of a trip, so we'll have to make a few stops along the way.'

He still looks confused but he doesn't argue. Instead he says, 'Is it nearly dinnertime? A man could eat the leg off a chair.'

I laugh. It's been ages since he's used that expression. 'Not too much longer. I'll get you a nice cup of tea and a biscuit as soon as we get to the motel and then we'll sort out something for dinner.'

'Motel, eh? Fancy.'

'Oh, not really. Just a cheap one, but I'm sure it will be fine.'

At least I hope it will. Once we hit the coast and pick up the Kombi we'll be right. We won't need to check in anywhere. Tonight's motel stay is the weakest link in my plan, but I really couldn't see a way around it. I chose Yass in the hope it would throw anyone looking for us off the trail. I figure once they work out where we stayed overnight they'll assume we're headed straight down the Hume towards Melbourne. At least, I hope they will.

'Is it dinnertime yet?'

I laugh again. 'Almost.'

It doesn't take long to reach the three-star motel I've booked. The car park is all but empty – a good sign for me. I park directly out the front of the office so I can see Frank if he decides to take a wander. 'You stay here for a minute. I'll be back in just a moment with the keys and then we'll have something to eat.'

He nods. 'Righto.'

The office is empty when I enter and I have to ring the bell on the counter before a middle-aged woman dressed in stretchy pants and an oversized T-shirt appears from a door behind the counter.

'Hello there,' she says brightly. 'I'm Sarah, the owner here at Traveller's Rest Motel. How can I help?'

'I have a reservation in the name of Miller.'

She clicks away on her keyboard and then nods. 'Ah yes, Mrs Miller. One night in a twin room.'

'That's right.'

'Lovely. The account comes to one hundred and nine dollars. That includes a complimentary continental breakfast. I can do you a cooked breakfast for eight dollars extra per head.'

'Oh, we won't be needing breakfast. We have an early start, you see. I expect to be heading off at first light.'

'Not a problem. If you like, I can do you up a breakfast basket and you can take it on the road with you. It won't be anything fancy – some fruit and yoghurt and pastries – but it'll fill the hole until morning tea time.'

'That would be lovely, thank you.'

'I'll make it up and bring it to your room in half an hour or so. And, seeing as you'll be leaving before the office opens in the morning I'll get you to settle the account now, if you don't mind?'

'Of course.' I dig around in my bag for my purse and pull out three fifty-dollar bills.

'Oh, I don't think I have enough change out here. I'll have to just pop in the back for a minute. Meanwhile, can you fill out this registration sheet?' She hands me a pre-printed form and a pen.

I nod and try my best to look unconcerned, even though my heart is beating a little faster than it was a moment ago. I hadn't counted on this. I fill out the name I've registered as, Peggy Miller, and use Francis Miller for Frank. I'm worried that if the woman calls Frank by completely the wrong name he'll argue with her. When it comes to the address I use a fake one – a holiday cottage in Moama we stayed in once when Fiona was little. We had such a nice time there and for some reason I always remembered the address. I fill out the car registration number – the motel owners can easily look out the window and see the numberplate, so there's no point in leaving that field blank. When Sarah comes back with my change I smile and hand her the completed form.

She returns the smile. 'Thank you. Now, if I could just see some ID, Mrs Miller, I'll get you your keys.'

I wasn't expecting this and my surprise obviously shows on my face.

'It's our policy when guests pay by cash to protect ourselves in case of theft or damage, that sort of thing,' she says apologetically.

'Of course,' I say as calmly as I can manage. I take my time to put the change back in my purse, then make a show of searching through its various compartments before looking up in dismay. 'Oh my goodness,' I say, 'I can't believe I've done this. In my hurry to pack I've brought the wrong wallet.'

Sarah looks at me blankly.

'It was just my birthday, you see, and I was given this lovely new purse.' Fortunately this is true. Fiona gave me the wallet for my birthday in August and I've only just started using it. If Sarah's taking notice she'll see that it looks brand-new. 'I grabbed it when I was packing and put all my money in it but I must have forgotten to transfer all my cards over.'

Sarah is nodding but somehow she doesn't seem convinced.

I sigh. 'What an idiot I am. It's just I really wasn't myself when I was packing. My husband's not very well, you see.' I drop my gaze for a moment. 'Dementia,' I whisper, as if it's some sort of shameful secret. I *am* ashamed, not of Frank's disease, but at how easily the lie I'm about to tell has come to me. I guess half a lifetime of deceit has been good practice. 'His sister is very ill with cancer and she doesn't have much time left. We got the call last night to come as soon as we could, so this morning I threw together a few things, got my husband in the car and got going.' I send another silent prayer for forgiveness to the heavens. Frank's sister, Patty, died years ago, so my lie can't hurt her.

Sarah's face softens. 'Oh, I am so sorry to hear that. Terrible thing, cancer. We lost my mum to it the year before last.'

I shake my head sympathetically. 'How awful for you.'

She nods thoughtfully. 'Let's not worry about the ID. I'm sure you and your husband aren't going to trash the room.' She laughs. 'Other than that, the ID is really only so we have something to give to the police if you turn out to be a criminal on the run. But you don't look much like an axe murderer to me.'

I laugh as convincingly as I can and finally say something that is true. 'I can solemnly promise you I'm not an axe murderer.'

She grins as she hands me the keys. 'Hmm, I don't know. They say it's always the ones you least suspect.'

Chapter 8

April 1962
Geelong

The look on Shirley's father's face when they told him was absolutely priceless. Frank had taken the liberty of buying a bottle of spumante to celebrate, so her mother seemed preoccupied with finding the right glasses in the crystal cabinet. But her dad just stood there grinning from ear to ear. Eventually he stepped forward, slapped Frank on the back and shook his hand. 'Welcome to the family, son. I couldn't have wished for a better man for our Shirley. You've made me a very proud and happy man tonight.' He drew Shirley in for a hug. 'Congratulations to you both. Now, excuse me for a moment, would you?' With that he disappeared into the hall.

Shirley looked across at her mother, who was walking towards the living room carrying a tray of drinks, and raised her eyebrows. 'What's got into Dad?'

He mother just shrugged. 'I'm sure I don't know, but we'd better wait for him before we have the toast.'

'Can I have a glass of spumante?' Wendy asked.

Her mother shook her head vigorously. 'Of course not. Sixteen is far too young to be drinking alcohol.'

'Oh, Mum, don't be such a stick in the mud. It's a celebration, and it's not as if I'll get drunk on one tiny glass. Tell her, Shirley.'

Shirley giggled, high on the excitement of what had just happened. Even though she'd anticipated this moment for ages, the reality was so much better than anything she'd imagined. He'd surprised her by being here when she got home from work – she hadn't expected him until late tomorrow night. He'd told her to get changed into her prettiest dress because he was taking her out somewhere special. She'd dressed and done her hair and make-up in record time, and soon they were in the car driving. She tried not to show her surprise when they bypassed town and headed out on the road towards Torquay. 'Where are we going?' she asked.

'You'll see soon enough.'

When they pulled up near the dunes at Bancoora Beach her heart swelled with emotion. He'd brought her back to the place they'd first met. It was dark now, but Frank insisted that they make their way onto the beach. Shirley hesitated for a moment, thinking about her new dress and the pink leather kitten heels she was wearing. 'This is such a romantic gesture, Frank. I only wish I was dressed more appropriately.'

'You're dressed perfectly for what I have in mind, my darling. You can carry your shoes if you like. I promise you your dress will be fine. Trust me.' He pulled a torch out of the boot of the car. 'Come on. I have a surprise waiting for you.'

She smiled then and pulled off her shoes. 'I do trust you, my love.'

They walked down the stairs to the sand. Shirley shivered in the autumn chill and pulled her cardigan tight. Why had Frank told her to dress up? This excursion would have been far more comfortable if she was dressed in pants and a jumper. She didn't want to be a wet blanket but the sand was freezing beneath her bare feet and she had goosebumps already. The beach was a romantic idea, but she hoped Frank had a late dinner booking somewhere and this was just a detour. Sitting on wet sand in the cold in her best dress wasn't really her idea of fun. Not that she'd dream of hurting Frank's feelings by saying as much. After all, it was the thought that counted.

Frank took her by the hand. 'Are you cold, sweetheart?'

'It is a bit nippy.'

'It won't be for long. Look, there's a fire down there. Let's go warm ourselves by it.'

Shirley looked towards the orange glow coming from a small bonfire a little way along the beach. As they walked towards it she realised there was another couple standing by the fire. Her heart sank. Perhaps tonight wasn't *the* night after all. Surely Frank wouldn't ask her to marry him in front of strangers?

'Seems like we don't have the beach all to ourselves,' she said.

'Soon we will, don't you worry about that.'

'What do you mean? We can't just ask people to leave, Frank.'

'Shh. Too many questions. Just come with me.' He laughed and broke into a jog, and Shirley had no choice but to follow him.

When they reached the fire she saw that the people were not strangers at all. Mary and her fiancé, Graham, stood with their backs to the fire.

Shirley forced a smile. Obviously she'd been wrong about the type of surprise Frank had planned for her. 'Well, hello, you two. I wasn't expecting to be on a double date tonight.'

Mary laughed. 'Graham and I can't stay, unfortunately. But I'm sure you two will do just fine without us.' She gestured to a blanket on the ground on the other side of the fire. A picnic blanket was laid out. A basket full of food sat at its centre and there was an ice bucket with a bottle of Barossa Pearl – her favourite fizzy wine – and two champagne glasses in it.

'What's all this?'

Mary shrugged. 'You'll have to ask Frank. We were just minding the spot until you arrived.' She turned to Graham. 'Hope you've been taking notice of this. Frank here sure knows how to treat a girl.'

Graham elbowed Frank. 'Now see what you've gone and done?' He grabbed Mary by the hand. 'Come on, Mare, let's leave these two lovebirds to themselves.'

Once they were gone Frank didn't waste much time. He bent down on one knee and asked her to make him the happiest man alive.

At last! At last it was happening. She was going to be a bride!

She could clearly picture herself walking down the aisle on her father's arm, wearing the dress she'd been coveting for months now. She had a scrapbook filled with ideas for everything from the bridesmaids' dresses to the cake. Until this moment it had been a fantasy, but now all her dreams were coming true.

'Shirl?' There was a worried note in Frank's voice.

'Oh!' Poor Frank. She'd been so busy picturing the wedding she hadn't actually replied. 'Of course I'll marry you, Frank. Nothing would make me happier.'

He'd jumped up and whooped before slipping the ring on her finger, and they'd laughed and danced and sipped champagne under the stars.

After a while they sat down on the picnic rug. Frank carefully draped a soft mohair blanket around her shoulders and served her the dinner he'd put together. He'd gone to so much trouble – finger sandwiches, little cubes of cheese on toothpicks with gherkins and pickled onions. He'd even packed some madeira cake for dessert. But Shirley was so excited she could barely eat a bite. She couldn't wait to go home and show her family the gorgeous ring Frank had picked out all on his own. It was absolutely perfect. Perhaps he'd had help from Mary . . . In any case, she loved it, and she couldn't wait to see the look on her sister's face when she showed it off.

Now she was home and everything was just how she imagined it would be. Her parents were ecstatic and Wendy was suitably impressed with the ring; less so with their mother's refusal to pour her a glass of bubbly.

'Shirley, tell Mum she's being an old fuddy-duddy. A girl should be able to celebrate her only sister's engagement.'

Shirley looked at her little sister with affection and then at her mother. 'Surely a little sip wouldn't hurt?'

Her mother grimaced. 'Oh, all right then. Just a little. But only if your father agrees.'

The man himself reappeared at that very moment. 'What am I agreeing to?'

'Can Wendy have a little wine to celebrate, Dad?' Shirley asked as Wendy slid her arm around his waist.

'Oh, I don't see why not. This is a big occasion indeed. And Mother and I have an announcement ourselves, don't we, dear?'

'What announcement?' Shirley looked at her mum, who just shrugged coyly.

Her father was revelling in the moment. 'Come on, everyone, into the lounge room. We can't have an important toast milling around in the kitchen.'

They all took their glasses into the lounge room. Shirley squeezed herself in between Frank and Wendy on the couch while her mum sat in her armchair next to the fireplace, but her father remained standing. He cleared his throat a little and then began. 'Shirley, firstly I'd like to say how proud your mother and I are of the fine young woman you've become. You've always been a good girl and done everything we've asked of you. We're thrilled that you've found an equally fine young man to love you and take care of you.' His voice cracked a little, and Shirley's eyes began to well at this rare show of emotion from her dad.

He gave a little cough before directing his gaze towards Frank. 'Frank, Margaret and I warmly welcome you into our family. From the moment Shirley first brought you home we had a good feeling about you. You've been respectful of us and of Shirley, and that's all we could ask. Well, that and that you follow the right football team, of course.'

Frank laughed. 'Go Cats!'

'Attaboy. I knew she'd picked a good one in you. Anyway, you two, here's to a long and happy marriage.' He looked at Margaret with affection. 'May you be as happy as your mother and I have been. Raise your glasses, everyone. To Frank and Shirley: may they live happily ever after.'

'To Frank and Shirley.' Wendy gulped down her wine in one mouthful, but neither of her parents seemed to notice.

Before taking a sip, Shirley's mum added her own toast. 'And may God bless your union with a large and healthy family.'

Her father nodded his agreement. 'Too right, Mother. Well said. Now, Frank, Shirley.' He looked at them each in turn. 'Your mother and I have long anticipated this day and we have a surprise for you both.' He reached into his back pocket and pulled out an envelope, which he gave to Frank. 'Go on, open it, son.'

Frank did as he was told, his eyes widening in surprise when he saw what was inside. 'Oh, good grief!' He passed the envelope to Shirley. 'This is too much. We can't possibly accept.'

Shirley's dad flushed with pride and her mum beamed from ear to ear. Shirley looked into the envelope to see a wad of cash. 'Oh my goodness!' It looked like there was at least one hundred pounds, maybe more.

'Let me look!' Wendy said. 'Wow. How much is it?'

Shirley frowned at her. 'Hush! You don't ask questions like that. It's not polite to talk about money.'

'Quite right, Shirley,' her father said. 'But because we're all family here I don't mind telling you there's two hundred quid in that envelope.'

Shirley gasped. 'Dad, that's too much! How did you ever manage . . .?

'Never you mind about that. Just use it wisely. There's enough there for a decent deposit on a house.'

Frank stood then and went to shake her father's hand. 'I promise you, Mr Miller, we will put this money to good use. And we'll build on the good start you've given us. I'll work tirelessly to make sure Shirley – and our children, when they come along – will want for nothing.'

'Enough of this "Mr Miller" business, Frank. I think it's about time you started calling us Mum and Dad.'

Chapter 9

Monday

Miraculously, Frank sleeps through the night. He was pretty exhausted after the drive yesterday and I slipped a splash of Phenergan into his after-dinner cup of tea for insurance. I had visions of him wandering off in the middle of the night, even though I was fairly sure he would struggle to open the locked motel-room door in the dark. The possibility that he might somehow manage to escape kept me awake half the night.

Despite my lack of sleep, I'm up before dawn. I quickly shower and dress in the motel's tiny bathroom, using the cheap hairdryer provided to dry off my hair. I give up on trying to style it – there's really no point. Between the hurried haircut I gave myself yesterday and the cheap dye job I did on it last night while Frank was sleeping, I've made a complete mess of myself. Nevertheless, I look at my reflection with satisfaction. I might look odd with my blue rinse and crew cut, but it's worked. I look nothing like myself.

I dress in the travel clothes I've bought especially for this trip: navy capris made from some sort of stretchy fabric and a pink polo shirt, topped off with a synthetic navy cardigan. A pair of sensible lace-up shoes completes my outfit. I look like every other grey nomad on the road. Or at least I hope I do.

I didn't bother with a new wardrobe for Frank. New things can stress him out and, besides, I didn't think it would achieve much. All old men dress much the same.

I boil the kettle and grab the thermos from my bag. I'd deliberated over whether it was worth bringing – it takes up a fair chunk of space in my little suitcase – but now I'm grateful. Tea has always soothed Frank, so it will be handy to have along the way. I need to be careful with the drugs today. I have a lot to negotiate and, while I need Frank to be calm, I can't risk him appearing heavily medicated.

My phone pings. It's a text from Fiona. She's up early. With a stab of guilt I wonder if she got any sleep either. I have a dozen or so missed calls – some from Fiona, the others from the nursing home. But it's the one from Lou that twists my stomach into a knot.

I love all three of my granddaughters equally, but Lou and I have always shared a special bond. I remember the first time I saw her – she was only a few days old. She arrived three weeks before her due date, so Frank and I weren't in Sydney for the birth like we'd planned to be. We'd raced up as soon as we heard the news and arrived in time to be with Fiona when she brought her second child home. Lou was cranky that day and Fiona – who looked like a washed-out dishrag – admitted she'd barely slept the night before. I put Gary in charge of our firstborn granddaughter, Frances, giving him strict instructions to take her out and keep her amused for at least an hour. Once they were gone, I encouraged Fiona to express as much milk as she could and then insisted she have some sleep while Frank and I got acquainted with our new grandchild. Lou settled quickly in my arms and from that day on I've always been the apple of her eye. Nan's the one who could make a boo-boo go away when she was little, and now she's in her last year of school, Nan's the one she comes to when life's not treating her right.

Frances (named for her grandfather, of course), is overseas right now so I doubt she'll have any idea what's going on. And sweet little Lila, who at fifteen is still a baby in all our eyes, is usually too caught up in her own social life to worry about much else. I'm sure Fiona's reassurances will be enough to stop her from fretting too much.

But Lou's a different kettle of fish. She's sharp as a tack and super-observant. Vague assurances from her mother will be of no comfort. I couldn't let Lou worry about Frank and me, so I left her a letter explaining myself without giving too much detail.

Dear Lou,

Please don't worry. Papa and I are absolutely fine. I'll be in touch as soon as I can. I promise by the time your HSC results come we'll be able to celebrate one way or another.

Love you,
Nan

I slipped the note into the pocket of her Coles uniform and I'm hoping she'll find it before her shift this morning. I didn't ask her not to show her mother – I would never put her in that position – but I have a feeling she won't. I figure it doesn't matter either way. It's not as if I've given her any clues as to where we are. In any case, Fiona's not stupid. I'm sure she will have her own ideas about which way we're headed.

Fiona's sent several texts and left a voicemail. Interestingly, Lou has left a message too. She once told me that only old people use voicemail. I decide not to listen to any of the messages now. I'm afraid that if Lou or Fiona sound distressed, my resolve will weaken. I turn the phone off, throw it in my handbag and grab the breakfast box that Sarah delivered the night before. It's packed full of goodies – more than enough to keep us going for hours – but there's no time to waste right now. We'll stop to eat once we've got some kilometres behind us.

The room's heavy floral curtains block out all light so it's hard to tell whether dawn has broken or not. I part them slightly and see that although the sun's not up yet, it won't be long. It's not pitch-black out there. I glance at my watch. Five-twenty. It'll be light by six. We need to get out of here.

'Frank,' I whisper, gently touching his leg. 'Time to go.'

He opens his eyes, blinking at me as he slowly comes to full consciousness. Once he's fully awake he sits bolt upright, his eyes betraying his fear and confusion.

'Where am I?' he demands. 'And who the hell are you?'

'Shh, Frank, we don't want to wake up the other guests.' I don't know whether there actually are any other guests – the car park was still empty when I'd taken Frank to the KFC drive-through to grab us some dinner. Nevertheless, I don't want him causing any sort of commotion. The last thing I need is some do-gooder knocking on the door to ask us if everything's okay.

Frank's glaring at me.

'It's me, Shir—' I start, and then stop mid-sentence. 'I'm Peggy.' I hate lying to him, but I console myself with the thought that it's a means to an end.

'Peggy? I don't know any Peggy.'

'We met at Sunset Lodge. You asked me to take you home.'

He stares at me for a moment then nods slowly. 'Oh. I beg your pardon, Peggy. I'm a silly bugger, aren't I? I forget things from time to time these days. So you're going to take me home. That's good of you.'

'It's my pleasure, Frank, truly. But we've got a bit of a long trip ahead, so we need to get going, if you don't mind. Let's get you up and showered and we'll be on our way.'

'Right you are. I'll just have a cuppa and bite to eat and then I'll be moving like greased lightning.'

'Actually, Frank, if you don't mind, I'd rather get on the road as soon as possible. I've got a big box of treats packed for us. You can snack on some fruit in the car and then we'll have a proper breakfast when we get a bit further down the road.'

He grins at me in that cheeky way that he still has. 'Well, yes ma'am. You're quite the bossy-britches, aren't you? That's all right, I like a woman who knows what she wants.'

I resist the urge to reply that this is news to me. Frank's a sweetheart and an old-fashioned gentleman, but he's always assumed that he knows best. Not that I blame him for that. It's just the way he is.

Getting Frank showered and dressed takes longer than I'd counted on. The sun is well up by the time we get going at quarter past six.

By seven we're almost at Bungendore. It's not far to Queanbeyan, which is where we'll leave the car. Our bus doesn't depart from there until twenty past eight, so we've got plenty of time to stop and have something to eat. As soon as I find somewhere suitable to pull over we'll have ourselves some breakfast.

Frank's been more animated today than I've seen him in weeks. He asks about the car and shakes his head when I tell him it's a Hyundai. 'Foreign rubbish. All those Japanese cars are tinny. Unreliable.'

'Korean,' I say.

'Eh?'

'Hyundai's a Korean brand, and, from what I'm told, a reputable one.'

He sniffs and tells me I'd be better off in a good, solid Australian-made car, like the ones built at the Ford factory, where he's a supervisor. Of course I don't mention that not only has he not worked at Ford for almost twenty years but that the Geelong plant has now closed down.

I spy a side road – not much more than a dirt track, really – and decide this is as good a place as any to take a break and have our picnic breakfast. A few hundred metres up the road it widens and I find a spot to pull over under a large gum tree.

Frank is happy to stretch his legs and makes a bit of a show of 'doing his exercises' (which consist of some toe touches and side bends) while I make us both a cup of tea. Frank sips his immediately – he's always liked his beverages piping hot – while I drag the breakfast box out of the back seat. I decide the yoghurt's too messy – I'd have to feed it to him to avoid spills and I'm not sure how that would go down with him. I want to avoid any sources of potential conflict, especially when he's in such a great mood. Even though I'd love nothing more than a tub of yoghurt to help settle my acid reflux (which has been in overdrive since yesterday afternoon), I decide the two thick slabs of banana bread are a better choice. Sarah's packed some little pats of butter and was even thoughtful enough to include a plastic knife. When this is all over I must remember to drop her a little thank-you note. That's if they let me write letters in jail.

I laugh at the thought of being behind bars. Surely no one would consider a custodial sentence for a harmless little old lady like me? I'm not even sure that what I'm doing is breaking the law. Frank came with me of his own free will, and I'm his next of kin. Fiona might hold the medical guardianship, but surely as Frank's wife I have rights. I should be able to spend time with my husband as I see fit.

Frank appears beside me. 'What are you laughing at?'

'Nothing really. I'm just happy, that's all. I'm enjoying being out here in the morning sun with you.'

He looks pleased with my answer. 'Well, that's good to hear. Now, what's a man got to do to get a feed around here?'

While we eat, I decide to broach the subject of the bus with him. I know how he hates change and I'm worried that the sudden switch in transport will throw him, especially since he hasn't had his risperidone this morning. I've slipped a half-dose of Phenergan into his tea, just to keep a lid on any problems. As much as I hate sedating him, I feel it's the wisest choice for this next leg of the journey. Hopefully it'll be enough to take the edge off without making him drowsy. And hopefully it'll be the last time I'll have to resort to such measures.

'So, I know you're keen to get home, Frank.'

'Too right. My girls will be missing me.'

'I have no doubt about that. Well, look, I'm really keen to get you where you need to go and I think you might be right about this car.'

He looks confused and I realise he's forgotten our earlier conversation. He cocks an eyebrow. 'How's that?'

'I'm not sure it's up to the task. We've got a long way to go and I think we need a new set of wheels to take us there.'

He walks around the front of the car and taps his hand on the bonnet. 'Flimsy, these Japanese models. Style over substance. Not like a Falcon. Now, there's a reliable car.'

I nod, not bothering to repeat the information about the car being made in Korea. 'I've organised to pick up a new car. Not a Falcon, but I think you'll like it.'

'A Ford, though?'

'Not a Ford. A Volkswagen.'

He scratches the stubble on his chin and nods. 'Well, if you're not going with an Australian car, a German one's the next best thing, I suppose. But I'm not sure one of those Beetles is the thing for a long-distance drive. Great for city driving—'

'I agree. That's why I've organised to pick up a Kombi.'

His face lights up. 'Shirl and I always wanted a Kombi van. We were going to take . . .' He flounders for a minute and I wonder if he's forgotten Fiona's name. He scrunches his brow and looks at me intently, and for a moment I think he recognises me, but the look is fleeting. 'One day we'll take our kids around Australia in a Kombi,' he says at last. But the joy has gone from his eyes. His scrambled memory has taken him back in time, but I don't know where.

I hope the Kombi is not a mistake. It's my gift to him. Part of my atonement. 'We're going to drop off this car and leave it for its new owner while we take a bus to pick up the Kombi. It won't take too long once we're on the bus.'

'Hmm,' he says, and I have no way of knowing whether he's taking all of this on board or not. I wonder how long the Phenergan will take to kick in. I pull a roll of antacids out of my handbag, pop two tablets in my mouth and begin to chew as I go over the next part of The Plan in my head.

According to Google Maps, we're almost at Queanbeyan. Once we're there, we'll leave the car at the local shopping centre – I think it'll draw less attention there than at the bus station. It's not a long walk from the shopping centre to the bus depot and it's not as if we have much luggage. I just have to pray that our faces haven't been plastered all over the media just yet. It's still early and I'm hopeful that even if we have made the news, not many people will have taken any notice. People these days seem to be in a perpetual hurry. I'm counting on most people being too busy, or apathetic, to commit the faces of a couple of old codgers to memory.

If we can get to Batemans Bay and pick up the Kombi without incident, I think we'll have a good chance of getting to our destination without being caught. The bus is a calculated risk, I know that, but it's only a matter of time before someone identifies the car we're travelling in, if that hasn't happened already. The sooner we can dump this vehicle the better. We only need to stay a few hours ahead of the authorities to get where we need to be.

'Come on, Frank, let's go.'

Frank gets himself back in the car, but seems confounded by the seatbelt, which has locked. He jerks it violently, muttering 'damned stupid thing' to himself. Luckily he's amenable to me assisting and I manage to sort that out before climbing in to the driver's side. Despite his height he shrinks into the seat, his earlier ebullience now gone. I wonder at the wisdom of giving him the sedative, but he seems lucid enough, just quiet and sad.

'Are you okay there, Frank?'

'Who's asking?'

'I'm Peggy, remember? From the nursing home. I'm taking you home. We're driving for a little bit and then we're going on a bus.'

He looks at me with complete disdain. 'A bus? What the hell would we want to do that for?'

I laugh. 'It'll be an adventure, don't you think?'

'An adventure? Well, that's one way of looking at it. But I'll pass, thanks. The last time I went on a bus I was still wearing short pants.'

'Is that a fact?'

He gives me a half-smile. 'Not really, but I was a young man. I work in the car industry. I've been a Ford man most of my life. Why take the bus when you can drive? That's what I always say.' It's true. He does always say that. Or at least he used to.

'I see. Well, I promise you that once we get off the bus we'll have another vehicle waiting for us.'

'That's a relief. Of course, I can see why you wouldn't want to drive too far in this thing.' He taps his hand on the dashboard. 'It's got about as much get-up-and-go as a matchbox car. Bloody flimsy Japanese rubbish.' He points to his wrist. 'Although people tell me the Japanese make good watches. Fancy that.'

We drive in silence for the next little while and before long find ourselves outside the shopping mall in Queanbeyan. I expect this car will be found pretty quickly once they know what they're looking for, but by leaving it here maybe it won't be immediately apparent that we've hopped on a bus. My hope is that by the time they find it we will have already left Batemans Bay.

We still have over half an hour until the bus leaves and I don't want to be standing around on the street for too long. I decide it won't hurt just to sit in the car for a bit. I can use the time to listen to the voicemails on my phone. I'll be throwing this phone in the bin before we get on the bus and activating the new phone I have all ready to go. I'm hoping it'll take the authorities a day or two to work that one out. I'm counting on them all believing that I'm inept.

I guess it largely depends on what information Ollie is prepared to divulge. He's the only person who has any idea of my technological skills. I'm no genius, but these days I know my way around a smartphone and a tablet. I honestly don't understand why people my age find modern technology so complicated. It's much simpler than some of the things we had to negotiate when we were young. Once upon a time I ran the switchboard at the Valley Mill. I'd like to see my granddaughters giving that a go. Or doing some of the other things we didn't think twice about – taking shorthand, for instance.

My daughter has no idea that I even own an iPad, let alone know how to use one. She's also blissfully unaware that I have a Facebook profile (under a pseudonym, of course) and a Twitter account. So far those things haven't been any help to me, but the community centre was running a social-media course and I figured it couldn't hurt to learn the basics. You never know when that sort of thing will come in handy. I find Twitter quite enjoyable, to be honest. But as far as Fiona's concerned, I'm hopeless with anything that was invented after 1980. Granted, I never did learn how to tape shows on the VCR, but that was simply a case of motivation. When video first became available I didn't have a lot of time on my hands. Catching up on missed TV shows was hardly a priority. And, besides, Frank was always the one in charge of what we watched.

The sun is shining through the windscreen, making the car warm, but not unpleasantly so. Frank stretches his legs out as far as they will go in this tiny car and closes his eyes. He's a man who loves the heat. Fiona and I used to joke that he had the blood – and the skin – of a blue-tongue. While Frank enjoys a moment in the sun, I check my phone.

First I open up the news websites. As I suspected, we've made the news, although we're not a top story and details of our disappearance are sketchy at best. More than one site has just a few sentences, ending with a promise of 'More to come'. Thankfully there seems to be no mention of the car yet. The *Sydney Morning Herald* is running a photo of us. I'm pleased to see it's one I approve of – taken at Christmas last year. Well done, Fiona. At least you haven't paid me back by giving the papers an unflattering photo, like that one taken at Frances's twenty-first where I have my mouth open and it looks like I have two chins. I was embarrassed to find Fiona had put that one in a frame and I insisted she change it for a better one. But in this case we are twice blessed: not only is the photo in the paper a decent one, it bears little resemblance to the way either of us look right now.

I sneak a glance at Frank and realise just how much he's deteriorated in the months since it was taken. Yes, it's a good photo, but it's also a fairly accurate depiction of how he looked on that day. Funny how you don't notice change when it's happening right in front of you. In the photo Frank's still a big man – solid and substantial, the way I always think of him. Looking at him now, I realise he's lost weight since then, and his tanned skin has become sallow. In the photo there's still a spark of life in his eyes. Yes, he was often confused, but just as often he was fine. He was still himself. There hadn't been any 'incidents' at that stage.

At first I didn't believe the staff at the home when they called us in six months ago to discuss Frank's new care plan in light of recent 'behaviours'.

'There must be some mistake,' I told the director. 'Frank simply wouldn't do such a thing. He's a gentleman. Don't take my word for it – ask anyone who's ever known him.'

'Mrs Sullivan,' the director said, in what I'm sure she thought was a sympathetic tone, but sounded patronising to me. 'Alzheimer's causes all sorts of behaviour in people. We understand how shocking this is to you, but it's part of the disease. No one is blaming Frank, but we do need to think about the other residents' safety. Surely you can understand that?'

'But no one's safety was at risk. You're all carrying on as if Frank has assaulted someone when he simply got into the wrong bed. It's quite easily done. I mean, all the rooms look exactly the same in this place.'

'Mum,' Fiona interjected, 'just listen, would you?'

I shot her a dark look, but she turned her head and pretended not to notice.

The director glanced at the social worker – who looked as if she was fifteen years old. The teenager smiled at me. 'Perhaps that is the case, Mrs Sullivan, but as you can imagine, Mrs Digby got a terrible fright. She was so distressed we had to call for the doctor.'

I resisted the temptation to roll my eyes . . . just.

So it transpired that Frank was moved from the regular part of Sunset Lodge into the high-security dementia unit. That's when I woke up to myself. I knew I couldn't just sit back and let this happen without trying to get him out of there.

With a sinking heart I realise that I came to my decision too late. I should have enacted The Plan months ago, when Frank was still enough of himself to appreciate it.

After scrolling through the news and reading Fiona's increasingly worried texts, I listen to my messages. The first few are from Sunset Lodge – each one more terse and urgent-sounding than the last. Then I listen to Fiona's. She sounds furious, which is her default position when she's worried. She spent most of her teen years snapping like a cantankerous Jack Russell terrier. Still, she doesn't sound too distraught, more incredulous that I could be so 'irresponsible'.

The sound of Lou's voice nearly breaks me. 'Nanny,' she says (she hasn't called me 'Nanny' since she was five), 'please be careful. I don't want anything to happen to you and Papa. You can call me if you need me. I won't tell Mum. You can trust me, Nanny, I promise.'

I cough to clear the lump that's formed in my throat and Frank's eyes open. 'What's going on?'

'Did you have a nice nap?'

He blinks a couple of times. 'Where am I?' he asks. 'And who the bloody hell are you?'

'I'm Peggy from Sunset Lodge and I'm taking you home.'

'I know that,' he says gruffly.

'Good. Well, we are going to grab our things and go for a little walk to the bus stop. How does that sound?'

He shrugs. 'All right, I suppose.' He doesn't look overly enthused.

'And then we'll hop on the bus and head across to the coast to pick up our Kombi.'

His mood visibly lightens. 'A Kombi, eh? Now there's a good choice. I've always wanted a Kombi.'

I grin at him. 'Is that a fact?'

I pop open the car's boot and retrieve our suitcase, and as soon as Frank sees it he insists on taking it from me. It's one of those ones with wheels, so it won't be too tricky for him to drag along to the bus stop. I pull out the handle for him and we make our way across the car park. Just before we hit the footpath, I spy a ute with Queensland numberplates and an idea strikes me. I pull my old phone out of my bag and, as we pass the vehicle, casually drop the phone in the ute's tray.

Hopefully the driver won't notice it until they are far away from here.

Chapter 10

14 March 1963
Geelong

It wasn't until she was changing into her going-away outfit that Shirley's nerves started to get the better of her. She sent June back out into the reception to get her a glass of champagne while Mary worked on unbuttoning her guipure lace wedding gown. Mary had beaten her down the aisle by two months and was now Mrs Graham Stewart. They hadn't had the double wedding Shirley had once imagined they might, but she'd been Maid of Honour for Mary and now Mary was her Matron of Honour.

It had been a beautiful day. The wedding had gone exactly to plan; even the weather had been picture-perfect. Shirley hadn't felt one ounce of trepidation for the whole day. In fact, walking down the aisle on her father's arm was quite thrilling. Everyone was looking at her as if she was a film star. She wished she could bottle the moment to keep forever. Frank's eyes shone as he lifted her veil. He whispered to her, 'You are the most beautiful girl in the world,' and right at that moment she felt as though she was.

At the reception all the girls from work had fawned over her, telling her how gorgeous her dress was and how lucky she was to have snapped up a handsome boy like Frank. She'd been floating on cloud nine all day.

Until now.

While she and Mary were alone, Shirley seized the opportunity to ask her friend the question that was the source of her apprehension. 'What's it like, Mare?' she whispered.

'What's what like? Oh . . .' Realisation dawned on Mary's face. She giggled a little. 'Honestly, Shirl, there's nothing to worry about. The first time is a little, well, strange. And a tiny bit uncomfortable when they first, you know' – she dropped her voice to a whisper – 'put it in.'

Shirley's stomach churned. Of course she knew the basic mechanics of sex but for some reason she hadn't ever stopped to think, *really* think, about Frank putting his . . . She shuddered. The idea of a part of Frank's body being inside hers filled her with terror, quite frankly. 'Does it really hurt?'

'Only a little. And then . . .' Mary blushed. 'I feel ashamed to admit this, Shirl, but once you get used to it, it's really quite lovely. In fact – God forgive me, I can't believe I'm saying this – but I actually can't get enough of Graham.' She giggled. 'I keep telling him it's because I so badly want a baby, but honestly that's only part of the attraction.'

'Really?' Shirley couldn't imagine how the act could possibly feel so good. She enjoyed kissing Frank, because it was an expression of their love for each other. Of course, Frank (being a man) seemed increasingly eager to go further. Recently she'd let him put his hands on her breasts – she wasn't a total prude, and they were engaged after all – and this seemed to increase his desire even more. As for her – well, she couldn't see what all the fuss was about. Frank's hands roaming over her bra felt . . . fine. His touch didn't bother her, but it didn't make her go weak at the knees either. 'What does it feel like, though? What makes it feel good?'

Mary giggled. 'Honestly, Shirl, I can't explain it. It just does. Don't worry, you'll see.'

June walked in with a tray of champagne glasses. 'She'll see what?'

Shirley shot Mary a warning look.

'Never you mind. Just old married ladies' talk,' Mary said.

'Right. Well, old married ladies, perhaps you'd like to raise a toast to all your single friends and wish them well in their quest to join your ranks.' She handed each of them a drink.

Mary raised her glass. 'To love,' she said. 'For us all.'

Later that night, in her brand-new home, Shirley took her time getting ready for bed. She couldn't quite believe her bedroom had its own ensuite. 'Oh my goodness, Frank, how fancy. Can we really afford this place?' she'd asked when he'd first taken her to see it.

'Let me worry about the money. You just worry about turning this place into a home.' She'd squealed then and kissed him. This house in Highton – one of Geelong's newer suburbs – was a dream come true. It was only a few years old, and was filled with all the modern things Shirley loved – a breakfast bar in the kitchen, which was open to the living and dining areas, lovely polished timber floors and beautiful exposed timber beams on the ceilings.

And so they'd bought the place and now they were finally here. It was sparsely furnished for now – just a bed, a couple of saucer chairs in the lounge room and a card table and camping chairs in the dining area. But Shirley didn't care. The house was theirs and that's what mattered. They'd put all their saved money into the deposit, so that their loan wasn't as enormous as it could have been. Frank had a good job now at the Ford plant, so making the loan repayments wouldn't be a problem. She was still a Valley Mill girl, for now. Of course she'd have to leave as soon as she was expecting, but until then all her wage would be spent on making the house look nice. They'd received some beautiful wedding gifts – lots of lovely glasses and things like that – and Shirley couldn't wait to start making this house into a real home.

'Are you right in there, Shirl? You've been ages,' Frank called from the bedroom.

'Making myself beautiful for you, my love.'

'No need for that. You're already beautiful. Come to bed.'

She quickly wiped away the cold cream, splashed her face with water and dried it on a soft new *Hers* towel from the set Aunty Mae had given them as a wedding present. She checked her reflection in the vanity mirror and flushed a little when she realised her nipples were completely visible through the sheer white baby-doll negligee she'd chosen for her wedding night. There was no need to be embarrassed, she counselled herself. Frank was her husband now. He was entitled to see her naked. And pretty soon the negligee would be coming off altogether.

'Coming,' she called. She slid the ensuite door open and struck a pose in the doorway. 'Well, Mr Sullivan, what do you think?'

Frank wolf-whistled. 'Ravishing, Mrs Sullivan, simply ravishing. Now obey your husband and get in this bed so I can have my way with you.'

Afterwards, Shirley ran herself a bath in the main bathroom down the hall. She lowered her body gingerly into the steaming hot water and waited for the pain to subside. Mary had forgotten to mention the bleeding. Of course she'd known about it from whispered conversations between the girls at work, but she hadn't expected it to be more than a drop. Now her brand-new sheets were soaking in the laundry trough and she'd had to put fresh ones on the bed so Frank could go to sleep. The whole thing had been messy and uncomfortable. How Mary could 'not get enough' of this activity was a complete mystery to her. It wasn't something she wanted to repeat in a hurry.

Frank certainly seemed to enjoy himself, although he hadn't lasted very long once he was inside of her. In fact, after half-a-dozen thrusts he grunted and collapsed on top of her. He lay there for a long time, stroking her hair and murmuring sweet things to her. When he finally prised himself away she felt something trickling down her thigh. Mary hadn't mentioned *that* either.

Still, Mary had warned her the first time was uncomfortable, so hopefully things would improve. If not, well, she'd just have to make the best of it. She wanted to be a good wife, and obviously Frank would expect marital relations on a regular basis. Besides, she wanted to be a mother more than anything, and there would be no babies without doing the deed. If it turned out suffering a few minutes of discomfort every night was the price she had to pay to make a family, so be it.

Frank knocked gently on the door. 'Shirley, honey, are you in there?'

'Come in, Frank.'

He opened the door and looked at her, his forehead creased with concern. 'Are you okay, sweetheart?'

She smiled. 'Never better. I just wanted to unwind a little. It's been such a big day.'

He leaned on the doorframe and smiled back. 'Best day of my life.'

'Mine too.'

The next day they were both up early for Sunday Mass. Shirley wandered into the ensuite to find Frank shaving. He grinned at her refection in the vanity mirror. 'Shame you're already up, Mrs Sullivan. I was going to bring you a cup of tea in bed.'

'No time for that if we're going to make it to church on time.'

He nodded. 'Fair enough. Tomorrow then.'

'I can't wait.'

They'd agreed on forgoing a proper honeymoon, instead opting to spend Frank's week of leave from work at home in the new house. 'There will be plenty of time to travel later on,' Frank had said when they were planning the wedding. 'In a few years' time, when we're a bit more on our feet, we'll do a big trip.'

Shirley agreed. It was stupid to waste money on a holiday when they had a beautiful new home that was crying out to be properly furnished. They'd be together and that was honeymoon enough. 'That sounds lovely, Frank,' she'd said.

He'd scratched his head. 'Of course, we'll probably have kids by then, so it wouldn't exactly be a honeymoon, Shirl.'

'A family holiday will be even better,' she assured him. 'Just imagine, Frank, you and me, and a couple of little ones strapped into the back seat of the car. It'll be heaven.' She'd leaned back into him as they sat together on her parents' couch. Mum was in the kitchen making a start on dinner and had sent Dad outside to pick some tomatoes for the salad. For the moment they had the room to themselves. 'Where would we take them?'

He'd grinned. 'Everywhere! You know what would be great, Shirl? We could get ourselves a van and travel all over the place.'

'A caravan?'

'Yeah, maybe. Or, even better, one of those new Kombi vans. We could pack the kids into the van and just take off for a few weeks at a time. Maybe we'd go north, to the Gold Coast. Wouldn't that be a treat?'

So that was the plan. Once the house was furnished they'd put away money for a Kombi van. It wouldn't have to be a new one. Frank assured her that between him and his mates they had enough mechanical knowledge to fix up a second-hand van and make it like it was new, so it shouldn't set them back too much. And once they had their little mobile home they'd be able to take their kids on lots of lovely holidays all over the country.

Shirley nudged Frank to move over so she could share the basin, and he gave her a cheeky tap on the backside. As she splashed water on her face she wondered if perhaps God had blessed them with a baby already. After all, lots of girls fell pregnant after doing it just once. The nuns at school had repeatedly warned them that if they allowed their bodies to be defiled before marriage there was a very great chance that they'd end up carrying a child out of wedlock. But now she was a married woman and her union was blessed by God.

She knew what she'd be praying for in church today.

Chapter 11

Monday

Thank goodness the coach is on time. The short walk from the shopping centre car park has done Frank good. He's looking happy and alert, and less frail than he did just a few hours ago. We popped in to the shopping centre to use the toilets before wandering to the bus interchange. I'm getting better at managing the bathroom situation so it's less upsetting for both of us. Being matter-of-fact and using a bit of humour seems to be the best approach. It's not unlike the methods I used to use to keep Fiona happy on outings when she was a toddler.

Comparing Frank to a toddler turns my insides to water and my confidence begins to wobble.

Am I crazy, trying to pull this off?

But there's no time for second thoughts now. We're in the thick of it. The thought of my once strong and capable husband being cajoled like a child has to be pushed to the back of my mind. Instead I focus on the positives: Frank's fed, watered and toileted, and as ready as he can be for two and a half hours on a bus.

The driver looks at us intently as we board the coach and my throat goes dry. I smile at him and he returns the gesture.

'Watch your step there. It's higher than you think.' He glances at the tickets I show him and he ticks off our names (Miller, party of two) on his list before diverting his attention to the next passenger. I realise he's not the slightest bit interested in us.

That's hurdle number one cleared. All morning I've feared we'd be pulled up at this point for some reason – recognised by the driver from the news coverage perhaps, or traced by my ticket purchase. I bought our fares online using the credit card Fiona doesn't know about after I discovered I could open a brand-new bank account using my maiden name. I used a bank neither Frank nor I have ever done business with before in the hope that it will take the authorities a tiny bit longer to join up all the dots. Of course, I'm sure in this brave new digital world we live in it won't be too long before the police trace it – and, through the credit card, these bus tickets – but hopefully we have a day or two before that happens.

The bus pulls out of the interchange bay right on twenty minutes past eight. More than half of the seats are empty, which is hardly surprising considering it's a weekday outside of tourist season. There are a few other oldies like us on the bus, a couple of scruffy-looking teenagers – maybe they're backpackers, I can't be sure – and a smartly dressed young woman who sits herself across the aisle from me.

The girl smiles and says hello. I smile tightly and turn my head. I could really live without any idle chitchat today. But Frank eyeballs her and gives her his most charming smile. 'Looks like it's going to be a nice day,' he offers.

His memory might be failing him, but the essence of who he is remains. Frank is a talker, a social being, and there's no distracting him from that. So he engages the young woman – Cait, she introduces herself – in conversation. She's headed to Batemans Bay for a job interview at the real estate agent there. She grew up in Batemans Bay but work there is hard to find. She moved to Queanbeyan for a job but misses her family. For once I'm grateful for the self-involvement of millennials – that's what they call the young people now, isn't it? Cait prattles on and on about her life and her family and doesn't think to ask us anything other than what we are doing in the area.

'Just here on holidays,' I say vaguely.

She smiles and says, 'It's a lovely part of the world,' before launching into another monologue. She talks about all the places she's lived along the coast and tells Frank about some good fishing spots she knows of. My ears prick up when she mentions Mossy Point, a secluded little spot just off the beaten track. Cait says it's mainly frequented by locals at this time of year, as well as the occasional backpacker. 'Although you'd probably need a car to get to the boat ramp,' she says. 'Are you staying with someone who could drive you?'

Her sudden question catches me unawares. 'No, it's just us,' I say, in what I hope is a breezy tone. *Damn it.* I need to be more careful and have a story prepared. Why didn't I invent a relative of some type? Or stick to the tale about Frank's sister?

But Cait seems unfazed by the idea of two elderly people taking themselves off on a holiday on the bus. She smiles indulgently, like we're a pair of adorable preschoolers. 'Never mind. There are plenty of other nice spots on the bus route.'

Thankfully, Frank doesn't correct her assumption. He seems to have forgotten all about the Kombi. At any rate, he doesn't mention it.

The trip is slow going as the coach crawls around the twists and turns of the mountainous road, but I'm beginning to relax. No one on the coach is even slightly interested in us. Not even Cait, now she's told us her whole life story. She's finally stopped talking and is engrossed in watching something on her phone. Frank's given up trying to keep her attention and is looking at the scenery through the window. I yawn. Now the adrenaline's worn off, the early start and stress of the morning is starting to catch up with me. There's still another three-quarters of an hour until we arrive in Batehaven, where hopefully Joachim and Petra will be waiting for us. My eyelids begin to droop and I allow myself a moment's shut-eye. The next thing I know, the bus's brakes are being applied and my eyelids flick open. We're in Batemans Bay already.

Cait stands to disembark. 'It was lovely meeting you both,' she says.

I notice with relief that she doesn't use our names. I'm not sure if Frank introduced himself, but I was careful not to, and the girl was so busy talking about herself she didn't seem to notice. Hopefully she'll forget all about us oldies once she steps onto the street.

'You too, love,' Frank says.

She turns back for a moment, a look of concern on her face. 'Which is your stop? I thought you were holidaying in Batemans Bay? Do you know where to get off?'

I plaster a reassuring look on my face. 'Oh, we're fine, love. Don't worry.'

'Yeah, we're right as rain,' Frank chips in. 'The boss here has got it all sorted. We're going on a road trip in a Kombi.'

Cait's eyes widen in surprise.

Shit, bugger, bum. Of all the times for Frank's short-term memory to function, why did it have to be now? We were so close to getting to our destination without giving away anything. 'You wish, you silly old bugger.' I look at Cait and shake my head. 'We're meeting some old friends at Batehaven,' I say, contradicting my earlier story. Her face creases in confusion and I try to come up with a plausible reason for not mentioning them earlier. 'They're old, like us. They don't have a car.' I sound ridiculous and I know it. 'We'll have a couple of days in a nice unit with them and then head on up north alone.' I nod towards Frank. 'He gets confused sometimes, so I try to keep things simple. Not give him too much information at once.'

I feel Frank deflating beside me and I hate myself for resorting to this public humiliation of him. What's the point of taking him away from that prison he was in if I'm going to inflict even greater pain on him?

For her part, Cait gives me a sympathetic smile. 'Well, have fun, you two. I'd better get going.' And just like that she's gone. I tell myself she poses no real danger. She'll be tied up all morning with her job interview and by this afternoon she'll have forgotten all about us.

I'm on high alert now, albeit a little too late. Thankfully the bus is nearly empty by this stage. The only people left on board are the scruffy teenagers, and they're too busy looking at their phones to be interested in us.

It doesn't take long to snake our way along the coast to Batehaven. My heart leaps as I spy a turquoise-blue and white Kombi parked near the playground in the beach car park. Surely that's Petra and Joachim. There's a flutter of anxiety – mixed with a tinge of optimism – in my chest. I know in my bones that if I can get the keys to that Kombi, I can get Frank back to where he belongs. I just have to hope that I can fudge the paperwork without the young German couple noticing.

I deliberately chose to buy from backpackers, figuring that they might be less concerned about the transfer of registration than others. Petra and Joachim are at the end of their holiday, apparently flying back to Germany next week. Originally they were reluctant to meet us here, saying they preferred to get rid of the van closer to a major airport. Luckily for me they were easy to persuade. As Frank always used to say, everyone has their price. I offered to pay for their flights to Sydney and added an extra five hundred dollars to the asking price for their trouble. After that they were happy to oblige. I'm hopeful that their enthusiasm for the deal will help them to overlook the fact that I don't have any valid ID.

The bus pulls up and I help Frank out of his seat. The driver asks me if we need help to retrieve our luggage from under the bus and I wave away his concern. 'We're fine,' I say. 'Thank you.'

As the bus drives away I look up at the bright-blue, cloudless sky and inhale the sea air. Frank is smiling. Right now he looks like himself, not some washed-out watercolour version of who he used to be. I take him by the hand. 'Come on, old man. Let's go start our adventure.'

Chapter 12

April 1964
Geelong

Shirley sat in the doctor's waiting room with her hands clasped in her lap. She smiled at the elderly woman sitting opposite her who was knitting a sweet little baby bonnet. She could hardly contain her excitement at the thought that her own mother would soon be engaged in the very same task. 'For your grandchild?' she asked.

The woman looked up. 'No, love. I don't have children. I knit these for the hospital, for the poor mothers.'

'Oh. How lovely of you.'

'Some people have no business bringing children into this world, but that don't seem to stop them. Still, not the poor wee babe's fault, is it? All babies deserve to have something warm to go home in, don't you think?'

Shirley nodded. 'Yes, of course.'

'What about you, love? Got any little ones at home?'

Shirley felt herself blushing. 'Not yet. But we're hoping we'll be blessed that way very soon.' Surely this was it. She'd missed her monthly twice in a row now, a fact she'd managed to conceal from Frank. She felt bad about the pretence that her cycle was normal but she didn't want him getting his hopes up unnecessarily. And she had to admit that the break in their nightly relations was a welcome one, especially with her breasts being so sore and swollen lately.

Her lack of menses and the tender breasts were good signs, she was sure, but they weren't the only ones. She was incredibly tired after work each day. By the time she'd made Frank's dinner she was ready for bed and could hardly keep her eyes open. Frank had joked that she must be getting old, because she'd fallen asleep watching *Pick A Box* several times now. Last month she'd had a bout of nausea that had lasted on and off for a couple of weeks. Combined, all these symptoms seemed to point to one happy conclusion.

She was very much hoping Doctor Downing would confirm her suspicions today. She'd taken the afternoon off work, claiming a headache. If the doctor gave her good news she'd head to the shops on the way home and buy something special for dinner.

She couldn't wait to see the look on Frank's face when she told him. They'd been married for more than a year now and, although he'd never said as much, she was sure he must be starting to worry that she was barren. She knew how much he wanted children and she hated to think what might happen if she couldn't produce them. Not that she believed Frank would leave her, or anything like that – he was the most loyal husband on earth – but it would be a sad life without children. Look at her Aunty Ellie and Uncle Bob. They hadn't been blessed with children, and the bitterness and jealousy that plagued her aunt had turned her into a meddling old cow. Instead of rejoicing in her nieces and nephews, she endlessly criticised them. 'Not enough to do with her time,' Shirley's mum was fond of saying. As for Uncle Bob, sweet man that he was, he looked perpetually sad. Was that what the future held for her and Frank if they couldn't have children?

They hadn't worried for the first few months. Frank had even joked that he was having so much fun 'trying' that he didn't mind her not being pregnant at all. But after six months of almost daily relations and no sign of a baby, Shirley had begun to worry. There was no one she could talk to about this. No one she knew was in the same situation. She didn't want to worry her mother, her sister was too young, and none of her friends would understand. Mary had given birth to a baby boy before her first wedding anniversary and all the other married girls she knew were either already mothers or well on the way. What was wrong with her?

Today, she hoped she'd find out there was nothing wrong after all.

'Mrs Sullivan,' the receptionist called. 'Doctor will see you now.'

Thirty minutes later Shirley left the doctor's office with a handful of pamphlets and a song in her heart. She was tempted to catch the bus to Chilwell so she could pop in and see her mother, but she couldn't share this news with anyone before she told Frank, so instead she made a detour via the butcher to get some steaks for dinner. Lately the meaty odours from the butcher's shop had made her feel off-colour and she'd been avoiding it as much as possible, but not today. Now she knew the cause of her squeamishness she was prepared to tolerate it to buy Frank's steak – in fact, in a perverse way she welcomed the sensation. Finally she was part of the club!

She dawdled home, stopping off at the greengrocer for baby potatoes and a bunch of daffodils. She couldn't remember ever being so happy, not even on her wedding day. At home she fussed about – setting the table, making a salad and preparing dessert – before heading into the ensuite to shower and change. She wanted everything about this evening to be perfect, including her appearance. She took her time in the shower, washing her hair even though it really didn't need it. Before she dressed in her yellow sundress (Frank's favourite), she took a moment to look at her naked body in the full-length mirror on the back of their bedroom door. Her breasts, which had always been on the smaller side, were full and large. She turned side-on to look at her stomach, to see if she could detect any difference. It still looked flat, but when she ran her hand over it she thought she could detect the tiniest bump. Maybe it was her imagination. Not that it mattered. She'd be sporting a real bump soon enough. She supposed she should make the most of this time while her clothes still fitted. In a month or two her wardrobe would consist of maternity smocks.

Doctor Downing had told her she would need to give up work. As soon as was convenient, he advised, but definitely before the sixth month of her pregnancy. Luckily she had a job where she sat at a desk, otherwise she'd have to leave immediately. She loved her job, but now that she was to be a mother she had to prioritise her family life. Baby came first, of course. Still, if there was no harm in it she'd like to work for a few more months. The money would come in handy for all the extra expenses they were about to incur: clothes, baby formula, toys, and of course there was the nursery to furnish.

The one bonus of having had to wait so long to conceive was that she and Frank were doing quite well for themselves. Frank had already been promoted to supervisor at the plant, and he was making pretty good money. Her wage helped too. They were easily making the mortgage repayments and she'd managed to furnish their house with beautiful things. A few weeks back, Mary had come to visit with her baby. She'd gushed over the new dining setting and told Shirley how envious she was of their lovely house. Shirley had truthfully replied she'd give it all up in a heartbeat to have what Mary had. And now her dream was coming true. She couldn't believe that soon she'd be cradling her own babe in her arms.

She must be the luckiest girl in the world.

Frank arrived home at five-thirty on the dot. She heard him park the new Falcon – his pride and joy – in the carport. His key turned in the front door just as she was putting the potatoes on to boil. She busied herself at the stove, not daring to look at him lest her face give her away. She planned to tell him over dessert; she'd made apple crumble, which was his favourite. He came up behind her and put his arms around her waist, kissing her neck at the same time. 'You smell good,' he said. 'Let me look at you. Is that my favourite dress? Turn around and let me see.'

She laughed and batted his hands away. 'Let me get on with this, would you, or there'll be no dinner. Why don't you go and get cleaned up?'

'Only if you give me a kiss first.' He twirled her around to face him and planted his lips on hers. When they parted he looked at her. 'What's up with you tonight? You look like the cat that's got the cream.'

She shrugged and shook her head without replying, but there was no hiding her news. She saw the realisation dawning on his face.

'Shirl, do you have something to tell me? You couldn't be what I'm thinking . . . are you?'

She couldn't stop herself from grinning. 'If you mean am I in the family way, well, the answer is a most definite yes. You're going to be a daddy at last.'

Frank let out an almighty whoop and lifted her off her feet, before kissing her hard on the lips again. Suddenly he set her down. 'Sorry. I should be more careful now you're expecting. In fact, should you be doing all this work? Why don't you go and put your feet up and I'll finish dinner.'

She laughed. 'Frank Sullivan, when did you suddenly learn to cook?'

He looked sheepish. 'Well, you can sit at the breakfast bar and tell me what to do. I'm sure I can manage.'

'There'll be no need for that. I'm pregnant, Frank, not an invalid. I can still cook us dinner.'

'If you're sure,' he said, looking relieved. 'But, my darling, you will have to take it easy now. Have you given your notice at work?'

She laughed again and shook her head. 'Frank, you're fussing. Firstly, I only found out a few hours ago, and secondly I don't need to give up work just yet. Doctor Downing said it was fine to keep working for a few more months.'

Frank frowned. 'Really? I'm not sure that's such a good idea.' He placed his hand gently on her stomach. 'We've waited so long for this, Shirl. I'd hate for anything to happen.'

'I know. Look, let's talk about this over dinner. Go and get cleaned up while I grill the steaks.'

He grinned again. 'You're the boss.'

They ended up having a lovely dinner, even if everything didn't quite go to plan. The steak was a tiny bit overdone, due to Frank insisting that they open the bottle of spumante his cousin Brian had given them at Christmas.

Shirley didn't feel much like drinking, but Frank's enthusiasm was contagious so she let him pour her half a glass. She was lightheaded after just a few sips, which caused her to momentarily forget all about the steak she had cooking in the vertical grill. It was definitely well done, but neither of them minded. At least the apple crumble was perfect.

Over dessert, Frank returned to the subject of her job. 'Listen, Shirl, we're doing all right, don't you think?'

'More than all right, I'd say. In fact, Dad told me the other day that he was so proud of what we'd achieved in such a short time. He might even have referred to this house as a "palace".'

Frank laughed. 'High praise indeed. Especially considering his reservations when we first bought the place. So, that being the case, do you really want to keep working these next few months? I'd be much happier if you were at home resting. I'm on a good wage now, and things are only going to get better. The bosses have told me they think I'm management material. How about that, huh? Not too shabby for a boy from the bush.'

'Oh, Frank, that's wonderful!'

'I'm sure none of the other managers have working wives. You'll have to give it up soon enough, so you may as well hand in your notice right away.'

Shirley had always known this day would come. Of course she wanted nothing more than to be at home with her baby. It was just that the idea of not going to work, not seeing the other girls in the office every day seemed strange to her. What would she do with herself until the baby arrived?

'I see what you're saying, really I do, but there will be a lot of expenses with a new baby in the house. Clothes, nursery furniture, a pram and a highchair. Mary says her little fella is sending them broke.'

'Still, wouldn't you rather be at home, resting up?'

She shrugged. 'I feel perfectly well at the moment. I mean, I've been a little bit tired, but otherwise I'm as fit as a fiddle. And it's not as if my job is physically taxing. I don't see how it could hurt. And I'm not sure what I'd do with myself all day, to be honest.'

'You'll be busy enough, I'm sure, what with decorating the nursery and shopping for all those things you've just said we need. You could spend some time with your mum. And Mary. It might be good to visit with her more often so you get used to being around a baby, eh?'

Everything Frank said made sense, but the stubborn streak within her resisted being told what to do. Yes, Frank was her husband, and yes, she'd promised to 'obey' him, but theirs wasn't that sort of marriage. They were a modern couple. Frank treated her as an equal.

'I'll tell you what, why don't I meet you halfway? Doctor Downing said I could work up to the sixth month of the pregnancy. He estimates I'm nearly three months along. What if I give four weeks' notice tomorrow? That way we'll have another month's wages and I'll be finished up by the time I'm starting to show.'

Frank nodded slowly. 'If you're sure that's safe. I want you to promise me that you'll take it easy.'

'Honestly, Frank, I'm fine. But I promise to be careful, and I'll stop work the second it gets too much.'

He smiled. 'All right then. Mother knows best. Now you go and put your feet up. I'll take care of the dishes tonight.'

Shirley's heart swelled. She'd married a good man. She took herself off to the bedroom and started her nightly beauty routine. By the time she'd slipped on her nightie and tucked herself into bed, Frank was ready to join her. He changed quickly and climbed in next to her. As she clicked off the bedside lamp he reached for her, as he did every night, his hand coming to rest on her lower belly.

'Shirl,' he whispered. 'Is it all right to . . . can we still . . .?'

She hadn't thought to ask the doctor about intercourse, and even if she had, she wasn't sure she would have been comfortable bringing up such an intimate matter. Of course, she knew that Mary and Graham had continued to have relations right up to the week baby Paul was born. Mary had joked that she'd begged Graham to make love to her in the last week of her pregnancy because she'd heard that intercourse brought on labour.

She patted Frank's hand. 'Probably best not to, darling, just to be on the safe side.'

Shirley floated through the next week on cloud nine. With her father still working at the Valley Mill she really couldn't risk handing in her notice at work until she'd delivered the news to her parents, so she and Frank paid them an impromptu visit after dinner on Wednesday night.

As expected, her parents were thrilled, and Wendy was over the moon. She insisted on everyone calling her 'Aunty Wendy' for the remainder of the evening.

On Thursday, she handed in her notice as she'd promised to Frank, and then she delivered the news to the girls in the office. Everyone congratulated her and June started planning her farewell party on the spot.

On Saturday she and Frank went into town to look at nursery furniture. Shirley just wanted to get some ideas and to work out what they were up for price-wise, but Frank couldn't contain himself. She kept telling him that they had months to go and that they really should take their time to look around and compare prices, but he insisted on buying a bassinette that Shirley had admired. 'If you like it, get it,' he said. It took a while to convince her but she was glad he did in the end. As soon as she finished working she'd be able to get started on sewing a layette to fit. After they'd had lunch in a new cafe on Ryrie Street, Frank bought her a pot of tea and excused himself. 'I've got a couple of tiny jobs to do. Nothing of interest to you, my love. No point you being on your feet more than necessary.

You stay here and enjoy your tea. I'll be twenty minutes or so, tops.'

Shirley agreed without questioning him. She figured he was off looking at something for the car. He was so obsessed with that Falcon that sometimes she joked that he loved it more than he loved her. In any case, she was happy to sit for a bit. Frank was right – she did tire more easily than usual these days, so it wouldn't hurt to have a break.

Frank returned within the half-hour carrying a brown paper shopping bag.

'What have you got there?' she asked.

'I'll show you when we get home. Ready to go?'

Despite her curiosity, she nodded and accepted the hand he offered to help her up. Clearly Frank had a surprise of some sort and he'd reveal it when he was ready, not a moment before.

Once they were home, Frank asked her to take a seat in the lounge room. He sat beside her and took a tiny wrapped parcel out of the shopping bag.

'What's this?'

'It's a gift for you, my darling. To show you how grateful I am for the gift you're giving me.'

'Oh, Frank. You shouldn't have.'

'Well, I have, so you might as well open it.'

She tore open the paper to reveal a tiny box from Duffs Jewellers. She opened the box and gasped. Inside was the most beautiful pearl pendant on a silver chain. 'Frank,' she breathed. 'It's gorgeous. But can we afford this?'

'You let me worry about that. Would you like me to put it on for you?'

She nodded eagerly, lifting up her hair so he could fasten the clasp. She went straight to the mirror to check her reflection and then rushed back to Frank to kiss him. 'Thank you, darling. I absolutely love it.'

'That's not all. I have something else here too. But technically this one isn't for you. It's for junior.' He handed her the shopping bag.

She reached in and found a soft toy; a white fluffy rabbit. 'Oh, how adorable. This will look gorgeous in the bassinette.'

'Speaking of which, I'd best get that inside and set it up in the nursery. Then we can pop this little fellow in bed and see how he looks.'

She placed her arms around his neck and kissed him properly. 'You are going to make the best daddy in the world.'

On Tuesday morning Shirley found herself unable to concentrate at work. Being pregnant was everything she had hoped it would be. The nausea had settled considerably now and her breasts weren't quite as tender as they had been. She was ashamed to admit it – even to herself – but having a plausible excuse not to have intercourse with Frank was a blessed relief. She wasn't even worried about the pain of labour. Mary had told her it wasn't so bad. She'd gone to birth preparation classes beforehand. Apparently there was some sort of special breathing you could do to help manage the pain. In any case, what was one day of pain compared to the lifetime of happiness a child would bring?

Frank might have been right to insist that she give up work sooner rather than later, though. Today she'd woken up with a sore back, and sitting all day had made it worse. She was looking forward to going home and putting her feet up. Frank had been so considerate of her since he found out the news. He insisted that he was perfectly capable of cooking dinner for them both if she needed to rest. Tonight she might even take him up on that offer. Surely he could manage eggs on toast? In fact there was a bit of bacon in the refrigerator too. That would have to do.

She fingered the pearl pendant at her throat and once again thanked her lucky stars for the man she'd been given. Normally she didn't like to skite, but she hadn't been able to resist showing off the pendant to the girls yesterday. There had been lots of *oohs* and *aahs*, but June seemed to have her nose out of joint. 'I'd be careful wearing that if I were you. You know pearls are for tears, don't you?' Sometimes June could be a right pain in the neck.

At least Nola had stuck up for her. 'Don't listen to her, Shirley. That's just a stupid old wives' tale. June's just jealous because she hasn't got anyone to buy her jewellery.'

Shirley told herself that she wasn't superstitious, but she had to admit June's words had unsettled her. She'd even thought about taking off the necklace, but what would Frank think if he noticed? No, Nola was right. June was jealous. She hadn't had any luck in love and was still single. No wonder she felt the need to lash out every now and then.

She glanced at her watch. Only five minutes till lunchtime. She really needed the ladies' but supposed she could hang on another few minutes. Even though he knew she was expecting, Mr Mason frowned upon 'excessive' bathroom breaks. Thank goodness she was leaving soon, because her bladder seemed increasingly sensitive with each passing day.

When the factory whistle blew for lunch she stood up quickly and was overwhelmed by a sharp cramp, not unlike the pain she often experienced during her monthly. Nola, who sat at the desk opposite her, heard her sharp intake of breath and looked up.

'Are you okay, Shirl?'

The cramp had eased now. 'I think so. I just need the ladies'.'

She pushed in her chair and had started to walk towards the bathroom when another powerful cramp took hold. She clutched her stomach in fear. Something wasn't right. She raced into the toilets and hoisted up her skirt. When she saw the blood in her knickers she began to cry.

Please, God, no. Please don't take my baby from me.

Chapter 13

Monday

I use my hand to shield my eyes from the glittering light reflected off the water and wait for a gap in the slow-moving tourist traffic. There aren't many cars about but Frank needs more time than me to cross, so I need to be careful. Finally we cross the road and walk towards the Kombi, but before we get there a young, blonde-haired woman walks towards us. 'Hello. You are Peggy, yes?' The German accent is thick. This must be Petra.

I smile and nod nervously. 'I am.'

She thrusts her hand out for me to shake. 'I am Petra. Pleased to meet you.'

Frank shuffles from foot to foot, his buoyancy from just moments ago diminishing. He's wearing a bewildered expression. 'This is Frank,' I say.

Petra smiles and shakes Frank's hand, then turns to call back over her shoulder, 'Joachim. They're here.'

A bearded young man appears from behind the camper and waves at us. Petra beckons for us to follow her. The camper's door is open, ready for our inspection. Joachim shakes our hands and invites us to get in and take a look. I'm anxious to get going but don't want to raise any suspicions so I go through the motions, asking about how the bed folds out and if the fridge works. Joachim is quick to assure me everything is in working order. 'The bus is old and a little slow, but good. We have had no problems.'

I'm pleased to discover the interior is even better than the photos I viewed online. It's compact, but has everything we need. Woodgrain laminex cabinets house a sink, a working stovetop and a small refrigerator. There's a two-seater couch upholstered in blue vinyl, which Joachim shows me how to fold out to make a double bed.

Petra lifts up the seat to reveal a storage space underneath. 'We keep the bedding in here.'

I nod. 'It all looks to be in order.'

'Let's take a look at her engine,' Frank pipes up and, despite my desire to be away as soon as possible, my heart swells. I don't know if his brain recalls how an engine works, but the fact that he even thinks to ask makes me hopeful. Underneath all the bewilderment, Frank is still Frank.

Joachim nods and he and Frank hop out to go take a look. Petra addresses me. 'You don't want to look?'

I laugh and shake my head. 'I wouldn't have the first idea of what to look for. Maybe we can make a start on the paperwork.'

'Yes,' she says. 'That would be good. If you are happy to go ahead? What if your husband is not satisfied with the engine?'

'Oh, don't worry about that. Frank just loves his engines. He'll probably be happy to find something wrong, just so he can tinker with it.'

She smiles and points to a picnic table. 'Should we go and sit so we can sort out the details? I'll go and get the registration papers out of my bag.'

I nod and make my way to the table, positioning myself so Frank is still in my line of sight. He's engaged in animated conversation with Joachim, pointing at parts of the engine as he speaks. He seems to be enjoying himself for the moment.

When Petra joins me she waves her phone. 'I can fill out my side of the paperwork online right now if you like? I think I just need to see your licence.'

I grimace. 'Oh, no. I can't believe I could be so stupid. I didn't bring it. I keep it in the glove box of my car at home.' My heart is really thumping now. I only hope my anxiety is not outwardly apparent.

Petra's smile fades, no doubt worried that the money she and Joachim are counting on is about to fall through. She scrolls around on her phone for a bit. 'Maybe we can work something out.' She reads for a moment and then her face relaxes. 'Look, I think this will be okay. I'm supposed to check your ID in case you're a scammer but' – she looks me in the eye – 'I trust you. I mean, you don't look like a criminal to me.' She laughs.

I give her my best grandmotherly smile. 'I've never even had a parking ticket.' This at least is true.

She nods. 'Good. If you just give me your full name and address, I'll fill this out and give you the registration papers. Once I've lodged this, you have fourteen days to transfer the vehicle to your name. Don't forget now, will you?'

I shake my head. 'Oh no, you can count on me. I'll do it just as soon as we get home.' This is also true. I will register the vehicle eventually. Well, if the authorities let me, that is. Maybe they'll take my licence away after this. Who knows? But there's no danger to Petra and Joachim. They've done the right thing and if anything untoward were to happen, like a speeding fine or – God forbid – an accident, Petra and Joachim will no longer be in the country, so there's no danger of any negative consequences for them. I give my name as Peggy Miller and make up a bogus address in Queanbeyan, which is where I've told her we're from.

A few more taps on her phone and she smiles. 'All done.'

I hand over an envelope full of cash, which she quickly counts before passing me the keys.

'Thank you, Peggy. I hope you and your husband enjoy the van. We have had a very good time in her.'

We wander back to where the men are. 'What do you say, Frank? Does she pass muster?'

He folds his arms across his chest and nods slowly. 'Yeah, the old girl's in pretty good nick, actually. There are a few tiny issues, but nothing major.'

'Good,' I say. 'Well, I think we should get going, don't you?'

'Where are you off to?' Joachim inquires.

I shrug. 'We'll probably head north, I guess. We've just got a few days to try the van out and then we'll head home.'

Joachim scratches his beard. 'There are some really lovely spots around here, if you feel like exploring before you go north.'

'Yes,' Petra pipes up. 'We've been camping at a place called Mossy Point. It's not too far from here. We parked down near the boat ramp for a couple of nights. It's beautiful, but quite isolated. Not somewhere to go for a party, but I suspect that won't bother you.' She laughs and I join in.

It's the second time Mossy Point's been mentioned in a matter of hours. I wonder if it's some kind of sign. I had planned on driving a little further south today, but Frank's had a big day already. It might be good to find somewhere off the beaten track to kick back and relax for the afternoon. 'So what's there?' I ask.

'It's just a lovely little beach. There's a jetty there. The water is beautiful, crystal clear. Joachim even went swimming yesterday, although it was too cold for me.'

Joachim grins. 'That's because you are not strong like me.'

She gives him a playful shove and I think what a lovely young couple they are. I wonder what's ahead of them. Will they always be sweet and playful with each other? Will they stay together no matter what life throws at them? Probably not. Young people don't do that these days. They walk away when things get tough. A lot of people my age would think that's soft, but I don't know. Sometimes there's merit in knowing when to give up.

Petra goes on. 'It's not an official camping ground but no one seems to worry about vans parking there. And there's a toilet block. No showers, but that didn't bother us.'

'Oh,' I say, 'that might not be suitable for us, then. I like a nice long shower at the end of the day. But thank you anyway. We might go for a drive there and have a look at the scenery before we head north.' I don't want them knowing my plans, just in case they are questioned about us later.

Joachim nods. 'You won't be sorry. It's very pretty, but hard to find the spot I'm talking about. I can show you on the map if you like?' He pulls out his phone.

Petra shakes her head as if Joachim is a complete fool. 'It would be easier to draw them a map.' She looks at me uncertainly. 'Unless you want us to put it into Google Maps on your phone? Do you have a phone?'

'I do, but I'm afraid I'm not very good with it. My granddaughters keep showing me how to send texts, but it seems very complicated to me.' I'm beginning to think I've missed my calling in life. Perhaps I should have taken up acting.

Petra smiles at me and orders Joachim to get a pen and paper. 'Draw Peggy a map, please.'

Joachim obediently rummages in his backpack for some paper and sketches a rudimentary map.

Once Joachim's done explaining the map to me I thank him and ask, 'Can we offer you a lift anywhere?' It's the least I can do after duping the poor young things.

Petra shakes her head. 'We've got friends with a van. They're meeting us here and taking us to the airport later. Thank you, though. Happy travels.'

'And the same to you.' We all shake hands and then it's time to go. I stow our suitcase in the back and, after checking Frank's all sorted in the passenger seat, I buckle my seatbelt, close the door and start her up. The engine is revving as hard as my heart. I haven't owned a manual car since I was in my twenties and, fearing that I'd forgotten how to drive one, I've spent the past three months having weekly lessons at a driving school recommended by Marcia from the community centre. I've finally managed to master the clutch, but the car I've been practising in is much smaller and much more modern than the Kombi. My hands are sweating as I shift the huge and unwieldy gearstick into first and take off. It's not the smoothest departure ever, but we're moving.

Once we're out of the car park and onto the road my confidence grows. We wind our way along the coast for a few kilometres and Frank rolls down his window to drink in the sea air. Suddenly he laughs and slaps my thigh. 'I don't know what your plan is, Boss, but whatever it is, I like it.'

Chapter 14

May 1966
Geelong

'Mail for you today, Mrs Sullivan.' The nurse dropped a blue envelope stamped with the words *By Air Mail* on the tray table in front of her.

A letter from June, no doubt, seeing as she was the only person Shirley knew who lived outside of Australia. She smiled at the nurse and picked up the wafer-thin envelope, turning it over in her hands while she decided whether or not she wanted to open it. June's aerogramme would no doubt be jam-packed with exciting news about her new life in London as a personal secretary to a notable British businessman. She was happy for her friend, but right now she couldn't help but feel the tiniest bit jealous. June was off seeing the world and meanwhile she was here in a hospital bed, twiddling her thumbs, in what was probably yet another futile attempt at keeping a baby inside her.

Four pregnancies so far (including this one) and nothing to show for it. She was beginning to wonder if it was all worth it. Maybe she wasn't cut out to be a wife and mother at all. Maybe God was sending her and Frank a message through all these miscarriages. Maybe children weren't to be part of their future.

Frank was such a wonderful husband and she hated that she couldn't give him the thing he wanted most in the world. After the first miscarriage he'd been upbeat, telling her not to worry. He was so optimistic that she'd be pregnant again 'in the blink of an eye' that he'd insisted that she leave work so that she could concentrate on starting a family. 'No point in going back, my love, when you'll be handing in your notice again in no time.' She'd been reluctant at first, worried about the drop in their income, but there was no need. Frank had worked hard and secured yet another promotion, so they made up the shortfall in no time. He thrived on being the breadwinner and she repaid him by being the best wife she could be: keeping a trim figure, making their home beautiful and cooking tasty meals each night. He often commented that he was the luckiest man he knew.

Now, she sighed. They both knew that wasn't true. Despite all their efforts, Frank wasn't a father yet. Lately she'd started wondering how much more disappointment their marriage could take. If this baby slipped away like all the others, would Frank still consider himself lucky? Would he wish he'd stuck with Libby Franklin, the girl he'd dated before her? Apparently Libby had two kids already and another on the way.

'You all right there, love?' Mrs Maguire in the next bed was talking to her.

'Fine, thank you.' She realised with a start that she was crying. She picked up her handkerchief and dabbed her eyes.

'Bad news?' Mrs Maguire laid her knitting in her lap and nodded at Shirley's letter.

'Oh. No. Just a letter from a friend who has moved overseas. I miss her, that's all.'

'Overseas? Fancy that. What does her husband do?'

'She's not married. She's gone to London to work.'

Mrs Maguire's eyebrows shot up comically, causing Shirley's lips to twitch in amusement. 'Oh dear. She'll probably have to marry an Englishman now.' Mrs Maguire made this sound as if it was a terrible punishment.

Shirley couldn't help having a bit of fun with the older woman. 'I don't think she's worried about getting married at all right now. She's too busy having a good time.'

'Hmph. That's the problem with young people these days. Too worried about having a good time and not worried enough about doing their duty. I pity her parents.' With that pronouncement, Mrs Maguire went back to her knitting.

The older woman didn't know it, but her grumpiness had cheered Shirley somewhat. All this lying around was making her morose. She was dwelling on the negatives, when she had so much to be grateful for. She had a husband who loved her, and a beautiful home. This pregnancy was far more advanced than her previous, unsuccessful ones. She only had four weeks to go now, and if sitting in a hospital bed was what it took to take home a healthy baby then that was what she would do. Her mother was right when she said God doesn't give us anything we can't handle. Everything else in her life had come easily. Maybe God needed her to prove to him that she *really* wanted a child.

She laid a hand on her swollen belly and felt her child squirm beneath her touch. This baby would survive. It had to. *Please, God, let this one live. I promise I'll never ask you for another thing. I'll be the best mother on earth, if you just give me the chance to prove myself.*

Satisfied God knew she really meant it this time, Shirley drifted off into a contented sleep.

When the familiar cramps woke her in the early hours of the morning, Shirley let out a wail. 'No!' she screamed. 'No, please, God, no. Don't take this one. Please. It's not fair.'

Mrs Maguire rushed over to hold her hand. The older woman must have pressed the call bell for the nurse, because before long the room was swimming with activity. One nurse shooed Mrs Maguire away and pulled the curtains around Shirley's bed for privacy, while another lifted her nightie to examine her. The cramp eased and Shirley was hopeful for a moment. 'Is everything all right?'

The large-bosomed nursed clucked her tongue. 'Well, Mrs Sullivan, your baby has decided it's time to be born. I know it's early, but I'm afraid there's no stopping the labour now. Time to take you up to the delivery ward.'

'Frank,' Shirley panted as another contraction gripped her. 'Please call my husband and let him know what's happening.'

The nurse gave a curt nod as she parted the curtain to exit. 'I'll be back in a moment to shave you and then we'll get an orderly to take you off to delivery.' She attempted a smile. 'Don't be afraid, Mrs Sullivan. This will all be over soon.'

Shirley began to cry then. That's exactly what she was afraid of.

The next contraction gripped her wildly and she heard herself grunting like an animal.

'Don't push, love,' Mrs Maguire called from the next bed. 'Otherwise that babe'll be born before the nurse comes back.'

After that the world ceased to make sense. Shirley could focus on little else but the pain. The nurse never did shave her, though, she was pretty sure. The orderly arrived and dragged her onto a trolley, and she yelled and moaned all the way to the delivery room, pleading for something to make the pain stop. The doctor greeted her with stern words about not making such a fuss, and then a sweet-voiced midwife took her by the hand and whispered in her ear that there was no time for pain relief but not to worry. 'Just relax and try not to fight the contractions. It'll all be over soon and then you'll be a mother.'

After what seemed like hours of indescribable agony, the baby was born silently. Shirley begged the doctor for some reassurance. 'Why isn't it crying?' she wailed. 'Please tell me my baby's okay.' The midwife squeezed her hand in response.

When Shirley woke her hand flew to her belly, lest it was all just a bad dream, but no. There was nothing there.

No baby.

No life.

No hope.

'Hey, sweetheart. How are you feeling?'

'Frank.' Her voice came out in a whisper. 'When did you get here?'

'Just before our daughter was born.'

A lump formed in her throat and she couldn't stop the tears spilling down her cheeks. 'A girl? She was a girl?'

Frank gripped her hand. '*Is* a girl. She's alive, our Fiona – if that's what you want to call her, still?'

Shirley pulled herself upright. Her head swam, maybe from the physical ordeal she'd been through, maybe from the news she'd just received. She sank back into the pillows and tried to make sense of what Frank was saying. 'What are you saying, Frank? Our baby's alive? How can that be? She didn't cry. I remember. And it's too soon. None of this is making sense.'

Frank laughed and shook his head. 'I don't know how but she's here. They've got her upstairs in this special incubator thing. She's little but not too little. Five pounds or so, which the doctor says is a good size, considering. They're watching her carefully but they seem to think the signs are good.'

'But she wasn't born alive. I remember . . .'

Frank's forehead creased and he hesitated before answering, seeming to weigh up whether he should say what he was thinking. He squeezed her hand and spoke quietly. 'The doctor said she needed to be resuscitated.'

'Resuscitated? How? Oh God. I don't remember that. I should have been with her. I should have—'

'Shh, now. There was nothing you could do. Our little one had the best of care. You don't remember because there was some sort of issue with your blood pressure, and you were so distressed at what was happening that the doctor thought it was best to sedate you. You'd been through so much and you needed some rest. After all, you're going to need all your strength to look after our little girl once we get her home.'

'She's really all right? You're not just telling me that?'

He shook his head. 'When have I ever lied to you? I'll admit that it was touch and go for a while there, but she came around, and apparently the paediatrician has said she's doing so well that they're going to try to take her off the oxygen supply in the next few hours. The nurses are all saying that she's a strong babe and the signs are good. I honestly think she'll be fine. In fact, I know it in my bones.'

Could it be true? Was she finally a mother? The beaming expression on Frank's face was pretty convincing. There was no way he could fake a smile like that. The tears spilling down her cheeks were now joyous ones. 'Fiona. Our little fair one. Is she fair? Oh, Frank, when can I see her?'

He laid a tender kiss on her forehead. 'I'll go get a nurse and find out, my darling.'

True to his word, Frank returned moments later with a nurse in tow. 'Let's get you up and showered, Mrs Sullivan, then we'll see about taking you up to the nursery to meet your baby. Mr Sullivan, time to make yourself scarce for a bit. Perhaps you have some phone calls to make?'

Frank nodded. 'Indeed I do. When should I come back?'

'An hour should be sufficient,' the nurse replied. 'Now, Mrs Sullivan, let me help you out of bed.'

An hour or so later, dressed in a fresh nightie and her pale-blue brunch coat, Shirley was wheeled to the viewing pane of the special-care nursery.

'There she is.' Frank's chest puffed out as he pointed to the scrawny, wrinkled baby with a clear tube protruding from her tiny nose and wires strapped to her chest. 'Isn't she beautiful?'

Shirley was glad she was sitting down. This wasn't at all how she'd imagined greeting her daughter. Through all these years of hoping and trying she'd had a picture of what this moment would look like. In her dreams, she was sitting up in bed, wearing her pretty new nightwear – at least she'd got that part right – and a nurse handed her a pink-faced cherub perfectly wrapped in a bunny rug (yellow in her fantasy, because she really didn't mind if the baby was a boy or a girl). The red-skinned infant she was looking at now was naked except for the giant nappy from which its spindly legs were protruding. She knew she should feel elation that this child lived at all, and she did, really she did, but the sight of her frail daughter was too much to bear. Her body began to convulse with sobs.

The nurse patted her back a couple of times. 'There, there, Mrs Sullivan, there's no need to cry. Your daughter is doing perfectly well. The wires are monitoring her heart rate, which is quite normal at the moment, and the tube in her nose is a feeding tube to ensure she gets the right nutrition. Nothing out of the ordinary there. She's doing supremely well for a premature baby. You may even be able to feed her yourself in a day or two.'

The thought of holding that tiny thing, let alone having it clamped to her breast, brought on a fresh bout of sobs.

'Goodness me, that's quite enough of that,' the nurse said, more sternly now. 'You are very lucky to have a live baby,

Mrs Sullivan. All indications are that your little one will be just fine but, nevertheless, your daughter will need you to be strong for her these next few weeks.'

Through all this, Frank hadn't taken his eyes off the baby. He patted Shirley's shoulder almost absent-mindedly. 'Listen to the nurse, Shirl. Our Fiona's a fierce little thing. She won't let us down.'

Frank had a brand-new love. Shirley could hear it in his voice. She hated herself for not being able to conjure up similar feelings of adoration. She *knew* she was lucky. Hours ago all she had wanted was a living baby. God had seen fit to give her this gift and she knew she should be grateful. This should have been the happiest moment of her life, and she was ashamed that she wasn't able to enjoy it. But right now she felt cheated. Her introduction to motherhood had hardly been idyllic. She tried to smile through her tears, to pretend that everything was fine, but it wasn't. She'd bargained with God for this. She'd made him a promise that she was already failing to keep. What sort of mother didn't feel an overwhelming sense of love for her child the first time she laid eyes upon her?

She bit her lip to try to quell the tears, but it was no good. No matter how hard she tried to stop, the sobs just kept coming.

'Right then. I think we'd best get you back to bed. This display isn't doing anyone any good.' The nurse swung the wheelchair around forcefully and began to push her back down the corridor. Shirley glanced behind her and saw that Frank hadn't moved an inch.

Back on the ward, Shirley noticed with relief that the beds either side of her were now empty. 'What happened to Mrs Maguire?' she asked when the nurse – a different one, thank goodness, to the previous old grump – came to take her blood pressure.

'Discharged while you were in labour this morning. She said to pass on her regards to you.'

Shirley nodded her head towards the other empty bed. 'And this one?' She hadn't been able to bring herself to talk much to the heavily pregnant young woman who'd occupied the bed to her right for the past twenty-four hours. Angela looked like she couldn't be more than eighteen years old, and already had a two-year-old 'brat' at home. She was almost at her due date and had been experiencing some rumblings, so had been put on the ward for observation.

'Gone up to delivery about an hour ago. Apparently she delivers quickly so she'll be back before you know it. You two girls can compare notes then.'

'Yes. I suppose we can.' Shirley couldn't think of anything worse than getting tips from a mother who was little more than a child herself, and yet seemed to be far more successful at this mothering thing despite her tender age.

She needed to pull herself together. Frank had called her parents and they'd be visiting tonight. Frank was heading home now to shower and change. He was going to work for the afternoon but would be back for the evening visiting hours. Everyone would be expecting her to be over the moon, and fair enough, too. What on earth was wrong with her?

She closed her eyes so the nurse wouldn't notice the tears welling yet again.

The nurse took off the blood-pressure cuff and patted her arm approvingly. 'Get some shut-eye while you can, love.'

When she opened her eyes again an unfamiliar face greeted her. A woman around her own age stood at the foot of her bed looking at her chart. She didn't appear to be a nurse, as she was wearing a pink woollen coat and her dark hair fell freely around her shoulders.

'Oh, I'm so sorry. I didn't mean to wake you. I'm just going off duty and I wanted to pop in and see how you are. I'll leave you in peace.'

The face might not have rung a bell but she'd know that voice anywhere. It belonged to the beautiful midwife who'd held her hand and kept her calm through her labour.

'No! Don't go. I didn't get a chance to thank you for your kindness this morning. I couldn't have done it without you.'

'Nonsense. You were doing fine all on your own, Mrs Sullivan.'

'Please, call me Shirley.'

To her surprise the woman moved towards her with her hand outstretched as if she wanted to shake hands. Shirley tentatively offered her own hand and the woman looked pleased as she gave it a firm pump. 'I'm Rita,' she said. 'One of the midwives here.'

'Very pleased to meet you properly, Rita. I really did appreciate what you did for me.'

'I'm pleased to see you looking so well, and your little girl too. I've just checked on her in the nursery and you'd hardly even know she was an early arrival. She's a bonny little thing.'

To her dismay, Shirley's eyes filled with tears yet again. This was getting ridiculous. She prided herself on being a brick, a girl who could face any setback with a smile. But not today. It seemed her emotions were on a roller-coaster ride. 'I'm so sorry.' She sniffed. 'I can't seem to stop the waterworks today.'

Rita handed her a white lace handkerchief. 'No need to apologise at all. You've been through the wringer. All those lost pregnancies, then weeks of bed rest, and then a pre-term labour. And I'm sure you were worried that you were about to lose this baby too.'

'Yes.' Her voice came out in a hoarse whisper.

'But honestly, you mustn't let yourself worry. Your daughter is one of the healthiest-looking premmies I've ever seen. I'm certain that she's going to be fine.'

Shirley mopped her tears with the handkerchief and was momentarily distracted by its sweet rose scent. 'Everyone keeps telling me that.'

'Well, you should believe it, because it's the truth. I wouldn't tell you otherwise if I wasn't convinced that your little one was going to make it. In fact, I think they'll be bringing her down to you for feeds sooner than you think. Maybe even tomorrow.'

The thought of feeding the baby terrified her. 'So soon? What if I'm not up to it?'

Rita took her hand and gently squeezed it. 'That's what we midwives are here for. To help you. You're going to be fine, Shirley. Better than fine. I'm sure you're going to make a wonderful mother.'

'But what if I'm not? What if I'm not cut out for the job? All those losses and this one was a near miss. What if God was trying to tell me something?'

'If that were the case, why would He let this one survive? You've just been unlucky, that's all. But now your time has come. You have a beautiful little girl.'

Shirley didn't know if it was Rita's kind voice, or the comforting touch of her hand, but somehow she knew she could trust this woman. 'I know I should be grateful, but . . .' Her heart beat wildly as she hesitated before making her confession. 'They took me up to see her before. I didn't feel . . . she wasn't what I expected. When I saw her I felt . . . well, cheated somehow.' The tears began to flow again. 'I mean what sort of person – sort of mother – does that make me?'

'A perfectly normal one. You have been through a major trauma – more than one, if you count the babies you've lost. Physically your body has just had to do one of the hardest things it is capable of, and now it's dealing with the end of the pregnancy and preparing for lactation.' Rita rubbed Shirley's arm soothingly. 'There's a hormonal tidal wave breaking inside you. All new mothers experience that, but most of them haven't experienced the emotional upheaval you've been through. I think you need to be less hard on yourself.'

Shirley smiled, touched by Rita's kindness. The fact that this experienced midwife didn't think she was a heartless monster was comforting.

'Give it a day or two. Once your baby is off all the monitors and is dressed up in a little outfit she'll look more like you imagined she would. And feeding her will help you to bond. You'll see.'

'I hope so.'

'Nothing that has happened is your fault, Shirley. You remember that. Things will start looking up, just you wait and see. I'll be back to see you tomorrow and I'm sure by then you'll be feeling a whole lot better.'

As Rita left the ward, Shirley found herself looking forward to tomorrow.

Chapter 15

Monday

Petra was right. Mossy Point is a perfect little camping spot. Apart from a few locals who head out fishing from the boat ramp, the place is deserted. Once we've settled on a camp site I decide to check out the amenities. I can't risk Frank wandering off so I insist he comes with me. He baulks at accompanying me into the ladies'. 'Have you gone mad, woman? Why on earth would I want to go in there?'

I try to appeal to his sense of chivalry. 'It's so isolated out here, anyone could be lurking inside. Please, Frank, can you come with me, just to be on the safe side?'

As hoped, this convinces him. 'Oh, pardon me. I didn't think of that. I'm happy to be of assistance.'

He follows me inside. The facilities are pretty basic, but they're adequate for an overnight stay. This place will do us nicely.

It took us no time to get here from Batehaven, despite having to stop a couple of times – once to stock up on a few supplies and then at a cute little cafe just up the road from the campground, where I grabbed us a couple of takeaway coffees and some sandwiches for lunch.

After our inspection of the toilets, I grab the carry tray with the coffees and the sandwiches from the Kombi. 'Do you think there might be some folding chairs in among that camping gear in the back? We could take them and eat by the water.'

Frank slides open the Kombi's door and stands staring at its interior. It strikes me that he may not even know what it is he's searching for.

'Let's look together,' I say. I put the tray on the ground and move past him into the van. After opening every storage compartment I realise we're out of luck.

Frank walks to the back of the van and opens it up. He lifts out a canvas bag. 'What's this?'

The bag is long and thin. I shrug. 'Maybe fishing gear?' He passes it to me and I open it up. Inside is not fishing gear after all but two folding camp chairs. 'Eureka! Frank, check out these beauties.'

Frank helps me set up the chairs on the shore, and then sits, rolling up his trouser legs to catch some rays. We sit quietly, enjoying our lunch and the sparkling vista before us. I briefly ponder whether it's a smart move to stop so soon after picking up the van. The day still has hours of good light left in it and maybe we should be using those to get as far south as possible. But, sitting here looking at the smile on Frank's face, I remind myself that this trip is as much about the journey as it is about the destination. If we're caught before we get home, at least Frank will have had a few good days. And I will have given it my best shot.

Frank puts his coffee into the chair's cup holder, leans back and closes his eyes. I've asked a lot of him today. This is a man whose biggest excitement in the past six months has been what's on the dinner menu. In the past twenty-four hours I've ripped him out of his familiar surroundings, made him travel hundreds of kilometres in no less than three different vehicles, made him complicit in a number of lies – not that he remembers that, but still – and altered his medication regime. No wonder he's tired. We definitely need to take this afternoon to recharge our batteries. We'll rest today and set off early in the morning.

Satisfied that Frank is napping contentedly, I slip back to the van for a moment to grab my new phone. Of course there won't be any messages, because no one has this number, but I can check the news for any updates. I take a seat in the shade near Frank – I can't afford to let my guard down lest he wakes up and wanders – and open the ABC News app, which I preloaded before I left home.

We're a bigger story now, higher up in the news feed, although still not the huge headline I'd imagined. Even though this is a relief I feel a tinge of surprise – or perhaps even slight disappointment – that we're not making front-page news.

The photo is unchanged, which bodes well for us I think, and no sightings have been reported, thank goodness. For the first time in forever I'm grateful for the apathy that pervades our current population. I'm never sure if it's due to life's busyness or an entrenched laziness, but these days people don't seem to worry too much about anything that doesn't directly concern them. In any case, it's working in our favour right now. Except . . . *damn it*. Towards the end of the news article there's a mention of Ollie. Not by name, of course, but by description.

Police wish to speak to a man who was seen leaving Sunset Lodge with the elderly couple.

I roll my eyes. *Elderly.* Is that how the world sees me? A helpless little old lady? If only they knew. I allow myself a small smirk.

It can only be a matter of time before poor Ollie is hauled in to a police station for questioning. Perhaps I should ring him – tell him to tell the truth? But then if the police ask if he's heard from me he'll be in an even more awkward position. And maybe they'll confiscate his phone. Track my number. The risk is just too great. Despite my desire to keep Ollie out of trouble, my desire to take Frank home is greater.

Surely he'll hand himself in, anyway? It's not like he's done anything illegal this time. Although, maybe he'll be too scared to come forward, given his record. God, I hope this doesn't fly in his face. I'm pretty sure his community service order is finished and that he just hangs around the community centre now to fill in the time until a job comes up. I don't think he's actually on probation or anything like that. Still, I should never have involved a third party. I should have found another way. Ollie's really turned his life around in the past year or so and I'll never forgive myself if my actions get him into trouble.

I read the article to its end. After a somewhat generic description of Ollie, Fiona is quoted saying she has grave fears for our safety. There is an emotional appeal from her for information regarding our whereabouts and she goes on to beg the man who 'took' us to hand himself in.

The thought of her fretting about our fate churns my stomach. I'd like to let her know she has nothing to worry about, that her parents are perfectly fine, but there's no way of doing that without the risk of giving ourselves away, so I have to comfort myself with the knowledge that her worry will be short-lived.

Then a second thought strikes me. Perhaps the emotional appeal is aimed at me. Perhaps she wants me to think she's distressed. She knows her unhappiness eats at me like a cancer. Long has she used that fact as a weapon against me in the battle of love and hate we've been engaged in since the day she was born. Maybe she's onto me, but wants me to think she has no clue what's going on in the hope that her perceived anguish will flush me out. If that's the case, I take my hat off to her.

Maybe I'm giving her too much credit. Or too little. I don't know. Sometimes it seems inconceivable to me that Fiona came from my body. She's always been such a mystery to me.

I watch Frank sleeping. His head has lolled to one side and his mouth is wide open. A trickle of drool runs down his chin. He may not be a child, but right now he's as vulnerable as a newborn babe. I realise that I have to make a choice. Reassuring Fiona will mean the end of this jaunt. Once she gets a whiff of where we are she'll stop at nothing to bring us back. I don't know what it is that drives her to win, but she's always insisted on having her own way. So many times throughout my life I've made the wrong choice. But not this time. Fiona might be my child but she is a grown woman. She'll cope no matter what happens.

This time I'm choosing Frank.

Chapter 16

March 1969
Geelong

Frank came up behind her and wrapped his arms around her waist. 'I think she's asleep already.'

Shirley pulled her gloved hands out of the sink and nodded. 'Thanks, love. The heat must have tired her out. I know I'm exhausted.'

He picked up the tea towel and began drying the dishes in the rack. 'Oh, really? Maybe you and I should have an early night.' He winked.

Shirley sighed inwardly. She really *was* tired. Surely she was entitled to one night off every now and then? Lately she'd been feeling completely wiped out at the end of the day. Being the mother of a toddler was a full-time job, and Fiona was an active little thing. Recently they'd decided to cut out her afternoon nap. They'd tried shifting her into a 'big-girl bed' but the lack of a physical barrier meant she was in and out like a yo-yo. If Shirley had the audacity to try putting her into her cot during the day she screamed blue murder. Inevitably Shirley gave in, worried that Fiona's cries would have old Mrs Harvey next door suspecting her of child abuse.

Fiona seemed determined to oppose her at every opportunity. She rejected the clothes Shirley set out for her, and would simply undress herself if Shirley somehow managed to get her into them. She demanded toast cut into squares and then cried because she'd really meant triangles. She tossed her vegetables onto the floor and threw her Alphabetti noodles at the wall. Not to mention the hullabaloo that occurred at bath time. Unless Frank was the one bathing her. Daddy's little princess never made a fuss when he was in charge.

When Shirley complained about her day, Frank just laughed and said Fiona was a spirited little thing, and weren't they lucky to have such a clever child. Of course, she always smiled and agreed. What sort of mother would she be if she couldn't appreciate the delights of her own child?

'Actually, Frank, I'm just going to pop over to Rita's for a bit, if you don't mind?' She kept her tone light and casual, as if it didn't matter whether she went or not, but in reality she was desperate to see her friend. The nagging worry that had plagued her for the past week or so was getting harder to ignore. One minute she dismissed her dark thoughts, telling herself that she was imagining the whole thing, but only moments later she was convinced her fears were true. Rita was strong and sensible. She would know what to do.

Frank turned away from her to place a dinner plate in the overhead cupboard. She couldn't see his face but she felt the atmosphere in the room chill, despite the stifling heat.

'She's helping me finish off the new bed linen for Fiona's bed. I think a pretty new bedspread might be just the thing to encourage her to stay in her big-girl bed.'

When he turned to face her his expression was soft. She'd won him over by claiming her motive was to make something for Fiona. If she'd said she was going to keep Rita company, or to get help with a new dress pattern for herself, she knew he wouldn't be so accommodating. Anything for his little girl, though.

As much as this irritated Shirley, she was grateful she had an excuse. Rita was the person she trusted most in the world. In the past couple of years they'd become firm friends. It had started when Shirley was in the hospital after Fiona was born. Rita had visited her every day. She tried to schedule her visits during feed times to reassure Shirley and assist with any problems. When Shirley was allowed to go home – without the baby for the first few weeks – Rita was a godsend. She took it upon herself to do the grocery shopping and the washing so Shirley could spend more time at the hospital. When Rita was on nightshift she kept an eye on Fiona after the staff forced Shirley and Frank to go home for the evening, which gave Shirley great peace of mind. It turned out Rita lived in Porter Avenue – walking distance from Frank and Shirley's house – which made it easy for the two women to keep in touch even after Fiona was allowed to come home.

Rita was unlike any friend Shirley had ever had. Three years her senior, Rita wasn't married and lived alone in a house she owned outright. Apparently her grandmother had left her a small inheritance, which she'd used to buy her cosy weatherboard home. Far from being a lonely spinster, Rita lived a full life, working and socialising. When Shirley had tentatively asked her if she was still hoping to get married, Rita had laughed. 'Marriage isn't for me, Shirl. I'm too selfish for it. I couldn't bear to have to answer to someone the way you do to Frank.'

Shirley had bristled. 'Frank's all right. He's not an ogre or anything. He treats me really well.'

'Oh, love, I didn't mean to hurt your feelings. Of course Frank's not an ogre. He's a wonderful husband and an exceptional father. Believe me, you bagged a good one there. In my line of work I see plenty of scoundrels. Men who treat their wives like possessions. It's the 1960s, for heaven's sake, not the Victorian era. What some women put up with . . .'

'Yes, I suppose I *am* lucky. Still, there are plenty of nice chaps out there. My friend Mary is married to a lovely fellow too.'

Rita smiled and lit a cigarette. 'I'm sure there are, but I'm not the marrying type. I value my freedom too much.'

'But what about children? You clearly love them. You're so good with Fiona. Sometimes I think you're better with her than I am.'

'Ah, you sell yourself short. Kids are always toughest on the ones they love most.'

'Seriously, though, you'd make a great mum, Rita. Aren't you worried about missing out?'

Rita's smile had faded then. 'I actually can't have children, Shirl. There are reasons . . . well, let's just say it's not possible for me. So you see, there's not much of an upside to marriage as far as I'm concerned.'

Shirley could have kicked herself for being so insensitive. 'I'm so sorry. I didn't mean to pry.'

Rita's face brightened again. 'No need to be glum. I have a great life. I answer to no one and I get to cuddle babies every day at work. I happen to think I'm a very lucky woman.'

Shirley had smiled and agreed, although at the time she couldn't help but feel sorry for her friend. On days like today, though – faced with Fiona's tantrums, Frank's amorous advances and the worry at the back at her mind that she'd spent the past week trying not to think about – she actually found herself envying Rita.

'Don't be too late, now, will you? I know what you two are like when you get nattering. I worry about you walking home alone after dark.'

She kissed his cheek and gave him a hug. 'Oh Frank, you worry too much. Rita always stands at her gate and watches me walk to the corner, and once I turn it I'm only a hop, skip and a jump away from here. Besides, we live in a safe neighbourhood. There's truly nothing to worry about.'

He squeezed her tight. 'Still, I can't have anything happening to my best girl, now, can I? What would we do without you?' He shuddered. 'I can't even bear to think about it. So just be careful, okay?'

She kissed him again, this time on the lips. 'Yes, Boss. Now, I'd better get going or we'll never get the project started, let alone finished.'

Rita propped open the screen door with her foot. She had a cigarette in one hand and a glass of wine in the other. 'Come in, come in. Let me get you a drink. There's a cask of riesling in the fridge.'

Shirley's stomach turned at the thought. She screwed up her nose as she followed Rita through the living room. 'I think I might just have a cuppa, if you don't mind? I'm not in the mood for wine.' She pushed an orange vinyl beanbag out of the way with her foot and stepped over a higgledy-piggledy pile of newspapers and magazines on her way to the kitchen. Housekeeping wasn't high on Rita's list of priorities, but then most of the time the only person she had to please was herself. Sometimes Shirley envied her that freedom.

Rita raised her eyebrows. 'Worried the other half might smell it on your breath? Come on, live a little.'

'Nah, it's not that – although Frank probably wouldn't be thrilled if he suspected I was out drinking wine in the middle of the week – I just don't feel like it, to be honest.'

‘Fair enough. I’ll put the kettle on. What’s that you’ve got there?’ She nodded at the bag of fabric Shirley was carrying.

‘My alibi. I told Frank we were finishing off Fiona’s new bedspread.’

‘Oh, I’ll get the machine out, shall I?’

Shirley laughed. ‘No, don’t bother. I finished it myself this afternoon. I just thought it was best to make up a valid excuse for coming around here. Frank’s been a little testy about me doing things without him lately. I think he might be jealous of all the time I spend with you.’

Rita raised her eyebrows.

‘He probably does have a point. I mean, the poor man works all day to put food on the table. I guess it’s not too much for him to expect his wife to spend a little time with him in the evenings.’

‘You spend far too much time worrying about what’s best for others. Frank gets plenty of your time and attention. It’s not as if you spend every evening here. And, anyway, what about what *you* want? Aren’t you entitled to be happy?’

‘I suppose so.’ Of course she was entitled to be happy, she knew that. But shouldn’t being with her husband and daughter – the child she’d had to fight so hard to get – make her happy? Admitting that she’d rather spend time with her best friend felt traitorous to her family.

‘So, to what do I owe this visit from you, then?’

‘What do you mean?’

‘When you called me earlier you said you had something to talk about.’

Shirley sighed as she settled herself onto a stool at Rita’s breakfast bar. She did want to talk, but she was afraid that once she told Rita her secret, Rita would insist on her taking some sort of action. And once that happened her worry would be a reality, not something she could push to the back of her mind the way she had been doing up to now.

Rita sat a cup of tea in front of her – weak and black, just the way she liked it – and folded her arms across her chest. 'Come on then, out with it. Whatever it is, it can't be that bad. In my experience, all problems have a solution.'

She stared into her tea. 'My period has been a bit erratic.'

'Okay. That can happen sometimes. Maybe you need a check-up. It's probably something minor. Have you been eating properly?'

Shirley shook her head. 'Not really. I've been a tad off my food. I keep having mild bouts of nausea.' She paused before blurting out. 'I'm worried I might be pregnant.'

Rita didn't speak immediately. Shirley looked up to see her waiting expectantly, as if Shirley had more to add. She hadn't.

Finally Rita spoke. 'Have you had a test?'

'No,' she said, with a heavy heart. 'I haven't been to the doctor yet, but my last two periods have been nothing more than a bit of spotting, my breasts are sore and the smell of coffee makes me want to retch. Just like all the other times, really.'

'I take it you haven't told Frank?'

She shook her head slowly. 'I don't want him to get his hopes up. You know, just in case.'

'In case you lose it?'

'Yes.' That was sort of the truth, although she was trying to spare her own feelings as much as Frank's. He would be overjoyed at the prospect of another child – perhaps this one might be a son! – and then she would have to bear the weight of his hopes and dreams along with the worry of the pregnancy.

'Shirley,' Rita said quietly, 'didn't the doctor warn you that it could be dangerous for you to have another baby?' She squashed her cigarette butt into the glass ashtray that sat permanently on the kitchen bench and pulled another smoke from its pack.

Shirley shrugged. 'I don't think there's any real threat to my health. I think he just meant that it would be unlikely I would carry another child to term.'

Rita shook her head. 'There's a real danger to you too. Your previous blood-pressure issues put you at risk of developing eclampsia, which, without trying to be too dramatic, could kill you. Fiona would be without her mother. If you choose to go ahead with this pregnancy, you'll need very careful monitoring and you'll need to take it easy. That's going to be hard with a toddler at home.'

'What do you mean, *if* I go ahead? What other choice do I have?'

'If you don't want to have this baby, you don't have to.'

'You mean . . .?' Shirley couldn't bring herself to say the word.

Rita lit her cigarette and drew back slowly. She turned her head slightly to avoid blowing smoke in Shirley's face. 'An abortion,' she said, as if she were discussing any other medical procedure.

Shirley leaned back, physically recoiling at her friend's words. 'Oh, I couldn't do that. I mean, they're not even legal, are they?'

Rita shrugged. 'It's a ridiculous law. One that needs to change, but until that time there are ways to procure an abortion – a safe abortion – without anyone knowing. They may not be legal but there are people who can help.'

'A backyard abortion? You can't be serious!' Shirley couldn't conceal her shock.

'You make it sound so seedy. I'm not talking about some old bastard with a coathanger trying to make a bit of cash. I'm talking about trained midwives like me, who will supervise an early induced miscarriage for women in need.' She reached across the counter and took Shirley's hand. 'I can help you with this if you want me to.'

As much as it shamed her to admit it, she really didn't want another baby. She didn't know how she could bear to go through all the sickness, pain and worry all over again. Yes, it had all turned out all right last time, but the chances of two healthy babies in a row were slim. The doctors had been very clear about that. In fact, they'd sent her home with a packet of the contraceptive pill. She'd kept that packet for months before finally throwing it out. It was a sin, after all. And even if she'd been prepared to take the risk of eternal damnation, Frank most certainly wasn't. He'd made his feelings very clear on the matter. 'I'm sorry, Shirl, it's just not right. This sort of thing isn't up to us, now, is it? Think about it. God won't give us another baby if we can't handle it. I know he won't. We can try natural methods if you're really worried, but I can't abide any of this other nonsense.'

So they'd used the rhythm method, which was sanctioned by the Church but, judging by the predicament in which she now found herself, clearly not that reliable.

She shook her head. 'As much as the thought of having another child scares me, abortion just isn't something I can consider.' She squeezed Rita's hand. 'Thank you, though. I appreciate the offer.'

Rita smiled. 'Fair enough. So, what's your plan?'

'Plan?'

'When are you going to tell Frank? Are you waiting to get confirmation from the doctor? You know they'll probably want to put you on bed rest.'

Shirley didn't answer immediately. Once the pregnancy was confirmed she would lose control over her body. Frank and the doctors would insist on bed rest and maybe even hospitalisation. What would happen to Fiona? Her mother would have to help. Poor Mum hadn't been that well lately. How would she ever cope with a firebrand like Fiona? 'You know, I didn't start showing with Fiona until I was more than four months along.'

Rita gave her a blank look.

'So, well . . . maybe I should just let nature take its course for a while. If God wants me to have this baby, then surely he'll look after it.'

'Let's take God out of the equation, shall we?'

Rita wasn't one for religion. She felt it made no sense, that the Bible contradicted itself. On a number of occasions she'd pushed Shirley to explain or justify the Church's teachings, and had even made her doubt her beliefs once or twice, but in the end faith was faith. She might not be able to explain hers, but it was real. They'd had to agree to disagree on the subject.

'I'm all for nature taking its course,' Rita continued, 'but it's not just the baby's life that's at risk here. Your history of high blood pressure in pregnancy puts you at risk in ways other than premature labour. If it gets out of control you could have a seizure, or even die. I don't think it's wise to go without medical care. If you've decided to go through with this pregnancy you need proper monitoring.'

Shirley sipped her tea and nodded. 'I guess you're right. I just feel like once I tell Frank, I'll be back on the roller-coaster and my life will be out of my control. I suppose I was just thinking that if I could have a bit more time, maybe I'd get used to the idea of having another baby. Once upon a time I wanted a whole houseful of kids. But the past few years have been hard, you know?'

Rita nodded sympathetically.

'If this baby is determined to be born then I'll cope – I'll have to. But if this is going to be another loss, I don't think I can bear watching Frank get his hopes up only to have me let him down yet again.'

'None of what has happened is your fault, you know that, don't you?'

Shirley shrugged. 'I guess so. I just don't want Frank to be disappointed in me. Sometimes I think he must look at me and wonder how he managed to pick such a lemon.'

'Frank looks at you like you are the most desirable woman on earth, and you know it.'

Shirley's cheeks burned. She hadn't realised Frank's ardour was quite so obvious. 'Maybe, but it's been such a struggle to give him what he really wants – a family. Fiona is the apple of his eye, but I'm sure he'd give his right arm for a son. It seems cruel to let him think there might be a chance of that. But you're right. It would be irresponsible of me not to seek the care I need. I can't risk leaving Fiona motherless. I guess I have no choice but to make an appointment at the clinic this week.'

'Unless . . .'

'What?'

'Well, I could keep a close eye on you for a month or two. I could monitor your blood pressure every few days, look out for any signs of trouble. That would buy you some time. If the pregnancy lasts those two months, then you probably won't be able to hide it any longer, and you'll be getting to the stage where you will need more care than I can provide.'

Shirley's heart swelled with gratitude. 'You'd do that for me?'

Rita shrugged. 'Of course. But you have to promise me that you'll do what I say. If your blood pressure gets too high, you'll have to go to the doctor. I'll call him myself if I have to.'

'I promise I'll do everything you ask me to.'

Rita stubbed out her cigarette. 'Well, no time like the present. Let me get my stethoscope and blood-pressure cuff.'

As Rita left the room, Shirley let her hand drift to her stomach.

Maybe this time things would be different.

Chapter 17

Tuesday

I wake to the sound of the Kombi door sliding open. Frank's headed out. 'Hey,' I say. 'Where are you off to?'

He lifts his head to look at me. 'Who the hell are you?'

I sit up in bed and rub my eyes. 'I'm Peggy, from Sunset Lodge. I'm looking after you.'

'This isn't Sunset Lodge.' He steps out of the camper.

'Hang on a minute.' He turns to stare at me as I swing my feet out of the bed. 'You're right, it's not. We're on a trip, Frank. I'm taking you home.'

He looks unconvinced. 'Right. Well, even so, I think I'll be off now.' He starts to walk away.

'Frank! Stop! Where do you think you're going?'

He looks at me with disdain. 'To relieve myself.'

'Hold on. Let me come with you.'

'I don't need you to help me pee,' he says gruffly and heads off, not towards the toilet block but towards the water.

I scramble to find the thongs I've packed and shove my feet into them while putting on my cardigan. By the time I get myself out of the camper I'm confronted with the sight of

Frank's bare bum. His pyjama pants and the incontinence pants are around his ankles and he's pissing into the water, apparently unconcerned that his saggy arse cheeks are out for all the world to see. Fortunately there's no one here but us right now, so I cross my arms across my chest and wait for him to finish. The Frank of old would never behave this way. His manners were impeccable. The mere thought of exposing himself in public would have been abhorrent. But, then again, once upon a time I would never have used the word arse, not even in my head. Time moves on, I guess. People change – dementia or no dementia.

When he's done, I bribe him with the promise of a cooked breakfast to come to the toilet block with me for a wash and a change of clothes. It's not pleasant in the toilet block and the water is freezing, but we make do. I'm out of diapers now. We picked up some supplies at the IGA in Tomakin on our way here yesterday, but my head was filled with what I could cook in the camper and I didn't think beyond food. Never mind, I'll get some next time we're at a supermarket. In the meantime I'll just have to make sure we stop for frequent toilet breaks.

I use the camper's little gas stove to make some scrambled eggs and toast. Frank takes the camp chairs and folding table down to the sand and we eat there, looking out across the river to the sea beyond. It's a cold but crystal-clear spring morning and the water is glassy. Our surroundings have a calming effect on both of us. I feel as if we are becoming the parts we are playing – a loving elderly couple on holidays. Maybe this is who we could have been. Maybe it's who we can be.

Except Frank doesn't know me anymore.

'You remind me of someone I used to know,' he says, between mouthfuls of egg.

'Is that right? Who?'

His forehead creases in concentration and then realisation dawns on his face. 'I know,' he says excitedly. 'My . . . my . . .' He clicks his fingers in frustration. 'Oh, I can't think of the word. She belonged to my wife.'

I'm confused for a moment. Is he talking about Fiona? We do look a lot alike and occasionally Frank will call her Shirley, but it doesn't make any sense that he would mistake me for her. Maybe he means Rita.

'You know, whatshername, the mum.'

Suddenly I understand. 'Do you mean your mother-in-law? Her name was Margaret.'

'Yes,' he says, visibly relieved he's made himself understood. 'You look like her.'

I'm taken aback for a moment even though I know it's true. I do look like Mum, although she was gone before she could reach the age I am now. It pains me that this is how he sees me. Today Frank's a younger version of himself and his wife is a young woman too, not a wrinkled old lady like me.

I'd hoped that once I'd got him away from that mind-numbing prison and stopped dosing him up on antipsychotic drugs his memory might pick up a little. I'm not a fool, of course. I understand that he has dementia and that it's progressive. But I've done some reading and there's research to suggest that stimulating the brain in certain ways can slow the rate of advancement. Life at Sunset Lodge could hardly be called stimulating.

I keep telling myself that this trip is all about Frank, but if I'm honest with myself it's about me too. He's dying. Maybe his body has a few more months left in it, maybe years, but his mind – at least, the mind of the Frank I knew – is almost gone. Before he disappears from reach there are things I need him to know. I need to explain myself, to make him understand why I did the things that I did. I need to let him know that it wasn't his fault.

It's funny how ageing changes a person's perspective on life. When you realise there are far fewer years in front of you than behind, it becomes easier to filter out all the trivialities and concentrate on what really matters. Atoning for the pain I've caused Frank matters to me. Maybe it's all that Catholic brainwashing. Once a Catholic, always a Catholic, I guess. I did try to break away from the Church for a while there but eventually I found my way back. Like it or not, it's part of me, and try as one might there's no escaping yourself.

A pelican glides in and lands on the water in front of us, buoying my spirits. I'm not sure why, but I love these birds. When Fiona and I would walk along the beach at Bancoora as we waited for Frank to finish his surf lifesaving drills, the sight of a pelican would always cheer me no matter how low my mood. It's a good omen for the day ahead, I think.

It's still early but I'm keen to get on the road. After I've filled the sink, I give Frank the job of washing up. There aren't many dishes and he likes to feel useful. I watch him use the sponge to clean a cup and once I'm satisfied he knows what he's doing I remove myself to sit in the driver's seat so I can check my phone for any news updates. I'm not quite used to this new phone and it takes me a moment to find my way to my favourite sites, but I get there eventually. We're still making news, but (hallelujah!) the prime minister has chosen today to do the first useful thing he's done since he's been in office. He's managed to get himself into some sort of high-level political scandal and it's dominating the news. My quick search brings up a handful of stories about us, but there are no significant updates. It doesn't seem that Ollie has been identified yet.

I try not to think about Fiona and the girls, waking up to yet another day not knowing where we are, because it can't be helped. Besides, it won't be forever. I expect by this time next week this whole thing will be over, one way or another.

A loud clatter coming from the rear of the camper shifts my attention away from the phone. Frank looks at me with a bewildered expression on his face.

'What's wrong?' I ask, as I climb out of my seat and make my way towards him. The skillet is on the floor and it's surrounded by dishwater. Frank's face is crumpling in shame and I smile to reassure him. 'No harm done,' I say. 'Nothing's broken.' I bend down to pick up the pan and I notice the wet patch on the front of his trousers. I suddenly realise the puddle on the floor is not water.

It takes me a while to clean up the mess and get Frank into clean pants. I put the wet ones in a plastic bag and throw them in the bin near the jetty. I'm going to have to find somewhere to buy Frank some extra clothes. We can't afford to be stopping to do loads of washing along the way.

As I pack away the last of our gear in the Kombi's storage compartments the wind whips up, causing little white caps to form on the water. The calm of the early morning has disappeared. It's time for us to go.

Frank is out of sorts after his accident and doesn't want to get into the passenger seat. 'I can't come with you,' he says. 'I'm waiting here for my wife.'

'Shirley asked me to bring you home, Frank. Come on now, hop in and let me help you with your seatbelt.'

'You know my wife?'

I smile. 'We're very close.'

'Well . . .' He pauses for some time before conceding. 'All right then.' He climbs aboard and allows me to buckle him in.

I've plugged the directions to our next stop into Google Maps on my phone, but I have the sound turned off because I think the voice directions might startle Frank. I've had a look at where we're going and it seems pretty straightforward to me. We'll stay on George Bass Drive until Moruya and then make our way to the A1. From there we'll head south until we find somewhere safe to park the camper overnight. It's a pleasant drive. The solid Kombi isn't affected by the wind, which appears to be dying down anyway, and we're free to enjoy the sunshine. Frank's subdued in the passenger seat.

'Penny for your thoughts,' I venture.

'Eh?'

'You're quiet there. What are you thinking?'

'I'm thinking it must be breakfast time.'

'We've had breakfast, Frank. Not long ago in fact.'

'You might have, but I most certainly haven't.'

We've only been travelling for about ten minutes but I don't want to argue with him. 'We'll stop soon, I promise.' I rack my brain for something to distract him. We need to cover some distance today while we're still flying under the radar in this camper. As much as I want Frank to enjoy the journey, we really can't be stopping every ten minutes or we'll never make it home. The Kombi's radio catches my eye. It's not the original one the vehicle rolled off the assembly line with, but it's not exactly new either. A good thing in my view. It means Frank should have no problems operating it. 'Feel like some music?'

Frank laughs. 'Do you want me to sing you a song?'

'Well, that's one option, but I thought maybe you might like to listen to the radio for a bit.'

He nods. 'Yeah, why not? A bit of music always livens things up.'

I press the knob on the radio and we're immediately blasted with the most god-awful noise. I swirl the knob left to turn the volume down and glance at Frank to see if he's okay.

His eyebrows have shot up but he's laughing. 'What in God's name do you call that?'

'Can't say I know. Change the station, see if you can find something decent.'

He stares at the radio for a moment.

'Try pushing one of those silver buttons underneath,' I say.

'Yes,' he says. He pokes tentatively at one, which results in the end of the thumping noise but replaces it with a talkback show. Frank screws up his face and makes a quacking motion with his hand. 'Pah. Gums flapping. Who wants to listen to that?'

I shake my head. 'Not me.'

The next push brings an ad for farming equipment so Frank tries his luck one more time. It's an old Beatles song, 'She Loves You'.

'That's more like it,' I say.

'Hmm, marginally better, I suppose. My wife would approve, but these blokes are overrated in my opinion.'

I laugh and then join in the song's chorus. Frank shakes his head at my singing. Some things never change.

When the song finishes an announcement proclaims the station plays 'the best of the '60s, '70s and '80s'. Frank settles back in his seat, satisfied with his choice. After a couple more boppy songs, the mood in the camper has lifted significantly. We're both enjoying the singalong. 'And now for a golden oldie from 1962, here's Andy Williams with "Stranger on the Shore".' At the first note, a lump forms in my throat, then Frank's rich baritone voice joins Andy Williams's and my eyes prick with tears.

Once upon a time this was 'our' song. It was playing on the radio in Frank's car that first night when he'd driven me home from the Palais. Now, as the song finishes, Frank's hand drifts to my knee. 'All right, old girl?' he asks, and I nod, unsure of who he thinks I am now. When I glance in his direction I see a husband's eyes looking into his wife's.

The moment passes with the beginning of the next song. This number is from the 1980s, and Frank screws up his nose and presses several buttons until finally he shuts the radio off. 'Must be time for breakfast.'

This time I don't bother to correct him. I'd planned to stop in Narooma, but we're driving into Bodalla and it's a charming little town so I pull over near the first cafe I see. 'Righto,' I say. 'How about we get a cuppa and something to eat here?'

Frank nods enthusiastically. 'Suits me. I'm starving. I reckon it's about time for breakfast.'

I laugh. 'Is that right?'

We take a seat in a sunny corner of the old-fashioned cafe. The whole town has a cutesy village feel and I'm pleased to see that the menu in this place is traditional too. No quinoa or kale here. Pots of English breakfast tea and scones with jam and cream are the menu staples. When Frank hears me order a Devonshire tea, he forgets all about eggs and bacon and decides to have the same. When the fat and fluffy scones arrive he claps his hands like a delighted child at a birthday party. 'Ooh, look at these. I haven't seen a decent scone like this in years. My Shirl's a beauty of a cook. Never seen a scone that could beat hers, but I reckon these might come close.' He takes a scone from the basket, cuts it in half and heaps jam and cream on top. His first bite brings forth a moan of pleasure.

'Good?' I ask.

He gives me the thumbs up sign. 'Bloody beautiful.'

After this we slip into a companionable silence. Frank seems so content right now that I'm reluctant to hurry him. When he pours himself a second cup of tea from the pot I force myself to remain quiet, despite my desire to be back on the road.

We while away forty-five minutes in all. When the pot is dry, I stand and say, 'I'll just go pay the bill and then we can get going.'

Frank touches my arm. 'Sit down,' he says. 'My treat. What sort of gentleman lets a lady pay for her meal?'

He reaches into his pocket for his wallet. 'Well, that's the strangest thing. My wallet's always in my back pocket, but it appears to be gone.'

'Don't worry,' I say. 'It's probably in the car. Maybe you put it in the glove box. Let me get this and you can pay for lunch.'

I have the wallet. In fact it's in my handbag right now. He hasn't needed it since he's been a resident of Sunset Lodge. It's a tatty old thing, probably best suited to the bin, but his brown leather wallet was so much a part of Frank's identity that I couldn't bear to throw it out. Silly, really. I consider handing it over and pretending that he dropped it earlier, but there's no money in it and the credit and debit cards no longer work, so that would probably just agitate him further. I make a mental note to surreptitiously remove the cards, put a fifty-dollar note in it and pop it in the glove box for Frank to find later. That would at least afford him the dignity of paying for a meal.

He nods graciously. 'That's very kind of you.'

After we settle the bill we walk out into the sunshine and Frank's attention is caught by some brightly coloured fabric flapping in the breeze outside a nearby shop. He wanders into the store and I hurry to catch up. The shop is filled with handmade items, candles, cushions and clothing made of gaudy tie-dyed material.

'Get a load of this,' Frank calls to me from the back of the store. He's holding up an orange and black patterned shirt. 'Shirl's always saying I should smarten myself up and wear brighter colours. I bet this one would knock her socks off.'

I can't help but laugh. Frank's always been a conservative man. He persisted with his neat white button-down shirts and short-back-and-sides haircuts well into the 1970s, long after his friends had started to grow sideburns and wear flares. 'Try it on,' I say on a whim. After all, he does need some new clothes. Why not get them here? I look around the shop and gather more items for Frank to try on, and while I'm at it I grab a few things for myself. I can safely say that there's not one thing in this shop that the Shirley Sullivan of yesterday would have worn, but maybe that's not a bad thing. We are fugitives on the run, after all. Surely it makes sense for us to disguise ourselves a little? Besides, these clothes will go better with my new hairstyle. I start to giggle at the thought of us as hippie bandits. I'm still laughing when I hand over an enormous wad of cash to the bemused sales assistant. We're both wearing some of our new purchases. Frank has on a black T-shirt paired with a pair of loose orange and black tie-dyed pants. He's carrying his shoes and socks and has slipped his feet into a pair of soft leather Jesus sandals. I've ditched my travelling clothes for a pair of pink and white yoga pants and a gauzy floral caftan affair. It's ridiculous how much I like it.

'We're going to keep these things on, if you don't mind,' I say to the shop assistant. She smiles politely. After all, Frank and I have just bought up half the shop. She bags up the rest of our new gear and starts to fold up our old clothes.

When she's done we amble back to the van, both of us grinning. As we climb into the Kombi I'm aware that we look like a pair of ageing hippies. Frank and Shirley Sullivan have totally disappeared.

Chapter 18

September 1969
Geelong

'When are you coming home, Mummy?'

Shirley kissed the top of her daughter's head. 'Very soon, my angel. Your little brother or sister will be here soon. Won't that be exciting?'

Fiona nodded. 'I'm going to be a big sister.'

'Yes you are, and I know you will be the best big sister ever. Daddy and Nanna say you have been such a good helper while Mummy's been in hospital. What a big, grown-up girl you are.'

Fiona beamed at her mother's approval and Shirley revelled in the moment. How had she got so lucky? She couldn't believe how her fortunes had changed in just over six months. When she'd gone to Rita to talk about her pregnancy, she was at her lowest. Back then she'd felt that her life was barely worth living. Although she could never have brought herself to take any action to terminate this pregnancy, she hadn't wanted to go through with it. Now, she felt ashamed of herself. Rita was the only one who knew about any of that and she'd been kind, telling Shirley that her feelings were completely normal.

This pregnancy had been so much easier than the last one. Everything had been almost textbook until last week, when her blood pressure started to creep up a little and her hands and feet began to swell. Doctor Downing wasn't overly concerned, but after consultation with the specialist obstetrician at the hospital it was decided she should be admitted, just to be on the safe side. She didn't mind. The baby was due in less than two weeks and she'd been assured by the medical staff – and Rita, who she knew wouldn't lie to her – that if it came along now it would be perfectly fine.

'Kiss Mummy goodbye, Princess,' Frank said. 'We need to get you home for your bath, and Mummy and Bubby need their rest.'

Fiona planted a sloppy, open-mouthed kiss on her cheek and then kissed her swollen belly. 'Goodnight, Mummy, goodnight, Bubby. See you tomorrow.'

Frank smiled at Shirley and kissed her tenderly on the lips. 'You are just radiant today, my darling. I wish I could stay but I need to get Little Miss home and into bed. See you tomorrow.'

Shirley glowed in the wake of Frank's words as she waved them goodbye. She *felt* radiant. Serene, almost. She was actually looking forward to the birth now. The pregnancy had been relatively uneventful and she felt certain the birth would be the same. Once she'd felt confident enough to announce her pregnancy, both Frank and the doctor treated her with kid gloves – insisting she take to her bed. It was hard, especially with Fiona being so little. Her mother and Rita helped as much as they could, but the biggest helper was Fiona herself. At three, she was really still a toddler, but she took to the challenge of 'looking after Mummy' like a duck to water. She loved being given the responsibility of dressing herself each day and bringing Mummy glasses of water when asked. Shirley's mum dropped by each morning to tidy up, collect the washing and cut sandwiches to leave in the fridge. At lunchtime, Fiona would switch off the TV and take a tray with the sandwiches to Shirley's room so they could eat together. They'd talk about all sorts of things – Fiona's favourite TV shows and toys, what sorts of things babies did and whether she would be allowed to push the baby's pram when he or she arrived. Despite her confinement, Shirley found she was loving this time, and she'd never felt closer to her daughter.

Rita dropped by as often as possible – pretty much every day. They'd grown exceptionally close in the early months of the pregnancy, when they were the only two who knew of the baby's existence. Rita had monitored her so carefully, checking her pulse and her blood pressure, and recording her weight gain to make sure everything was as it should be. When she'd first felt the baby move, Rita had been with her and she seemed every bit as excited as Shirley was. As time went on, Shirley noticed that the baby seemed to respond to Rita's presence. It moved more when Rita was in the room and became more active when Rita laid her hands on her belly. It was odd, she supposed, but it almost felt as though the baby belonged partly to Rita.

After a month of complete bed rest at home and with everything looking perfectly normal, Rita suggested that she ask the doctor if partial bed rest might be an option. He agreed, so she'd been able to do some light housework each morning and then she and Fiona would rest in the afternoon, Fiona 'reading' her picture books for her entertainment.

Now the pregnancy was almost over, and once the baby was safely born, everything would be perfect.

This time when a nagging ache in her back awoke her in the middle of the night she only felt excitement. Soon she was going to meet her baby – little Andrew or Nicole – and she could hardly wait. As the first pain took hold she calmly pressed the buzzer for a nurse. She pulled herself up to a sitting position and panted through the pain, just as she'd been taught in her childbirth classes. As the wave of the first contraction ebbed she realised the sheet was wet beneath her. Obviously her waters had broken already. That was a good sign. Rita had talked to her lots about the progression of labour and she knew that the rupture of waters should speed things up. Hopefully this labour would be short and sweet, and she'd be able to greet her baby before the break of dawn. At that thought the nurse arrived, along with another contraction.

The nurse shone a torch in her face. 'What is it, Mrs Sullivan?'

'My . . . labour . . . has . . . started,' she panted. The pain was awfully strong for early labour, but she didn't mind. Surely that meant it would be over quickly.

'Very good. Let's have a look then, shall we? See how far along you are, so I can let Doctor know.' She pulled back the bedcovers and lifted Shirley's nightgown, then quickly turned on the overhead light and pressed the emergency call button next to the bed. 'Looks like you'll be going to delivery right away, my dear.' She glanced over her shoulder. 'I'm just going to get Doctor to have a look at you. I'll be back in a moment. Don't you worry, dear, we're going to take good care of you.'

Shirley winced in pain as yet another contraction gripped her. 'Can you please call my husband to let him know?'

'Yes, yes, of course.' The nurse bustled out of the room and Shirley heard her call down the hallway, 'I need help in here.'

Obviously the baby was coming even more quickly than she imagined. The hospital had just started allowing expectant fathers into the delivery room and Frank was very much hoping to be present when the baby was born. She hoped he wouldn't miss it. They had both Rita and Shirley's mum on standby to look after Fiona. Seeing as it was the middle of the night and Rita was on day shift this week, she'd get the job. She lived closer than Shirley's parents, so it wouldn't take her long to get to the house. Still, the way these contractions were coming – relentlessly, with barely a break between them – Shirley feared there wouldn't be enough time for Frank to make it before the baby's arrival.

As the latest contraction eased, Shirley noted she felt odd. Her head was woozy and she felt nauseated – probably because of the pain. She was relieved to see the nurse rushing back into the room with the doctor and someone else . . . maybe it was an orderly . . . or was it Frank? The pain was making it hard for her eyes to focus properly. An intense contraction tore through her and she let out an involuntary cry. The nurse gripped her hand as she writhed on the bed.

A male voice said, 'Mrs Sullivan, you're in advanced labour. Don't worry, we're taking you up to delivery right now.'

A halo of blue light surrounded the figures at her bedside and the conversation became unintelligible. Shirley felt detached from all that was going on around her and, while she struggled to stay lucid, the fatigue was too great. She wanted to beg the doctor not to let anything happen to her child, but she found herself powerless to speak. A strange floating sensation overtook her. She felt oddly disconnected from her body and the commotion surrounding her. Shirley put herself in God's hands and closed her eyes.

'Shirley? Can you hear me? Oh, thank God.' Frank's face hovered above her as she opened her eyes.

She blinked a few times to help her focus and then tried to sit up, but found her head swam as soon as she lifted it from the pillow. When she tried to respond to Frank's question she realised an oxygen mask covered her mouth and nose. She lowered it and found her voice. 'Frank,' she croaked. 'What happened?'

'Put the mask back on, love. You've had surgery.'

She ignored him and placed a hand on her stomach. No baby, but her belly was still swollen and tender to touch. 'Surgery? What sort of surgery?' She searched her memory but came up blank. She could remember hanging on through a powerful contraction, one that had made her think the baby was about to be born any second, and a nurse telling her not to push just yet. She tried again to pull herself up to a sitting position, but a searing pain prevented her from moving. 'Frank, where's the baby?'

'Your blood pressure got too high, love, and it made you have a funny turn, a fit of some sort. The doctor needed to get the baby out quick so they had to give you a caesarean.'

'Oh.' A wave of relief washed over her. That explained her sore tummy. 'So, don't keep me in suspense. Do we have an Andrew or a Nicole in the nursery?'

Frank squeezed her hand tightly and his eyes glistened with tears. 'Maybe I should get the doctor.'

'Frank,' she said, her pulse quickening. 'What is it? Is something wrong with the baby?'

'It was Andrew,' he said, his voice breaking. 'I'm so sorry, my darling, but little Andrew didn't make it. He was stillborn.'

'No,' she whispered, so quietly even she couldn't hear it. 'No! That can't be true. I could feel him kicking right before I went into labour.' Why was Frank saying this to her? She didn't believe him. 'Where is he? I want to see him!'

Frank's face drained of colour. 'That's not possible, Shirley.'

'Where is he? I want my baby! Take me to him.'

'Andrew's gone, my love.' Frank wiped away a tear. 'They buried him yesterday.'

'Yesterday? But . . . he was only just born. You're not making any sense.'

'You've been in the critical care unit for three days, Shirl. Our boy never took one breath. The doctors said you might not pull through. I was beside myself . . .' Frank tried to take her into his arms, but she batted him away.

'Don't touch me,' she screamed. 'This is your all your fault! I never wanted another baby. I knew, do you hear me? I *knew* this would happen. I wanted to take that pill but you wouldn't let me. You said God would protect us, that he wouldn't give us another baby we couldn't keep.'

Frank looked stricken. 'Shirley, please . . . I'm sorry. I didn't—'

'Didn't what? Didn't think what this would be like for me? Didn't *care*?'

'I didn't know . . .' Tears streamed down his face, but she couldn't think about Frank's emotions right now. All she cared about was her child.

'Get out.'

'Shirl, please. I know this is hard but—'

'Get out, get out, get out!'

Her shouts brought a nurse, who'd been hovering nearby, rushing to her side. 'Mr Sullivan, I think it would be best if you stepped outside for a little while. Now that Mrs Sullivan's properly lucid, Doctor will want to have a look at her. I'll let you know when you can visit again.'

Frank's shoulders slumped but he nodded and walked slowly out of the room.

The nurse put a sympathetic hand on Shirley's shoulder. 'Dear girl, you have had a terrible time of it. I know you're hurting. But I need you to try to calm down a bit. We can't let that blood pressure come back up.'

The ball of anger inside her deflated and grief took hold. A sob escaped her lips, quickly followed by another. The kindly nurse rubbed her back. 'That's the way. Let it all out. Have a good cry now. I'll pop off and get you a cup of tea and then we'll fetch the doctor. Is there anything else I can get you, dear? Would you like me to call your mother?'

'Rita,' Shirley said. 'I need to see Rita.'

It was hours before Rita arrived and Shirley refused to see anyone else that day. Her parents and sister came to the hospital, but she had one of the nurses turn them away. 'Tell them I'm too sick. No, wait . . . I don't want them worrying. Just tell them I'm not up to seeing visitors. Maybe tomorrow.' The young nurse, who'd just come on shift, nodded sympathetically and went off to do her bidding. When she returned, carrying a huge bunch of white freesias from Shirley's mother, Shirley inquired about Rita's whereabouts. 'The message has been passed on and she said she'll be here as soon as she possibly can.'

Rita would know what to say, or what not to. One of the reasons she couldn't bear to see her mother was because she could already imagine what she would say. 'These things happen for a reason. We don't always know what God's plan is for us, but we must trust that He knows best.' What sort of a plan was it to take the life of an innocent baby? At least Rita wouldn't spout rubbish like that to her.

Maybe Rita was right. Maybe there was no such thing as God. Maybe He was just a fairy story, like Father Christmas and the Easter Bunny. If he did exist he was cruel and vengeful, not loving and kind as she'd been brought up to believe, and right now she couldn't bear to listen to anyone claiming otherwise.

The doctor arrived with a team of younger doctors – medical students, the nurse explained quietly – behind him, and after a curt acknowledgement of her loss, went on to explain in detail what had happened to her. He used a whole lot of medical jargon, some of which Shirley understood (hypertension, seizure) and much of which she didn't (eclampsia, placental something-or-other). She stopped paying attention halfway through his little speech when she realised it wasn't really aimed at her. It seemed he was more concerned with using her 'case' as a lesson to his young students. When he was done checking her wound and consulting her chart, he looked at her sternly. 'I strongly advise no more children for you, Mrs Sullivan. Really, given your history, this pregnancy was a foolhardy venture. Thankfully your blood pressure is going the right way now and we expect you to make a full recovery. Next time you might not be so lucky.'

The young nurse squeezed her hand before following him out of the room.

One of the painkillers they had her on made her drowsy, and when her eyelids drooped she gave in, sinking into the pillows to embrace the welcome state of sleep. In dreamland there was no pain or grief, and if she were lucky she might wake up and realise this was all just a nightmare.

When she woke, Rita was sitting in the chair beside her. The look of pain and pity on her friend's face told Shirley all she needed to know. It wasn't a dream. Her baby really was dead.

'Rita,' she said, and she began to cry.

Rita took her in her arms and cradled her. She didn't say, 'Everything will be all right.' Nor did she say she knew how Shirley felt. In fact she said nothing. She just held Shirley until the flow of tears was stemmed.

Finally Shirley composed herself enough to say, 'I'm so glad you're here.'

'I'm sorry I took so long. I worked nightshift last night. I checked in on you but you weren't really with us yesterday.

This morning I had a few errands and then I went home for a sleep. I didn't hear the phone the first time the hospital called.'

'That's okay. You're here now.'

'How are you?'

Shirley didn't know what to say. There weren't words to describe the pain she was feeling right now. Instead she asked the question she was desperate to know the answer to. Rita was her friend and she knew she would tell her the truth. 'How? How could this happen? What did I do wrong?'

'Oh, lovely girl, you did nothing wrong. This isn't your fault.'

'Well, whose fault is it then? I don't understand what happened. The baby was strong, I know he was. He was kicking right up until I went into labour. How could he be dead? Did the doctors do something wrong when they were getting him out?'

Rita shook her head sadly. 'No, I can assure you that the medical team did everything possible to save your baby. It's not bloody fair, but it's no one's fault.'

'Why, then? It just doesn't make any sense.'

Rita gently broke their embrace and sat back in the armchair. She reached out and took Shirley's hand. 'Has the doctor not spoken to you?'

'He has, but I didn't understand half of what he said. It was all medical gobbledegook.'

'Would you like me to explain? I've spoken to one of the nurses who was there when the baby was born and I can tell you everything she told me. It doesn't have to be right now if you don't think you are ready to hear it.'

'I want to. I need to know what happened.'

Rita nodded. 'Your blood pressure got too high again, like it did in the last pregnancy.'

'But they were monitoring it right up until I went into labour. Everyone thought I was going to be fine this time.'

'Yes, that's true, but the doctors seem to think your intense labour caused your blood pressure to rise. So you went from having "pre-eclampsia" – the condition that gave you the high blood pressure and the puffy hands and feet – to full-blown eclampsia, which caused you to have several seizures on your way up to the delivery suite.'

Shirley shook her head. 'I don't remember having any seizures.'

'No, you wouldn't.'

'I was having trouble seeing, I remember that. I just thought it was because of the pain. I should have said something to the nurse.'

Rita gave her a sympathetic look. 'It wouldn't have made any difference, Shirl, honestly. By the time it got to that point there was nothing anyone could do except keep you safe during the seizure.'

'So the fit killed my baby. Is that what you're saying?'

'Well, not exactly. It's a little more complicated than that. Unfortunately they weren't able to control the seizures and you had another one. This one was longer and it damaged your placenta. You might have heard the doctor say something about a placental abruption?'

'Yes, he did say something about that, but I didn't really understand what he meant.'

'It's when the placenta comes away from the womb. It's dangerous for the baby because it can cut off their supply of oxygen.'

'And the seizure caused that?'

'Yes, they think so. It's hard to tell the absolute cause. You'd had very intense contractions and some bleeding before that second seizure, so maybe there was a partial abruption already, but after that second fit there was massive bleeding and the only way to try to save the baby – and you – was to do an immediate caesarean section. The baby was born without a pulse, Shirley. Val, the nurse who was there, said the paediatric staff did their very best to revive him, but they were unsuccessful. I'm so sorry.'

The tears had stopped now. Shirley was all cried out. 'Frank says they've buried him already. Is that right?'

Rita gripped her hand. 'Yes. It's the hospital's policy to send stillborn infants for burial as soon as possible.'

'Did nobody think about me? That I might not want that? That I might want to say goodbye to my baby? Why didn't someone stop them?'

Rita's eyes glistened. 'I'm so sorry.'

Shirley shook her head. This wasn't Rita's fault; she wasn't even here when Andrew was born. But Frank was. Why hadn't he tried to do something? 'Did they ask Frank? Do you know?'

'I don't know. That's something you'll have to ask him. But Shirl, I want you to know the midwives did their best for your boy. Val knew you were my friend and she called me as soon as she could. She told me she had wrapped the baby up in a bunny rug and placed a bonnet on his head. She wanted me to let you know Andrew went off clean and warm and with a kiss on his cheek.'

Shirley was unable to speak. She was so overcome with conflicting emotions she thought her heart might burst. On the one hand there was gratitude that her baby had been shown love, on the other hand despair that she had been denied the opportunity to be the one to provide that love.

Rita let go of her hand for a moment and pulled a small parcel out of her bag. 'Here,' she said. 'This is for you. It isn't much, but Val and I hoped it might bring you some small measure of comfort.'

Shirley unwrapped the brown-paper package to find a pale-blue jewellery box. She flipped it open and found a gold heart-shaped locket inside. Rita meant well, but no piece of jewellery could bring her comfort right now. She forced herself to smile. 'Thank you,' she said, as graciously as she could manage. She set the box down on the bed beside her.

'You might not want to open the locket now – or ever – but I want you to know there's a lock of Andrew's hair in there. I asked Val to cut a little of his hair so you would have something to remember him by. I hope I did the right thing.'

Shirley snatched the box back up and carefully removed the locket. With her heart pounding she prised the heart open and there, behind a thin sheet of clear plastic, was a wisp of black hair. Her baby had black hair, just like his daddy.

'Oh, Rita, you have no idea what this means to me. Thank you.' She held her arms open.

Rita embraced her once more. 'Anything for you, my darling girl.'

Chapter 19

Tuesday

We laugh and sing our way to Narooma, where we're forced to stop on the bridge at the town's entrance to let a commercial fishing vessel pass. Frank has asked me at least a dozen times who I am and where we're going. Each time my reply is the same: I'm Peggy and I'm taking him home.

Frank watches as a section of the bridge lifts to allow the boat through. 'Look at that engineering,' he says. 'Simple but brilliant.'

Not being one with any knowledge of such matters, I simply agree.

Once the boat has passed the span lowers and the boom gate goes up. As we continue driving across the bridge Frank's leg starts to jiggle up and down impatiently.

'Everything okay?' I ask.

'I could use a toilet stop.'

Inwardly I sigh. I should have insisted he go when we were in Bodalla. Or stocked up on incontinence pads. I'm torn on the whole diaper issue. Frank still has enough self-awareness to find wearing one humiliating. The whole point of this trip is to free Frank from humiliation, so I'm reluctant to make him wear the incontinence pants when it's not strictly necessary. But the accidents are embarrassing for him too, and the need to keep stopping for bathroom visits will slow us down. There's no easy answer. 'I'll find somewhere to stop as soon as I can.'

I pull over into the first parking space I find, which happens to be outside a pub. Frank's jiggling has become frantic so there's no time to look for a public toilet. The pub will have to do. We make our way inside and find the bathrooms. Frank dashes into the gents' and I stand awkwardly outside, not sure whether I should follow him in or not. It's not quite lunchtime and the pub is almost empty. Frank's probably in there on his own. While I'm still debating what to do he appears, happy as Larry. I quickly check his appearance and, satisfied that all is in order, ask him if he's washed his hands.

His answer is indignant. 'Of course I washed my hands. Not that it's any business of yours.'

'Right. Well, let's get back on the road, shall we?'

But something has caught Frank's eye, and when I follow his gaze I can see what. The pub sits on top of a hill and has impressive views of the water. Frank walks through the bistro towards the deck at the back and I follow. The sun is shining down on the rippling water and it shimmers. Fishing boats and catamarans move below us.

'Are you after a table on the deck?' the young woman behind the bar calls to us. 'Just sit anywhere that doesn't have a reserved sign on it.'

I turn to say we're not staying, but Frank is opening the glass door and heading outside. He turns to me, his face shining. 'Get a load of this view, eh? Reminds me of when I was growing up. Pop had a boat, an old tin thing – it wasn't much to look at but it did the job. Sometimes in summer he'd take me to Lakes Entrance or Marlo and we'd spend the day on the water, fishing. Pop was the one who taught me to love the water, and to respect it.

He showed me how to spot a rip and what to do if I got caught in one. Ah, he was a good man, Pop. Hard, mind – he never took any rot from us kids – but he was fair.'

Of course I know all about Pop and I've heard this story many times before, but the joy in Frank's voice as he reminisces about his grandfather moves me. Time-wise The Plan is going to hell in a hand basket, but what does it matter? I try to let go of the inner voice telling me we have to get back on the road. If this trip is *really* about Frank, then I need to take my cues from him. 'Fancy getting a drink and maybe sitting a while?'

He nods enthusiastically. 'I'd love a beer.'

This takes me by surprise. Frank's never been much of a drinker. He's not a complete teetotaller – in fact, over the years he's developed a taste for fine wines – but I can't ever remember him drinking beer by choice. 'Are you sure you want beer?'

He nods. 'A place like this deserves a toast. Sometimes when I'd been fishing with Pop we'd pull the boat up outside the Metung Hotel and we'd go have a drink in the beer garden – beer for Pop, lemonade for me. Did I ever tell you about Pop? He was my grandfather.'

I smile and nod, encouraging him to go on.

'I couldn't wait for the day I was old enough to have a beer with him, but the old man died when I was just fifteen. Too young for a beer. But I can have one now and drink a toast in his memory.'

'Fair enough. How about you choose us a table and I'll go to the bar to order?'

He seems pleased with this arrangement and sets about weighing up the pros and cons of the assorted seating possibilities. Inside the pub I engage in a bit of meaningless chatter with the barmaid – is that what they're called these days? The term sounds wrong, somehow, even to my old-fashioned ears. Barperson, perhaps. Whatever she's called, she's a friendly little thing. She looks to be around Frances's age, and for a moment my thoughts flit to my eldest granddaughter, who I haven't been in touch with for a while. I wonder if she's pulling beers in some pub overseas, like this young woman.

She brings my attention back to her by complimenting me on my hair (which is a similar shade to her own), and she also remarks favourably on my top. I resist the urge to tell her that this gaudy number isn't my standard attire. I order a beer for Frank and a lemon, lime and bitters for myself.

'What sort of beer would your husband like?'

I stare at her blankly. 'Oh, goodness. I'm not sure. He's not much of a beer drinker usually.' I glance out at the balcony, where Frank is still wandering around the tables.

'We have Tooheys New on tap. It's very popular.'

'That will be fine, I'm sure.'

'Schooner, middy or glass?'

Again I'm stumped for an answer. Who knew ordering beer took such expertise?

The young woman grins at me. 'Small, medium or large?'

'Oh. Best make it a small one, I think.'

'Right, a glass then.' She pours the beer from the tap and then looks under the counter. 'I'm so sorry. We're out of lime cordial, but I'm sure there's more in the stock room. I'll be back in a flash.' She rounds the bar and then disappears from sight. I decide to take Frank's beer to him while I'm waiting, but as I turn to make my way outside I'm distracted by the news update on the pub's oversized TV screen.

There's a huge photo of Frank and me on the screen, behind the newsreader. It's the same one I saw online, and even I'm surprised at how different the image is to the way we look now. The funny thing is, I actually feel different too. My hair and the clothes I have on now are so far away from Shirley Sullivan (wife, mother, grandmother and model citizen) that I feel quite removed from her.

Liberated, in fact. Rita's voice pops into my head. '*You worry way too much about what other people think, Shirley.*'

Not for the first time, I wish I was more like Rita.

The newsreader's smooth voice informs viewers that there have been no reported sightings of us since we left the nursing home on Sunday.

I walk closer to the TV so I can better hear what the newsreader is saying. My heart begins to gallop as I see a photo of Ollie appear onscreen.

'The man wanted for questioning in regard to the disappearance of old-age pensioners Frank and Shirley Sullivan—'

Pensioners! Frank and I are self-funded retirees, thank you very much.

'—handed himself into police early this morning, but has since been released. Our crime reporter, Janet Leong, is outside Sutherland Police Station with an update. What's the latest in this case, Janet?'

'Well, Brock, as we reported to viewers in our morning bulletin, twenty-four-year-old Oliver Petrakis handed himself in here' – the reporter gestures to the building behind her – 'to Sutherland Police Station early this morning. We believe he was questioned for a short time before being released without charge. Police are not giving much away at this stage, other than to say that Mr Petrakis is helping them with their inquiries and is not a suspect at this point in time.'

I exhale and my heart rate slows a fraction. Thank God they didn't charge him, although I don't like the sound of 'at this point in time'. What does that mean? Surely Ollie has told them the truth. I'm suddenly gripped by fear. What if the police don't believe him?

Get a hold of yourself, Shirley. Nothing will happen to Ollie. If he is charged with anything I will hand myself in. I haven't gone completely mad, after all.

This thought comforts me until the reporter crosses to some footage shot earlier. Ollie is leaving the police station, his hands thrust deep into his pockets and his eyes on the ground as he hurries towards a waiting car. Janet Leong leads a group of reporters who chase him and ask him for a comment. 'Where are Frank and Shirley?' Janet asks as Ollie squeezes into the car (which, I note, is driven by the same young woman who picked him up on Sunday. They're clearly an item. Good for him!). The expression on Ollie's face is grim as he's driven away, and I'm once again filled with remorse for having involved him.

But regret is quickly replaced by anxiety when a photo of a white Hyundai hatchback flashes up on the screen. The reporter's tone is sombre as she announces, 'It is believed the elderly couple—'

Again with the 'elderly'.

'—are travelling in a white Hyundai Getz like the one pictured here. The car in question bears the New South Wales numberplate LR-00-DI. Police are asking the public to report any sightings of this car to them immediately. Back to you, Brock.'

It had to happen sooner or later, but now that the car has been identified it won't be long before it's found. Once that happens it will be easy for the police to track our movements. I'm pretty sure that the bus had a security camera in it. Forget savouring the moment. We need to get back on the road, pronto. I place Frank's beer on the table beside me, but before I can move the newsreader informs me that my family have just held a press conference. I hold my breath as Fiona appears on the screen. She's seated at a table on a raised platform and is flanked by Gary on one side – that's an interesting development – and a grim-looking woman in a grey suit (presumably a police officer) on the other. Fiona is pale, and there are obvious bags under her eyes. Her forehead is creased and her mouth is set in a hard line, like she's concentrating hard on a maths problem she just can't solve.

Before she speaks the police officer whispers something to her and she nods and rubs her eyes. She looks into the camera and reads aloud from a prepared statement.

'My parents, Frank and Shirley Sullivan, were last seen on Sunday afternoon when they left Sunset Lodge Nursing Home in Kirrawee, where my father is a resident. We now know that they left in a car driven by my mother. We have no idea why they would take this action or where they were headed.' Her voice is shaking with emotion. To the general public it probably seems like distress, but I'm her mother and I hear it for what it is: unbridled anger.

'My mother is elderly,' she continues, and despite everything, I shake my head in irritation. 'She's not a confident driver and prior to Sunday she had not driven a car for over a year.'

Wrong! I'm tempted to shout at the screen.

'She is quite nervous in traffic, so I can't imagine what would possess her to drive my father away from his home. Perhaps she was coerced by someone or perhaps she is suffering from some kind of medical condition that has affected her mental state.'

I roll my eyes.

Fiona continues. 'My father suffers from several medical conditions, including dementia, and is quite fragile. I can only imagine how distressed he must be right now. I'm told by his carers that he left the nursing home with sufficient medication for one day only, so obviously that is very concerning.' She stops reading now and looks directly at the camera. 'I have grave concerns for my father's wellbeing. If anyone out there has seen him, I urge you to contact your local police station.'

It's a message for me. She's furious and she wants me to know it. Fiona's not stupid. She knows I'm solely responsible for Frank's 'abduction' and she probably has a fair idea of where we are going. The sense of urgency I felt moments earlier returns twofold.

We need to get back on the road, and fast. Frank will have to go without his beer for now. I turn to make my way outside to collect him and my heart stops.

Frank is nowhere to be seen.

Chapter 20

March 1970
Geelong

Shirley sat on a park bench at the edge of the playground, watching as Rita pushed Fiona on the swing. Rita must have been tired – she'd just come off a night shift – but she still seemed to have enough energy to tolerate Fiona's delighted demands. 'Higher, Aunty Rita, higher!' The attention was more than Shirley could offer her child right now.

She didn't seem to have energy for much at all these days. Two weeks ago she'd visited the clinic for a check-up. Doctor Downing had been firm. He'd written her a prescription for some iron tablets – her iron levels had been low since Andrew's birth – but his advice was clear. Stop moping about. 'I know you've had a bit of a rough trot, Shirley, but time heals all wounds. It's been six months now. I know it's hard but you have to put the past behind you. Focus on all the good things in your life. You have a healthy little girl. Keep yourself busy. Lots of fresh air and exercise, that's the ticket.'

Doctor Downing wasn't the only one. Her mother, Mary, even Frank, they all thought it was high time she bucked up and got over herself. 'You just need to keep busy,' her mother had said. 'It's a shame you can't have any more children, but at least you have Fiona. Think of all those poor women who can't have children at all.'

Shirley had wanted to scream. She'd wanted to say that she was grieving. That her child was dead and no other child could replace him. But she knew her mother would consider that sort of outburst ungrateful and unseemly. It was easier just to agree.

It seemed no one wanted to talk about Andrew and, worse than that, no one wanted her to talk about him either. Everyone thought it best that she didn't dwell on what had happened. In fact, it seemed as if people thought that if no one ever talked about it she would somehow magically forget that she had lost her child.

At first she'd tried her best to play along. She'd cleaned the house from top to bottom, sewed Fiona a whole wardrobe of new clothes and spent hours in the kitchen baking treats. None of it had helped. Sometimes she managed to push the pain to the back of her mind during the day, but as soon as her head hit the pillow at night it all came rushing back. Her mind wouldn't stop going over and over all the ways things might have been different. She barely slept, and when she did her dreams were filled with terrible images of her baby lost in limbo. She could hear him crying for her and she called to him, telling him she would find him, but no matter how hard she tried he was always out of reach.

The only person who understood was Rita. Perhaps it was because she was experienced in this sort of thing, being a midwife and all, or maybe it was just because she understood Shirley better than anyone else. Whatever the reason, Shirley was more grateful than ever for her friendship and she found herself seeking out Rita's company more and more.

After that first manic month, exhaustion had set in. One morning she had found herself unable to get out of bed. Frank had been understanding that first day. 'Don't worry, love. You stay there and have a good rest. We'll manage.' But the next day he'd frowned. 'Look, Shirl, how about I make you a nice cup of tea? But I'll have to get going to work then. I was late yesterday, which was fine because it's never happened before, but I can't go making a habit of it.'

She'd nodded and dragged herself out of bed. That day she'd managed to make Fiona breakfast and lunch, but that was about it. When Frank came home he found the two of them sitting on the couch in their pyjamas, watching an episode of *The Lucy Show*. 'What's for dinner?' he'd asked, and Shirley had shrugged. He'd banged around in the kitchen then and, after half an hour, announced dinner was ready. Fiona was thrilled, canned tomato soup and toast for dinner. What a treat! But Frank barely said a word during the entire meal. He sent Shirley off to bed straight after dinner, like she was a naughty child. 'Don't worry about the dishes, Shirley. I'll clean up. You go have an early night so you are ready to face the day bright and early tomorrow.'

His message was loud and clear. Moping about would not be tolerated.

She'd done her best since then to stay on top of things. She cooked and cleaned and did everything a good wife should do.

Well, except *that*.

At first Frank had left her alone. She was recovering from surgery and so sex was out of the question for six weeks at least. Frank was patient. He didn't attempt to touch her until three months had passed. She'd tried to let him down gently, but really there was no easy way to say what was in her heart.

'Frank, I just can't.'

'I understand, my darling. You take all the time you need.'

'No, Frank, you don't understand. I can't risk getting pregnant again.'

'I know that, Shirley. And of course I don't want to do anything that could cause your life to be at risk. But there are things we can do, ways to prevent that from being a problem.'

'Ways? Like what?'

'Well, there are natural methods.'

A burst of anger flamed in her chest. 'Natural methods got me pregnant with Andrew, and look how that turned out.'

Frank looked taken aback, but he wasn't about to give up. 'Well, there are other ways. There's an operation you can have to get your tubes tied. I think considering your delicate . . .' He cleared his throat. '. . . medical condition, God would understand you taking this precaution.'

Shirley was outraged. What the hell? Frank was the horny one, the one who wanted to have sex, but *she* was supposed to have surgery to facilitate this? 'No,' she said flatly. 'I'm not having surgery.' Where were Frank's high and mighty morals, his religious objections, now? 'In any case, Frank, I thought contraception was a sin in your eyes. Aren't you afraid we'll both go to hell?' Shirley looked at him, truly interested in his answer. She no longer feared hell herself, because she knew there was nothing worse than what she was living through right now.

Frank cleared his throat. 'Well, I had a chat to Father Michael about all this.'

Shirley's eyes widened and for the first time in forever she felt a smile forming on her lips. The thought of her uptight, conservative husband discussing his sex life with the priest tickled her fancy. But she kept a straight face as she replied, 'Is that right? And, what, pray tell, were Father Michael's words of wisdom on the matter?'

Frank dropped his gaze from hers. 'Well, er, he seemed to think that there was a bit of a grey area where married couples were concerned, particularly when there was a chance of a woman's life being at risk if she were to fall pregnant. He said that if that couple already had offspring then there was a chance God would understand them taking measures to prevent endangering the woman's life. He believes God wouldn't want to rob Fiona of her mother. Maybe if you come back to church, Shirl, he could explain all this to you himself.'

Shirley sighed. That wasn't going to happen. God had abandoned her when she'd needed Him most. She wasn't about to waste any more of her life mouthing empty prayers to a deity who clearly wasn't listening. Conversely, Andrew's death seemed to have renewed Frank's faith, or at least caused him to be a more regular churchgoer. Prior to Andrew's death, she'd occasionally had to nag him to get up early for church on a Sunday. Since they'd lost their baby he'd been there every week and he'd made sure Fiona was by his side. At first Shirley hadn't been well enough to attend, and now that she was physically able she just couldn't bring herself to go.

Given Frank's renewed religious devotion, she was taken aback at his eagerness to find a method of contraception. Before Andrew's conception he'd baulked at the idea. But now, faced with a life of celibacy, he seemed prepared to compromise his beliefs. She supposed it shouldn't come as a surprise to her that Frank was prepared to risk embarrassment or even condemnation from Father Michael by seeking his approval to go against the Church's teachings. He was a man, after all, and men had needs that women didn't. It was as simple as that.

Despite everything, she still loved Frank. He was a good man, a kind man, and the most caring and devoted father she'd ever seen. She knew Andrew's loss must be affecting him too, but no matter how often she tried she couldn't get him to talk about it. Maybe he thought he was supposed to be strong for her, or maybe he thought that she would see him as a failure if he opened up about his grief. Maybe he simply couldn't bear to think about it. Whatever Frank's reasons, he kept his grief to himself.

Sometimes Shirley craved the comfort of physical contact. Some days she longed to have Frank take her in his arms and whisper sweet things in her ear. But she kept her distance. She didn't want to lead him on. Tender embraces inevitably led to more intimate ones and she just could not go there. Even the slightest risk of pregnancy was too great for her to bear. If they were to be together again as man and wife there could be absolutely no chance of conception.

She'd talked about her fears to Rita – there were no secrets between the two of them – and Rita had told her that there were doctors in Melbourne who performed vasectomies for contraception. They didn't advertise the fact, because the procedure was still considered illegal if used solely for contraceptive purposes. Rita believed that this would change very soon, as the procedure was becoming more and more popular due to its effectiveness. It might be an answer to their problem.

'Well, Frank, that being the case, maybe there is an option. There is a procedure called a vasectomy. I'm not one hundred per cent sure how it works, but it's an operation a man can have on his penis to prevent him from impregnating a woman.'

At the mention of the word 'penis', Frank visibly paled. 'You can't be serious?'

The flash of anger she'd felt before returned. 'Why wouldn't I be?'

'You can't expect me to have surgery on my . . .'

'*Penis* is the word I believe you're looking for. And I can't see why not. You thought it was perfectly fine for me to have surgery.'

His face went beet-red. 'It's not exactly the same thing, is it?'

'I don't see that there is any difference, actually. For heaven's sake, Frank, I'm not asking you to cut the old fella off.'

'That's enough. I've never heard you speak so crudely. I'm trying to be understanding, Shirl, because I know you've had a hard time of it lately, but this really is going too far. I'm not having any sort of sterilisation procedure and that's that. Where did you even hear about such a thing?'

'Goodness, Frank, to hear you speak, anyone would think we were living back in the 1930s. Get with the times. Rita says these operations are becoming more and more commonplace.'

He shook his head and sighed. 'Ah. Rita. I should have known she was behind all of this.'

'What on earth is that supposed to mean?'

'I know she's your friend, but Rita isn't exactly an expert on marital relations, now, is she? I don't see why she has to go sticking her nose into other people's affairs.'

'She's a nurse, a medical professional, and I asked her for her opinion.'

'And of course whatever the great Rita says, Shirley takes as gospel. Sometimes I wonder if she's the right sort of company for you. I mean, she's not married, all that drinking and smoking, and goodness only knows whatever else she gets up to.'

'"Whatever else she gets up to?" What are you insinuating, Frank?'

'Rita is not a good influence on you, and I think you could stand to see less of each other.'

Now that's where he was wrong. The one thing that Shirley absolutely couldn't bear would be to see any less of Rita. 'Are you trying to tell me who I can and cannot be friends with?'

'Of course not. I just think maybe you need to prioritise your family at this time. Rita doesn't have a family so she can do what she wants. You, on the other hand, are a wife and mother.'

'So I'm not allowed to have a life?'

'Lower your voice,' he said. 'You'll wake Fiona.'

She started to cry then. 'Don't ask me to give up Rita, Frank. She's my friend and I need her.'

Frank looked stricken at her tears. He reached across and squeezed her hand. 'I'm not asking any such thing. I'm just asking you not to accept everything Rita says as gospel.'

'I'm not an idiot, Frank.'

'Of course you're not. I know that. I just think you're blowing this all out of proportion, Shirl. I'm sorry, I shouldn't have pushed the issue. It's too soon since your surgery for us to make love. I see that now. In a few weeks' time you'll start to feel better, I'm sure.'

She shook her head in frustration. 'No, I won't. A few weeks isn't going to make this problem go away. I don't want another baby. I can't take the pill because of my blood pressure. I don't want to go under the knife again so soon after my last surgery and I very much doubt the doctors would approve of that anyway. The way I see it there are two solutions. You can have a vasectomy or we can get single beds.'

Three months had passed since that day and they were still at a standoff. They hadn't resorted to single beds but it was almost as if there was an invisible line down the centre of their mattress, which neither of them was able to cross. Frank still kissed her good morning and good night, but there was no passion in their daily exchanges.

They were at a stalemate and Shirley didn't know what to do about it. Feeling guilty about her marriage just added to her exhaustion. She wondered how many other couples were living this half-life, pretending everything was fine to the outside world, while behind closed doors it was anything but. Maybe this was just the way life was, and all her romantic notions of married life were nothing more than the fantasies of a silly schoolgirl. But when she thought about the way Mary and Graham still looked at each other after seven years of marriage, and three kids to boot, she knew it wasn't this way for everyone.

Fiona touched her hand. 'Mummy, Mummy, want to come down the slide with me?'

She sighed and gave her child a half-hearted smile. 'You go, sweetheart. I'll watch you from here.'

'Come on, Mummy. It's really good fun.'

Rita took Fiona by the hand. 'Come on, Poodle, Aunty Rita will come down with you. We'll wave to Mummy. Okay?'

Fiona glanced at her mother hopefully one more time and Shirley smiled. 'That's a great idea, don't you think?' She threw Rita a grateful look.

'Come on, Poodle, I'll race you to the slide. Last one there's a rotten egg.'

With that, Fiona was off like a shot. She could never resist a challenge.

When the novelty of the slide finally wore off, Rita took Fiona by the hand and sauntered back to Shirley. 'Miss Fifi here says she's hungry. Shall we get going?'

Shirley nodded reluctantly. She dreaded going home. Rita might stay for a cuppa but then she'd head home to sleep and Shirley would be left to fill in the hours until Frank came home by doing the things that a wife and mother should do. To think just a few short years ago this was the very life she'd craved. She should be grateful, she supposed, but it wasn't enough. The menial tasks that filled her day didn't occupy her mind, and with her thoughts free to wander she couldn't help but focus on all she had lost.

'All right then, let's go.' She looked at her watch and then at Fiona. 'If we're quick we might catch the end of *Here's Humphrey*, and then if you're a good girl you can watch *Play School* too.' Frank didn't approve of daytime television. He believed it should only be allowed when the weather was inclement or in times of sickness. But Fiona loved her shows and Shirley couldn't see the harm in indulging her every now and then. Besides, with Fiona's attention diverted she and Rita could chat more freely.

Fiona clasped Rita's hand and pulled her towards the footpath. 'Come on, Aunty Rita. Let's go!'

Rita grinned. 'Looks like you've said the magic words.'

'Are you coming back for a cuppa?'

Rita checked her watch. 'I don't think so. I'm on nightshift again tonight. I really need to get home and do a few chores before I hit the pillow.'

'Oh.' Disappointment washed over her. She'd hoped to have Rita's company for another half an hour at least. 'Of course. I understand. We shouldn't have kept you for as long as we have.'

Rita fell in step beside her and draped her free arm around Shirley's shoulders. 'You didn't keep me. I stayed because I wanted to. Surely you know you two are my favourite people in the whole wide world?'

It was ridiculous, but Rita's words caused a lump to form in her throat. Shirley thought it was just about the nicest thing anyone had ever said to her.

Fiona let go of Rita's hand and skipped ahead, calling out, 'You're *my* favourite girl, Aunty Rita,' as she left them behind.

'Thanks, Poodle,' Rita called after her. She looked at Shirley. 'You know, maybe I have got time for one quick cuppa after all.'

Chapter 21

Tuesday

I run outside to the deck to be sure, but Frank is not there. To my dismay I realise the deck wraps around the side of the hotel and there's direct access to the street via a side pathway. I run down the path onto the street and look both ways but there's no sign of Frank anywhere. Panicked, I race back into the bar, where the bemused barmaid is standing with a bottle of cordial in her hand, watching me. 'I wondered where you'd got to,' she says.

'My husband,' I say breathlessly. 'Have you seen him?'

'He's on the deck.' Her gaze shifts to where Frank had been sitting. 'Oh . . .'

'I have to find him. He's not well. He has dementia.'

It seems both of us have the same thought at the same time. *The water.*

We rush outside to the deck and stand up against the glass balustrade, both of us scouring the car park below for any sign of him. 'I'm sure he wouldn't have fallen off the balcony,' she says. 'The barrier is quite high. He would have had to drag a chair up here to climb over.' She looks around. 'There's no sign of a chair and, besides, if he had . . .'

There's no need for her to finish the sentence. If he'd managed to get over the barrier he'd be lying on the concrete below us, most likely dead. It seems more probable that he's wandered into the street. I retrace my steps down the side pathway with the barmaid in tow.

'Hang on,' she says, 'maybe he's inside somewhere. He could have walked down the path and entered the pub again without being noticed. Maybe he's in a bathroom or a storeroom.'

I nod. It's possible.

She touches my arm kindly. 'Don't worry, he can't have got far. I'll go inside and have a look and I'll get one of the kitchen hands to help. What's your husband's name?'

'Frank,' I say, my voice shaking.

She scrutinises me, like she's trying to work something out. Maybe she's wondering where she's seen me before. Not that it matters. The jig is most certainly up.

'Okay, and what's your name?'

'Shirley,' I say. No point in lying now, is there? The Plan isn't important anymore. Frank's safety is the only thing that matters. At the mention of my name I think I see the barmaid's eyes widen slightly and I wonder if she's realised who I am, but when she speaks she gives no indication that she recognises us. I tell myself I'm being paranoid.

'I'm Sophie,' she says gently. 'Shirley, why don't you go and check the shops close by then come back here? If he doesn't turn up here or in one of those places then we might have to call the police.'

My heart pounds. *No!* I want to scream. *Not the police.* 'Is that really necessary?' I say, but even as the words form I know she's probably right.

'Don't worry,' Sophie says in a comforting tone. She probably thinks I'm a timid old woman who doesn't want to bother anyone. 'I'm sure it won't come to it, but if we have to involve the police, I'll handle it.'

I'm reminded of the time I lost Fiona at the Royal Melbourne Show. I completely panicked and allowed others to take charge. Thankfully, she was found safe and well in the animal nursery, completely oblivious to the fuss she'd caused. She was only gone five minutes but it felt like hours to me.

I start off towards the florist next door. This whole plan of mine was ill conceived. Crazy, in fact. I can't believe I've been so stupid – and arrogant – as to think I could pull it off. Of course we were always going to get caught. I had hoped that I might have given Frank a few carefree days, not memories of course, because he's already forgotten what happened an hour ago, but I had thought we could have a nice time. Even if he didn't remember it, I was hell-bent on giving him the holiday he's dreamed of all these years. But instead of that I've put his safety at risk. I've been a fool and this whole trip is a self-indulgent farce. There's no making up for the past. I have to live with the choices I've made.

I push open the florist's door, where I find a young woman wrapping up a bouquet as she chats to a middle-aged customer. She looks up and smiles. 'I'll be with you in a moment.'

'Sorry to interrupt,' I say, 'but this is urgent. My husband has wandered off and he has dementia. You haven't seen an old man looking lost, have you?'

The young woman's face fills with sympathy. 'Sorry, no, but I'll keep an eye out.'

The customer turns to look at me. 'What's he wearing?'

I give a silent prayer of thanks for Frank's loud clothing. 'Orange and black tie-dyed pants and a black T-shirt.' The women both eye my outfit and I squirm with discomfort. 'We're on holidays,' I add, as if that explains everything.

'Oh,' the customer says. 'I *have* seen him. I noticed the pants. It was a few minutes ago. He was crossing the road to go to the service station.'

Crossing the road? Lord have mercy! 'Thank you,' I call as I hurry back out the door. I stand at the kerb waiting to cross. There's a truck coming one way and a stream of cars behind a four-wheel drive towing a mammoth caravan coming the other. I shield my eyes with my hand and look across to the service station. I can't see him, but maybe he's inside. The building seems to hold a cafe and a newsagency as well as the usual petrol-station offerings. As soon as the traffic clears, I trot across the road as fast as my arthritic knees will take me. Inside, I accost the leather-faced man at the till. 'My husband,' I say breathlessly, 'he's missing. He's in his eighties. Tall and thin. Frail. Wearing bright orange and black pants.'

'Sorry, love. Haven't seen anyone like that in here.'

I scan the shop for hidey-holes but there don't seem to be any. The place is empty and there's no sign of Frank anywhere. 'You're sure?'

He nods. 'I see everyone that comes into this place. They've gotta walk right by me, see? And we've been pretty quiet this morning. Reckon I'd remember someone wearing bright-orange pants.'

'Okay, thank you. If you do see him could you please let Sophie from the pub know?'

'No worries, love. Hope you find him.'

I leave the service station and head to the brightly painted building next door. The Soldiers Memorial School of Arts, according to the sign on the front. I try the heavy timber doors, but they appear to be locked. Perhaps there's another entrance?

'Shirley!' Sophie calls to me from across the road and for a moment I think she's found him. But I look back at her and she shouts, 'Any luck?'

I shake my head and her shoulders slump. She beckons for me to return to her. Once again the through traffic holds me up and I shudder at the thought of Frank crossing this road. When

I'm back outside the pub I say, 'Someone in the florist saw him heading across the road, but there's no sign of him now.'

'Well, at least we know he was headed away from the water. That's reassuring, don't you think?'

I nod. I know she's right, but as each minute ticks by without him I feel less and less reassured. Frank has no judgement. He could be anywhere, with anyone. I shudder to think.

'Come back inside.' She places a hand gently on my elbow and steers me towards the entrance, and I allow myself to be guided. My composure is crumbling. I'm ready to give up now, to confess all if I must. I just want Frank back in one piece. 'I think we should call the police now, don't you?'

I know she's right but I shake my head. 'I hate to cause a fuss. Is there no other way?'

She shakes her head. 'It's okay, there won't be a fuss, I promise. The longer we wait the more chance there is that Frank could place himself in harm's way.'

I sigh and nod my agreement.

Once we're inside Sophie calls over a young man, the kitchen hand I presume, and asks him to make me a strong cup of tea. She pulls out a chair and gestures for me to sit. 'I'll go make the call, Shirley. You just sit tight for a minute.'

I nod again. What else is there to say?

She disappears behind the bar. There are no other patrons in the bistro yet so I'm alone for the moment. I cover my face with my hands, defeated. If Frank has come to harm I will never forgive myself. And neither will Fiona.

She'll never understand that she drove me to this.

She's a formidable woman, my daughter, and I'm proud of her. I like to think that I did something right to produce such a confident human being. Not that she would give me any credit for the way she's turned out. I'm well aware that my mothering has fallen short of Fiona's expectations. She was fourteen when

I first realised the depth of her contempt for the way I was living my life. Apparently I was letting my whole gender down.

As I entered the high school canteen, my partner for the shift, Helen Thompson, looked at me with concern. 'Should you be here?'

I smoothed my hair self-consciously and wondered if my eyes were still red-rimmed. It was the day after Andrew's tenth anniversary and I'd spent the previous twenty-four hours in a state of melancholy, but there was no way Helen could know that. 'I think so. I haven't mucked up the roster again, have I?'

'No, it's just I thought you must have been on death's door.'

'Why would you think that?'

'Well, when you weren't at the girls' debating competition yesterday I was concerned. It's not like you to miss one of Fiona's events. I asked her where you were and she said you were too sick to come, so I half-expected to find a replacement here today.'

I tried not to let my surprise show on my face. This was the first I'd heard about a debate. 'Oh, I was just laid low by a bug for twenty-four hours. Nothing serious. I'm as right as rain now. Disappointed of course to have missed the debate. How was it?'

'They were fabulous. Your Fiona was utterly amazing. She wiped the floor with the opposition. It's a shame you didn't get to see her, but of course you'll get the chance when they represent the school at the regional finals.'

'Yes.' I struggled to keep my tone light and even. 'I'm certainly looking forward to that.'

After school I ambushed Fiona. 'Why didn't you tell me about the debate?'

She shrugged. 'It wasn't a big deal. I didn't know parents could come.'

'I find that very hard to believe. Linda's mum was there, so obviously she knew all about it. Didn't you want me there?'

She walked to the fridge and opened it without bothering to look at me. 'Didn't think you'd want to come. I thought you'd be too busy lighting candles or planting memorial roses or something.'

The bitterness of her words rendered me momentarily speechless.

She poured herself a glass of milk and began heaping teaspoons of chocolate Quik into it. 'Anyway, even if it hadn't been on Andrew's "special" day, I didn't think it would be your cup of tea.' She rolled her eyes as she said the word 'special' and I fought back the urge to slap her face. How have I raised a child who thinks nothing of using her mother's grief as a weapon?

But I wasn't going to be so easily baited. 'Why not? You know I'm always interested in everything you do.'

'No, you're not. You come because you think you have to. You're only worried about proving to the world that you're the perfect mother.'

'That's ridiculous,' I said, my cheeks burning. 'Whatever would make you say such a thing?'

She shrugged again. 'Just calling it the way I see it. Anyway, the debate was on women's rights. If Aunty Rita wasn't working I might have invited her, but I never considered asking you. I didn't think the subject would be of any interest whatsoever to you.'

I tried to contain my hurt. It's not Fiona's fault she sees me as letting down the side. She doesn't know the truth. She's too young to understand the complexity of my life. To her I'm a boring old housewife, a study in how not to be rather than a role model. I can't tell her that the sacrifices I've made have all been for her. She doesn't know that I yearn for things to be different. 'Why not? I'm a woman, aren't I? Haven't I always raised you to believe you can do whatever you want? That you're just as good as any boy?'

She stopped stirring and looked up from her drink to meet my eyes. 'But not one particular boy. No matter how hard I try, I can never be Andrew.' She tossed the teaspoon she'd used into the sink and walked away, leaving me to deal with the drips of chocolate milk she'd left behind.

If I'm honest with myself, I know I did let her down in those first few years after Andrew's death. The hole he left inside me couldn't be filled – not by her or anyone else. I did my best but in a lot of ways I was just going through the motions. The wounds suffered in those early years of Fiona's life never fully healed. Frank and Rita tried to pick up the slack but now I realise their intervention merely papered over the cracks in our relationship. I had hoped that when she became a mother herself she'd begin to understand, but if anything the gap between us widened as Fiona set out to prove she was nothing at all like me. And now, without Frank and Rita to fill the space between us, it seems there's not much hope of bridging that expanse.

Rita would never have let things get out of hand like this. She would have talked to Fiona, cajoled her into seeing sense. If only I had Rita's strength. If only I'd stood my ground about staying put in Geelong after the incident with the house, we wouldn't have had to run away like fugitives and Frank wouldn't be missing.

If only . . .

'Shirley!' The excitement in Sophie's voice snaps me out of my ruminations and I look up at her. 'The police have him, or at least they think they do. A man matching Frank's description went into the cottage behind the School of Arts building. There was a painting workshop in progress and Frank – if it's him – wandered in for a look. The teacher was a bit concerned about him because he seemed disorientated, so she called the police. Apparently they're with him now. If we hop to it we can get to him before they take him back to the station.'

My relief is so great that for a moment I don't even care that this is the end of our adventure. I tried. We've had a couple of mostly nice days and while it wasn't what I'd hoped for, it was something. Of course this latest mishap has proved Fiona right: I'm not capable of caring for Frank alone anymore.

My heart sinks. I feel as if I've just signed Frank's death warrant.

Sophie touches my shoulder lightly. 'Shirley, are you coming? We need to hurry.'

'Yes, yes, of course.' I push myself up out of the chair, feeling every one of my seventy-nine years.

Sophie, sweet girl that she is, puts a hand on my elbow to steady me. 'Are you okay, Shirley? You look pale.'

'Just the worry catching up with me, I think.'

She nods. 'Perfectly understandable.'

Thankfully the road is clear when we reach the kerb, so we cross and Sophie leads the way to the 'cottage'. As we round the corner of the arts school I see two uniformed officers with their backs to us. They are talking to someone I can't yet see, but I know it's Frank. I can hear him and he's not happy.

'Mind your own beeswax, would you? I'm fine and I'm not going anywhere! Go on then, off you trot. Go and make yourselves useful elsewhere. Find some criminal to arrest and stop bothering innocent people.'

My gut clenches at this tirade. The law-abiding, courteous man I know Frank to be would be horrified at this outburst. I can only surmise that his words come from a place of fear. 'Frank,' I call, 'it's okay. I'm here now.' I hurry to his side.

He looks at me with a bemused expression. 'I know you, don't I?' He clicks his fingers. 'Nope, it's gone. I can't think of the name.'

I place my hand on his shoulder. 'It's me, Shirley.'

Frank grins. 'Well, I'll be. That's my wife's name too.' I leave my hand on his shoulder and the pressure of it seems to soothe him a little.

I turn my attention to the policemen, or rather police-children. Honestly, one of them doesn't look old enough to shave. He looks as if he's dressed up as a policeman for a birthday party. And the other one has a tattoo visible above his neckline. Since when was that allowed? No wonder Frank's not taking them seriously.

'I'm his wife.' The baby constable raises his eyebrows, so I feel the need to explain. 'My husband has dementia. He doesn't always remember who I am.'

'Ah, I see.'

Tattooed officer butts in. 'Frank, you say?'

'Yes, that's right.'

'He wouldn't tell us his name.'

So they don't know who we are yet. Maybe there's a chance we can still get away without anyone realising we're on the run. I give the officers what I hope is a reassuring smile. 'The dementia can make him uncooperative at times. I'm so sorry for your trouble.'

'No trouble. I'm Senior Constable Bartlett and this is Constable Turner.'

I nod and ignore the pause. Obviously *Senior* Constable Tattoo is waiting for me to introduce myself, but I feign ignorance. I'm just an old lady, after all. And I've had a shock. I can't be expected to be in my right mind now, can I?

'Your husband seems quite disorientated. Do you think he needs medical assistance? We can call an ambulance or accompany you both to the hospital, Mrs . . . sorry, I didn't catch your name.'

Well played, senior constable. I try for an innocent looking smile. 'Oh, I'm sorry. How rude of me. Shirley Miller,' I say. The name slides easily off my tongue. I tell myself it's not a lie. I am Shirley Miller, or I once was.

'I think we should get some medical assistance for your husband, Mrs Miller.'

'Oh, no. He's fine. He's just a little distressed because of the unfamiliar surroundings. Once I get him back in the car he'll be as good as gold.'

'Nevertheless, it can't hurt for Frank here to have a check-up, can it? I'll feel better if he's seen a doctor.'

I smile again. 'Thank you for your concern, senior constable.' I use his title, hoping the flattery will win him over. 'But Frank finds medical settings particularly distressing. He really will be much better off if I can just get him back into our camper.' *Damn it.* Why didn't I say *car*? I've just given away our mode of transport. Too late to take it back now. I continue on, trying to make my voice sound calm and convincing. 'Once he's in more familiar surroundings he'll settle down.'

Senior Constable Tattoo looks unsure. 'Well, maybe the ambos could give him a look over.'

My shoulders slump and I sigh as I resign myself to the fact that I'm not going to win this one. 'Is that really necessary?'

Frank is sitting quietly now and Constable Babyface is shifting from foot to foot, clearly keen to move onto something more exciting. Tattoo stares at Frank for a moment, seemingly weighing up whether he can risk letting us go without follow-up.

'Hey, Darren,' Sophie pipes up. 'How about this: what if I take Frank and Shirley back to the pub and give them some lunch? That'll give Frank a chance to settle down. He seemed perfectly fine before he wandered off. Honestly.'

Tattoo looks at me then. 'Hmm, but he did wander off, didn't he? We can't risk that happening again. We're just lucky the old bloke didn't get hit by a car or something.'

I feel the sting of both accusation and dismissal in his words. And the truth.

Sophie answers confidently. 'If there are any issues I'll call the ambos myself. Promise. I'm sure you guys are busy enough today.' She smiles sweetly at him and the skin around his tattoo goes pink.

Babyface looks up at Tattoo hopefully.

'Yeah, all right,' he concedes. He focuses on Sophie, holding her gaze for a fraction longer than necessary. 'So long as you promise you'll call me if you need any help at all.'

'Promise,' she says brightly and she turns her attention to Frank. 'Hey, Frank, fancy a nice chicken parmigiana for lunch?'

He looks up and I see a twinkle in his eye. 'My word I do. You certainly know the way to a fella's heart.'

Sophie grins. 'Indeed I do. Come on now, let's get you back to the pub.' She offers Frank her arm and he accepts it without question.

I can't believe that we're getting away with this, but I'm not going to look a gift horse in the mouth. I smile at Tattoo and Babyface. 'Thank you so much for your help, officers. I promise you we won't be troubling you again today.'

Tattoo gives me a begrudging nod. 'Look after yourselves, now.' He turns to Sophie. 'I'm counting on you to keep an eye on them.'

She winks and gives him a flirty look through her eyelashes. 'I won't let you down, Officer.'

Chapter 22

February 1971
Geelong

Shirley walked away from the school gate, blinking back tears. She was proud that Fiona wasn't one of the clingy kids who'd wailed and begged their mothers not to leave them, but part of her was disappointed that her only child was so untroubled at the thought of being separated from her. Not that she was terribly surprised. Fiona had been playing 'school' with her dolls and teddies and counting down to the big day for months now. Shirley only hoped the experience lived up to her expectations.

The day stretched out before her endlessly as she dawdled home. She could feel the heat from the footpath coming up through her sandals, even though it was only just past nine o'clock. Yesterday had been a scorcher and the temperature had barely dropped overnight. It looked like today would bring more of the same. Now that Fiona was at school there was so little to do. Her housework was all up to date, she'd planned on sliced ham and salad for dinner – it was too hot for a cooked meal – and there wasn't enough washing to warrant doing a load. Perhaps she'd make a start on one of the library books she'd picked up in town last week. It was really too hot to do anything else, and it would fill in the time until *Days of Our Lives* started. But first she'd pick some tomatoes and a fresh lettuce from the garden for tonight's salad – she didn't want them getting scalded by the sun.

She was surprised – and immediately cheered – when she rounded the corner of her street to find Rita standing at her gate. 'Hello,' Shirley called, as she picked up her pace. When she reached her friend she grinned and gave her a hug. It wasn't normally her style to be so demonstratively affectionate, but she was so pleased to see Rita she simply couldn't help herself. 'This is a nice surprise indeed. Aren't you working today?'

Rita shook her head. 'I swapped shifts with Val. She wanted tonight off because it's her hubby's birthday. I knew it was Fiona's first day at school and I thought you might like some company.'

'Oh, that's lovely of you. Yes, I was just wondering how I was going to fill in the day. Fancy a cuppa?' She pushed open the gate and signalled for Rita to go ahead.

'Love one.'

Shirley left Rita to make the tea while she picked what she needed from the vegie patch and lowered the bamboo blinds Frank had recently installed to help keep out the heat on days such as these. Once those jobs were done they took their tea into the lounge room. Shirley had kept the venetian blinds closed for the past couple of days, so the room was dark and still reasonably cool. She put the tray carrying the teapot and two cups down on the teak coffee table and began to pour. There was no need to ask Rita how she took her tea – she'd lost count of how many cups they'd made each other over the past few years. While she was pouring, Rita asked how Fiona had gone and Shirley proudly relayed how she'd marched off into the classroom without so much as a backwards glance.

Rita gave a satisfied nod. 'Good. She's a smart little cookie. School will be the making of her.'

Shirley sighed. 'I'm sure you're right, but I honestly don't know what I'm going to do with myself without her here.'

'Have you given any thought to getting a job? Even something part time?'

Shirley shook her head. 'I want to be here to walk Fiona to school and pick her up again. I don't want her to think I've abandoned her.'

'I'm sure she wouldn't think that, especially if it wasn't full time. Besides, you'd be a good role model for her, showing her that women can be more than just wives and mothers.'

Shirley agreed with Rita in theory, but she knew Frank would never put up with her working outside the home. He'd see it as a direct attack on his masculinity. Maybe if everything else in their marriage were perfect she'd be able to convince him, but they were still celibate more than a year after Andrew's death. The lack of sex was hard on Frank, but he accepted it, which she was grateful for. In all other ways their marriage was a good one. They enjoyed each other's company, had similar ideas about childrearing (although admittedly Frank mainly left that up to her) and they never, ever fought. Shirley was loath to do anything that would upset the balance of their bland but comfortable life. 'Maybe when she's a bit bigger,' she said. 'Right now I think it's important to give her some stability, at least until she's settled in at school.'

Rita looked unconvinced, but she didn't argue. She always conceded that Shirley's knowledge of parenting was superior to hers considering that she didn't have any children of her own. 'Fair enough. So, if not a job, what are we going to do to get you using that brain of yours?'

'I don't know. Maybe I could take on some charity work of some kind.'

Rita opened her mouth and then closed it again, giving a little shake of her head.

'What? What were you going to say?'

'Well.' Rita looked sheepish. 'I was going to suggest you join my women's group, but I don't think it's such a good idea.'

'Aren't all the women nurses?'

Rita shook her head. 'Not anymore. The group did start as all midwives who wanted to advocate for mothers' rights, but it's got much bigger than that and there are all sorts of people now – teachers, factory workers, housewives . . .'

To Shirley's shame, she'd never paid too much attention when Rita talked about her 'women's group'. In fact at the beginning of her friendship with Rita, she and Frank had joked about it a little. Shirley had lamented that Rita would never find a bloke when she spent so much of her free time hanging out with other women. Frank had winked and said perhaps that's what Rita liked. She'd blushed then and hit him with the tea towel. She'd actually thought Rita's women's group was a professional thing, nurses trying to improve their working conditions and the treatment of the women they cared for. She had no idea the group had members outside the profession. 'So what does the group do? What's it all about?'

'All sorts of things, really. We have social get-togethers where we have a few drinks and talk about current affairs. Sometimes we might have a guest speaker at those. Other times we talk about books or films – especially ones that are important to raising awareness of women's issues. Even though the group has expanded the majority are still nurses, so we focus a lot on working towards improving women's healthcare – access to health checks and contraception for all women, not just married ones, that sort of thing. Lately there's been a bit more focus on education for women. We've been talking about different topics – ways to increase participation in and access to university education for women who want it, and, at the other end of the spectrum, some of the group are interested in preschool education and childcare.'

Shirley was impressed and slightly alarmed. She knew about the women's liberation movement, of course. She'd seen their protests on TV and, while she agreed with many of their complaints, she thought some of their tactics were quite uncouth. Not the sort of thing a married mother like herself should be involved in. And she didn't know what to think about Rita's involvement. She knew what Frank would say if he discovered Rita was 'one of those women's libbers'. He would say, 'I told you that Rita was a bad influence. Best steer clear of her.' Still, the group did sound interesting. The film and book discussions might be fun – she loved to read – and she was definitely interested in improving educational opportunities for girls. She'd loved school herself and was sad to leave. Fiona was such a clever little thing; she was already teaching herself to read. Shirley wanted her to have the chance to finish high school and go on to university if that's what she wanted. She didn't want her daughter dependent on a man – even a good man – the way she was. 'I had no idea your group did all those things. To be honest, I thought it was just an excuse for a bunch of nurses to get together and drink.'

'Well, there's a fair bit of that too.' Rita laughed. 'But we do try to do some worthwhile things as well. The group's growing and it's quite diverse, so it's interesting.'

'When you say you advocate for certain things – what does that mean, exactly?' Shirley had seen footage on the news of women throwing away their bras. Apparently this was to protest women's oppression, but it just seemed like a big waste of money to her. Bras weren't cheap, and going without one was unthinkable. She hoped Rita wasn't involved in anything like that.

'We write letters to the newspapers, and sometimes there are protests that we attend, but it's not all about agitating for change. We support each other too. We raise funds for women in need, organise childcare, that sort of thing.'

'Why haven't you talked to me about this before?'

Rita shrugged. 'It's really taken off in the past six months or so and you've been . . . well, you've had other things on your mind. But recently I've been thinking maybe you're ready to use your experiences to help others.'

'What do you mean?'

'Think about all the women who would be better off if they had access to reliable contraception. Even though the pill's been available in Australia for around ten years, we still have restricted access to it. And who controls our access? Men, that's who!' Rita was warming to her topic, her voice increasing in volume and excitement as she spoke. 'Women should be in charge of their own bodies, their own fertility – not required to get permission from their doctors, husbands or even their priests before they can use contraception. Don't you agree?'

Rita had a point. Shirley hadn't wanted another baby, she'd wanted to take the pill, but Frank had said no and that was that. Of course once she was pregnant with Andrew she'd fallen in love with him, and look where that had got her. She'd loved and lost her child, and her life would never be the same. Maybe it was unfair, but deep down she still partially blamed Frank. And she hadn't set foot in a church since Andrew was born. 'Yes, I suppose I do.'

Rita lowered her voice again. 'Shirl, it's not just about preventing pregnancy, it's about treating women with the respect they deserve. What happened to you in the hospital after Andrew was born shouldn't happen to any woman. You should have been allowed to farewell your baby properly.'

A familiar watery feeling settled in her chest. It happened whenever she thought about her baby being carted off to be buried without her by his side. She found herself unable to speak.

Rita looked stricken. 'I'm sorry, Shirl. I didn't mean to upset you. I was right in the first place, I shouldn't have brought up the women's group. It's still too soon for you to be thinking about all this. Let's change the subject.'

Shirley shook her head. 'No. It's fine. I want to talk about it. What happened to me – to my baby – that day has changed my whole life. My marriage suffered, it was months before I could be a proper mother to Fiona again, and even though I'm feeling better now there will always be a sense that there is a hole in my life that can never be filled. I can't bear to think of that happening to another woman, but I'm not sure what I can do to help. It's not like I work at a hospital or have influence with anyone. I'm not even sure Frank would approve of me writing letters to the paper. I mean, what if his boss read it? Frank could get the sack, and then where would we be?'

Rita was ready with her answer, nodding as she spoke. 'I understand your concerns. Really I do. That's why we need broad, systemic changes in our society,' she said.

Rita was beginning to sound like one of those militant types Shirley had seen on the television. This women's group was becoming less appealing by the minute. 'That sounds a bit dramatic, to be honest. I'm not really into politics or anything like that. Maybe the group isn't for me.' Shirley tried to imagine herself holding up a sign and shouting slogans like the women she'd seen on the news. The whole idea was unseemly.

Rita shrugged. 'Well, I won't pressure you, but maybe you should come to a meeting sometime and see for yourself. You can participate as much or as little as you want.' She laughed. 'No one's going to insist on you burning your bra.'

'Goodness, I should hope not.' She put her hands either side of her not-as-pert-as-they-used-to-be breasts. 'These girls need all the help they can get.'

Rita dug around in her handbag and pulled out a book. She pushed it across the table to Shirley. 'Here, take a look at this. You can borrow it if you like. I was going to loan it to one of the girls at work, but she can wait a week or two. It won't take you long to read it once you get started. I couldn't put it down.'

She picked up the book and read its title: *The Female Eunuch*, by Germaine Greer. She knew who Germaine Greer was, of course. It would be hard not to. It seemed she was on the TV every other night, talking about women's rights and . . . sex. She seemed to talk a lot about sex. Shirley carefully placed the book back on the table. 'I don't know, Rita. I don't think this is my kind of thing. I mean, what does it even mean, the *female eunuch*? How can a female be a eunuch? It doesn't make sense.'

'It does when you read the book.'

'Frank would have a fit.'

'Best Frank doesn't read it then. Shirl, you're a smart woman. This stuff is important. I'm not asking you to agree with her, I'm just asking you to read it and then make up your own mind. Don't you think you owe it to Fiona to keep informed about current issues?'

'I guess so.'

'Good.' Rita patted the book. 'That's settled then. This book will change your life. Mark my words.'

Shirley needn't have worried about the day dragging – she was still reading when three o'clock rolled around. Not wanting to be late to pick up Fiona on her first day, she reluctantly put the book away – in her underwear drawer, where no one else would find it – and headed to the school. Her head was so filled with provocative new ideas that the walk seemed to take no time at all. She felt herself blushing at the thought of what she'd been reading, but Rita was right, she hadn't been able to put it down. It was the most challenging thing she'd read since leaving school. She generally preferred to read romance novels or the latest blockbusters the library had on offer. They were easy reads, some of them might have been slightly risqué – not the sort of thing her mother would read – but nothing she'd read before compared to the book she'd consumed today. Germaine Greer was so matter-of-fact in her use of language to describe not just body parts but feelings as well. It was a compelling, though not easy or comfortable, read. She'd actually had to drag out an old dictionary to look up the meaning of some words. And then there were words she knew the meaning of quite well, but she'd never seen them in print before. Frank would be shocked if he knew, and she thought her mother would probably have a heart attack if she clapped eyes on the language in question.

The school bell sounded and moments later a gleeful-looking Fiona raced towards her, babbling the news of her day even before Shirley had the chance to ask how it was. Apparently the teacher had been so impressed with her reading that she'd awarded Fiona a gold star *and* made her a milk monitor, which was a much-coveted position among the Prep children. Shirley put the book out of her mind and focused on her daughter.

There wasn't time to read again until the following day – another scorcher. Frank had suggested that to celebrate Fiona's school success they buy fish and chips for dinner that night and have their meal at Eastern Beach. Ice cream was also hinted at. Fiona was thrilled to bits, and Frank equally pleased his suggestion was such a hit. Shirley thought the beach would be packed, but it meant a night off cooking, so she kept that thought to herself. Without an evening meal to prepare there would be more time for reading.

She finished the book an hour before school got out and found herself most unsettled. She really had no clue what to make of Greer's work. At times she found herself nodding in agreement, but a page or two later she'd be shocked at the ideas the author put forward. She phoned Rita, hoping that she'd be awake even though she'd worked a nightshift the night before, but there was no answer. She hung up disappointed. She'd have to wait until tomorrow, when Rita had a day off, to discuss what she'd read. But as it turned out, Rita was waiting at the school gate when she arrived. Shirley grinned at her friend. 'I just tried to call you at home. What are you doing here?'

'I popped in to see a new mum and her bub – one of the women from my group, actually – and she lives just around the corner. Seeing as I was already in the neighbourhood I thought I'd come and surprise Miss Fiona after school, maybe take her for a milkshake.'

'Ooh, she'd love that, I'm sure.'

The sun was blaring down on them as they spoke. Rita stepped away from the gate into the shade of a nearby tree. 'So why were you trying to call me?'

Shirley followed her into the shade. 'Oh, it's about that book you lent me. I've finished it.'

'Already? Wow, you charged through that. Although I did tell you it was hard to put down. So did you love it?'

Shirley took off her floppy straw hat and fanned herself. 'I don't know. It was compelling, I'll give you that, but I really don't know what to think about it.'

Rita grinned. 'But it's got you thinking, right?'

'I guess so.'

'Look, you should come to our get-together on Saturday night. We have a guest speaker from Melbourne. I think it'll be an interesting discussion, and there will be wine and cheese too.'

'I don't know. I'll have to see what Frank says.'

Rita sighed. 'For goodness sake, Shirley, Frank's your husband, not your keeper. Make up your own mind.'

It was all very well for Rita to say that, but she wasn't married. The reality was that married couples needed to consult each other. It wasn't a matter of being kept, it was a matter of courtesy. 'To be honest, I'm not sure if all this women's lib stuff is for me. There were some pretty confronting things in that book.'

'I agree. That's the point. The book's supposed to be confronting. It's supposed to make you think. And as for women's lib, if you're a woman, it's for you. It's all about choices. Come to the group and see. If you don't enjoy it, you don't have to come again.'

'I'll think about it.' Shirley eyed the throng of students pouring out into the schoolyard. 'Look, here comes our girl.' As predicted, Fiona was delighted to see Rita and ran to embrace her. Shirley tried not to mind that the greeting she got wasn't quite as enthusiastic. Rita was a fun 'aunty', not a boring old mum.

Shirley waited until after dinner to broach the subject with Frank. They sat on a blanket on the sand among scores of other families. Fiona had finished her fish and chips and was paddling in the shallows, under strict instructions from her mother not to go any further than knee-deep.

'I'll be there in a minute to take you out deeper,' Frank promised. He looked at Shirley. 'She's a good little swimmer. Let's not get too over-protective, eh? We don't want her to turn into a Nervous Nelly.'

Like her mother. Frank didn't have to say the words for her to know what he was thinking.

'I know. I just couldn't bear it if anything happened to her.'

His face softened and he touched her hand. 'I won't let anything happen to her. I promise.'

She resisted the urge to tell him not to make promises he couldn't keep. She knew only too well that life as they knew it could be ripped away from them in the blink of an eye. Instead she changed the subject. 'Do you have any plans for the weekend?'

'I thought I might start work on building that barbecue in the backyard if it isn't too hot. Jeff from work has offered to come over and give me a hand. If we get cracking we might even finish it this weekend. We could invite a few people over next week if you like. Jeff and his wife, and maybe Mary and Graham – we haven't seen them for a while. And you can invite Rita if you want. I'll ask Brian to come. He's at a bit of loose end since Sandy broke off their engagement. Who knows, maybe he and Rita will hit it off.'

That gathering sounded like a recipe for disaster. Jeff's wife was terribly shy, so hard to entertain. And suffering through an evening of Mary and Graham behaving like a pair of newlyweds – kissing and making gaga eyes at each other all night – would be bad enough, but watching that oaf Brian (so uncouth, always making lewd jokes – no wonder Sandy left him) make a play for Rita would be intolerable. Instead of pointing any of this out, though, she said, 'Oh, that sounds like a fabulous idea, Frank. I'll talk to Rita about it when I see her.' She'd think of some excuse for why the barbecue couldn't go ahead later, but for now it suited her to keep Frank happy. 'Speaking of Rita, she's invited me to a girls' do on Saturday night. I said I'd check with you to see if you minded.'

'Girls' do, eh? What is it this time? Not more Tupperware I hope. We've already got a cupboard full of that stuff.'

'Um, no, not Tupperware.'

'Something new, is it?'

'I'm not really sure. Rita said something about a guest speaker. Perhaps it's a poetry reading or something.' She laughed. 'I'm really only going for the supper. Do you mind?'

He shook his head. 'No. I'll probably have an early night. I'll be worn out from working all day. How are you getting there, though? Do you need me to drop you off?'

She smiled at him and thought how lucky she was to be married to such a considerate man. This women's group might be okay for single girls and women married to ogres, but she really didn't see what it could possibly offer someone like her. She'd go this one time because she'd promised Rita, but that was it. 'No thank you, darling. I'm going with Rita.'

Chapter 23

Tuesday

Back in the pub, Sophie settles us at a corner table with a view – inside this time, where Frank can't easily escape – and hands us each a menu. 'Choose whatever you like,' she says. 'On the house.'

I shake my head. 'Absolutely not. You have done more than enough already.'

'Don't be silly. I'm honoured to help.' She lowers her voice. 'Anything to help a fellow Sherbie's family.'

A Sherbie? What the heck is that? Obviously my bewilderment shows on my face because Sophie goes on to clarify. 'You're FrankandShirley,' she says, running our names together like they're a single word. 'Miss Lulu's grandparents, right?'

'Miss Lulu?' I say, confused.

Her face falls. 'Oh, maybe I'm wrong. Forget I said anything.'

Then something sparks my memory. I know that name. *Miss Lulu* is Lou's online alias! 'Sorry. It took me a minute to catch up with you there. How do you know Lou – Miss Lulu, I mean?'

Sophie's face breaks into a wide smile. 'Oh, I don't really know her. Like, not in person or anything. We're both

"Sherbies" – members of the same online gaming community. Miss Lulu is one of our most popular members.'

This doesn't surprise me. Lou is an adorable girl, of course she is popular. 'Right. I see . . . well, actually, Sophie, I don't. How did you know we're related to Lou, I mean Miss Lulu?'

'You're FrankandShirley,' she repeats unhelpfully. She makes the silly hashtag sign with her fingers. '#oldsontherun.'

I shake my head, still not comprehending her meaning. She chuckles and glances back at the bar. 'I'll show you in just a moment. Why don't you give me your lunch order and I'll let the kitchen know. I'll come back in a minute with my phone and then you'll see.'

Frank, who's been quiet for a bit, pipes up. 'What's a man got to do to get a drink around here?'

Sophie laughs. 'I do believe I owe you a beer. Coming right up.'

I give her our lunch order – fish of the day for me and chicken parmy for Frank – and glance at my watch as she heads back to the bar.

Frank cocks an eyebrow in that comical way that never fails to make me smile. 'What's your hurry?'

I shrug. 'No hurry.' I try to make myself believe it. Our close call with the law has made me anxious to be back on the road again, but I'm also mindful of the fact that Frank is happy right now and that's something to be savoured. Live in the moment. Isn't that what all those new-age experts – the ones you see on the morning TV shows – are always telling us?

Sophie's back in a flash, putting a beer down in front of Frank (I make a mental note to insist he goes to the toilet before we leave) and a lemon, lime and bitters on a coaster for me. She fishes in her pocket, pulls out her phone and starts to scroll around a bit. 'Here,' she says, handing the phone to me. 'Take a look at this.'

I slide on my reading glasses and stare at the screen, not quite comprehending what it is that she's showing me. There's a tiny square in the corner with a photo of a girl (at least I think it's a girl) dressed up as some type of Pokémon. Although I don't know its name I recognise the character; it's the same one I made a costume of for Lou when she went to a gaming convention earlier in the year. Fiona made such a big deal about how she was too old for dress-ups, and that she should be spending more time worrying about studying for her HSC and less time worrying about stupid video games. The hurt in Lou's eyes was heartbreaking. I'm not sure why Fiona insists on criticising the poor kid so much.

Suddenly it dawns on me. The girl isn't just dressed like Lou, she *is* Lou. I touch the photo and it opens a new page with an enlarged version of the same photo and some information about her.

Miss Lulu
Sherbie rank: Ultimate expert
Games of choice: *Everblade*, *Crimson and Autumn* and *Spellstar*
Other interests: drawing, making Animated Music Videos, watching Anime

I smile at her sweet face and turn to Sophie. 'That's my' – I glance at Frank – '*our* granddaughter.' I feel bad about the slip of the tongue, but Lou has always been mine. I love all three girls but I can see into Lou's soul and she into mine. I have the relationship with her that I always wanted for Fiona and me.

'Yes,' Sophie says, and suddenly I feel like an old fool.

'Sorry, you said that before. So explain what I'm looking at here, Sophie.'

Sophie looks around the bistro. The lunch crowd has started to filter in but there's another staff member serving and it's not too busy yet. She takes a seat next to me. 'This is a forum on Sherbet. Sherbet is an online community for gamers. Are you with me so far?'

I nod. Lou has explained this before and Ollie taught me how to search forums for information. I joined one, Knitting World, for practice, and then I spent time searching travel forums, which is how I found Petra and Joachim. 'Yes. I've used forums before, but they looked different to this one. Of course I was using a big screen, not my phone, to access them, so maybe that's why.'

Sophie looks pleased and she nods. 'Exactly. That would make a difference. But also Sherbet has a kind of unique layout and design, and we talk to each other using lots of acronyms and code, so I imagine it's quite different to . . .'

'Knitting World,' I offer.

'Yes.' She grins. 'It probably doesn't look much like Knitting World. But even though it might look different and talk about different things, it's essentially the same. We talk about our games, have competitions among ourselves, design new settings and world builds, that sort of thing.'

'I see,' I say, and I mostly do. Lou has talked about her online gaming friends to me a little.

'Sherbet is the biggest gaming community in Australia. We have members all over the world but the Aussie community is really strong. We sometimes have IRL meet ups – IRL means In Real Life – and we really feel bonded to each other. So when a Sherbie has a problem, we like to help out if we can.'

'And Lou asked for the community's help to find us?' What sort of a grandmother am I to have put the girls through this? I didn't want to involve Lou, didn't want to put her in a difficult position or drive a wedge between her and her mother. But now I realise that was a mistake. I should have told her what I was planning.

Sophie shook her head. 'Not to find you. To *help* you.'

'I don't understand.'

‘Here,’ she says, taking the phone from me and scrolling some more. She thrusts it back into my hand. ‘Read this.’

Miss Lulu
Monday 3.14 am

HELP NEEDED! **NOT TO BE SHARED OUTSIDE THIS GROUP**
Hi everyone, I’m posting this because I need your help.

Last night my grandfather went missing from his nursing home. You might see a news story about this sometime tomorrow. Or not. Apparently the police told my mother that the case is not high priority. Which is a good thing really, because it was my grandmother who took him.

Papa has dementia. He and my nan came to live with us a while back and then, about a year ago, my mum put him in a home. He hates it there. Every time we go to visit him he begs us to take him home. My mum always changes the subject or pretends not to hear him, but my nan squeezes his hand and tells him one day they’ll go home again.

I’m not really sure how she did it but it looks like Nan has made good on her promise. My grandparents (Frank and Shirley) come from Geelong in Victoria and I think that’s where they’re headed. My nan is a smart woman and she loves Papa. She’ll look after him. Obviously they can’t stay on the run forever but it would be great if Papa could see his home town again and visit the places he loved so much before his memory completely fails.

So this is where I need your help. If you see them DO NOT report them to the authorities. Give them some local tips about places to stay that might be off the beaten track. Help them to fly under the radar. And please let my nan know that she has my support. PM me if you see them!

Thanks Sherbies!
#FrankandShirley #oldsontherun

Lou, bless her heart! I look up to see Sophie looking at me expectantly, and I wonder if she's the first "Sherbie" we've encountered on our travels. 'Thank you for sharing this with me, Sophie. You can let Lou know we're safe and on our way to our destination. Maybe don't tell her about Frank's misadventure today, though. I don't want her to worry.'

'Of course not. But you can tell her yourself if you like. That is, if you have a smartphone?'

I nod. 'I do, but Lou won't have the number.' I pause for a second, wondering how much to tell her. Lou trusts these people. She's asked them to help us. 'I threw my old phone away so we couldn't be easily traced. I have a new phone but I don't want to use it to call anyone in case it leads to us being caught.'

I hear a trace of admiration in Sophie's voice as she replies, 'Smart thinking. But I didn't mean for you to call her. I can set you up with an account on Sherbet and you can talk to her via the message board. I'm sure you'd get the hang of it in no time.'

I consider this idea for a moment and decide the risk of us being caught is minimal. I mean, let's face it, who on earth is going to think that an old nanna like me would have an account on an online gaming forum? It's actually a tiny bit genius. I dig in my handbag for my phone and hand it over to Sophie. It takes her a few minutes and several questions before the account is ready to use, but eventually she says, 'There you go. All done.' She hands me the phone and points at the screen. 'Your username is FrankandShirley, all one word.'

Before I can ask her how to post, a surly-looking young man dressed in black and white chequered pants and a white top smeared with food stains plonks our meals down on the table and looks at Sophie. 'Theo says to ask you if you're planning on finishing your shift today or if you've decided you'd rather socialise than get paid.'

Sophie shakes her head and sighs. 'Righto, I'm coming now.' She looks back at me. 'You'll work this out, Shirley, I have no doubt. Good luck to you. My username is Paradise. Feel free to send me a personal message if you need anything.' She stands, gives my shoulder a gentle squeeze and heads back to the bar.

Frank's knife clatters on the table and I look up to see him thumping his fist in frustration. I pick up the knife. 'Here. Let me help you with that.'

For a moment I'm not sure he'll accept my offer. He gives me a withering look but then sighs and allows me to take his plate and cut up the meat into bite-sized pieces. I assume his desire to eat has overridden his desire for independence. Moments after I push the plate back in front of him he's eating heartily, as though the outburst never happened.

'Bloody good tucker,' he says with a smile. 'Best meal I've eaten in ages.'

'Good to hear,' I say, and it is. It's the simple things in life, after all, that bring us happiness. And that is what this whole trip is all about.

Chapter 24

February 1971
Geelong

Bubbles of anticipation fizzed in Shirley's stomach as she sat at her dressing table putting on her make-up. She felt as if she was headed off on a first date. She'd chosen her outfit carefully – a floral, halter-neck maxi dress, with platform shoes. No bra. This dress was designed to be worn without a bra, a fact she hadn't really considered when she'd fallen in love with the fabric and bought it. When she'd realised her error she'd shoved the dress to the back of the wardrobe. She'd never been game enough to wear it in public until now. She looked in the mirror and hesitated. Perhaps wearing it tonight was a mistake. But it was too late to get changed. She'd wear her pink crocheted bolero jacket over the top to be on the safe side.

Fiona sat on Frank and Shirley's bed, watching her mother apply pale-pink lipstick. 'You look really pretty, Mummy.'

'Thank you, sweetheart. Would you like some lipstick?' Fiona nodded eagerly and Shirley beckoned for her to come closer so she could apply it. 'Be a good girl for Daddy tonight, won't you? I've left you some chocolate biscuits for supper as a special treat. I've told Daddy that if you behave yourself and do everything he asks, you can have those with a glass of milk before bed, okay?'

'I'll be good, I promise.'

A car horn sounded in the driveway. 'That'll be Aunty Rita. I'd better get going.' She grabbed the jacket and her handbag, collected the plate of devilled eggs from the kitchen and raced to kiss Frank goodbye. 'Don't wait up. I'm relying on Rita to bring me home and I'm not sure what time it'll be.'

Frank gave her a distracted kiss and went back to watching the telly.

'Look at you,' Rita said as Shirley slid in and sat down, placing the devilled eggs on the seat between them. It was seven o'clock, but the sun hadn't gone down yet and the bench seat in Rita's Holden was still warm.

'What?'

'Nothing. You just look very pretty, that's all.'

'Fiona said the same thing. Maybe I should wear make-up more often.'

Rita laughed. 'You always look great, Shirl, make-up or not. Ready to go? I don't want to be late for the speaker.'

Shirley nodded and Rita backed out of the driveway. Shirley still wasn't sure what she'd let herself in for tonight, but Rita's face was alight with excitement and she didn't want to spoil that by letting on how nervous she was.

'You look nice, too.' It was true. Rita was dressed casually, in a white halter top and denim shorts. Her long black hair, so often pinned up in a bun, hung loose and her make-up-free face glowed. Maybe make-up was frowned upon in this group. Perhaps she'd gone overboard. She tried not to worry about it. 'I like that top. It shows off your tan.'

Rita grinned. 'Thanks. God knows how I've managed to get a tan this summer. I worked so many hours it feels like my skin barely saw the sun.' She pulled over and parked behind a

Morris Minor. 'Glennis's house is up the hill a little but it looks like this is as close as we'll get.'

The street was lined with cars and Shirley's stomach churned in nervous anticipation. They were greeted by Glennis, who, far from the joint-smoking hippie of Shirley's imagination, was a rather ordinary-looking woman with short curly hair and a pinafore apron covering her shift dress. She embraced Rita and kissed her cheek. 'Hello, darling. So pleased you could make it.' She turned her attention to Shirley. 'And you must be Shirley. I'm glad you could come along.' She glanced at the devilled eggs. 'Oh, and you brought a plate. You're definitely a keeper. Come on through and I'll show you where to put it.'

'Is the speaker here yet?' Rita asked as they followed Glennis up the hallway to the kitchen.

'Bad news, I'm afraid. She called half an hour ago. She can't make it.' Turning to Shirley, she explained, 'We had booked a gynaecologist from Melbourne to come and speak to us – she specialises in treating women who have complications after traumatic births or backyard abortions – but unfortunately she's been called to an emergency.'

Rita put the bottle of wine she'd brought into the fridge. 'That's disappointing.'

'Yes, but she promised to come to the very next meeting she can. The perils of having a working doctor as a guest, I suppose.' Glennis handed each of them an empty wine glass. 'Help yourself to wine, ladies. There's a cask open in the fridge.'

Rita grabbed Shirley's glass and poured their drinks. 'So will we have a directed discussion tonight, Glen, or just leave it as a social gathering?'

'I don't know. Got any ideas for a topic?'

Rita shrugged. 'Perhaps we could talk a bit about *The Female Eunuch*. I think most of us have read it now. In fact, Shirley's just finished it.'

Glennis gave Shirley an approving look. 'Good for you, Shirley. All right then, Rita, if you're happy to lead the group, we'll make a start in ten minutes or so. Why don't you take Shirley into the lounge room and introduce her to everyone. I'm just finishing off the pav and then I'll be in.'

A diverse group of about twelve women were packed into Glennis's front room. Chairs were set up in a circle around a low coffee table laden with biscuits, cheese and dips. All the women seemed to know each other and the room was filled with chatter and raucous laughter. The majority were young – Shirley's age or younger – but there were a couple of middle-aged women and one, Betty, who looked about the same age as Shirley's mum. Rita made some quick introductions and then disappeared back into the kitchen.

'There's a seat here, love.' A plump woman who looked to be in her forties patted the folding chair beside her.

Shirley smiled and took a seat.

'Dot, in case you've forgotten,' the woman offered. 'I work with Rita.'

Before Shirley had the chance to answer Rita and Glennis appeared and Glennis asked for a bit of shush. 'For those of you who are unaware, I'm sorry to report that Doctor White is unable to make it tonight due to an emergency; however, she has given her word she'll attend a future meeting.' A murmur of disappointment went around the room, which Glennis quickly quelled. 'Never fear, we have a replacement speaker. Our very own Rita has kindly offered to lead a discussion on Germaine Greer's book, *The Female Eunuch*.'

The room burst into spontaneous applause, and Rita laughed. 'Settle down. I haven't done anything yet. Now, before we begin, is there anyone here who hasn't read the book? It's going to be an awfully dull night for you if you haven't.' No one raised their hand so Rita went on. 'Good. I thought we'd start by summarising the book as a whole, just to refresh our memories, and then we'll go back and look at each section in more detail. If anyone has any questions or comments just go ahead and call them out as we go.'

Shirley sat back and watched Rita with a sense of awe. Her summary of the book was articulate and insightful, clarifying some things that Shirley had wondered about. She managed the debate that ensued with grace and humour, so that, despite the many different opinions offered, the conversation remained civil. Shirley was actually surprised at the level of disagreement about the book. She'd expected all of the women to agree with everything Greer said, but they didn't. Some thought she didn't treat women fairly, that her brand of feminism was 'my way or the highway', and that angered them. Others thought she was a genius, who'd opened their eyes even further to the daily injustices suffered by women. It was a no-holds-barred conversation, with many of the women sharing intimate details of their lives. Shirley had never experienced anything like it.

'What about you, Shirley? What do you think?' Glennis asked after the conversation had been going for a while.

'Me? Oh, I don't know. I don't really feel qualified to offer an opinion.' She downed the remaining wine in her glass.

'Nonsense,' Glennis replied. 'You've read the book, that's enough qualification for me. Everyone's opinion has equal weight here.'

'Well,' said Shirley, smiling as Dot topped up her glass. 'I guess it did open my eyes to a lot of things. Things I hadn't thought about before.' She took a large gulp of wine.

'Like what?' Glennis persisted.

'Sex,' she blurted out. Her cheeks burned. Why had she said that? What a fool she was. As if these women needed to know about her lack of knowledge in that department. She took another swig of her wine in an attempt to hide her shame.

But as she swallowed it she realised many of the women were nodding.

'Yes,' Glennis said with an encouraging smile. 'I think this book has been illuminating for many of us in that regard. Was there something in particular that informed or moved you?'

Emboldened by the wine and the encouragement, Shirley surprised herself by elaborating. 'The whole idea of women being eunuchs, in that they have had their sexuality cut off, spoke to me. I feel ashamed to admit this, but . . . well, it's never really occurred to me that I should covet satisfaction in the bedroom. I've always seen that as my husband's domain.' More nods and knowing looks from around the room. Shirley felt as if she'd just unlocked a secret room full of treasure. She wasn't the only one! There were other people who felt the way she did. 'This probably sounds terribly naive, but I figured if I didn't like what was happening then it was because there was something wrong with me. It never occurred to me that the issue might lie elsewhere. I've been feeling guilty all these years that I didn't like sex better. After reading the book I'm beginning to think it's not entirely my fault.'

'Absolutely,' Dot said. 'We women take the blame for everything.'

'I think the main thing I got out of the book is that I need to get in touch with my own feelings – my own body – and maybe take some responsibility for my own pleasure,' one of the younger women said. 'I need to be more assertive, inside the bedroom and out.' She grinned.

'Right on!' Glennis said, and everyone clapped and cheered, including Shirley.

She was surprised to find herself talking again. 'Actually, I haven't wanted to have sex with Frank in a long time. Not since . . .' She found that she was unable to complete the sentence. Rita shot her a sympathetic look. Shirley shook her head.

'Well, let's just say it's been ages. I was beginning to feel guilty about that, but after reading the book I feel a bit more at ease. I mean, I have a right to feel how I feel, don't I?'

'Of course you do,' Glennis said. 'In some ways I feel like Greer is the voice of everywoman in that regard. She's put voice to feelings we'd buried so deep some us didn't even know we had them.'

'I did find her take on the nuclear family a bit hard to swallow, though,' Shirley said.

Rita smiled knowingly, as if this came as no surprise to her. 'How so?'

'Well, the bit about children, actually. The author seems to think mothers pay too much attention to their children, and I just can't agree with that. Children are precious gifts and can't be given enough attention in my opinion.'

There were murmurs of agreement, but Rita shook her head. 'I interpreted that part differently. I thought Greer was saying children deserved the attention of many different caregivers, and that the nuclear family robbed them of that opportunity.'

The discussion then moved on to Greer's idea of communal living. There were some aspects of that concept that appealed to Shirley: the company and division of chores immediately came to mind. But the idea of sharing her child with other women did not appeal to her at all.

'I'm happy to share the cooking and the cleaning,' Dot offered, 'but heaven help the woman who lays a hand on my Bruce. That sexy beast is all mine.'

The room erupted in raucous laughter.

Glennis stood. 'On that note, shall we make our way into the dining room for supper? Thanks to everyone who brought a plate, we have a lovely spread. Go help yourselves, and please continue these great conversations with each other. The night's still young.'

Dot filled Shirley's glass yet again. 'So, what did you think of your first meeting, Shirley?'

'It's been terribly interesting and lots of fun too.'

'Good to hear. Shall we get something to eat?' Without waiting for her answer, Dot stood up and made her way into the dining area.

Shirley went to follow her but as she stood she found herself feeling lightheaded. All these bodies crammed into the small space had made the room stuffy, as well as hot. She decided to go out to the garden for a moment to take in some air.

She wandered back through the kitchen and found a sliding glass door, which led to a large patio. She stood with her hands on the white iron railing, looking out over the sloping backyard. It was finally dark. The sky was clear and star-filled, and there was a slight southerly blowing, the first sign of the long-awaited cool change. She breathed deeply, enjoying the fresh air and the scent of the summer garden below. A little garden bench positioned under the lemon tree called to her. Surely no one would mind if she took herself off for a few minutes?

For the first time in a really long time Shirley felt happy. Elated, really, as if she'd suddenly discovered the meaning of life. It was the wine, of course. Somewhere in the recesses of her mind she knew that it was an artificial happiness that wouldn't last, but she didn't care. She'd take it.

She sat on the wooden bench looking at Glennis's moonlit garden. The heat had wilted her hydrangeas but it didn't matter. Everything seemed soft and beautiful.

'Shirley?' Rita's voice came from the patio above.

'Over here. Under the lemon tree.'

Rita made her way down the back steps with two glasses in her hands. Why had she never noticed how beautiful Rita was before? Why on earth did Rita not have a man in her life? She was like a gazelle, with those long graceful legs of hers. The top she was wearing tonight left nothing to the imagination – her flat midriff was on show as well as her full yet still-pert breasts – the benefits of not having borne a child. Rita was definitely sexy. Shirley giggled at the thought. Were friends allowed to think that about each other?

Rita walked down the path and took a seat beside her. 'There you are. I thought you might have slipped off home without telling me. What are you doing hiding away down here? Are you okay?'

Shirley laughed again. 'I'm great. Best I've been in ages, in fact.'

Rita smiled and handed her a glass of water. 'You're drunk.'

Shirley shook her head. 'Not drunk. Just a little bit tipsy. How about you?'

'I might be a little bit tipsy too.'

Shirley reached over and took her by the hand. 'I really want to thank you, Rita.'

'What for?'

'For bringing me here tonight. For being my friend. For not giving up on me. For everything, really. My life has been pretty tough lately. Without you, it would have been intolerable. You're the best friend I've ever had.' She turned to give Rita a hug and their eyes met.

'You're welcome,' Rita said.

Their eyes remained locked. A surge of electricity coursed through Shirley's body. Without thinking or intending it, she moved closer and touched her lips to Rita's.

At first Rita stiffened, but after a long moment she kissed her back, tenderly at first, then deeply. Every inch of Shirley's skin tingled. She wanted to touch Rita's satin skin and feel Rita's hands on her. She tentatively reached up and cupped Rita's perfect breast with her hand. Rita moaned but, only a heartbeat later, pulled away.

Shirley pulled back immediately. 'I'm so sorry. I thought you . . . I thought you wanted to.'

'I *do* want to. I've thought about this more times than you can imagine, Shirl. But this only works for me if you want it too. I don't want you to regret this tomorrow. You've had quite a bit to drink. Maybe I should take you home. We can pretend this never happened, and things will be the same as they've always been between us. If we go any further, I'm afraid there will be no going back.'

Shirley thought about it for a moment. Was it just the drink? Plenty of times she'd gone to bed with Frank after having consumed a few wines and, while it did make the sex more tolerable, she'd never felt like this. Rita kissing her was the most exquisite thing she'd ever experienced and she didn't want it to stop. She didn't want to go back to a place where she would never feel like this again.

She placed her hand high on Rita's thigh and leaned in. 'No regrets. I promise.'

Chapter 25

Wednesday

I wake up to the sound of pounding. I sit up quickly – no easy feat at my age – and look to the motel door. My pulse is racing. It's then I realise that the pounding I can hear is coming from my own heart. I breathe deeply and focus on steadying my heart rate. I can't afford another cardiac 'episode'. Not this week, anyway. If anything happens to me, Frank will be in all sorts of trouble.

I tell myself to calm down. We are safe here in this little motel.

The events of yesterday have rattled me, yet made me more determined to see this thing through to the end. I feel as though we've been tested and come through, if not with flying colours then at least unscathed. The police let us go. The fact that we got away without them finding out our true identities has given me confidence. Maybe, just maybe, we can make it all the way. On Sunday I prayed for God's protection, not expecting Him to listen. I mean, why would he? I'm hardly a model Christian. In fact, I might just be one of the most hypocritical Catholics in existence. (Apart from the child abusers, of course.) But God works in mysterious ways. Apparently these days he's using online gamers to do his bidding.

After Frank's adventure in Narooma we drove all afternoon to make up the lost time. Frank slept most of the journey, which, although a blessing in some respects, worries me a little. Before I emancipated him I thought he was sleeping so much each day partially out of boredom and partially due to the heavy-handed medication routine they had him on at Sunset Lodge. But it seems even without those things he spends much of his time in slumber. It's hard to reconcile his dozy state with the fit and active man he was just a few years ago.

I messaged Lou via the Sherbet message board before we left the pub at Narooma and there was a reply waiting for me the very next time I checked my phone. She'd been hoping to hear from me, she said. She sent me here to this safe haven, where her online friend Sylvie works. I'd intended to drive a bit further, maybe even make it across the border yesterday afternoon, but when I stopped for a toilet break and found Lou's message, I figured this place was a safe bet. Even without Sylvie's help, Merimbula would have been a good choice because of all the grey nomads in town. Nothing suspicious about an old couple in a campervan here.

I chose the motel over a campground because it's owned by Sylvie's parents. She's been a godsend, checking us in using false names and giving us her mobile number so we can call her directly if we need anything.

The room itself is lovely – a twin overlooking the lake – but the decor is . . . let's just say not my style. The motel is probably three stars at best, but compared to the Kombi it's positively luxurious.

I'm too old to go without life's little comforts. Frank would say I've never liked to rough it, but that's not exactly true. When Wendy and I were little, Mum and Dad would take us camping at Bright for four weeks every summer. We'd pack the caravan on Christmas Eve, and then, after celebrating Christmas with all the extended family, we'd head off early on Boxing Day. We spent the hot summer days floating on inner tubes with our cousins in the shallows of Morses Creek, while Mum and the aunties sunbathed on the pebbly banks.

I'd always thought I'd continue the Bright camping tradition with my own family, but it never happened. When we were first married Frank only took the bare minimum of holidays. He was focused on getting ahead, so there was no time for leisurely camping trips. The summer before Fiona started school he finally relented. He declared he was taking three weeks' leave and he booked a campsite at Breamlea. It was only twenty-five minutes away from home, which meant that if there was a disaster at the plant he could whiz back to Geelong for the day to sort it out. It wasn't Bright, but it was something.

Fiona was thrilled at the prospect of camping a stone's throw from the water. Frank had been teaching her to swim since she was a toddler and she'd taken to it like a fish. 'My little mermaid', Frank called her, and he was right. She took after her Daddy.

Despite not being a beach lover, I had a wonderful time that summer. Frank and Fiona swam or surfed in the mornings, while I pottered around the campsite, doing a little bit of tidying up before settling down on a banana lounge in the shade to read my book. We befriended the family at the site next to us and all agreed we'd return the following summer. In fact, we returned five more times before Frank and I argued about the Kombi.

After that we never went camping again.

For heaven's sake, Shirley, stop living in the past. All this pondering is a complete waste of time. I need to focus on the present.

That thought galvanises me into action. I slide on my glasses, grab my phone from the bedside table where I've left it charging overnight and turn it on. I go straight to the Sherbet community and log in. Immediately I see there's a private message, or a DM as the youngsters call it. (I feel quite chuffed with myself for knowing this.)

> Hi Nan,
> I'm so glad you made it to the motel safely and managed to meet up with Silky.

Silky is Sylvie's online persona.

> You're going to have to be more careful from now on, though. Things are hotting up here. The police have found the car you were travelling in and then a girl reported seeing you and Papa on the bus to Batemans Bay a couple of days ago. BTW she's given the cops an updated description of you, so you might want to change your hair colour again. Although would you mind sending me a selfie first? The thought of you with blue hair is kind of funny.

I smile and snap a shot of myself before I forget. I'll send it later on. The idea of dyeing my hair again doesn't appeal much. I certainly haven't got time for that this morning. I'm thinking a hat might be an easier option.

> Mum was already onto you, of course. She knows you're heading back to Geelong. But until yesterday no one really knew which way you'd go. I think you'll need to stay out of sight as much as you possibly can from now on. You're safe where you are right now. Am I right in assuming you'll be passing through the Bairnsdale area? I had a look at the map and it seems like a logical place to stop, so I've put a call out on the message board for any

members around there to come forward. If you check the board before you leave Merimbula hopefully there will be some offers of help, which you can take advantage of if you need to.

Nan, I know you're trying to take Papa home to Geelong, but I'm not really sure exactly where you are headed once you get there. Mum contacted her old friend from school, Carol someone. Apparently this lady is a police officer in Geelong now. Carol promised to keep an eye out for you.

Fiona's got all the bases covered. I guess I expected that but the confirmation brings me no joy.

Well, it's late now and I need to go to sleep. I don't need Mum coming in here and yelling at me about 'screen time'. She still treats me like I'm ten.

Don't forget to check the message board before you make any more plans.

Love from Lou xxx

I throw back the garish bedclothes and will my stiffened limbs to life. I've neglected my morning stretches these past couple of days and that, coupled with my backside being planted in the driver's seat for far too many hours, has resulted in my arthritic joints being even more obstinate than usual. I shuffle to the window and open the drapes a crack, not wanting to wake Frank. The morning light is soft and hazy but I can see the lake. It's so still. The deep-blue water is framed by the mountain range beyond, making it seem more like a painting than reality. The sky has an almost imperceptible pink tinge to it. Looks like it's going to be a nice day.

The bedside clock tells me it's almost seven, and I've ordered breakfast for seven-thirty. Frank usually eats breakfast around that time and he gets cranky if he has to wait too long to eat. If I hurry, there's probably time for a shower. I haven't had a proper one since the day before yesterday. I was too tired to be bothered last night, and too worried that Frank would do another runner.

He was agitated last night and didn't sleep well, maybe because I only gave him a smidge of Phenergan at bedtime. I've been trying to keep the drugs to a minimum. He was up at midnight, then again at three, yelling and demanding to know where he was. He made such a fuss that I was terrified someone would make a complaint. Luckily the motel wasn't full last night and I'm fairly sure Sylvie has kept the rooms either side of ours empty.

The first time he woke I sang to him, like I used to do for Fiona when she was woken by nightmares. He ignored me initially, but eventually the familiar tunes settled him. It took me ages to calm him down the second time. I tried talking, singing, being firm, but nothing worked. Finally I hit upon the idea of making him a cup of tea. I slipped some more Phenergan into his brew in sheer desperation. Half an hour later he finally nodded off and I haven't heard a peep from him since.

I have no idea what sort of mood he'll be in when he wakes, but he's fast asleep right now, so it might be the only chance I have to use the shower. If I leave the bathroom door open I think it should be okay. I've put the privacy chain on the door, so he'd have to negotiate that before he could get out of the unit and I figure that will make enough noise to alert me. Like me, he doesn't move too quickly first thing in the morning so I think the risk of a stealthy escape is fairly low.

I deliberate over whether to put the bathroom fan on or not and in the end decide that it's safer to leave it off. I open the window a little to give the steam an escape route and turn the shower on.

The hot water is therapeutic, washing away the tension of the past few days along with the dirt. My hair is slightly damp from the shower spray and I long to put my head under and let the water cascade over me. My hair could definitely use a decent shampoo too. Dare I risk it? I can see the end of Frank's bed from here. He hasn't moved a muscle yet. There's no way he'll make it out of bed and out the door in the short amount of time I'll have my eyes closed. I step back and close my eyes for a few seconds. When I open them again Frank has moved, but I can see him – well, I can see half of him. He's pulled the covers off and is sitting on the side of the bed.

I call out to reassure him he's not alone. 'I'm in here. In the bathroom. Won't be long.'

'What?' He stands up and comes to the bathroom door.

'Just saying I'm in the bathroom.'

'I can see that. I need to pee.'

I still haven't managed to buy any more incontinence pants. Most of the stores were closed by the time we got here last night and I was too tired to traipse around town looking. I noticed the beds here have a rubber-backed mattress protector, so I figured if Frank had an accident in his sleep it wouldn't matter. If he's gone the distance overnight – and as far as I can tell it looks like he has – I don't want to him to have an accident now. 'Come on in and use the toilet then.'

He shifts from foot to foot, seemingly unsure of what to do.

'It's okay. I won't look.' It seems a ridiculous thing to say considering all the times I've had to accompany him to the bathroom these past few days, but for all I know Frank doesn't remember any of that.

Eventually he shrugs and totters in. We've never been one of those couples who had an open-door bathroom policy. Using the toilet has always been a private affair, but Frank's dementia has meant a loss of many things besides his memory. His right to privacy has slowly been chipped away, and these days it seems no part of his life is off limits.

While Frank relieves himself I take the opportunity to lather up my hair. I give it a good scrub and tip my head back under the water to rinse. When I'm done I open my eyes to see Frank staring at me. He's stripped off his pyjamas and is standing naked before me. Strangely, this doesn't make me uncomfortable. In fact it feels like the most natural thing in the world.

My instinct is to open the shower door and invite him to join me. Our whole married life Frank sought comfort in my body and I offered that to him when I felt up to it, which was probably far less often than he would have liked. Looking back, I don't think either of us fooled the other, no matter how hard we tried. Frank did his best to give me what I needed, and I appreciated the gesture no matter how misguided. For my part I tried to make it look like his efforts weren't entirely wasted. Our sex life has always been a well-intentioned lie.

Sometimes the truth is overrated.

I shake my head at my own stupidity. Clearly I'm overthinking this. Frank's not seeking comfort from my body now. He doesn't even know who I am.

'I'll be out to get you breakfast in just a moment,' I say.

'Shirl,' he says, and my heart stops. I wipe the water from my eyes and look at him. My husband returns my gaze. Frank's come back to me and I know that I must make this moment count.

I open the shower door and take Frank by the hand.

Chapter 26

February 1971
Geelong

The sun streamed through a crack in the venetian blinds and seared into Shirley's temple as Frank snored beside her. She rolled onto her other side to escape the heat and realised that it wasn't the sun causing her pain. She couldn't believe she'd let herself get so drunk last night. She needed water, aspirin and a shower before Frank or (God forbid) Fiona woke up.

Gingerly she pulled back the covers and tried to sit up. It took a couple of minutes of concentrated deep breathing before she was game enough to toss her legs over the side of the bed. Once she could focus properly she looked around her bedroom to find the evidence of her drunken return home. There was a shoe in the doorway, and the dress she'd worn the night before lay in a crumpled heap on the floor. Her handbag was open beside the bed, its contents spilling out onto the polished boards.

Dear God. Had Frank woken last night when she arrived home? She couldn't remember getting into bed, so she had no idea. Maybe not. He was a sound sleeper. When Fiona was a baby her nocturnal crying had never woken him. These days

Shirley often came to bed after him, hoping he'd have fallen asleep first so the sex thing wouldn't be an issue. Most times he didn't move a muscle when she slipped in beside him. Hopefully last night was no different. Frank mustn't be allowed to see the aftermath of her shame.

She stood and tiptoed around the room, collecting the detritus as she went, each step causing a vibration of pain to reverberate through her body. In the ensuite she dumped her clothes in the hamper and examined her panda-eyed reflection in the mirror. With trembling hands she filled a glass with water and opened the medicine cabinet to search for aspirin. Then, as the painkillers dissolved, she turned on the shower and wriggled out of last night's underwear. Clearly she hadn't managed to get herself into any proper night attire before she'd fallen into bed. As her undies fell to the floor she unearthed another memory of the night before . . . her underwear around her ankles.

No. That couldn't be.

She shook the memory off as she gulped down the aspirin and then stepped into the shower. Soon the combination of the hot water and painkillers helped to dull the thudding in her head and she began to piece together the events of the night before.

It'd been fun. She'd enjoyed the conversation about Germaine Greer's book, and the company. She'd laughed a lot. And drank. She remembered going outside for some fresh air and . . .

Oh God.

Rita's perfume, sweet and citrus.

Rita's lips tasting of moselle.

The soft peach-like flesh of Rita's breast.

And the mind-blowing explosion that had racked her body as a result of Rita's touch.

Her knees buckled.

Shirley put a hand on the tiled shower wall to steady herself as nausea overwhelmed her. She retched violently, bending her head to allow the disgust to pour out of her and down the drain until all that was left was bile.

After she'd cleaned herself and the shower, Shirley wrapped a towel around her body, carefully blow-dried her hair and did her make-up. She stared into the mirror and made a promise to herself. Enough was enough. She'd spent too much time wallowing in her grief. She'd pushed her husband – a wonderful, kind, loving man – away because of her pain. But that was done now. Last night she'd gone too far. If she continued down that path she would be beyond salvation. She knew what she had to do. From this moment on she would focus on being the perfect wife and mother. Anything less was unacceptable.

She slid the ensuite door open to find Frank sitting up in bed listening to the 7.30 news bulletin on his clock radio. He smiled at her. 'Good morning. You're up early for a Sunday.'

She nodded. 'Yes. I thought it was time I came back to church.'

His eyes lit up. 'Really? Oh, Shirl, I can't tell you how happy that makes me.'

'I thought you'd be pleased. So up and at 'em, Frank Sullivan. I'd like to be there in time for confession.'

Being back in church was like coming home. There was such comfort in the familiar rituals. The standing, the kneeling, making the sign of the cross. Confession beforehand had been excruciating, of course, but Father Michael had been kind under the circumstances. She'd told him the truth. Well, perhaps not *everything*, but enough. She confessed to keeping her distance from her husband, and her preference for spending time with her friend. To the drinking. She said she was unclear what had happened after that, which was technically true. Sure, she'd had flashes of what might have happened, but there were whole blank spots in her memory too. How did she know that the visions in her head were accurate? So she'd confessed the absolutes. The things she knew to be true. The other stuff? Well, maybe she'd hallucinated it.

Father Michael told her she'd suffered greatly and that God would forgive her sins now she'd confessed them. God knew she was remorseful and would remove the stain on her soul provided she toed the line from now on. As she made her way down the aisle to receive her communion wafer, Shirley felt full of optimism. Everything would be all right.

After Mass they stood in the churchyard chatting to the other parishioners. Frank held her hand, beaming at the people who came to kiss her and welcome her back. In the midst of all this attention, Fiona pressed against her leg, claiming her in a way that made Shirley's heart swell. The events of last night softened in her mind. She'd imagined them, surely? Rita would never have done such things. She would never have allowed it. It was all just a silly hallucination. The by-product of drinking too much. But all that was behind her now. Last night she'd hit rock bottom. The good thing was there was only one way to go from there – up. She'd learned her lesson. Self-indulgence got you nowhere. Family, faith and service: these were the things happiness was made of. Tonight she would give herself back to her husband, body and soul.

And perhaps Frank was right. Perhaps she had been seeing too much of Rita lately. That silly book had filled her head with nonsense.

Fiona tugged on her skirt. 'Mum, I'm hot. Can we go to the pool?'

'I'm sorry, sweetheart, but we're going to Nanna and Pop's house for lunch.'

'After lunch, then?'

Frank squatted down to Fiona's height. 'The pool will be packed on a day like today. How about Daddy takes you to the beach instead, and we'll let Mum have a rest. She had a late night last night.'

Shame heated Shirley's cheeks. Did he know? Had he seen her stumbling home like a drunken whore? She searched his face for a hint of reproach, but there was none. Frank was as happy as she'd seen him in a long time. She squeezed his hand. 'I'll come too, if you like.'

'Oh, love, that's nice of you to offer but it's so hot. You'll just get sunburned. Why don't you have an hour or two to yourself? You don't mind if Mum stays home, do you, Princess?'

Fiona shrugged. 'Not really. Mum can't swim anyway so she's really no fun at the beach.'

'Hey, that's enough of that. If you're going to be rude to your mother then I might just change my mind.'

'Hush, Frank, she's right.' Shirley hated the beach in summer. It was so crowded and there was no respite from the sun. Even when she took care to put on sunscreen and sit in the shade, more often than not she still ended up sunburned. And Fiona *was* right. It wasn't like she could swim, so she really wasn't much use to anyone on beach outings. Frank had tried his hardest to teach her but her fear always got the best of her. Not Fiona, though. She was a water baby. She loved the sea almost as much as her father. A trip to the beach usually meant Fiona and Frank spending hours in the water while Shirley looked on anxiously from the shore. 'If you're sure you don't mind, then I might take you up on the offer of a few hours to myself.'

He kissed her cheek. 'Not at all. Have a nice rest and then we'll all have a lovely dinner together.'

She slid her arms around his waist and hugged him. It was the most intimate embrace they'd shared in a long time. 'I'll make that potato salad you like.'

Frank looked into her eyes and grinned. 'Right. Now that's all sorted, let's make a move.'

Lunch at her mother's was a cheerful event. It was as if Shirley's return to church had lifted a huge weight off everyone. Her parents' palpable relief caused her to feel a little ashamed. She'd had no idea her actions had been causing so much worry. When she kissed her father goodbye at the gate, he squeezed her tight. 'Good to have you back, my girl.'

She hugged him back. 'It's good to be back, Dad. I'm sorry it took me so long.'

On the drive home she let her hand rest lightly on Frank's thigh and a couple of times she caught him furtively glancing at her as if he was trying to work out whether he was reading more into her gesture than was there. So when he bundled Fiona back into the car to head off for the beach, Shirley kissed him in a way that needed no interpretation.

After two more aspirin, a bubble bath and an hour's nap, Shirley felt almost human. Never again would she allow herself to drink like that. The consequences just weren't worth it. Still, all things happened for a reason, as her mother would say, and Shirley knew what the lesson was from this unfortunate incident. Happiness came from hard work and sacrifice. Marriage took work. Her whole life she'd wanted nothing more than to be the perfect wife and mother, and she'd been given that opportunity. She was so lucky. She was married to an attractive, hard-working man. They had a beautiful, healthy daughter and a home to be envied. So much more than so many others.

She dressed in a cool cotton shift and headed into the kitchen to set about chopping the potatoes she'd boiled earlier as per her grandmother's recipe. As she prepared the salad she thought about the evening ahead. She would make the mayonnaise from scratch, just the way Frank liked it. She'd put on lipstick and wear her hair down. When Frank complimented her on her cooking or her dress she wouldn't bat the compliment away, instead she'd thank him and give him a meaningful look. After dinner, once Fiona was in bed, she'd slip into the pale-blue negligee he'd bought her for Christmas a few years ago – it was still in its packaging at the back of her wardrobe – and let Frank know she was ready for things to go back to normal between them. She hoped God would protect her from another pregnancy, but if not she accepted now that was His choice for her and she had no right to fight it.

She tossed the cubed potatoes into a salad bowl and was searching the pantry for a tin of condensed milk to make the mayonnaise when the phone rang. She rounded the bench and hurried to the entry hall to answer it. 'Hello?'

'Hi, Shirley, it's me, Rita.'

Immediately she felt her pulse thudding in her temples. 'Oh, hi Rita. You just caught me in the middle of getting dinner ready.'

If Rita got her hint she wasn't taking it. 'How are you feeling today?'

Shirley took a seat at the telephone table. 'Oh, fine now. I was quite seedy this morning though. Felt like I'd been hit by a truck to be honest. What about you?'

'Well . . .' she hesitated for a moment, maybe choosing her words carefully. 'I didn't drink quite as much as you, so I was pretty clear headed actually.' She emphasised 'clear headed', but Shirley pretended not to understand what she was getting at.

'Oh, good. Well, if you don't mind, Rita, Frank will be home soon so I'd better keep going with dinner.'

'I do mind.' Her tone was impatient. 'Come on, Shirley, are we going to talk about what happened last night or not?'

This morning's blinding headache returned with a vengeance. Under no circumstances could they talk about last night. If Rita said the words, then it would be true and Shirley would be a slut who'd cheated on her husband.

'I don't think there's anything to talk about. I'm a little embarrassed by how much I had to drink. I can't really remember most of the evening so I hope I didn't make a fool of myself in any way.'

'You don't remember anything? Really, that's what you're going with?'

'I really don't know what you mean. If I did anything to offend you, Rita, I sincerely apologise. I certainly won't be drinking like that again in a hurry.'

'You didn't offend me last night. But I can't believe you have no memory of the evening at all. Please, come over after dinner and we'll talk about it. I understand if you're having second thoughts, really I do, but please don't pretend that nothing happened.'

'There's nothing to talk about, Rita. Just leave it alone. Please. I think that's Frank pulling up now,' she lied. 'Must be off. Talk to you later.'

She put the receiver back in the cradle and bit her lip as she thought about Rita's bewilderment. She pictured her friend – her *best* friend – standing at her kitchen bench, phone in hand, too stunned to even hang up. If there was any other way to move forward she would take it, but she simply couldn't think what that might be. If she admitted to Rita that she did in fact remember the feel of her skin beneath her hands, the taste of her lips, and the whispered declarations of lust – and love – they'd exchanged, then she'd have to explain to Rita why that could never happen again. Rejecting her best friend was unthinkable. If they were to salvage their friendship – and she wasn't sure that was even possible – then denial was the only option. She'd done the right thing.

Or had she? She leaned back against the wall. A bead of sweat trickled between her shoulderblades, dampening her dress. At times like this she wished she smoked, like Rita. She thought about Rita drawing back on a cigarette and slowly, seductively blowing the smoke in her face.

She closed her eyes, but more thoughts of Rita came. Rita's lips on hers. Rita touching her, stroking her hair, whispering in her ear, as they explored each other's bodies.

When the sound of Frank pulling up in the driveway startled her back to reality, she realised her hand had drifted to her breast. She pulled it away and quickly stood up and smoothed her dress. This shameful affair was over. She would not think about it again. If that meant never seeing Rita again, so be it. She wasn't about to risk her family for the sake of a drunken mistake.

'Wow!' Frank's eyes skimmed her body appreciatively. 'Wow. God, Shirl, how's a man supposed to resist you in that get-up?'

She did a little twirl so he could get a look at the whole package. 'Who said you had to resist?' She kicked off the kitten-heeled slippers she'd finally been game enough to wear. Boudoir shoes, Mary had called them when, giggling like a couple of schoolgirls, they'd both bought a pair. It was years ago now, back when she was trying to get pregnant with Fiona.

Frank looked pleased but somewhat bemused. 'What's got into you all of a sudden?'

She shrugged as she climbed in beside him. 'I guess I just stopped feeling sorry for myself. Terrible things have happened to us, but in a lot of ways we're lucky. *I'm* lucky because I still have you.'

He drew her into his arms and kissed her tenderly.

Frank was considerate, touching her gently, taking his time, and repeatedly asking her if she was okay.

'I'm fine,' she kept replying. When he didn't seem convinced, she embellished. 'Better than fine. It's wonderful, darling, truly. I'm just a little out of practice.' She willed her body to respond, but no matter how hard she tried, his touch left her cold. How could it be that this man, who she loved so much, could not elicit the faintest stirring of desire within her? She had to make this work for the sake of her family. Frank had been patient. He'd waited more than a year for her to be ready, but he was a man and men had needs. He wouldn't put up with a sexless marriage forever.

She closed her eyes and pictured Rita.

Chapter 27

Wednesday

This leg of the journey has been challenging. Earlier today I was trawling the internet looking for messages posted especially for me, feeling like an adventurer searching for a secret code. This morning I was snapping selfies and deluding myself I was young and cool again. But four hours later reality has set in and I feel like the stupid old woman that I am.

When we left Merimbula I was full of optimism after a morning spent with the man I love. Frank was the most lucid he'd been in months.

We held each other in the shower for what seemed like forever. I'd let him run his hands all over my body as he breathed my name. 'I miss you, Shirley,' he'd said. Rivulets of water poured down our faces as our lips tentatively found each other's and then our bodies went on autopilot, moulding to each other in a way that was as familiar as breathing.

Afterwards, he told me he loved me and then asked me where on earth we were. I explained everything as simply as possible and he seemed to understand.

'I'm so sorry, Frank, that things turned out the way they did.'

'I knew,' he said. 'I knew you would come for me.'

I'd planned to be in Bairnsdale by the end of the day. From there it's about five hours' drive to Geelong. Just one day away.

But nothing has gone right. The weather has turned on us – it's gone from a beautiful morning to a gusty day with intermittent rain, which has made for slow-going on these twisting, turning roads. The tarmac is greasy and visibility poor. I've got my eyes peeled for fallen tree branches and other debris, and as a result my neck is aching and my eyes are stinging from the effort. To make matters worse, I think there's something wrong with the Kombi. The old girl seems to be losing power and with each new hill climb I fear she won't make it to the top. We're not too far from Cann River, so I'm planning on stopping there to see if we can get some mechanical help. If we get that far.

Frank has slipped away from me again. We'd only got as far as Pambula – not even ten minutes from the motel – when he asked me where we were headed. 'And who are you again?' he'd asked. My vision had blurred with tears then. Stupid, I know, but I'd hoped to keep my Frank for just a little while longer.

Right now he's snoring beside me. I'm not sure how, given the noise coming from the engine, but that's one small mercy. At least I can focus my attention on the road. The last thing I need is him stressing out about whatever is wrong with the van. I'm doing enough worrying for the both of us right now. If the Kombi dies completely, we'll be in trouble. It's not like we can just buy a new car in Cann River. From all accounts it's a one-horse town. But according to the road signs there's a service station there, so hopefully there'll be someone who can help us out.

We just need the camper to get us as far as Bairnsdale. Lou has more of her Sherbie friends lined up to help us there. And Bairnsdale's a big town. Frank and I went there a few years back for the funeral of one of his friends. I remember there were lots of shops, and car yards. Once we're there we can sort something out, but if we break down out here it'll be a disaster.

Cann River 5, the road sign says. Thank God. We can probably walk into town if the van conks it before we get there. Now I'm just praying the service station will have a workshop in it. I hit a pothole in the road and Frank wakes with a start. He rubs the whiskers on his chin, and I realise I should have helped him shave this morning while we were in that nice motel. 'Who are you?' he asks.

'I'm Peggy,' I say wearily. 'I'm from Sunset Lodge. I'm taking you home.'

He looks out the window. 'I thought you looked familiar. Where are we, then?'

'Almost to Cann River.'

'Good. I'm starving. Let's stop there and get something to eat. I haven't had breakfast.'

Despite my melancholy, I laugh. 'You're always starving, Frank. I don't know where you put it all. You don't have an ounce of fat on you.'

He pats his tummy. 'I've got good . . . good . . .' He clicks his fingers together in frustration.

'Metabolism?' I offer.

He shakes his head. 'No, no. When you get something from your family.'

'Genes?'

His face lights up. 'Bingo! My grandfather ate like a horse, he did. Granny always served him first and us kids got the scraps that were left over. The old man could really put it away, but he was a wiry old bugger.'

I wouldn't call Frank wiry, not with his broad shoulders. He had quite the body on him when he was young. Even when he moved into management at Ford and spent a lot of time sitting on his backside, he never turned to fat. Not like me. Ever since the change of life hit me I've had to work at keeping slim. Rita used to laugh at my Pilates classes and walking group, and roll her eyes every time I passed up dessert. 'For heaven's sake, Shirley, you're over seventy years old. Nobody bloody cares what you look like. Eat the cake,' I remember her saying.

'*I* care. Besides, it's not all about looks. I know I'm not getting any younger. I need to look after my health. And so do you.'

She shrugged and scooped up another spoonful of chocolate cake – with cream, mind you – and looked me in the eye. 'I'd rather drop dead of a heart attack than deny myself life's little pleasures. You only live once.'

I shake my head at the memory.

'What are you shaking your head at?' Frank asks.

'Nothing. I'm just a bit tired, that's all. I'll be glad to get out of this van and stretch my legs.'

'Looks like you're in luck then.'

We pass the town-population sign and the main street comes into sight. I breathe out a sigh of relief. At least we won't be stuck on the highway. The van gives a loud cough and Frank looks at me. 'This van of yours doesn't sound too good.'

'I know. She's been giving me a bit of grief today. I'm going to stop at the service station and see if I can get someone to take a look at her.'

'Pah, why on earth would you do that? I can handle any mechanical problems myself.'

I pause for a beat to think about how to handle this. Frank has forgotten how to read. He struggles to tie his own shoelaces. I'm not sure how he thinks he's going to repair the Kombi. Still, I don't want to hurt his feelings. 'But you don't have any tools. Let's just let the people at the service station have a look while we have some lunch. There's a bakery just over there, see?'

Frank shakes his head. 'I don't need tools to have a gander, though, do I? What's been going on? What have you noticed?'

Despite my reservations, I answer the question honestly. 'It keeps losing power. I feel like it has no get-up-and-go when I put my foot down.'

He scratches his chin and nods. 'Could be a few things. Spark plugs is my guess, though.'

'How will we know?'

'I'll know as soon as I take a look.'

Seems I have no choice but to let him have a go. 'Okay. I'll pull up at the petrol station and you can have a look, but we'll probably need a mechanic with some tools to do the job no matter what.'

'We'll see.'

I pull into the service station and find a spot to park away from the bowsers. Frank opens the engine cover and I head off to see if I can find someone to help. I keep my eyes carefully trained on Frank while the apologetic owner informs me there's no one on site who can assist us. There's a mechanic in town, but unfortunately he's taken his son to Bali on a surfing holiday and won't be back until next week. She suggests we call the RACV and I thank her, not wanting to explain why that's not really a great option for us.

Frank's attention is still firmly on the engine, but he has company now. A middle-aged man dressed head to toe in khaki has sauntered over and is standing beside him. I hurry back outside to see what's going on. Khaki man introduces himself as Steve. He explains he's on his way to a 'sweet little fishing spot' along the Bemm. 'I thought I'd come over and lend a hand,' he says. 'I used to own a Kombi and I know my way around the engine.'

'I know what I'm doing,' Frank says.

Steve shrugs. 'No doubt, but in my experience another set of eyes – and hands – doesn't hurt. So what do you think is up?'

Frank stands up straight and wipes his hands on his trousers. 'She needs a new set of spark plugs.'

'Mind if I take a look?'

Frank steps back. 'Knock yourself out.'

Remarkably, Steve confirms Frank's diagnosis. 'A new set of spark plugs and this old girl will be right as rain,' he says. 'If you can get a set here, I'll help you change them over.'

Back inside the service station shop my hopes for a quick solution are dashed. The owner shakes her head. 'You won't find those here. Eden would be the closest place.'

I look at her in dismay. 'Really? Is there nowhere closer?'

'Sorry, love, but I don't think so. If Mick was in town he might be able to scrounge some up, but I can't help you.' She bites her lip. 'You know what, though? My son works in Eden. I could call him and ask him to get a set of plugs for you and bring them back tonight. The only problem is he doesn't get back here until about six, and then it'll take you a little while to put the new ones in. If you don't want to be on the road after dark, you're probably best to stay here overnight. If you can get the campervan started there's a lovely little caravan park just over the bridge. It's free to camp there at the moment.'

I really don't want to spend the night here and I wonder whether we should just keep going, get as close to Bairnsdale – or at least somewhere bigger than this place – as we can. I look at Frank. 'Do you think we can risk driving the van the way it is?'

Frank shakes his head. 'Not advisable.'

In the absence of any ideas I sigh inwardly but smile at the woman behind the counter. 'Doesn't look like we have much choice. If your son could get the plugs I'd be incredibly grateful. I can call the auto shop and pay for the parts with my credit card over the phone, if you like?'

She shakes her head. 'No need to worry about that, love. I'll let you know how much they are when Jackson gets home from work. Do you want to give me your mobile number so I can give you a call when he gets in? Or I can just send him to you at the camping area if you think that's where you'll be.'

'If the van starts we'll definitely go and park it in the camping area, but I'll give you my number just in case. Thank you so much for your help.'

She smiles. 'Not a trouble. I'm Cheryl, by the way. I'll give you my number too. Just call me if you need anything at all while you're in town.'

'I'm sure we'll be fine, but thank you, that's incredibly kind.'

'Like I said, no worries at all. I'd hate for my mum and dad to be stuck somewhere with no one to help them.'

After swapping numbers with Cheryl we go outside and give Steve the news. He hangs around long enough to make sure we can get the camper started. It takes a few goes, but to my relief the engine finally splutters to life. Steve gives us a cheery wave and we putter off over the bridge to the camping area. At least we won't have to camp in the petrol station's car park overnight.

The free camping ground is actually quite lovely. There's a basic amenities block, even a little camp laundry. If we have to be stuck somewhere, this place is as good as any. There's a huge motorhome set up here, but no sign of the occupants; otherwise, the place is empty. It's still relatively early in the day, though, so perhaps it will get busier as the day goes on.

The weather has cleared a little now. It's still breezy but the rain has stopped and the sun has managed to poke its head through the clouds a couple of times, so I'm hopeful we're through the worst of it. Once we've parked and used the bathroom, I dig around in the back of the van for our raincoats – first time we've needed them this trip.

'Here, Frank, put this on.'

He waves me away. 'What do I need that for?'

'We're going to walk up the street and get a bit of lunch.'

His face brightens. 'Right you are.'

It's just a short walk back into town and soon we're sitting at a table in the bakery, eating pies for lunch, and Frank couldn't be happier.

'This pie's a ripper. I can't remember the last time I had such a good one.'

He's not wrong. It's been years since I've eaten a pie – pastry goes straight to the hips – but I'm enjoying this one immensely. Maybe Rita was right about life's small pleasures. It's a shame I didn't realise that when she was around to appreciate my about-face. I smile at him and nod. 'Should we get a vanilla slice to take back to the van for afternoon tea?'

He rubs his hands together in anticipation. 'Ooh, good thinking.'

Chapter 28

April 1971
Geelong

Shirley's hands gripped the steering wheel as she sat motionless in the Safeway car park. It was a crisp autumn day, the chill in the air a reminder that winter was on its way. Even so, Shirley's blouse was damp with sweat. She didn't know how to deal with what had just happened.

Eight weeks had passed since *that* night, and Shirley had barely seen Rita. She'd called around one morning while Fiona was at school and Shirley had been polite but cool. The visit had caught her by surprise and she hadn't known what else to do. She didn't want Rita getting the wrong idea. Rita had played along, keeping the conversation light. They talked about Fiona and the weather. It was tense, awkward small talk that squeezed Shirley's insides with a mixture of longing and regret. She ended the visit as soon as she could without being rude, claiming she had shopping to do. Rita looked hurt but she didn't protest.

The next time they saw each other Rita was blunt. 'I'm here to talk about what happened between us and I'm not leaving until we do,' she said when Shirley answered the front door.

Shirley ushered her inside, fearful that she'd cause a scene that Mrs Harvey might overhear.

'I'll make us some tea,' she said.

Rita sat on one of the stools at the island bench, like she had so many times before. Once the tea was poured Rita was the first to speak. 'We need to clear the air. I can't bear this cold war.'

Shirley laughed nervously. 'There's no war.'

'For God's sake, Shirley, you need to stop this. I thought you cared about me at least enough to be honest.'

'I do care about you.'

'This is exactly what I was worried about. I warned you, remember? I said I didn't want you to regret it. I didn't want to ruin our friendship. You promised me no regrets.'

Shirley couldn't meet her gaze. Rita was right. Rita had warned her and it was Shirley who'd pushed her to continue. She was the one who'd wanted to take things further. 'I'm sorry. I was wrong. It was a mistake.'

'Where does that leave us? I know I said I couldn't go back to us being just friends but I don't want to live without you in my life. If that's all we can ever be, I promise you I'll get over my attraction.' She laughed a little. 'Well, at least I'll try to. But I swear to you I will never act on it again if you don't want me to.'

That was the problem right there. Part of Shirley *did* want her to. Thoughts of what they'd done, how Rita had made her feel, flashed into Shirley's head at the most inappropriate moments – waiting at the school gate for Fiona, in the grocery store and, shamefully, every time she was intimate with Frank. She couldn't trust herself to spend time with Rita the way they used to. It would only be a matter of time until she gave in to her weakness and she simply couldn't let that happen.

It wasn't as if she hadn't considered the option. She fantasised about a real relationship with Rita over and over. In her fantasy she told Frank and he gave her his blessing, moving his things into the spare room. Rita then moved in with them and they all lived together as one big happy family, reminiscent of the communal living Germaine Greer had advocated in her book. But of course that was ridiculous. It could never happen. In reality, if she dared to admit her feelings to Frank he would be appalled. He'd likely kick her out of the house. Of course she could go and live with Rita, but what about Fiona? Frank would never give up his daughter, and it wasn't as if any court would give her custody, maybe not even access. A woman who left her husband to live with her lesbian lover would be considered an unfit mother, of that she had no doubt. Losing her child wasn't something she could risk.

She reached across the bench and put her hand on Rita's. 'I'm so sorry. I just don't think things can ever go back the way they were. It's not that I don't care about you. I do. But we can't change what happened and I don't see a way forward for us. I don't think of you the same way anymore. I wish that wasn't true, but it is.'

Rita withdrew her hand and walked down the hall and out the door, leaving her unfinished tea behind.

Shirley had cried for an hour and then it was over. She resolved to put the whole sorry mess behind her.

For the next few weeks she focused on her marriage, cooking all Frank's favourite meals, maintaining the house to an even higher standard than usual and making sure she took the time to put on some make-up and a pretty dress before he came home from work. She'd also made herself available in the bedroom as often as she could tolerate. As much as she wanted to put Rita out of her head, she found the only way she could bear to be intimate with Frank on a regular basis was to conjure an image of that evening with Rita. She was deeply ashamed of the places her imagination took her, but Frank seemed happy with the increased frequency in their lovemaking so she allowed herself this one indiscretion and prayed for God's forgiveness.

It was the right thing to do. The only thing. She was a married woman and a mother. She was lucky. Think of all the women who'd love to have everything she did – a loving husband, a healthy child and a beautiful, modern home. God had seen fit to give her a child against all the odds. He'd given her the life she'd dreamed of as a young girl, and her response was to want something different. Who was she to reject His plan? She'd made a stupid, drunken mistake. She wasn't about to ruin her life – or her child's – because of it.

As the weeks went by the pretence got easier. Sure, the sex wasn't great, but subjecting herself to Frank's attentions once or twice a week was a small price to pay for the life they had. On balance they had a happy marriage. So what if one little piece of it wasn't perfect?

Occasionally a voice popped up in her head. Sometimes it belonged to Rita, and other times it was Glennis or one of the women from Rita's group who spoke to her. *You deserve more*, the voices told her. But that was a lie. How could there be more than what she already had? The only way she could have more was if she could have Rita and keep Frank and Fiona too. And that was impossible. Not to mention wrong.

The only way forward was to stay away from Rita. That strategy had been working perfectly well.

Until today.

She'd been doing her weekly shop, pushing her trolley purposefully around the store, her mind cluttered with thoughts of packed lunches and evening dinners, when she realised she'd neglected to put cream on her list. She was planning a pineapple upside-down cake for dessert, and Frank preferred cream over ice cream with his pudding. She swung the trolley around and wheeled back to the refrigerated section.

She heard Rita's laugh before she saw her. Deep and throaty, it was unmistakable. Shirley stared into the dairy case to collect herself. Maybe she could slip away before Rita saw her. But what if she already had? Maybe she should be the one to approach Rita. She could smile politely and say hello as she walked past. Show Rita there were no hard feelings. Before she'd had the chance to make a decision, Rita was standing in front of her, making eye contact, and she wasn't alone. By her side was a pretty young brunette wearing a nurse's uniform identical to the one Rita wore.

'Hi, Shirley. I saw you there and thought I'd better say hello, just in case you'd seen me. I didn't want you to think I was avoiding you.' She finished with an awkward little laugh.

Shirley's chest constricted with grief at what she'd lost. Rita had been there for her during her darkest times. She'd never been closer to anyone. Rita knew the true, imperfect her and loved her anyway. Or she had. Now they couldn't even make proper small talk. But there was nothing to be done about it. 'Hello, Rita. Just finished work?'

Rita nodded. 'Yes. Robyn and I have just knocked off. We were thinking we might go on a picnic this afternoon, so we've come to get supplies. Although, it's chillier outside than I imagined so we might end up having an indoor picnic instead. What do you think?' She turned to the brunette, who simply shrugged in reply. 'Oh, sorry, how rude of me. Shirley, this is my friend, Robyn. Robyn, this is Shirley. I helped deliver her daughter a few years ago now and it turned out we live in the same neighbourhood so we see each other from time to time.'

Robyn smiled prettily. 'Hello.'

Shirley swallowed hard in an attempt to dislodge the lump forming in her throat. It was what she'd asked for, but to hear the status of her relationship with Rita reduced to that of acquaintances was hard to bear. 'Nice to meet you, Robyn,' she managed before she felt the heat of tears pricking her eyes. 'I don't mean to be rude, but I'm afraid I'm in a hurry. I'm cooking a special dinner for my husband tonight so I really must get home.'

'Oh, by all means. Don't let us keep you,' Rita replied. She was smiling, but the frostiness in her tone was unmistakable.

'Nice to meet you, Shirley,' Robyn said by way of dismissal. She put a hand possessively on Rita's arm. 'We should get going too.'

With that simple gesture Shirley's heart shattered. She tossed the bottle of cream into her trolley and hurried away to the checkout without bothering to finish the remainder of her shopping.

Now she sat in her car in the car park filled by an emotion she'd never encountered before. At first she wasn't able to identify what it was that had heated her blood and caused her to shake at the same time. She'd asked Rita to leave her alone, advising her to move on. And Rita, quite clearly, had followed that advice. That one touch had said it all. When she thought about Rita taking that slip of a girl into her arms, kissing her tenderly on the lips, Shirley trembled with rage she didn't know where to direct. She wanted to shake Robyn, to tell her to keep her hands to herself, but that was ridiculous. It was hardly the girl's fault that she was attracted to Rita. And what right did Shirley have to claim Rita as her own? None. She'd pushed her away. Told her they could no longer be friends, let alone anything else.

And yet here she was. Shaking and sweating and ... oh God, now she was crying. She had to pull herself together before somebody saw her.

No good could come of this sort of behaviour. She needed to get over herself. She would go home, put the casserole in the oven and bake the special dessert. She would pick up her child from school, make Fiona afternoon tea and listen to her read. She would set the table and change into a pretty dress for dinner. After dinner she would watch TV with her husband and laugh at his jokes. She would be the perfect wife.

And she would not ever think about Rita again.

The next morning after she'd accompanied Fiona to school she found herself walking to Rita's house. She told herself she hadn't meant to go this way, that her feet had just tramped this route out of habit. Of course she wouldn't go in. She would walk right on by. She had washing to hang out at home.

She hadn't slept a wink the night before. Every time she closed her eyes she saw Robyn pawing at Rita and it made her blood boil. No matter how much she tried to put the image out of her head, it persisted. This feeling was absolute torture and she wondered how long it would last.

She pulled her coat tightly around her to keep out the icy wind and hurried along, not lifting her gaze from the footpath. When she reached Rita's driveway, she paused to catch her breath. Rita's clapped-out old Holden sat in the driveway, so she was home. Later, Shirley would swear that it was some type of supernatural force that moved her from the street to Rita's front porch. She would never have made that decision of her own free will. Nevertheless, here she was knocking – no, banging – on Rita's door. Rita opened it a crack. She stood there in her short silky dressing gown, looking stunned.

'Shirley . . . is everything all right?'

'No,' she sobbed. 'Nothing is all right. Everything is wrong, in fact, and I don't know what to do about it.'

Rita held out her hand and Shirley grasped it, allowing herself to be pulled in from the cold. They stood silently in the hallway among the boxes of books, discarded shoes and the rest of the assorted debris that made up Rita's life. After what seemed like a lifetime, Rita spoke. 'What have you come for, Shirley?'

'You,' she said in a whisper. 'I'm here for you.' She reached up her hand to touch Rita's cheek but Rita recoiled.

'Shirley, I told you once before, I can't do this unless you're one hundred per cent sure. I'm not going to beat about the bush. Your rejection shattered me and I won't put myself through that over and over again. I'm not your plaything. I'm not here for you to toy with while you work out what you want.'

'I want you.' As she said the words she knew they were true. She didn't know how this would work, but she knew that living without Rita in her life was not an option.

'How can you be sure? You said that last time and then went running for the hills.'

Shirley's cheeks burned with shame at how her cowardice had hurt Rita, and also at what she was about to confess. 'I'm so sorry. I just didn't want what I felt to be true. I don't know how to live in the world like this. I don't know what it means to love you, but I know now that I do. When I saw you yesterday with that girl I felt like my heart was being ripped out of my body. I wanted to physically push her away and claim you as my own. I honestly don't know how to make this work, but I know that my life is not worth living without you in it.'

Rita pulled her close and as she did so the robe slipped. As Shirley laid her head on Rita's bare chest she knew she was right where she belonged.

Chapter 29

Wednesday

As we walk back to the camping area, I'm chastising myself for thinking a Kombi was a good choice for this trip. A modern camper would have been far more sensible, but I was trying to make a grand gesture by giving Frank the trip he'd always wanted. I should have known a Kombi would be nothing but trouble.

I'll never forget the day Frank brought one home.

Fiona was around ten at the time. It was a hot day, not long before Christmas, and Frank called me from work to say he was coming home early with a surprise for Fiona and me. I remember hoping that it wasn't a puppy. Fiona had been asking for one for months and Frank had started to warm to the idea, even suggesting we get her one for Christmas. I wasn't convinced, mainly because I figured I'd be the one saddled with walking it once the novelty wore off for Fiona. It would be just like Frank to come home with a dog without telling me. I was so preoccupied with being annoyed about the imaginary dog it never occurred to me that the surprise might be something different. It's fair to say I was completely blindsided by the Kombi.

'What are we going to do with this, Frank? We both have perfectly good cars.'

He laughed. 'It's not to drive around. It's a campervan. We can use it instead of the tent. It's got all the mod cons. Step inside and have a look.'

He slid open the side door and Fiona and I climbed in. She grinned and said, 'Wow, look, Mum, there's a little sink and it's even got a stove for you to cook on! It's great, Dad. I love it.'

I struggled to conjure the same sort of enthusiasm. It was nice enough, but I couldn't see the point, really. The tent had plenty of room and we cooked on the barbecue. The sink was a nice touch, I supposed, but the interior was tiny. Did he expect us all to sleep in there together? I could think of better ways to spend the thousands of dollars he must have forked out for this. Still, if Frank liked the idea, what was the harm? He worked hard to give Fiona and me a comfortable life, so if he wanted to splurge a little cash on a fully kitted-out sardine can, who was I to argue? Fortunately I'd become an expert at concealing my true feelings by then. I smiled and kissed his cheek. 'It's lovely, Frank.'

It wasn't until after Fiona was in bed that the full extent of Frank's surprise came to light. The Kombi wasn't just for camping at the beach. He was due for long service leave and could take three months on full pay. He wanted to travel around Australia early the following year. Frank explained that we could leave during the school holidays to minimise the amount of school Fiona would miss.

Three months without Rita? I couldn't bear it. We had so little time together as it was. Three months was unfathomable. It would be hard for me, but it would break Rita's heart.

I shook my head when he finished outlining his plan. 'No, I don't think so, Frank. It simply won't work. What about Fiona? She can't miss that much school.'

'Of course she can. She's a smart little thing. She'll catch up.'

'And what if she doesn't? They'll keep her down a grade. It'll be humiliating for her.'

'I doubt that will happen. Think of all the things she'll learn from travelling. But if you're really worried we'll get some work for her to take. You can supervise her lessons while we're away.'

'Oh, can I now?' My voice rose along with the level of panic I was experiencing. I couldn't just leave for three months. It was unthinkable. 'You're so bloody selfish, Frank Sullivan.' I didn't know if it was my tone, the swear word or my accusation that caused the look of shock on his face, but I was too far gone to stop. 'You look at three months on the road as an adventure, a holiday, and for you it will be. But what about me? When is it my turn to have a holiday? Did you ever think to ask me what I like? I hate camping, Frank. Every year you drag me to the beach for a holiday. I can't swim, I hate the sand and I'm left to do all the things I do here – cook, clean and wash – in primitive surroundings. It's no bloody holiday for me, let me assure you.'

'Keep your voice down,' he said. 'You'll wake Fiona.'

I should have walked away then, but I didn't. Instead I allowed my usually well-contained fury to get the better of me. The anger at all the injustices I'd suffered to be a wife and mother – the lack of meaningful work, the joyless sex, the terrifying pregnancies, life-threatening labours, the toll on my physical and mental health, not to mention that I'd given up the very essence of myself to fulfil this thankless role – overwhelmed me at that moment and I found myself yelling like a madwoman. 'If you want to traipse around the country living like a hobo for three months, go right ahead. But if you think I'm coming with you or letting you take my daughter, think again!'

The look on his face almost broke me and I instantly regretted my words. I didn't want to hurt him, but I couldn't leave Rita for three whole months. More than anything I wished there was a way to make both of them happy. Maybe I could talk Frank into a shorter holiday . . .

There would be no more discussion that night. Frank had already taken himself off to the spare room. I decided that wasn't such a bad thing. We both needed some time to cool down. I'd sleep on it and come up with a solution in the morning.

But it was too late. When I woke the next morning the Kombi was gone and so was Frank. I spent all day wondering whether that was it. Whether I'd driven him away. When he wasn't home by six I feared the worst, but ten minutes later he arrived home with a black curly-haired puppy under his arm and a 'don't argue' look on his face. Fiona was so delighted by the gift of Harriet – the name she gave to the pup as soon as she saw her – that the Kombi was pretty much forgotten. When she asked about it a few days later Frank explained that we wouldn't be camping this summer because Harriet wasn't permitted in the camping park, which seemed to mollify her.

We never camped again.

By the time we get back to the van a couple of hours have passed since we first drove in to town. The sun is shining and it's actually quite pleasant in the camping park. I pull out the folding chairs from under the bench seats in the back of the van and place them in the shade of a big gum. I grab my phone and check the signal, which thankfully is strong here. I need to get in touch with Lou and let her know what has happened, and also with 'Chazar' and 'Bandit', who are my Bairnsdale contacts. I fully expect Frank to nod off in the sun and leave me to it, but he rolls up his pants, stretches out and says, 'You wouldn't be dead for quids, would you?'

My breath catches in my throat. Frank might not recognise me anymore, and tomorrow he won't remember this moment, but right now he's happy and that's something. Maybe this delay isn't such a bad thing – provided we don't get caught – because in two days' time we'll be home and then . . . well, then I don't know what. We can't go on like this forever, but the thought of Frank going back to that nursing home is more unpalatable than ever.

I reach over and squeeze Frank's hand. 'No, you wouldn't.'

He squeezes back then gently pulls his hand away. 'Look at that! Up there in the tree.' He points to a pair of rosellas. 'What a pair of beauties.'

'Yes, they are pretty. As long as they stay up there and don't come near me.'

He lets out a loud belly laugh then. 'What is it with you women? My wife is terrified of birds. One got in the house once and she locked herself in the bathroom until I got home from work.' He laughed again and shook his head. 'It was a sparrow! As if a tiny little thing like that could cause any harm. Still, each to their own, I guess. Everyone has their weaknesses.'

Before I can stop myself I ask him a question I have no right to, considering he has no idea who I am. 'What's she like, your wife?'

He stops laughing then and the creases in his face soften. 'She's the most beautiful creature alive. Honestly, I have no idea how I got so lucky. I was just a ruffian from the bush when I met her and she . . . well, she was the belle of the ball. I didn't think I had a chance with her.'

I'm so caught up in the romance of his story that I almost forget he's talking about me. 'How did you meet?'

'Well, it was a fair piece of luck, I'll tell you that much. Some might even call it fate. I was at the beach, you see. I was a lifesaver back then. I was visiting my cousin in Geelong and he took me down to Bancoora beach. I'd had my eye on this group of girls who were splashing around a bit in the shallows. Lookers, all three of them, but one of them had that something special. She had a bit of Grace Kelly about her, you know? She was wearing this black and white polka dotted bathing suit and had a matching tie thing in her hair. Stylish, I thought. Anyway, there I was just appreciating the view when Shirl – that's my wife – was knocked over by a wave. They were only in water up to about here' – he puts his hand to his waist to indicate the depth – 'but Shirl couldn't swim. Still can't. She doesn't like the water.'

'So you saved her?'

He laughs. 'She thinks so. But between you and me, she was never in any real danger.'

'And she thanked you by going on a date with you?'

He shakes his head and explains about the dance that night and how I had another fellow lined up to take me home. 'I had no right to cut in on him, and I knew she deserved better than me, so I made a pact with myself that if I could win her heart I'd work my guts out – pardon the expression – to be worthy. I promised myself I'd do everything in my power to give her the life she deserved.'

It's hard to contain my emotions at hearing him confess this. I take myself back to that night and try to conjure up how I felt about him. I was flattered by the attention, of course. Frank was handsome and a good dancer. Was I deeply and madly in love with him? Not straightaway, maybe not even on our wedding day. But he was kind and decent and ready to settle down. I was twenty-one, it was time to find a husband, and Frank was a more than suitable candidate. My parents and sister loved him, my friends thought he was a 'catch' and I loved the *idea* of being in love with him. But did I feel the way he did? No, I didn't.

'So you ended up with the girl. Was she worth it?' I ask softly.

He seems surprised by the question. 'My word, she is.' He leans forward a little in the chair and turns to look at me. 'Oh, we've had our ups and downs, like any couple.' He drops his gaze to the ground. 'We had a boy, you see. Andrew. He was stillborn and Shirl took that pretty hard. She kind of withdrew from me after that. I blame myself for that now. The doctors all told me the best thing for us to do was to forget about the baby, focus on our daughter. So that's what I did. I didn't let Shirl dwell on what had happened. I brushed it under the carpet. Maybe that was a mistake. Shirl was a right mess for about a year or so and then she seemed to pull herself out of it. Still, things were never quite the same after that.'

It's taking all my willpower not to cry. 'I'm sure she knows you did the best you could under the circumstances.'

He shrugs. 'Maybe.'

I know I should leave well enough alone, but I have to ask. 'Are you happy in your marriage, Frank?'

He looks back at me again and his smile is broad. 'Absolutely. Yes, there was that sadness with Andrew, but otherwise I don't think we could be luckier. We've got a beautiful daughter, Fiona. She's sharp as tack that one. She'll end up being the first female prime minister of this country, I reckon.'

I smile encouragingly and neglect to mention that Fiona didn't end up going into politics, and that even if she had, Julia Gillard had taken the honour of being Australia's first female PM.

'I've got everything a bloke could ask for. When I was a little fellow, I didn't have much of a family life. My mum died just after I was born and my dad took off and left my poor grandparents to raise me and my sister. By the time I was ten, Granny had died too, and Pop didn't really know how to look after a couple of kids. He kept an eye out for us, but he couldn't keep us with him. I was split up from my sister and passed around between the aunties. Nobody wanted us. As soon as I was old enough, I got a job so I didn't have to rely on anyone. Old Mrs Grumley took pity on me and gave me a room at her boarding house. That woman was the closest thing I ever had to a proper mother. And as for my father? God only knows what became of him.'

I don't say a word. I don't want to do anything that will discourage him from continuing. In fifty-plus years of marriage he hasn't talked much about his early life. Oh, I already know the bare bones of it. He briefly talked about his family when we first met, and over the years my beautiful sister-in-law, Patty, filled in some of the blanks for me. But Frank has never willingly talked about his early life.

'I made a pact with myself when I was just a kid. I promised I would be the best husband and father a person could be. I would never leave my wife or child and I'd work as hard as I could to provide them with everything they could ever possibly want.' He sits up straighter in the chair. 'And I've done that. All I ever wanted was the honour of providing for my own family. Shirl's made us a lovely home and given me a daughter I'm proud of. I've held up my end of the bargain by providing for them both. Fiona's had a good Catholic education and she's off at the university. She's smart that one. Going to be prime minister one day.'

Suddenly I don't mind so much that Frank no longer remembers me. He's happy where he is. Maybe he's living an edited, happier version of our marriage, but who am I to deny him that? I've come to the realisation that there's no point in me confessing my sins to him now. Maybe the exorcism of my secrets will make me feel better, but they will do nothing for Frank but hurt him in the moment. And ten minutes later he won't remember what I've said anyway.

The time for truth-telling has passed.

Chapter 30

July 1977
Geelong

'Disneyland? Fuck. And you've told him yes?' Rita sat up in bed and pulled the covers over herself.

Shirley rolled onto her back and stared at the ceiling. 'Of course I said yes. What else could I do? I mean, I can't refuse to go on *every* holiday Frank suggests. I don't think he's ever got over me killing his dream to go around Australia in that damned campervan.'

Rita didn't answer. Instead she said, 'How long will you be gone for?'

'We leave on the fifth of August and we'll be gone for a month. Fiona's having the last two weeks of term off and we'll be gone for the school holidays as well.' Shirley waited for Rita to do the calculation in her head.

'Will you be back for my birthday?'

'The day after. I'm so sorry, I really tried to make sure I was back in time but the flights didn't work out that way.'

Rita was quiet for a while. Eventually she said, 'You know it's my fortieth, right?'

Shirley sat up and looked at her. 'I know. I promise I'll make it up to you when we get back. Maybe I can work out a way for us to have a weekend away together as part of my gift to you.'

Rita's voice was cold. 'Don't promise things you can't deliver, Shirley.' She threw the covers back. 'I'm going to have a shower. I start work at one and I've got a few things to do before I leave.'

Shirley grabbed her by the hand and pulled her back down on the bed. 'Don't. Don't run off in a huff. Let's talk about this.'

Rita blew out a long breath. 'I'm not sure you want to hear what I have to say.'

'Whatever it is, I do.'

Rita swung her legs up onto the bed. 'I'm sick of always being your second choice, Shirl. When is it my turn to be the centre of your life?'

'You are the love of my life, you know that.'

'No, what I am is a fool.'

'That is not true.'

'It is true. You squeeze me into your life and I'm supposed to be satisfied with that. I love being with you, but I feel like an afterthought. Today you'll go home to your family and I'll be left here with only the cats for company. I want someone to share my life with, Shirley. Not just a visitor a few days a week.'

'You know you mean more to me than that.'

'Prove it then. Tell Frank you can't go on this holiday.'

'I can't do that. We've already booked everything – flights, accommodation, we've even organised for Harriet to be put in a kennel . . .'

Rita gave her a withering look.

'. . . and besides, we've told Fiona. Imagine how heartbroken she'd be if we backed out now.'

Rita's shoulders slumped. 'It just feels like this whole relationship is one way – your way. I've played by your rules for six years now. Made it easy for you, haven't I?'

Shirley couldn't deny it. She'd set the ground rules. There was to be no physical contact in public and definitely none in Shirley's home. Rita was still welcome there, of course. Rita loved Fiona and Shirley didn't want to deny the pair of them their special bond – no birthday party would be complete without Aunty Rita. But Shirley had made it clear all romantic gestures (from meaningful glances through to physical touch) were strictly off limits. Their relationship didn't exist outside of Rita's home. So far this had worked perfectly – well, at least it had for her. Rita was becoming less and less enamoured of the arrangement. 'You've been a rock, Rita, and I really wish it could be different, but I have to think of my child.'

'Yes, Fiona. Of course.' There was an uncharacteristic bitterness in her voice. 'You've got it all, Shirley. The husband, the child and the lover. You get to have a life with your family, but what do I get? We can never do anything together. Never go on a proper holiday, never make plans for the future.'

'I wouldn't say we never do anything together. We have this. We have our craft group.' Shirley winced at the euphemism, wishing she could take it back. She'd taken to calling the Geelong Women's Alliance *the craft group* in front of Frank, because she knew he wouldn't approve of her belonging to a feminist group. The group had grown significantly since those early days when she'd gone along with Rita. There were several branches now, each focused on lobbying for a different aspect of women's rights. Shirley found herself drawn to the women's education branch, although she was really only a fringe-dweller in terms of what she contributed to the group. It wasn't as if she could attend marches or anything like that. (Imagine if Frank saw her on the news!)

Rita was deeply committed to the women's health lobby and spent a lot of her free time involved in their activities. The wider group held regular social functions – often in members' homes – and these provided the one public place where Rita and Shirley could be 'out' as a couple. At first Rita thought the sewing-circle label was funny but recently she'd made a few snarky comments about the hypocrisy of lying in order to be 'allowed' to attend a group that lobbied for women's rights.

Rita's eyes flashed with anger. 'You barely even come to the events anymore.'

'That's not fair. I couldn't come to Noelene's party because I had the Mothers' Club fundraiser dinner. I'm the president of the club so I could hardly give it a miss. And the women's clinic fundraiser clashed with Fiona's choir performance. You know I would have come otherwise.'

'I just feel like I'm never your first priority.'

'I don't know what to say. What can I do to make this better?'

'Leave Frank,' she said. 'Move in with me. I earn enough to support the two of us.' She paused for a moment. 'Fiona too, of course.'

Shirley sighed. 'We've been over this. You know I can't just leave. I'd lose Fiona. Frank would never allow me to have custody of her. And even if he did I couldn't do it to her. She'd be crucified at school for having a "lezzo" for a mum. You know that, right?' She softened her tone. 'I know how much you love Fi and I can't believe you'd want her to suffer that way.'

Rita shrugged. 'Change has to start somewhere. Why not with us?'

'Because this' – she pointed to Rita and back at herself – 'is *our* choice. Not hers. I don't want my decisions to impact negatively on my child. I'm not going to sacrifice my child's happiness for my own and I really don't think that's what you want either.'

'Of course I don't, but she won't be a child forever. What about when she grows up? I need to know that someday our time will come; that eventually we can be together properly. Right now I'm not sure that's what you want.'

'Things will be different when she's older.' Even as she said the words Shirley wondered at their truth. Because her reluctance to leave her marriage wasn't just about Fiona. Being married to Frank wasn't perfect, but it wasn't bad either.

She loved their home and their life together. They were compatible in almost every way. They were both house-proud and enjoyed making improvements to their home. (Rita's house frequently looked like it had been burgled, and those damned cats left hair on absolutely everything.) She and Frank liked to eat home-cooked meals, and spent their evenings on the couch watching TV together. If they had a night out it usually involved getting together with another couple to play cards. (Rita preferred to eat Chinese takeaway and her idea of a great night out was to see a band at the local pub, or a drunken get-together with friends from their women's group.) And Frank and Shirley shared one love that Rita, no matter how hard she tried, would never completely understand – Fiona.

There was no doubt in Shirley's mind that she loved Rita and wanted her in her life. But sometimes she wondered how long their relationship would last if they put it to the test by living together. Rita's intellect, her creativity and her passion were incredibly sexy, but would they be such attractive qualities on an everyday basis? Would things fall apart if Shirley had to constantly pick up after her? If she had to sit and listen to her rant and rave about the patriarchy every night, when all Shirley wanted was to sit in front of the telly and watch *The Sullivans* in peace? (Rita's TV was permanently tuned to the ABC.)

Did she blame Rita for wanting more? Of course not. But her own feelings were more complicated. Maybe it was selfish of her, but she was happy with things the way they were, even if deep down she knew they couldn't go on like this forever. Right now she knew she'd have to do something to mollify Rita because her feelings of injustice were growing. Rita was many things, but she was not a pushover.

'What if there was a way for us to be together now? Not all the time, of course, but for a few days at a time.'

'How?' Rita's scepticism was obvious.

'Fiona's becoming quite independent now, and she'll be in high school next year. She'll be catching the bus to Sacred Heart, so she won't need me for transport, and I could freeze her school lunches ahead of time. I could leave some casseroles in the freezer too.'

'And Frank? How would you explain this to him?'

Shirley shrugged. 'I'll think of something. Maybe the sewing group. We've always talked about going away for a girls' weekend. Maybe I could tell him it's finally happening, but instead of a weekend we're going for a whole week. So long as he's fed, I think he'd be okay with that.'

Rita fell back against the pillows. 'God, it'd be great, wouldn't it? A whole week of sleeping in the same bed; of going out to dinner together, of not having to clock-watch. It'd be wonderful. Where would we go?'

'Anywhere you like, my love. Somewhere faraway from here, where no one knows us. Maybe we could go interstate, even.'

'Yes. Queensland maybe. I haven't been there for years.' It was clear Rita was taken with the idea. Hopefully it would be enough to keep her happy with the way things were, at least for the time being.

'If that's what you want then that's what we'll do.'

'Do you really mean it? This isn't just some bullshit empty promise to shut me up, is it? Because you know I love you, Shirl, I've always been clear about that. But I'm not going to live my whole life being your second choice.'

'You are not my second choice, ever. It's just that I have responsibilities. My life isn't simple. But there's nothing complicated about how I feel about you. Now come here and kiss me before I have to go.'

Chapter 31

Thursday

The sound of a kookaburra laughing wakes me at dawn. Frank's in a dead sleep beside me so I grab my reading glasses and my phone, and creep out of the camper to go to the toilet block. The sun is rising in a soft-pink sky and I know that soon the dew on the ground will evaporate and the smell of wet eucalypts will give way to a drier scent of early summer. This has always been my favourite time of year; the air is full of the promise of the season yet to come.

Inspired by yesterday's realisation that this journey is all about embracing the moment, I decide that after breakfast Frank and I will start the day with a long walk. We can stop by the bakery on the way and pick up some more of those vanilla slices to take on the road.

After I've relieved myself and splashed my face with cold water I wrap my cardigan tight around me and duck into the laundry room to check my phone. I can see the van from here so there's no chance Frank can escape without my knowledge, but in here I can scroll around without fear that one of those stupid videos will start playing automatically and wake him. I'm keen for him to get as much rest as possible. He had a pretty big day yesterday. The young fellow, Jackson, who brought the parts for Frank to fix the Kombi, was quite the talker. It didn't take long for the two of them to change the spark plugs and test the van, but then the young bloke was on for a chat and the next thing we knew he'd talked us into joining him for a meal at the pub, along with his parents, Cheryl and Peter.

A child's cry comes from the caravan parked closest to the amenities block. The sudden stirring of life reminds me that Frank will wake soon. I need to look at my phone while I have the chance. Lou has left me a message:

> Nan, you need to leave where you are and get to my friends right away. Mum's offered a reward for information about your whereabouts. A lady from a shop you went to reported seeing you. She called Crime Stoppers and gave the police a description of all the clothes you bought.

Well, at least I can ditch the tie-dyed clothes. It was fun playing dress-up while it lasted, but the hippie look has never been my style.

> Now it's come out that the police in Narooma had you and let you go. The cops are being taunted in the media, which isn't good. You're not likely to get away with a stunt like that again.

I wince at this. Poor Tattoo and Babyface. I hope they're not in too much trouble.

> You and Papa have become a big story. It was on the news tonight and *News in Focus* called Mum and she's going to be on their show too. She's telling everyone you

are 'vulnerable' and that you and Papa have multiple health issues.

Oh, well played, Fiona. Invoke the sympathy card.

People are going to be on the lookout for you now so you have to be careful who you trust. Chazar and Bandit can hide you overnight on their farm outside Bairnsdale. Bandit's left you a message explaining how to get to her place. The Sherbies will do their best to get you home safe, Nan, but you have to be extra cautious now.

I force myself to take a few deep breaths and steady my heart rate. I make a mental note to take my medication as soon as I get back to the van. We're so close now. I haven't taken all these risks to falter in the final stretch. So much for savouring the moment. There's no time to spare for long walks.

I get out of the forum and go to my favourite news site. It takes me a mere moment to find a link to the news footage.

'A pair of elderly runaways gave police the slip at Narooma yesterday. Married couple Frank and Shirley Sullivan left the nursing home where Mr Sullivan is a resident last Sunday to attend a family party. Staff at the nursing home became concerned when Mr Sullivan had not returned by the end of the day. After initial fears that the couple had met with misadventure, it soon became clear that the old-age pensioners had simply done a runner.

'A reported sighting at Bodalla led to the discovery that Narooma police had spoken to the couple on Tuesday before allowing them to leave. Police were called to assist in reuniting Mr Sullivan with his wife after he wandered off from a hotel where they'd been having lunch. A police spokesperson confirmed that the Sullivans were not asked for identification at any stage during the incident, and an investigation is underway into why normal protocols were not followed.'

Maybe I should write to the police and put in a good word for Tattoo and Babyface once this is all over. Although maybe an endorsement from me, an old woman who managed to outwit them, will do more harm than good.

'The pair, both of whom suffer from medical conditions, are believed to be travelling south along the coast between Sydney and Melbourne, possibly in a campervan of some type. The couple's daughter, Fiona, believes they may be heading to Geelong where they lived for a number of years. She is urging anyone who encounters her parents to contact Crime Stoppers immediately, and has offered a ten-thousand-dollar reward for information that leads directly to her parents' whereabouts.'

I click away from the story and back to the message board, where I find Bandit's private message giving me directions to her farm near Lindenow. I read over her instructions several times, trying to commit them to memory. I don't want to have to make unnecessary stops to check the directions. I haven't come this far to be caught.

Chapter 32

June 1986
Shelley Beach, near Caloundra, Queensland

'Here, take this, would you?'

Shirley opened her eyes to find Rita standing over her with a glass in her hand. She peeled her bare back from the banana lounge and sat up. 'Goodness, is it happy hour already? I must have drifted off for a bit.'

Rita handed her a gin and tonic. 'It's four-thirty. I thought I'd better wake you so you have time to get ready before we go to the surf club for dinner. I know how you like to titivate yourself for dinner, even when it's not necessary.'

Shirley picked up her towel and made her way across the spiky grass to the outdoor setting on the back patio. She eased her bikini-clad bottom onto the timber slats of a wonky chair and placed her glass beside the platter of nibbles Rita had set out. 'There's no harm in looking one's best.'

Rita readjusted her sarong and took a seat beside her. 'I hardly think it matters here. Half the people in the bistro will be in shorts and T-shirts. It's one of the things I like most about this place.'

Shirley didn't doubt that. Rita was no fashion plate; she thought the beauty industry was enslaving women. Which was fine for her – Rita had been blessed with good genes and was ageing well. Her olive skin remained relatively unlined, especially considering how much time she'd spent sunbathing over the years. She ate what she wanted and never did any sort of formal exercise ('No time for that sort of nonsense, Shirl!') yet her figure remained trim. Even the grey hairs that flecked her cropped dark hair didn't detract from her beauty. By contrast, Shirley worked hard to keep up her appearance. She regularly visited the local hair salon to keep her smooth blonde bob free from grey. (A fact she'd managed to conceal from both Rita and Frank so far.) She dieted, exercised regularly and dressed in age-appropriate 'figure-flattering' fashions. She was aware that her obsession with her appearance amused and frustrated Rita in equal parts.

'I dress to my own standards, thank you very much. What's wrong with that?' Shirley speared a cheese cube with a toothpick and popped it into her mouth.

Rita shook her head. 'Nothing at all. I just like to see you relaxed. You don't have to impress anyone here, you know.'

Shirley cocked an eyebrow. 'Oh no? I thought I was here to impress you.'

Rita leaned across and placed a hand on her thigh. 'You don't have to dress up to do that, my darling. In fact, I'm far more impressed when you take your clothes off.'

After a quick glance at the back fence to make sure the neighbours hadn't made a sudden appearance, Shirley moved her hand to the back of her neck and pulled on the tie that fastened her bikini top. The top fell forward, exposing the milky white skin of her breasts.

Rita's hand found the second tie and undid it. 'You're a little sunburned,' she said, as her finger traced the line where white skin met pink. 'Maybe we should get you inside. Let me rub some lotion on that skin before it starts to sting.' She brushed her lips to one breast, while her hand cupped the other.

Shirley was gripped by a bolt of desire. After all these years Rita could still turn her insides to liquid with a single touch. She parted her legs and gently guided Rita's head lower.

Rita paused and looked up at her. 'Are you sure you don't want to go inside?'

She shook her head. 'The backyard's private. The neighbours would have to climb up on the fence to see us. And if they want to look, that's up to them.'

Rita laughed. 'I love how this place brings out your adventurous side.'

'That's the whole point of being here, isn't it?'

Afterwards, while Rita showered, Shirley threw on a pair of shorts and a T-shirt and walked down to the phone box on the corner to call her family. This annual trip to Caloundra was Rita's time. For two weeks a year they got to experience life as a couple without baggage. Here on the Sunshine Coast they were free from the fear of being caught, and free from the restraints of Shirley's daily life. For the other fifty weeks of the year Rita put up with a lot, and mostly without complaint. From time to time she grumbled about coming second in Shirley's life, but it didn't happen often. In fact, their lives had settled into a lovely sort of rhythm. They saw each other as many weekdays as possible, working around Rita's shifts and Shirley's family and volunteering commitments. Weekends were usually off limits, but that wasn't such a bad thing. The forced break helped to keep their relationship fresh.

Since they'd started having this annual holiday together, Rita seemed more content in the relationship. She looked forward to it all year, and would often fantasise about the two of them retiring to their own little 'piece of paradise' in the north. So while they were here Shirley tried her best to give in to the fantasy and pretend that it was just the two of them. She kept conversation about – and contact with – her family to a minimum. But today Fiona had started her mid-year university exams and Shirley wanted to see how she'd got on.

Frank was unusually brusque on the phone, cutting her short to say he was in the middle of getting dinner so he'd put Fiona on. Fiona was not much better. All Shirley's questions were met with monosyllabic answers.

'Darling, you sound upset. Are you sure the exam went okay today? It doesn't matter if it didn't. One bad grade isn't the end of the world.'

'The exam was fine. I'm annoyed, if you must know. Dad has no clue what he's doing in the kitchen and he keeps interrupting my study every five minutes. Honestly, Mum, I don't know why you thought it would be a good time to go swanning off on a holiday in the middle of my exams.'

'Oh, sweetheart, I'm sorry, but you know Aunty Rita and I always come up here around this time of year.'

'But this is the first time you've been away for my exams. I wish you'd thought about that. If you'd just waited a couple of weeks, I could have come with you. I would have loved a holiday in the sun to recover from all this stress.'

Shirley bit her lip in amusement. It would never occur to Fiona that she might not be a welcome addition to her mother's holiday plans. 'Sorry, darling, but we book the cottage a year in advance. I wasn't to know that it would be an inconvenient time for you.'

'Well, it *is* inconvenient. I have enough on my plate without having to look after Dad as well.'

Shirley's amusement evaporated. How had she managed to raise such a self-centred young woman? 'Sorry, darling, I have to go. I'm running out of coins.'

There was silence for a moment and Shirley wondered if they'd been cut off. She regretted having made the call. Neither Frank nor Fiona had bothered to ask a single thing about her trip. The idea of one day retiring somewhere with Rita was beginning to seem more appealing. Not here, though. Somewhere where she could still visit Frank and Fiona. They were her family, after all.

'Mum? Are you still there?'

'Yes, darling, I am.'

'I miss you, Mum. Bye.'

Shirley stood cradling the phone for a full minute after Fiona rang off. This was a moment worth savouring.

Chapter 33

Thursday

Bandit said she'd be waiting for us at the turn-off to her farm, but after twenty minutes of driving down single-lane gravel roads with potholes as big as ponds I'm beginning to wonder if I've taken a wrong turn somewhere, or if we've been sent on a wild goose chase. Up ahead is a fork in the road. I veer left towards the ancient gum with the red marker on it (just like the directions said, so we must be in the right place) and after a minute or two we leave the bush behind and drive into open farmland. Up on the right-hand side there is a big four-wheel drive ute flashing its lights at me. I pull up alongside it and a young woman gets out from the passenger side and comes over to me. 'Shirley?' she asks.

The woman, who is wearing a purple floral dress and a pair of Blundstones, has magenta hair and is sporting a nose ring. She's not at all what I expected a young farmer to look like. 'Are you Bandit?'

'Yes.' She smiles. 'You can call me Brianna if you like. That's my husband, Charlie, over there in the ute.'

Husband? Good grief. How can this slip of a thing be old enough to be married? I look across to the boy in the ute and he grins and waves.

'If you follow us now we'll lead you to our farm.'

The farm is tucked away down a long driveway off a narrow lane. I'm filled with renewed confidence that everything will be all right. We couldn't have asked for a better place to hide overnight. Brianna directs us to the granny flat, which is set back along a small driveway about a hundred yards away from the main house. We park out the front and Brianna comes to let us in.

'You'll be comfy in here,' she says. 'This used to belong to Charlie and me when my mum and dad had the farm. Now we use it as an Airbnb.'

'Do you get many people coming to stay?' I can't imagine many tourists coming this far off the beaten track.

She shrugs. 'You'd be surprised.'

I am surprised at the flat's interior. It's like a plush hotel room. Frank disappears into the bathroom. 'Look at this view,' he calls. 'You can watch the cattle grazing while you take a dump.'

My cheeks burn with humiliation at his crudeness. 'That's enough of that, Frank. We don't want to hear bathroom talk.' I turn to Brianna. 'Sorry about that. Frank's dementia causes him to have no filter at times.'

She grins. 'No worries. I say worse things than that and I haven't got dementia.'

'He used to be such a gentleman. And still is in lots of ways, but the old Frank would never have said something like that in front of a woman.'

She gently touches my shoulder and my eyes mist slightly. 'So, I'll leave you to settle in, but once you're ready come on up to the main house. I've made some lunch and I thought you might like to use the computer while you're there to contact Miss Lulu, or for anything else you need to sort out. The wi-fi signal can be a bit patchy out here.'

I reach out and squeeze her hand. 'Thank you. For everything.'

'It's cool, Shirley. I know how Miss Lulu feels. I loved my nanna too. Although, I have to say, she wasn't quite as badass as you.'

This makes me grin. Rita would laugh at the idea of me being called a 'badass', but I like the description and I'm not going to argue.

Frank and I both use the bathroom. I realise he's had no accidents since we left Mossy Point, which makes me feel I've been justified in my belief that ditching the antipsychotics and providing a stimulating environment would be good for him. He's been particularly upbeat today, chatting away about the Kombi and cars in general. Changing the van's spark plugs has given him a tangible boost. I realise it's been a long time since he's had any real purpose in his life.

Frank has always worked. Even in retirement he kept himself busy, playing bowls, serving on the committee at the club and volunteering at the local community centre with a group of 'at risk' young men. Of course he had to give up his committee position at the bowls club once the dementia made itself known, but he was still playing bowls and helping young men discover the mechanical workings of cars when Fiona swooped in and took us to Sydney. When we get home I'll make sure he has something meaningful to do, even if it's only planting a vegetable garden.

I change into a fresh set of clothes. Now that the woman from the hippie shop in Bodalla has described our purchases I've gone back to my nondescript travelling clothes, but I haven't been able to convince Frank to do the same. He's in love with his new colourful clothing, which is ironic, really, considering how conservative he's always been. I remember how horrified he was when I bought him a safari suit for Christmas one year back in the 1970s. ('I'm sorry, love, I know they're all the rage but it's just not my cup of tea.') So his attachment to his orange tie-dyed pants is kind of amusing. Never mind, there's no harm in his attention-grabbing outfit out here. For the moment we can both relax.

Inside the house we meet Charlie, who is covered in tattoos. I pray that Frank won't say anything derogatory, but as Charlie shakes his hand Frank's only comment is, 'Good grip you've got on you there, son. Nice to meet a young fellow with a decent handshake.'

Brianna invites us to take a seat at the table and then proceeds to load it up with home-cooked food. There's meat pie, oven-roasted vegetables and home-baked bread. Frank claps his hands with glee. Over lunch we talk about the farm and how Brianna came to inherit it from her parents, who've taken off on a 'round-Australia' holiday after her mum was diagnosed with breast cancer. 'The minute she finished her treatment they were off,' Brianna says. 'It's always been their dream, and Mum decided life was too short to put it off any longer.' She walks to the fridge and removes a postcard from beneath a large, banana-shaped magnet. She hands me the postcard, which depicts a beautiful white sandy beach. 'They're in Airlie Beach right now. Been there for a couple of months. Mum says it's beautiful there.'

'You must miss them,' I say.

She shrugs. 'I do, but I'm happy for them. And this place keeps us busy.'

'Will they come back here to Lindenow?'

She shakes her head. 'Mum's always wanted to live on the coast. I think they'll eventually choose somewhere up north to settle, which will be great for them and will give us somewhere to go on holidays. So it's a win-win, right?'

I nod and think about the loving and healthy relationship that Brianna appears to have with her parents. I'm hit with a wave of sorrow – and shame – that I don't have that with Fiona.

I realise Brianna is still talking. '. . . and that's why when I heard about your road trip I wanted to help in any way I could. Our society just doesn't know how to deal with ageing properly. In other countries they look after their elders, care for them in their own homes and even revere them in some cultures. We shove people away in nursing homes like they're past their use by date. It's shocking. I really admire what you're doing, Shirley.' She nods her head at Frank, who's engaged Charlie in conversation about his tractor. 'I mean, look at this bloke. He doesn't need to be in a home. If he was living here he'd be out helping Charlie on the farm and keeping active. People need to be useful to be happy, don't you think?'

Brianna continues telling me her thoughts. She's got opinions on everything, from the healthcare system to education, and isn't shy about expressing them. Charlie appears to be a much gentler soul. He's talking to Frank in a calm, quiet voice, asking his opinion about mechanical things that I'm fairly certain he knows the answer to. As I watch them together I think about Andrew and what he would be like now. Would he and Frank have had lots in common? What would he look like? Would Frank have accepted it if he'd come home covered in tattoos like Charlie? Of course, Andrew would be years older than the boy Frank's sitting with now. He'd be fifty, a middle-aged man. Would he have married? Had children? I try to picture him as he would be now, but of course that's impossible.

Brianna asks if we'd like dessert and naturally Frank is up for it. I offer to help her in the kitchen, but Charlie says he's on dessert duty. He starts clearing the table and Frank gets up to help. I'm starting to think that my plan to keep Frank with me isn't crazy at all. In fact it's perfectly feasible. We'll have a garden he can work in and I can get him to help me with simple tasks like doing the dishes and making the bed. If I can get someone to sit with him while I go out to do the grocery shopping that's probably all the help I need with him right now. These past couple of days he's shown me that the man I've always known and loved is still in there. I won't give up on him.

Chapter 34

March 1994
Geelong

Shirley gasped as Fiona walked out into the living room in her wedding gown. The pale-pink silk dress had puffed sleeves, a fitted bodice (which showed off Fiona's waist beautifully) and a full skirt complete with a train. Fiona was modelling it with the headpiece and veil. She even had her wedding shoes on so that Shirley and Rita could get the whole picture.

The result was breathtaking.

Shirley had been mildly surprised when Fiona and Gary announced their engagement. They'd been living together for a couple of months and Shirley assumed that Fiona had decided to eschew the 'old-fashioned' institution of marriage – much to Frank's dismay. But one night Gary had popped the question and Fiona had said yes. She'd been sporting a ridiculously large diamond engagement ring for the past eighteen months. A huge waste of money, if you asked Frank. 'With the money they spent on that they could have just about put a deposit on a house,' he complained on more than one occasion.

'Oh well, Fiona likes it, and that's what matters,' Shirley would reply. Of course Fiona liked it. She'd picked it and paid for it herself, something that both Shirley and Fiona had neglected to share with Frank.

If the engagement surprised her, then the fact that Fiona wanted a full traditional wedding came as a complete shock. Shirley had been imagining a registry-office affair for her no-fuss daughter. Even an elopement wouldn't have come as a total bolt from the blue. She'd prepared herself for something simple – a barbecue in the backyard perhaps, the guests all in jeans – so when Fiona and Gary announced they were hoping to be married at St Mary's with a reception at Sladen House, you could have knocked Shirley over with a feather.

She'd taken Fiona aside at the engagement party. 'You don't have to get married in the church if you don't want to, love.'

Fiona shrugged. 'It'll make Dad happy. And Gary's parents are Catholic too, so they'll be pleased. Besides, I don't want to risk a garden wedding. What happens if it rains?'

Now here she stood before them. The perfect bride.

Shirley's eyes misted. 'Oh, darling, you are simply stunning.'

'Breathtaking,' Rita agreed. 'Let me get my camera out of the car so I can snap a few shots for posterity.' She placed the half-empty champagne flute she was holding on the coffee table and made for the front door.

Fiona grinned. 'Don't worry about it, Aunty Rita. Relax and finish your drink. Between the photographer and all our friends, I'm sure there'll be plenty of photos taken tomorrow.'

'True, but I want to remember this moment right now. It's special being here, just the three of us, don't you think?'

Fiona nodded. 'It really is. Okay. Go find your camera and then I'm going to change out of this get-up.'

Once Rita was out of earshot, Shirley said, 'Thank you for allowing Aunty Rita to be here for your final try-on. You mean the world to her, you know.'

Fiona nodded. 'I do know. She's always been like my second mother and I really wanted to acknowledge that.'

Rita returned, brandishing her old Kodak Instamatic, and the three of them spent the next five minutes giggling as they took turns to pose for the camera. 'It's a shame Dad's not here,' Fiona said. 'He could have snapped a shot of the three of us.'

'Oh, you know he didn't want to see you in your dress before the big day. He thinks it'll spoil the surprise,' Shirley said. The truth was slightly different. Frank hadn't quite reconciled himself to the fact that Fiona was getting married (it seemed there was no pleasing him where Gary was concerned), so Shirley had sent him off to visit her dad, rather than have him spoil Fiona's evening with his grumpiness.

Looking at her daughter now brought back memories of the night before her own wedding. How optimistic she'd been about the future back then. She could never have predicted the things that were ahead of her. She hoped that Fiona knew what she was in for.

'What's the matter, Mum? You look like you've got the weight of the world on your shoulders.'

Shirley shook her head and said the first thing that came to her. 'I'm just thinking about being with Nanna the night before my wedding. Oh, Fiona, she would have loved to see you like this.'

Fiona's eyes filled with tears. 'I know. I miss her so much.'

'Come on, you two, enough of that,' Rita interjected. 'I didn't know your nanna well but I do know she would want you' – she paused and looked at Shirley – '*both* of you, to be enjoying this evening, not sitting around being sad.'

Fiona nodded. 'You're right, of course. Mum, why don't you come and help me get out of this dress while Aunty Rita pours us another drink?'

'Good plan,' Rita said. 'Although if I have any more, I'll have to leave the car here overnight and walk home.'

'Dad can drive you home in it when he gets back. I'm sure he won't mind walking home from your place.'

Rita and Shirley exchanged a quick glance. They both knew Frank would be less than thrilled with that proposition. After all these years he tolerated Rita but that was about it. Still, he'd do anything for his little girl.

Rita smiled. 'Good plan, Fifi. Now go get out of that dress so we can celebrate properly.'

In Fiona's childhood bedroom Shirley carefully unbuttoned her daughter's dress and helped her out of it. She sat on the bed while Fiona threw on a T-shirt and wriggled back into her jeans. All day Shirley had been wrestling with herself over what she was about to say. On the one hand Fiona was a grown-up – much more mature than she had been on the eve of her wedding to Frank – on the other hand, Fiona was her daughter, and she deserved at least a modicum of truth about marriage from her mother before she took this monumental step.

'Darling, you know I love Gary—'

'If this is going to be a "we don't think he's good enough for you" speech, you can save your breath. I've made my choice.'

'No, no. Not at all. This is not about Gary. As I said, I love Gary.' It was true. He was a lovely young man. A little unambitious, maybe, but polite and respectful, and he clearly loved Fiona with all his heart. 'I just want to make sure that you're getting married for the right reasons.'

Fiona laughed. 'I'm not pregnant, Mum.'

Shirley shrugged. 'I wouldn't mind if you were, so long as you were happy about it, but that's not what I meant. I just don't want you to think that this is something you have to do to make Dad and me happy.'

'I'm not doing it for you.' She was beginning to sound annoyed.

Shirley hesitated for a moment before deciding to push on. She needed to say this. 'Good. I'm pleased. It's just that, well, marriage is a big step and I want you to be sure. If I'm being totally honest with you, I have to admit that I really didn't think too hard about marrying your father. It was what was expected of me – to get married and have children – and I did it without question. Not that it hasn't turned out well, of course, but still. These days you have so many other choices.'

'I know I do, and I'm choosing to get married *and* have a career. Those two things aren't mutually exclusive, you know. I won't be stuck at home with a child like you were. I know it was tricky for you when I was little, but these days men are much more involved in child-rearing, and there's always childcare.'

Shirley bit her lip at her daughter's casual use of the word childcare – as if it was something simple and expected, something that hadn't taken the blood, sweat and tears of the women in Shirley's generation to achieve so that the women who came after them could take it for granted. 'It wasn't just about access to childcare. I wanted to be involved in your life. I wanted you to know how loved you were.'

'I know you thought staying home with me was essential to my wellbeing, but it really wasn't. I would have turned out just fine if you'd gone off to work. In fact I might have been better off if you'd been a less *involved* parent. I mean, did you ever think about the pressure it put on me, knowing that your happiness depended entirely on me being the perfect daughter?'

The accusation stung. 'That's not true. I never put pressure on you. I only ever wanted the best for you.'

'Exactly. I had to be the best at all times. If I wasn't achieving at school, if I had problems with my friends or boys, it wasn't just me who was miserable. You were bereft at the slightest indication that there might be an issue. In primary school I used to make up stories about being popular just to please you.'

Was this true? Of course she'd wanted Fiona to be happy, but had her mothering been excessive? She'd been so determined that her relationship with Rita wouldn't impact her family life that perhaps she'd overcompensated. She'd run herself ragged at times, trying to be a perfect wife, mother and lover. Now it was apparent that those efforts had all been in vain. 'Oh, Fi, I never meant for you to feel that way. All mothers want the best for their child.'

'I know that, but most mothers have more than one child.'

Shirley's eyes began to water and Fiona's face reddened at the sight.

'I'm sorry, Mum, that was uncalled for. I didn't mean ... I wasn't thinking.'

'It's all right,' Shirley said stiffly. 'Dad and I would have loved to give you a sibling.'

Fiona's voice softened. 'I know that, Mum, and I realise how hard that must have been for you. But no one ever seemed to realise that it was hard for me too. I was all you had. I had to be good enough to make up for what you'd lost. At least Dad had his work, but your world revolved around me. Maybe if you'd gone out and got a job, things would have been different. Maybe you would have been happier.'

'I don't know what you mean. I was always happy being your mum.'

'That's my point, right there. I didn't – I *don't* – want to be responsible for your happiness. You need to be in charge of that. I want my kids to know that their mother has her own life, independent from them. That way they'll be free to be whoever they want.'

Shirley looked at her feet. Fiona was right. She'd failed at the one thing that mattered most to her. 'I'm sorry,' she whispered. 'I did the best I could.'

Fiona wrapped her arms around her. 'Oh, Mum, I'm sorry too. I shouldn't have said anything. They say weddings bring out all sorts of emotions. I just want you to know that I'm fine. I'm living my life my way, just like you and Aunty Rita have always told me to.'

'Well, that's settled, then. Obviously you know what's best for you. We probably should go and have that drink.'

Fiona kissed her cheek. 'You know, Mum, maybe it's time you took some of your own advice.'

'What do you mean?'

'Maybe it's time you started to live life the way *you* want to. Maybe worry a little bit less about what people expect of you.'

Shirley smiled. 'I thought I was supposed to be the one giving out the advice here. How did you get to be so smart?'

Fiona shrugged. 'I don't know. Maybe I take after my mum after all.'

Chapter 35

Thursday

After lunch Charlie takes Frank out to have a look at the tractor they've been discussing while Brianna sets me up at her computer. She says to relax and take my time doing whatever I need to, as she has some chores to take care of.

I go straight to the Sherbet message board and scroll through the messages. There is an entire thread dedicated to #oldsontherun and I'm touched by the number of supportive messages there are for us. Many messages are offering practical help, and I take note of those who might be useful to me once we get to Geelong. Obviously it won't take long for Fiona to discover our whereabouts once we get to Rita's house. In fact, my plan is to call her as soon as we get there and let her know what's going on. We can't run forever.

I check my personal messages and, as expected, there's one there from Lou.

Hi Nan,

Hopefully by the time you read this you will have made it safely to Bandit and Chazar's farm. You just need to keep a low profile for one more day and then you and Papa will be home!

I overheard Mum talking to Dad last night. (BTW, Dad's staying here at the moment. Not sure if that's permanent or not because as usual nobody tells me anything. When I asked Mum she just said, 'We'll see.') Anyway, I heard her saying that if the police can't do anything she's going to pursue legal options.

My stomach churns as I read these words. I should have known it would come to this. Part of me fumes at her audacity. How dare she think she knows better than me? But then, in a lot of ways, this is a mess of my own making. I've kept secrets from Fiona for her whole life, and I'm beginning to see how that's contributed to the distance between us. I can't blame her for distrusting me.

Maybe I should have tried harder to rebuild our relationship while I was living with her in Sydney, but my focus was on Frank's welfare. Once I was well enough to start thinking clearly about things I raised the issue of going back home.

'You can't go home, Mum. You know there's nowhere to go to.'

'Not to the old house, of course, but there's no reason we can't buy something else in the area. I'd like to get the ball rolling as soon as possible.'

'I don't think you're well enough to even be thinking about this, Mum. Your doctor says you shouldn't have any stress. Let's talk about it again in a few weeks.'

She fobbed me off for weeks before finally telling me that there was no way that she would agree to Frank leaving the nursing home.

'I know you think you're fine, but you're simply not capable of looking after Dad anymore. After what happened I really don't think there's any question of that fact.'

'That wasn't my fault. I didn't mean to leave him on his own for that long. It was an emergency.'

'But you did leave him on his own. That was a huge error of judgement; one that Dad almost paid for with his life. I can't risk something like that happening again. Besides, Dad's getting the best of care. You don't have to worry about him now.'

'What do you mean by that?'

'You can please yourself from now on. Won't that be nice? Maybe once you're fully recovered you could go on some sort of holiday. A cruise perhaps? Perhaps one of your sewing friends would like to go with you. And if you stay here with us you won't have to bother about getting anyone to water your garden.'

'I get seasick,' I said, before walking away.

Apparently 'pleasing myself' didn't include having any say over where Frank and I lived. Is it any wonder I took matters into my own hands?

Now I've proved to myself that I can look after Frank. If she wants a fight, I'm ready. I have the financial means to battle her in court if that's what it takes. And it seems I have a team of supporters who can help out in practical ways. Surely that has to count for something.

I go back to Lou's message and bang out a quick reply telling her not to worry, all will be well, and assuring her that her mother has our best interests at heart. The last thing I want to do is drive a wedge between the two of them.

As I'm finishing up my message Frank and Charlie come back inside.

'What have you two been up to?' I ask.

Charlie gives Frank a gentle pat on the shoulder. 'This man's a genius. I've been having trouble with my tractor for weeks and Frank managed to fix it in under an hour.' He turns his head to look directly at Frank. 'Mate, I should give you a full-time job as a farmhand.'

Frank beams at the compliment and his happiness is infectious. I can't help but grin back at him.

'Frank was telling me he grew up around here,' Charlie says.

'Up the road a bit, on Rubys Lane,' Frank interjects.

It never ceases to amaze me how Frank can't remember what happened yesterday, but remembers the distant past with such clarity. 'Yes, that's right.'

'So I was wondering if it would be okay to take Frank, and you too of course, Shirley, for a short drive around the place. Frank can give me a bit of a history lesson and I can show him how the place has changed.'

I hesitate for a moment. We're so close to home now that I'm reluctant to take any unnecessary risks, but Frank's eyes are sparkling with anticipation and I don't want to disappoint him.

As if reading my mind, Charlie says, 'We'll be careful, I promise. We can even stay in the car the whole time if you like. If anyone happens to ask any questions I'll just say you're my aunt and uncle visiting from Melbourne. But we're not likely to come across anyone else where we're going anyway.'

This may be the very last time Frank is in his home town. How can I deny him the chance to visit his childhood home? 'Okay, but on one condition. Frank, you need to get out of those loud clothes. I don't want you drawing any unnecessary attention to us.'

Frank grimaces, but agrees. 'Righto, Boss, if you say so.' He looks at Charlie. 'She's a hard taskmaster this one. Would hate to be her husband.'

Charlie chuckles. 'Do what the lady says, Frank. That's my advice, for what it's worth.'

Once Frank's changed his clothes (under my strict supervision) the three of us pile into Charlie's big ute for an excursion. Brianna has more work to do around the farm so she waves us farewell, telling us to have fun. Now we're committed I'm actually excited to see the place where Frank grew up. We've visited Bairnsdale a few times in our married life but I've never seen Frank's childhood home.

We turn right out of the farm gate and head down a long, narrow dirt road with miles of farmland on either side. Eventually we come to a sealed crossroad and turn onto that. It's beautiful countryside, reasonably green considering the drought that's plagued the eastern states these past couple of years. I say as much to Charlie and he nods.

'Yeah, we've had some decent rain this spring, thank God. Next worry is the bushfire season, though. They reckon it's going to be a long, tough one.'

'Oh, the thought of that must be terrifying.'

He shrugs. 'All part of living in the bush. We take precautions, prepare as well as we can and hope for the best.' He flicks on the indicator and slows to make a left-hand turn. In the passenger seat beside him Frank calls out, 'Turn here, turn here. This is it.'

The lane is gravel and littered with potholes, so I'm glad we're in the four-wheel drive and not the Kombi. We drive for a bit until the old house in the distance becomes more visible.

'There it is. Granny's house,' Frank calls.

Charlie gets as close as he can to it without trespassing on private property and then pulls up. We all get out of the car and lean against the post-and-wire fence.

'Is it still the same?' I ask.

Frank nods. 'Yeah, I reckon, except for that big square room out the back. They must have added that at some point. It was only a tiny place when I lived here. Two bedrooms. One for Granny and Pop and one for us kids.'

'Happy memories here, Frank?' Charlie asks.

Frank nods. 'Here, yeah, I guess. We were a wild bunch. Patty and I used to walk to school with the Murphy boys who lived up the hill a little. We'd sure get into some scrapes along the way.'

Charlie looks impressed. 'You walked all that way every day?'

'Pffft, wasn't that far. Took us about three-quarters of an hour. Bit more, maybe, because of the mucking around. We were dirt-poor back then but happy enough.' He chuckles. 'I remember thinking we were the richest family around because we had a gold door.'

'A gold door?' Charlie asks.

Frank laughs again. 'Yeah. When Pop finished a tin of tobacco he used to stick the gold foil liner on the door. After a while the whole door was covered in them.'

After the farmhouse on Rubys Lane we drive into town to look at the school, which has changed 'a bit', according to Frank, and the church, which has not. We drive past the pub and Frank reminisces about nights spent there celebrating football wins. 'I never was much of a drinker, but those nights with all the boys together, well, they were a lot of fun. I really felt part of something then, like I truly belonged.' Our last stop is a visit to a bridge over the Mitchell River that Charlie wants to show Frank. There's not another car in sight, so we park in the middle of the bridge for a moment. I'm taken with the beautiful vista but Frank's gone quiet. I lean forward in my seat and touch his shoulder. 'It's pretty here,' I say.

'Hmm,' he replies without turning to look at me. He points in front of him. 'I used to live up there, on Rodericks Road, with my Aunty Doris, old bitch that she was.'

I can't help but draw in a breath at his language. Not that I haven't heard, or even used, worse in my time, but coming from Frank it manages to shock me.

'After Granny died they split me and Patty up. Patty went to Aunty Gwen, because she had little kids that needed looking after. I got sent to work on Aunty Doris's dairy farm.'

'How old were you, Frank?' Charlie asks.

'I reckon I would have been about ten.'

'Working on a dairy farm's hard yakka for anyone, let alone a ten-year-old.'

Frank shrugs. 'Truth be told, it wasn't the work that bothered me; it was the lack of school. The old bag said I could only stay with her if I worked full time, so she pulled me out of school. The teacher – Mr Davies, his name was – he came up here one night with the town copper to tell Aunty Doris the law said I had to go to school unless I was sick. So I got to go one day a week and she'd send me with a note saying I'd been sick the other days. That way no one could do anything about it. We had sport on Fridays, so I'd beg her to let me go on that day and she'd hold it over my head all week. She had a real mean streak, that one. She'd use the horse whip on you if you stepped an inch out of line.'

My hand covers my mouth as my heart tears at the thought of my sweet Frank being treated so cruelly. All these years and he never said a word about this. I knew he'd lived with his aunt on a dairy farm, but no more than that.

Charlie shakes his head. 'How long did you live there for?'

'I ran away when I was twelve and Doris never bothered to come after me. I didn't go far, just to the Murphy's place. Old Man Murphy contacted my granny's sister, who was a well-to-do lady, and she sent me off to boarding school in Sale. Patty too. I loved it there. Everyone complained that the Brothers were harsh, but after what I'd been through it was heaven.'

'But you came back here, didn't you?' I asked. Frank was living out this way when we met.

'Yeah, I did. The boarding school only lasted a few years. I came back to the Murphy's place for school holidays. The summer after I turned fifteen I got a job painting houses with Mr Murphy's cousin. I lived at Mrs Grumley's boarding house in Bairnsdale for years after that. She was like a mother to me. Then when I turned twenty-one I rented a little cottage out this way because it was cheap. A few years after that I met my Shirl.

She was the one. I knew it right from the start. She was a looker, but it wasn't just that. She dressed well and spoke nicely. I knew she was from a good family. And more than anything, that's what I wanted for myself, a family. I knew she'd make a good mother.'

Charlie turns and gives me a tender look, as if he understands how hard this must be for me to hear. And it is, but probably not for the reasons Charlie might be imagining.

Chapter 36

August 2008
Geelong

'Open your eyes now!'

Shirley obeyed Rita's command and saw an iced sponge cake lit up with at least two dozen candles on the table in front of her. She smiled. 'All those candles make me feel old.'

Rita chuckled. 'You're lucky I didn't put the whole sixty-eight on.' Then she started to sing 'Happy Birthday' in her off-key, gravelly voice and Shirley couldn't help but laugh. 'Pink icing, I see. My favourite.'

'Of course, what else? Now hurry up and blow out the candles so we can cut it.'

Shirley did as she was told and then took the knife that Rita handed her and cut into the cake.

'Don't touch the bottom or you'll have to kiss the nearest girl.'

'Too late.'

'Oh darn. Looks like you'll just have to kiss me then.'

Shirley complied with a peck and a giggle and then leaned in to kiss Rita properly. 'Can we eat it now?'

'Of course.'

After the cake Rita brought out a pile of beautifully wrapped presents and Shirley rubbed her hands together in excited anticipation. She had always loved birthdays, probably because her mother had made such a fuss of them when she and Wendy were little girls. The first few birthdays after her mother's death had been so painful she'd told Frank she was too old to be bothered with all the nonsense that went along with celebrating the event, and Frank was only too happy to comply. But Rita had persisted, taking over where her mother had left off. And as Fiona matured she stepped up and made an effort each year too, so these days Shirley looked forward to her special day.

This year Fiona was flying down with the girls to spend the weekend with her. Time with her beautiful granddaughters – and her daughter of course – was the best gift she could possibly imagine. Except that Frank hadn't seemed all that excited when she'd told him. Actually, he'd been downright grumpy about it. Which seemed to be par for the course these days. Frank had been almost unbearable to live with these past six months. He seemed irritated by the smallest things and frequently lost his temper – not usually with her, but still, the outbursts were getting harder and harder to live with. And despite having all the time in the world on his hands since his retirement, he seemed to be doing less and less around the house. Last time she and Rita had gone away on holiday together she'd come home to a pigsty. She'd cleaned up the mess and said nothing. If this was Frank's silent protest at her absence then so be it. She wasn't going to take the bait.

Some days she wondered if this new behaviour was because he knew about her relationship with Rita. After all these years they were still using discretion, although Shirley had to admit it wouldn't be too hard to work out that she and Rita were much more than friends. They'd dropped the pretence that their trips away were with the fictitious 'sewing ladies' two decades ago.

It wasn't Frank she was worried about fooling back then; it was Fiona. The older her daughter got, the more questions she asked, and Shirley knew that sooner or later she'd work out that she'd never once met any of these so-called 'sewing friends'. So one year Shirley had casually mentioned to Frank that none of the other sewing ladies could make the trip away this year and it would just be her and Rita. Neither Fiona nor Frank had batted an eyelid. Why would they? These days lots of women went on holidays with their friends. There was nothing suspicious about it. At the time Shirley wondered why she'd bothered concocting the more elaborate lie in the first place. Holidays with Rita became a standard annual event and occasionally they managed to get in the odd weekend away or overnighter in between. Frank had been unfailingly good-natured about the whole thing. But last time when she'd arrived home to a mess and the silent treatment, she waited for the accusation to come. In a way she would have welcomed it. Fiona was middle-aged now, with a family of her own, and would be horrified of course, but would cope. And Frank – well, she didn't know how he would cope. It would be the end of their marriage, of course, but after more than forty years of dedicated service to him she figured she'd paid her dues. Still, thinking about him in their house all by himself made her stomach churn.

Rita had long since given up asking her to leave Frank. Well, almost. Every year when Rita's birthday was approaching Shirley would ask her what she wanted and her answer was always the same. 'Move in with me.' But then she'd laugh and say she really wanted the latest book by Helen Garner, or the box set of whatever TV show she was currently addicted to.

There'd been that one time, just after Fiona's wedding, when the issue had almost cost them their relationship. Rita had waited until their annual holiday to bring up the topic.

'Can we talk?'

It was an odd question. After five nights away together it seemed to Shirley that the two of them had done plenty of talking. 'Of course, my darling. What's on your mind?'

Rita handed her a mug of tea and settled herself on the couch beside her.

'I've been patient, Shirley, but lately our living situation has started to get to me. Being here with you is wonderful, and it makes me want more. I understood you staying with Frank when Fiona was little, but she's a married woman with her own life now. Don't you think it's time for us to stop living a lie?'

A lie? Was that what her life was? It didn't feel that way to Shirley. She loved Rita and she loved Frank too. Being with both of them seemed like the only solution to her. 'Rita, you know I love you . . .'

'But?'

'But it's not that simple.'

'I love you, you love me. Doesn't seem that complicated to me.'

Shirley sighed. 'What will people think?'

Rita's eyes flashed with anger. 'I don't give a fuck what people think.'

'I wish that I didn't either, but I can't help but worry. I keep thinking about my dad and sister. I'm sure they'd disown me if they knew. And I really have no idea what Fiona would make of us being together. There's a very real chance we could lose her.'

'Fiona's a modern young woman. She'll understand.'

'I don't know about that. I think she'll see our relationship as a betrayal of Frank – which it is – and she'll punish me for that. She's always been a daddy's girl.'

'You're underestimating her.'

Maybe Rita was right, but there was one person's reaction she was completely sure of. Frank would be totally heartbroken. 'I can't leave Frank all alone.'

'Why not? Why are Frank's feelings more important to you than mine?'

'Oh, my darling, they're not. But you have a full life without me. You love me, but you don't need me. It's not the same for Frank. I can't bear to think of him rattling around in our house on his own. He's put up with a lot from me over the years, Rita. He's a good man and he doesn't deserve to be abandoned.'

Rita didn't reply. Instead she placed her mug on the coffee table and headed to the bedroom, where she pulled out her suitcase.

'Where are you going?'

'I need to be on my own to think for a bit. I told you once I wouldn't spend my life being your second choice, and yet it seems that I have. I don't know if I want to do that anymore.'

Shirley didn't see her again until their flight home two days later, when Rita tearfully fell into her arms at the departure gate. 'I want to hate you, Shirley, but I can't. You said I didn't need you, but you're wrong about that. I can't imagine a future without you in it.'

Rita's voice jolted her out of her reminiscence. 'Well, come on, aren't you going to open them?'

Shirley grinned. 'Give me a minute. I'm taking a moment to appreciate all this beautiful wrapping. You did a good job.'

'I can't lie. I took them to Sue's place and had her do them. You know she's got a gift for decorating.'

This was no surprise. It wasn't as if Rita was known for her patience or attention to detail when it came to this sort of thing. She was far more likely to grab a gift bag from the supermarket than to spend time meticulously matching paper and ribbons. 'Well, thank you for taking the trouble to get Sue involved. I appreciate the effort.'

'You're welcome. Now please open them.'

Shirley carefully unwrapped each gift: the newest Kate Atkinson book, a gorgeous silk scarf, her favourite vanilla-scented hand cream and a leather handbag she'd admired when they'd had a weekend away in Sydney a couple of months before. 'The bag! Good grief, Rita, wasn't it expensive? You shouldn't have.'

Rita hugged herself and grinned. 'Are you surprised? I went back and got it when you were browsing in the bookshop. Remember I said I had a headache?'

'Oh, you sly thing. I thought you were just bored.' She leaned in and kissed her. 'Thank you again, my darling. These are all just beautiful. So, what are your plans for the weekend? Will you come by on Saturday night for the birthday dinner? I know Fiona and the girls would love to see you.'

'I don't think so, Shirl. I don't want to intrude. It doesn't feel right, stepping into Frank's domain like that.'

'I know we don't normally see each other on the day, but this year's different. It's not like Frank and I will be on our own.'

'Still . . .'

'I know – why don't you pop by for coffee and cake afterwards? You don't have to stay long. I want you to see how big the girls are getting.'

'If you insist, but just for a little bit, okay?'

'Okay, good. Well now that's settled, I have a present for you.'

'For me? But it's not *my* birthday.'

'Which makes it even better, right?'

Rita laughed. 'I guess so. All right then, where is it?'

'Right in front of you.'

'I don't understand.'

'Me, my darling. I'm giving myself to you.'

Rita laughed. 'Oh, I see. I wasn't sure you'd . . . I mean, don't you have to get home soon?'

Shirley shook her head. 'Not like that. Goodness, Rita,' she joked, 'get your mind out of the gutter.'

'Well if not *that*, what are you talking about?'

'I'm leaving him, Rita. You finally get your wish. I've made up my mind that I'll tell him just as soon as the girls go home. So you might want to start clearing out a few drawers, because this time next week I'll be here for good.'

At first Rita didn't respond. Then she began to cry. 'Are you serious? Please don't mess with me, Shirley. I'd come to terms with the fact that it was never going to happen.'

'I'm serious. I've always loved you and wanted to be with you, you know that. But I never wanted what we had to hurt my family. And Frank has always been so good to me, such a devoted husband, that I just didn't think it was fair to break his heart. But lately things have changed. I'm not really sure why – perhaps he's guessed at what's really going on between us – but for whatever reason I feel Frank no longer loves me the way he used to. That being the case, I think it's time he and I set each other free.'

In hindsight, inviting Rita to her family party had been a mistake. Frank made it clear he wasn't impressed with her presence and was borderline hostile to her from the minute she arrived. Then poor little Lila spilled a drink and he yelled at her like a madman. Of course she started crying and Fiona had to spend ages settling her, so the night ended on rather a sour note.

The next morning Frank behaved as if nothing had happened. He seemed surprised when Lila was wary of him. He managed to win her over with a promise of ice cream later and right now he was playing a game of hide-and-seek in the backyard with all three girls. Sometimes it was as if he was two different people.

'Sit down, Mum, and I'll make you a cuppa.'

'I'll make it, love. You're the guest, after all.'

'I hardly think I'm a guest. Please, Mum, you've been bustling around ever since we got here. I'd like you to just sit still for a bit so we can talk about something.'

'All right then.'

Fiona put the kettle on and then sat beside her at the table. 'Mum, have you noticed Dad's behaviour is a bit, well, odd?'

Shirley sighed. 'I'm sorry about him yelling at Lila last night. I honestly don't know what got into him. Maybe he was put out because I invited Rita to a family party. You know how he is about family.'

Fiona nodded. 'Mmm, but it's not just him yelling at Lila. It's all sorts of things. I've noticed that when I talk to him on the phone he tells me the same stories over and over – sometimes in the same phone call.'

'We're getting older.' Shirley laughed. 'I probably do the same thing.'

Fiona shook her head as she got up to make the tea. 'You might repeat yourself occasionally, but not the way Dad does.'

Shirley thought about what she was saying. Frank did have a tendency to repeat himself lately. She'd just assumed it was because now that he'd retired he didn't have as much going on in his life, so he didn't have as much to talk about. 'Perhaps it's because he doesn't see you all the time, love. He forgets what he's told you last time.'

Fiona placed a cup of tea in front of her. 'But that doesn't explain the other changes in his behaviour, like the angry outbursts. It's not like Dad at all. He's always been so measured and calm. I can barely remember having an argument with him, ever.'

Unlike me. Shirley thought about the dozens of ways she and Fiona had clashed over the years. It had been a source of major irritation to her that Frank never backed her up. 'Come on now, you two,' he'd say, 'there's no need for all this unpleasantness.'

'And there was all that nasty business at the bowls club,' Fiona continued.

Shirley didn't like the way this conversation was heading. 'That was all a misunderstanding. Your father made the decision to step away from the committee of his own accord.'

'I've been worried for a few months now and this visit has confirmed my fears. Mum, I think we have to face the fact that there's something wrong with Dad and we need to get him some help. I'm going to call Gary and tell him I'm not coming home just yet. I want to take Dad to the doctor next week to get to the bottom of this.'

'So it's confirmed?' Rita asked.

Shirley blinked back tears. 'Yes. Alzheimer's disease. It's still in the early stages. The doctor said it's hard to predict how rapidly it will progress. Some people progress slowly and can live for up to twenty years with it. Others deteriorate quickly and are gone within a year or two. In Frank's case, it's been diagnosed early so there are lots of interventions we can try to slow the progress of the disease and to make sure he has good quality of life. But of course this means I can't . . .' She couldn't hold in the tears any longer.

Rita took her into her arms. 'Shh, it's okay. I understand. Everything is going to be okay. We'll deal with this together.'

Chapter 37

Thursday

Brianna has cooked a full roast dinner and Frank is like a kid in a lolly shop, helping himself to seconds of everything. He seems very settled here, the most relaxed I've seen him since we left Sydney. Whether it's the familiar landscape that's soothed him or the company of the delightful young people we're with, I'm not sure. Either way, he's happy and I feel relatively calm. Tomorrow will be a big day, but I'm confident of getting Frank back to his beach. Beyond that, I'm not sure what will happen. I know Fiona will come for him. Whether or not I can stop her remains to be seen. One way or another, tomorrow night I will sleep in Rita's bed, and the thought of that brings me great comfort.

The scent of baked apple and cinnamon wafts from the kitchen as we eat the first course. 'Is that apple pie I smell?' Frank asks.

'Indeed it is,' Brianna says with a grin on her face. 'But I won't be offended if you can't fit it in, Frank.' She winks at me and laughs.

'Oh, I'll make room, don't you worry about that.' Frank pats his belly. 'I have a special stomach for dessert. There's always room for apple pie.'

Everyone laughs and Charlie gets up to clear our empty plates.

'Oh, Shirley,' Brianna says, 'I almost forgot! Lulu – sorry, I mean Lou – messaged me to remind you that her mum is going to be on *News in Focus* tonight.' She glances at her watch. 'We'd better get a wriggle on with that pie. It starts in twenty minutes.'

Once we've eaten dessert – two helpings of pie for Frank – Charlie turns on the TV for us and then retreats to the kitchen to help Brianna with the dishes. 'Call out when she's on,' he says.

We sit through stories about shonky builders and exorbitant council rates before they announce Fiona's segment is up next. Brianna and Charlie join us in the living room, and Charlie turns up the volume as the segment comes on.

'Tonight we're talking to Fiona Stevens, daughter of Frank and Shirley Sullivan, the so-called "Runaway Seniors". For viewers who might have missed the beginning of this unfolding story, here's Clay Barry with some background.'

They cross to a reporter standing outside Sunset Lodge and he talks about the day Frank failed to return after being taken by me to a fictitious family party. Then he talks to some of Frank's carers.

'Mr Sullivan is a lovely old man. Very sweet. He adores his wife and would do anything for her.'

'Frank's a sweetheart. He's easily upset, though, and can get agitated when he's feeling stressed. I just hope he's okay.'

'His wife? She seemed nice enough. Well-dressed lady. Not a hair out of place, and lovely manners too. Always spoke pleasantly to the staff.'

They cut away from the nursing home then and show footage of the community centre. The reporter gives a list of all the courses I've taken there since I moved to Sydney. At first I seethe at this invasion of my privacy, but then my heart sinks because I know what is coming next. There's Ollie leaving the centre and heading for his car. He puts his hand out and shakes his head, unwilling to answer the barrage of questions directed at him. He steadfastly refuses to be drawn in until the reporter asks:

'In your opinion, is Shirley Sullivan mentally stable?'

Ollie pauses and looks straight at the camera.

'Shirley Sullivan is one of the smartest and most sensible people I know.'

My heart squeezes at his words. *Thank you, Ollie.*

The reporter talks about our 'escape' from the police in Narooma. Mostly it's a rehash of older reports, but there is one piece of new information.

'Yesterday police were hopeful that the pair would soon be located after Mrs Sullivan's phone was tracked to a property in south-east Queensland. A forty-six-year-old male resident of the property was questioned and released without charge. There's some speculation Mrs Sullivan may have intentionally planted the phone in the man's ute in an effort to conceal the route she was taking.'

Clay Barry grins as he throws back to the host in the studio, and I can't help but smile too. My plan worked, didn't it? Not bad for a 'little old lady'.

The host of *News in Focus* isn't smiling, though. Her face is deadly serious as she addresses my daughter.

'Welcome, Fiona. Both your parents have been missing since Sunday and you say you have grave fears for their wellbeing.'

'Yes, that's correct. As your reporter just explained, my father suffers from dementia. He finds unfamiliar environments extremely distressing. He takes a range of medications for his condition. My mother has a serious heart condition and needs daily medication to manage this.'

I let out an irritated sigh. I had a minor heart episode brought on by shock. I had surgery to correct it, and I'm perfectly fine now.

'Fiona, at first there were fears that your parents had met with some sort of misadventure, but there have been several reported sightings of them in recent days. As strange as it is to be saying this about senior citizens, it seems that they have simply run away from home. Can you give us any insight as to why that might be?'

'My mum has never really come to terms with my father being in a nursing home. I'm sure she believes she is doing the right thing by taking him away from there, but unfortunately her actions put them both at risk.'

'I think I know that woman on the telly,' says Frank.

'Shh,' I say, trying to hear the host's next question. Frank glowers at me, but quietens down.

'Would you care to explain further? From all reports they are a wily pair. Exactly how are they at risk?'

'Well, as I mentioned, my father has Alzheimer's disease and is very frail.'

Frail? She wouldn't say that if she'd seen the dinner he'd just wolfed down.

'He's prone to wandering and he can make poor decisions at times. My mother is not capable of caring for him. He was placed in a nursing home after a serious incident where he almost died while in my mother's care. I understand her desire to look after him, but the fact is she's almost eighty—'

I've only just turned seventy-nine. I'm not 'almost eighty'.

'—and not in good health herself. She's simply not capable of being my father's sole carer. In any case, I have medical guardianship of my father, which means that legally I'm the one who gets to make the decisions about his care. My choice is to have him cared for in a facility near my home so that I can maintain a close relationship with him while overseeing his care.'

'There seems to some support for your mother's actions. In fact, social media has been flooded with messages of support for their adventure. The idea of two pensioners on the run seems to have captured the imagination of the Australian public. What would you like to say in response to that?'

'My parents are good people, not criminals, and I understand the temptation people might feel to turn a blind eye if they see them, or even to actively help them to avoid detection. My mother can be extremely charming when she chooses to be, and I'm sure she has been able to talk people into helping her along the way—'

I glance at Brianna and Charlie, but their faces are unreadable. What if Fiona has convinced them Frank is in danger? Will they call the police as soon as we go back to the granny flat?

'—however, I would like the public to know that my father is a resident in a very highly regarded care facility. He is well looked after and we visit him regularly. I know with all the dodgy nursing homes in the news lately it's probably easy to think that he's been mistreated, but that is definitely not the case. He is very much loved and missed by me, and his granddaughters, and we just want to see him – and Mum, of course – safely back home where they belong.'

Well, my darling girl, we are on the same page there at least. All I want is to take your father back where we belong.

'Thank you for your time, Fiona. And just a reminder to our viewers to please call the number displayed on the screen below if you have any information about Frank and Shirley. Fiona is offering a reward for information leading to their whereabouts. The last reported sighting of Frank and Shirley Sullivan was yesterday evening at the Cann River camping area. At that time they were driving a blue Kombi campervan like the one pictured on your screen now. We hope this adventurous pair can be reunited with their family soon.'

'Well,' says Charlie, 'that's concerning.'

My heart flutters in anticipation of what he might say next. Has he changed his mind about hiding us overnight? 'What do you mean?' I ask. 'What's concerning?'

'They know about the Kombi. It's probably not safe for you to drive it back to Geelong.'

‘Oh,’ I say, relieved for a moment that he’s not about to turn us in. But then I realise what he is saying. The public will be on the lookout for us now. ‘Oh . . .’

‘Perhaps there is another way,’ Brianna says. ‘We could drive you to Bairnsdale and put you on the train. I can book the tickets online for you if you like.’

I nod slowly, trying to think of how this might work. I haven’t caught the Geelong train for years. What will happen when we get to Geelong station? Will we be able to get a cab to the beach from there? Will the taxi driver wait for us? What if he recognises us? Maybe we can get one of those new Uber things. But I don’t know how. Maybe Brianna knows . . .

‘What about your nan’s old car?’ Charlie looks at Brianna. ‘It’s just sitting there in the shed.’

Brianna looks unsure. ‘Um, I don’t know about that, Charlie.’

‘It still goes okay. It’ll be fine.’

I sense Brianna’s reluctance and, as much as I want to borrow the car, I don’t want to put pressure on her when she’s been so kind already. But I am desperate to find a solution. ‘I’m happy to buy it from you. I wouldn’t expect you to just give up a car for nothing.’

She smiles and shakes her head. ‘It’s not the money. It’s just, well, I was really close to my nan. She always loved me and accepted me just the way I was. Even when I was a rebellious teenager getting into trouble all over the place I could always count on Nan to take my side. I know this sounds stupid, but sometimes I go and sit in her car just to feel close to her again.’

‘That’s not stupid at all,’ I say softly.

‘What if we drove you there?’ Charlie offers, sweet boy that he is.

But I can’t in good conscience accept his offer. Not after I’ve seen how Ollie’s being harassed. I couldn’t bear to be the cause of trouble for Charlie and Brianna too. ‘Thank you, but I won’t allow you to do that, Charlie. You could get into trouble. The Kombi's got us this far. Frank and I will just have to take our chances.'

'What if you just borrowed the car?' Brianna says.

Charlie looks confused. 'How would that work?'

'Shirley could take the car tomorrow to get home and then, in a week or two, when all this has settled down, we can drive her Kombi back to her and swap the cars over. It'll be a nice weekend away for us.'

'That's a great idea,' I say.

'Right,' says Charlie, 'that's settled then. I'll just pop out to the shed and give her the once-over. Make sure she's in good working order. Coming, Frank?'

Frank rubs his hands together. 'Too right I am. I'm up for anything.'

Chapter 38

June 2018
Geelong

Shirley opened the sliding door leading to the backyard and looked down at the vegetable patch where Frank was kneeling. Weeding, she presumed, but who knew? Maybe he was planting. He'd lost all sense of what needed to be planted when, but what did it matter? So long as he was happily occupied she didn't mind. 'Frank, I'm just going up the shops for a minute. I won't be long. Just going to grab some ingredients so I can make us some lamb shank soup.'

Frank didn't look up. She sighed and walked down the concrete path to where he sat. 'Frank, did you hear me?'

He waved his hand dismissively. 'Yes, yes, soup. I'm busy here.'

'Okay, love. I won't be long, I promise.' She went back into the house, made sure the front door was deadlocked so Frank couldn't easily wander off into the street, and then grabbed her handbag and keys. Frank looked like he'd be occupied for a while now – he could spend hours digging in that garden – so she had time to drop by Rita's place on the way to the shops. Rita had been feeling poorly for a few days. 'You need to go to the doctor,' Shirley had told her when she'd called yesterday to say she wouldn't be round for lunch.

In the years since Frank's diagnosis their routine had changed. Now Rita visited Shirley's house on a daily basis so she could help out with Frank. She arrived mid-morning and stayed until early evening most days. On Friday afternoons a carer came in to give Shirley a break and this was now the only time they had alone together. Shirley felt guilty that Rita was making such a sacrifice for her, but Rita simply said, 'That's what love is – being there for each other in times of need.'

Shirley had to admit these past ten years would have been hell without her. Especially recently. Frank had been fairly stable for quite some time after his diagnosis. He'd had every type of intervention possible – medication, physical therapy, art and music therapy, and more. Rita made sure they were across the very latest treatments and, as a consequence, the progression of the disease was slow in Frank. So much so that Shirley began to wonder if he would defy his prognosis, but eventually the deterioration came. The past twelve months had been particularly difficult. The medications had ceased to have much effect and Frank forgot how to do many of the things he loved. Things like reading the newspaper and going out for unaccompanied walks became a thing of the past. He grieved these losses in his life and at times his frustration manifested in temper outbursts, not unlike the ones he'd experienced when he was first diagnosed.

Rita was a godsend. Her years of nursing came in handy, especially when Frank was being cantankerous. She didn't put up with any rubbish from him and seemed to know just what to say or do to keep him in line. Frank had actually become quite fond of Rita these past few months.

Yesterday, Rita had called to say she was going to sleep for a few hours and wouldn't be over as usual. 'I'm going to take some Panadol and have a good rest – see if I can knock this thing on the head.' She laughed at Shirley's insistence she see her GP. 'It's just a headache, my love. I probably need to get new glasses, that's all.'

But today she hadn't been answering her phone and Shirley was beginning to worry. Hopefully she'd changed her mind and gone to the doctor. A visit to the medical centre would explain why Shirley hadn't been able to contact her. You could wait hours in that place, even with an appointment. And Rita was not one of those rude people who would answer her mobile phone in the doctor's waiting room.

Shirley parked her little Mazda in Rita's driveway behind Rita's old bomb of a car. That put paid to the doctor theory. If the car was here, so was Rita. Shirley used her key to let herself in. 'Hello. Anybody home?'

When no answer came she went straight to the bedroom, her heart pounding. At their age anything was possible and she hoped she wouldn't find Rita unconscious – or worse. But thankfully the room was empty. She tried the bathroom, and then the rest of the house before heading outside to the garden. Rita was nowhere to be seen. Where on earth could she be? Shirley dug her mobile out of her bag and tried ringing her again but, just like the last four or five times, the call went straight to voicemail. The cats had followed her from the house into the backyard, both of them mewing pitifully. 'What's wrong with you two?'

She went back inside with the cats at her heel. Mittens ran to her food bowl and looked at Shirley pointedly. Surely Rita wouldn't have gone anywhere without feeding the cats? She treated her 'fur babies', as she called them, like royalty, always feeding them before taking care of her own needs. Nevertheless, Mittens was insistent. 'All right, all right, I'll feed you. I suppose a second breakfast won't kill you even if you have been fed.' She poured some kibble into their bowls and watched them both attack the food with gusto. It wasn't like Tux to overeat, so perhaps they hadn't been fed after all. And now that she thought about it, the house was in an even greater state of disarray than usual. It looked like Rita hadn't cleaned up for days. The sink was full of dishes and there were overflowing ashtrays on the coffee table. It wasn't unheard of for Rita to go to bed without doing the dishes, but she always cleaned the kitchen before she left the house. Rita's house wasn't always tidy, but it was usually clean. It really seemed like she'd gone somewhere in an awful hurry.

Shirley was at a loss as to what to do next. Maybe she could shoot by the medical centre on her way to the shops to see if Rita was there. But she'd have to be quick – Frank had already been home alone for twenty minutes and she hadn't even got to the shops yet.

She was just getting in the car when she noticed Janet Peterson, Rita's neighbour, hovering by the gate. She gave her a quick nod and tried to duck into the car without any further engagement. Janet was a talker and Shirley had no time for that this morning. She closed the car door but wasn't quick enough to escape Janet, who'd sprinted up the drive and was now tapping on the passenger-side window.

'Hello, Shirley, I don't want to keep you but I just had to come over and see how Rita is doing.'

'Rita isn't home, Janet.'

'No, well, I didn't expect her to be. Have you come to get her things for her? How is she this morning?'

'Sorry, I don't understand. I haven't seen Rita today.'

'I just assumed you'd come to get her things to take to the hospital.'

'Hospital?'

'Oh, goodness me, don't you know? Sorry, I thought someone would have called you. The ambulance came and took her away last night. About eleven o'clock, I think it was.'

Shirley's hand flew to her mouth. She *knew* there was more going on than Rita was letting on. She should have checked on her last night. 'Do you know why?'

Janet shook her head. 'Sorry. I thought you'd know.'

'She'd been having headaches,' Shirley said quietly. 'Sorry, Janet, you'll have to excuse me. I need to get to the hospital.'

Except that she couldn't go right to the hospital because Frank had been alone for almost half an hour, which was really pushing the boundaries of what was safe. If she didn't get home soon he'd start looking for his lunch and might even attempt to leave the house to find her. She'd have to go home and collect him first. She backed out of Rita's driveway like a madwoman and sped along Porter Avenue, taking the corner into Belle Vue Avenue far too quickly. When she heard the siren her heart sank. Being pulled over by the cops would just eat up more time. She looked in the rear-vision mirror and was momentarily relieved to find there was no police car following her. In fact, the siren's wail was getting louder. She realised the sound was coming from in front of her, not behind.

That's when she noticed the smoke; a thick cloud of grey up ahead.

Please, God, no.

She turned the corner into her street and was confronted by a chaotic scene. There were two fire trucks, an ambulance, and a police car was just pulling up – that must have been the siren she'd heard. There were people everywhere. Her neighbours were out on the street, all looking at the source of the smoke.

Her house was on fire.

She stopped the car in the middle of the street. Where was Frank? The deadlocked door and padlocked gate would have prevented him from escaping. She jumped out of the car, not bothering to close the door, and ran towards the house.

'Frank!' she screamed, her chest constricting with fear. 'Frank!'

Someone caught her arm. It was Anjali, the young woman from next door. 'Shirley, you can't go in there.'

'I have to find Frank. I left him home by himself. I was only gone for a few minutes. Do you know what happened? Where he is?'

Anjali shook her head. 'I don't really know.' She pointed to the woman who lived across the road. 'Senem called the fire brigade when she noticed smoke coming from the kitchen window. She said she tried to get into the house but the front door and the gate to the yard were both locked.'

Oh God, the kitchen. Frank must have tried to make himself something to eat. It seemed he was always hungry these days. More than once she'd caught him putting a tin of food into the microwave, and another time he'd tried to put the electric kettle on the stove to boil. Why, oh why, had she left him alone?

'Shirley, you don't look well. You need to sit down. Here, let me help you.'

Shirley shook off Anjali's hand and looked at the house she and Frank had built together, and raised their daughter in, as smoke billowed from the front windows. Despite the firefighters' efforts it was well alight. If Frank was inside that house he was lost to her.

Her chest squeezed even tighter and she thought that she might vomit.

'Shirley!'

Anjali's anguished cry was the last thing she heard before she collapsed onto the bitumen.

When she woke from her 'cardiac event', the very first thing the nurse told her was that her husband had suffered some smoke inhalation but was alive and well, and in a room just down the corridor. She said she'd arrange for Frank to come and visit as soon as possible.

It would be two more days before she received the news that Rita was gone; her life support had been turned off by her nieces while Shirley was unconscious.

Shirley had always known God would punish her for her unfaithfulness, and now her time had come. His vengeance was to take Rita and let her live.

Chapter 39

Friday

My dearest darling,

If you're reading this I am gone. Please don't waste time being sad. I'm grateful for the long and happy life I've had. I feel blessed to have loved and to have been loved by you. I know at times I pushed you to give me more than you were capable of, but I want you to know in my heart of hearts I always understood.

Your love has sustained me all these years and I leave with no regrets.

The house is yours to do with what you will. Please look after the cats.

You'll never be alone in this world, my love. If you need me, just close your eyes and think of our little cottage in Caloundra. I'll be there waiting for you when your time comes.

Forever and always yours,
R x

I've taken Rita's letter from my handbag and slipped it into my pocket. Even though I know the words by heart, I want to keep it close today. Having Rita's scrappy handwriting on my person makes her feel closer somehow, like she's part of this. In many ways she is. We certainly wouldn't be here without her.

We left Charlie and Brianna's place at six. Even with the change of car, I thought getting on the road early was our best chance of making it to our destination undetected. And now we're here. Well, almost.

Frank's face lights up as we pass the old Ford factory on our way into town. 'You can drop me here, thanks, love. This is where I work.'

'Oh, I know,' I say, 'but the plant's closed today.' I don't offer any further explanation. I've learned that sometimes simplicity is best.

'Hmm. Well, where are you taking me then?'

'We're going to the beach.'

Frank claps his hands together. 'Wacko! My favourite place.'

'I know, but listen, Frank, there's a place I want to take you first. I promise we'll spend the day at the beach, but there's something I need to do.'

'Righto, Boss. Whatever you say.'

We drive around the waterfront and as I take in the familiar sights of Cunningham Pier and Eastern Beach, I feel the coil of tension inside me unfurling.

'Not this beach,' Frank says, suddenly agitated. 'This one's no good. No surf.'

'Not this beach,' I agree. 'We'll go to Bancoora. We just need to make a couple of stops first.' I turn right onto Garden Street and follow it to Ormond Road, until I see the little flower shop. We park out the front and I ask Frank to come inside with me. I can't afford to lose him now. He's in his element in the florist, looking at all the pretty blooms. Ironic, really, when he spent so much of his gardening time digging up my flowerbeds to make room for his vegies.

I have the florist make me up two bouquets – one with bluebells and the other a mix of white peonies and sweet peas. When she's done, I cajole Frank back into the car and we head off again down Ormond Road. I turn left when we get to Humble Street and park the car outside the cemetery.

Frank gives me a confused look. 'What are we doing here?'

'I had a friend who died a little while ago. She was someone I loved very much. Unfortunately I never got to say goodbye to her.'

'I'm very sorry to hear that,' Frank says.

A lump forms in my throat. Rita's family had waited more than a week before burying her, in the hope that I'd be out of hospital by then, but my little bypass operation had kept me incapacitated for longer than I'd hoped. In the end, Fiona told Rita's niece they should just go ahead without me.

'Thank you. I wasn't able to go to her funeral to pay my respects, so I thought I'd visit her grave today and put some flowers there.'

'I can wait here, if you like? Give you some privacy.'

I shake my head. 'No, I'd be glad of the company.'

He nods, and fumbles with his seatbelt to release it. It's taken me some research, but I've found the exact location of Rita's grave and have the details written on a scrap of paper in my purse. It's a bit of a walk from where I've parked; in fact, it's on the other side of the cemetery completely, but after all the sitting we've done today I figure the exercise will do us both good. Frank isn't as fit as he used to be and I have to slow my pace significantly for him to keep up. Now that I'm here, I want to run to her, to lay prostrate on top of her bones, to feel her essence rise up out of the ground and embrace me.

Rita never believed in God, but she did believe in an afterlife. 'You can't watch as many people die as I have and not believe that there's something more than this,' she once said. 'I believe memories are proof of life after death. You know how sometimes a memory of someone you loved just pops into your head for no apparent reason? That's our loved ones visiting us, telling us they're okay. I believe those we love never truly leave us, and they come to us when we need them most.'

I need her today and I hope she'll come through for me.

It takes us a good ten minutes to reach Rita's grave, and when we get to the spot I am felled by fresh grief. It's not an actual grave, but a bronze memorial plaque. Rita has been cremated. There's no body, no bones, no essence – nothing. She is gone. On my knees in front of her plaque I weep. I'm not sure how long this goes on for, but eventually Frank puts a hand on my left shoulder.

'I'm so sorry,' he says. 'You must have loved her very much.'

I reach across with my right hand and squeeze his fingers. 'Yes, I did.' And in that moment I hear Rita's voice, as clear as a bell, saying, 'You told him at last. Well, better late than never, I guess.' I sob and laugh at the same time.

I sit there a moment longer before placing the bouquet of peonies and sweet peas next to the plaque. 'I'm lost without you, Rita,' I whisper. 'You sacrificed so much for me. I always thought there'd be time to make that up to you. I'm so sorry . . .' There's much more I want to say, but maybe now is not the time. Not with Frank looking over my shoulder. 'Goodbye, my love. I'll be back.' I blow her a kiss and then say a quick prayer, feeling her roll her eyes as I cross myself. In my peripheral vision I see Frank echoing my action.

By the time I stand up I am composed. I hand Frank the bunch of bluebells and begin the walk back to the other side of the cemetery. 'You know, my friend was a very smart woman.'

'Is that so?'

'Yes. She was smart and she was kind, which is probably the best thing you can say about a person, don't you think?'

He nods his agreement.

'She was a nurse for many years and she helped countless people throughout her life. As well as helping others in her role as a nurse, she advocated for women in the healthcare system and helped to bring about lots of changes, like making sure that mothers got to keep their babies in the same room with them in hospital.' I take a breath and then launch into what I really want to say. 'One of the most significant things she lobbied for was for the right of mothers to say a proper goodbye to their stillborn babies. It used to be that when a baby died at birth it was whisked away from its family, but that doesn't happen anymore.'

Frank stops walking for a minute and shakes his head. 'It's a bloody terrible thing to lose a child like that. We – my wife and I – lost a baby. A little boy. You know, you just don't get over a thing like that. Nearly killed my Shirl. Oh, in the end she got on with life, you know . . . she learned to live with it, I guess, but it damned near broke her.' His shoulders sag a little. 'Me too, to be honest. Not that anyone would ever have known. I had to be strong for my girls, but at night I thought about that little boy. I wondered where he was. Whether God had seen fit to admit him to heaven, on account of the fact that we never got to baptise him.' His voice cracks as he speaks, and I step closer to him and take his hand in mine.

'Frank, my friend Rita showed me something very special before she died. I wanted to show it to you right away, but I got sick and then . . . well, I haven't had the chance until now. There's a special place right here in this cemetery that I'd like to take you to, if you'll allow me?'

I'm not sure if he's guessed at my meaning but he nods, and then we walk in silence to a section of the cemetery close to where I'd parked the car. I stop at a park bench bookended by a pair of marble bunny rabbits. 'Here we are,' I say.

'What is this?'

'It's the Children's Memorial Section. This is where they buried the babies, Frank.'

His face is ashen as I lead him to the same spot Rita had brought me just a week before she died. 'I had this made for you,' she'd said. 'Fiona helped me organise it. You can change the plaque to say whatever you want; I just didn't want to bring you to an unmarked grave.'

Now I read the perfect inscription to Frank.

Andrew Francis Sullivan
Dearly beloved son of Francis and Shirley
Brother of Fiona
Born sleeping

Frank's eyes fill with tears. 'My son,' he says simply, and I nod.

We're both silent for a while and then he turns to me and says. 'Thank you. You don't know what this means to me.'

'Actually, I think I do.'

After our visit to the cemetery I expect Frank's mood to be sombre at best. I'd prepared myself for the possibility that he may even be distressed. But he seems fine. In fact, when I remind him we are heading to the beach his mood is positively jovial. I consider making a stop at the supermarket in Newcomb to pick up some picnic supplies but decide I don't want to waste the time. Instead we head to the drive-through at Hungry Jacks and order up big. Frank digs into the bag and stuffs fries in his mouth as we zip along Barwon Heads Road. 'Want some?' he asks.

I shake my head. 'I can't eat and drive.'

Laughing, he starts feeding me chips one at a time. I wish Fiona could see him right now. How happy and carefree he is.

I know she loves her dad and only wants the best for him. I think if she could see him this minute she'd realise the best place for Frank is with me.

This thought gives me an idea. I know how to make her see. We'll be at the beach in a few minutes and I can enact my plan as soon as we're there.

As we drive up Breamlea Road a wide grin settles on Frank's face. 'Oh, it's so good to be here,' he says. 'I can't wait to get in the water.'

I baulk at this for a moment. I hadn't thought about him swimming. In fact I haven't even packed any bathers for him. I can't believe my own stupidity. Of course he will go in the water. When has Frank ever visited this beach and stayed on the shore? And it's a beautiful, sunny November day. There's not a cloud in the sky. The water will be cold, no doubt, but it won't take long for Frank to warm up once he's out. So what if he hasn't got bathers? He's an old man. No one's going to care about him swimming in his briefs. I smile at him. 'Nice day for a swim.'

We park near the surf club in the near-empty car park.

'Frank, you can go in the water soon, I promise, but you really should let your lunch go down properly first. Let's sit on the beach for a bit, eh?'

Frank agrees to this more easily than I expect. 'Yeah, okay. I don't mind sitting on the beach. Especially this one. I met my wife here, you know.'

'Really?' I say. 'How lovely.'

His face clouds over for a moment. 'Does Shirl know I'm here?'

'I promise you she does.'

He looks relieved. 'She doesn't really care for the beach. Well, not the way I do. Our little girl, though, she's a water baby. Chip off the old block, so to speak.'

The beach is almost deserted, save for a young woman walking a large boxer and a couple of surfers way out the back.

We find a spot on the sand and spread out the beach towels Brianna insisted we borrow once I told her about my plans for today. I plonk myself down and pat the space beside me. 'Sit with me for a minute.'

Frank obliges me. He pulls off his shoes and socks and rolls up his trouser legs. I've already discarded my sandals. I dig in my handbag and grab a tube of sunblock, and offer it to Frank. 'Pah,' he says. 'I'm not putting that muck on. A little sun never hurt anyone.'

I laugh and squelch a big blob into the palm of my hand. 'Suit yourself.' Once I've covered myself in sunscreen I grab my phone. 'Come a bit closer, Frank. I want to take a photo of us.'

He scoots over next to me and puts his arm around my shoulders. 'Don't show my wife this, she might get jealous,' he jokes.

I turn on my phone's camera function and press the button to flip the lens the way Ollie taught me. It takes me a few goes to get us both in the 'selfie' and by the time I manage it both Frank and I are roaring with laughter. It's a great snap. I find Fiona's number in my contacts, take a deep breath and then send the photo to her before I can change my mind.

It takes less than a minute for the phone to ring. 'Hello, Fiona.'

'Mum, for Christ's sake, where are you?'

'Language, Fi,' I say automatically.

'Jesus. Mum, is Dad okay? Do you have any idea how worried I've been?'

'Fiona, please calm down. As you can see from the photo, both your father and I are perfectly fine. You can speak to your father in a moment if you like.'

'I would like,' she snaps. 'I honestly can't believe you seriously thought that abducting Dad was a reasonable thing to do. What on earth were you trying to prove?'

'I didn't abduct your father, he came willingly. I'm his wife. I have every right to take him on a holiday if I wish.'

She snorts. 'Actually, I think you'll find you don't have that right. I have medical guardianship of Dad, and I get to choose how he's cared for.'

I sigh. 'You were given guardianship when I was sick, but I'm well now and perfectly capable of caring for my husband.' I pause. I was going to tell her that if she won't allow me to care for Frank that I'll take her to court, but Frank's sitting beside me and I don't want anything to spoil this day for him. 'Let's not do this right now. Your father and I are at Bancoora and we're having a lovely time. I only wanted to let you know that we are safe and well, and you are not to worry.'

'Put Dad on the phone right now.'

'Just a moment.' I turn to Frank. 'Your daughter Fiona is on the phone. Would you like to speak to her?'

Immediately his face takes on that gooey expression he reserves especially for her. 'Yes, of course.' He takes the phone from me. 'Hello, Fi, love. How's university?' He pauses for her answer and then speaks again. 'Me? Oh, I'm good as gold. I'm at the beach with this lovely lady who gave me a lift here.' He narrows his eyes and looks at me carefully. 'She's a bit of a bossy boots, but I like her a lot.' He chortles. 'You better not tell your mother that. She might get jealous.'

I'm imagining the expression on Fiona's face, and I wish that we were FaceTiming instead of talking.

'Yep, all right then, love. I'll see you then.' He hands the phone back to me.

'Are you still there, Fi?'

'Yes, of course I am. Where are you staying? I'm getting on the next plane to Avalon.'

'All right, my darling. It will be lovely to see you. We'll be at Rita's house.'

'Oh, Mum, have you lost your mind too? Aunty Rita is dead.'

It warms my heart to hear her say Aunty Rita with affection in her voice. Rita loved her as if she were her own. I'm glad Fiona still feels fondly towards her. 'I know that, love.'

'Well, you can't just go and stay in her house. It belongs to someone else now, Mum.'

'She left it to me, Fiona.'

'To you? Why on earth . . .?' She trails off.

'Because she loved me.' This is the truth, plain and simple. How Fiona chooses to interpret it is up to her.

'Well,' she says eventually, 'I didn't expect that. I suppose you are planning on staying there permanently?'

'Yes, that's my intention.'

'What about Dad?'

'He's staying with me.'

'Mum, please be sensible. You can't look after him. You're not well enough.'

'I've managed all right these past few days.'

'Even so, I won't allow it. I have the legal right to insist he come back here.'

'I don't want to fight you, Fiona, but I will if you force me to. He's my husband and I have a right to a say in his care.'

'What I don't understand is why you would want to go and live back there on your own. Dad's not who he used to be, Aunty Rita is gone and all your family is up here. Do you really detest me so much that you'd rather live on your own?'

Her words shock me. 'Detest you? What on earth would give you that idea? I love you, Fiona. I don't agree with this ridiculous insistence on your father being in a home, but that doesn't mean I don't love you.'

'You can't bear to be with me, that's obvious. When I was a kid you smothered me with love, but as an adult your disappointment in me is clear.'

‘Fiona, that’s simply not true,’ I say, but she’s on a roll now and won’t listen.

‘I don’t blame you. I’m disappointed in myself. Being a mother isn’t easy. I get that now. I know I’ve been hard on you at times and pushed you away, but I love you, Mum, and I want us to be closer than we are. Dad’s illness has taught me how short life truly is. I don’t want us to spend the rest of your life fighting.’

‘I don’t want that either.’

‘I need you more than ever now, Mum. I don’t know what I’m doing. My marriage is a shambles and I’m a terrible mother.’

‘Fi, that’s ridiculous. You have raised three beautiful girls.’

‘Have I? Frances is off swanning around the world trying to “find herself”. She failed last semester at uni and I think she’s into party drugs. I’m terrified that the next call I get will be from the police or the Department of Foreign Affairs to say she’s in jail . . . or dead.’

‘Oh, Fi,’ I say, but she’s nowhere near finished.

‘I’m pretty sure Eloise hates me. And she has no friends. She spends her whole life holed up in her bedroom staring at a screen.’

I want to interrupt to tell her that Lou has many friends, in fact, but she’s sobbing now and still hasn’t finished.

‘As for Lila, well, I have no idea how I’ve screwed her up yet, but I’m sure I will have done something wrong.’

‘Sweetheart, you have raised three lovely daughters. They might have the odd problem or two, but who hasn’t? I’m sure none of this is as bad as you think.’

‘Look, Mum, I know this might come as a surprise to you, but I need you. I know you think that this is all about Dad, but the reason I wanted him in the home up here was so I could be closer to you.’

This statement is hard to digest. Fiona has always been 'Daddy's girl'. I'm ashamed to say that factoring this news into the equation is shocking and thrilling to me in equal parts. 'Oh, darling, why didn't you just tell me that?'

There's silence for a moment and then she responds like a sulky teenager. 'I don't know. I didn't want you to think I was a failure.'

'Fi, I would never think that. You're my daughter and I love you. I *want* you to ask for my help. You can always talk to me. Anytime. All you have to do is to pick up the phone.'

She sniffs. 'I guess I wanted you there for my girls, too. I can relax a bit more with you in the house. God, Mum, don't make me humiliate myself more than I already have. You were right, okay? Being a mother – being a woman – isn't easy. I got caught up trying to prove that I was different to you. That I could have a stellar career and be the perfect mother as well. Turns out I was wrong.'

I'm totally bewildered by this turn of events. 'Oh, Fi,' I say, 'you're not a failure, you're human. And I've loved spending time with you and the girls, but I simply can't let your father spend another minute in a nursing home. You should see him, love. He's so happy here.'

She sighs. 'Maybe we can work something out.'

Frank tugs at my hand. 'Sweetheart, I have to go. I'm glad we talked. We can sort all this out when you get here.'

She agrees and says her goodbyes. I would love to keep the conversation going. It feels like we are finally making a start on closing the gap between us. There are so many things I want to tell her. But there'll be plenty of time for talking later. Right now Frank needs my attention. He's started to take off his clothes.

'Ready to go in the water?'

'I am,' he says. 'Are you coming?'

I shake my head. 'No, I can't swim.'

'Huh, you and my wife would make a good pair. She can't swim either. In fact, I saved her life right here on this very beach.'

'Is that a fact?'

Frank undoes his trousers and lets them drop to the ground. 'It is indeed.' He takes off his shirt and then his singlet. Finally he pulls off his underpants. I open my mouth to protest and then close it again. There's no one here to complain. The girl with the dog is a distant figure now and the surfers are too far out to notice. I'll stand at the water's edge with his towel so that if anyone else appears I can cover him as soon as he emerges.

He strides towards the shore breakers, his shoulders back and his gait steady. He seems a different man to the one who shuffled around the cemetery just an hour ago. I follow him with the towel and stand in the shallows as he steps out into the chilly water. He doesn't flinch or hesitate for a moment and he doesn't look back. When the water is at waist height he dives in, ducking under a breaking wave. The wind carries his laughter back to me and I smile.

He's swimming now, disappearing under the waves as they break over him, going further and further out to sea. I realise with a start that he's not turning back. He's getting harder for me to see. 'Frank,' I call, but I'm too far away for him to hear me. I wade out just a little further. The hems of my shorts are soaked and the end of the towel dips into the water. I cup one hand to my mouth and yell as loud as I can, 'Frank!' but it's useless. Panicked, I turn around and look to the shore, hoping to see a surfer or someone – anyone – who can help me, but the beach is empty.

I don't see the wave coming.

I tumble face first into the water and the towel tangles itself around me. I struggle to stand but my feet can't find the sandy bottom. I feel myself being dragged out and for a moment

I fight it, but I realise the sea will deliver me to Frank. I relax and let myself be taken.

There is one perfect moment of peace before I hear Rita and Frank's voices in chorus. 'Stand up, Shirley,' they say.

And I do.

Author's note

The Secret Life of Shirley Sullivan is a combination of two separate sources of inspiration.

Many years ago I read a newspaper article about an elderly couple who had escaped from their nursing home and gone on the run from the law. At one point police captured them but they managed to escape and continue their journey. This plucky pair really captured my imagination. I wondered how they had orchestrated their escape and, more importantly, where they were headed. For years their story lingered in the back of my mind, waiting to become fully formed. Then, last year, I came across a box of my parents' love letters. There were over sixty of them and there was roughly an equal number written by each of my parents. The letters were written in the early 1960s when my mum and dad lived hundreds of kilometres apart. They document their romance from the first meeting until their engagement. I was entranced by the historical details in these letters, the language and the everyday minutiae of life in the 1960s. I suddenly realised that I could use the letters as inspiration for the backstory of my elderly couple.

Once I had my characters and setting I knew I needed a divisive secret. From there the novel pretty much wrote itself.

Although this is a work of fiction, I used many details from my parents' (and my own) life in the historical section. The house that Frank and Shirley live in is based on my parents' home, some details of Frank's childhood come from my dad's experience, and the mill where Shirley works is where my mother and grandfather were employed.

I loved researching the present-day storyline. I did the exact road trip Frank and Shirley embark on, albeit in a Jeep rather than a Kombi. Imagine my excitement when, stopped outside a pub in Narooma, I saw a Kombi identical to the one described in the book!

This truly is the book of my heart. I hope readers will enjoy reading it as much as I enjoyed writing it.

Book club discussion notes

1. *'Elderly. Is that how the world sees me? A helpless little old lady? If only they knew. I allow myself a small smirk.'*
   Shirley uses her 'little old lady' persona to her advantage. She understands that people will underestimate her abilities due to her age, and she plays on this. Do you think we as a society stereotype people as they age? If so, what are the consequences of this?

2. Despite her age, Shirley is depicted as a woman who learns quickly and copes well with modern technology. Do you think this is realistic? Do you know anyone like Shirley?

3. Even though Shirley acknowledges that Sunset Lodge is a good aged care facility, she doesn't think it is suitable for Frank. Is she right to think this? Do you think she made the correct choice when she decided to remove him?

4. Shirley and her daughter have a fractious relationship. Why do you think Fiona is so hostile towards her mother?

5. Why do you think Fiona chose to place her father in an aged care facility? Do you have any sympathy for her decision?

6. Shirley takes Frank on the road trip he's always dreamed of. If you had the opportunity to take off in a Kombi, where would you go?

7. Fiona worries about the amount of time Lou spends online and sees her as a social misfit, whereas Shirley sees another side of her granddaughter. When Lou manages to galvanise her online community, the Sherbies, to provide practical aid to her runaway grandparents, Shirley is proud of Lou's popularity and success within the group. Do you think online communities can provide real social benefits? Have you ever had an online association that evolved into a real-world friendship?

8. When Shirley meets Rita, her world opens up. Her friendship with Rita and their subsequent relationship allows Shirley to become her authentic self. Given this, why does Shirley stay with Frank, especially once Fiona leaves home? Do you think she made the right decision?

9. Rita is completely comfortable in her own skin and makes no apology for her sexuality, but she is forced to keep her relationship with Shirley a secret. Shirley's inability to fully commit to Rita eventually causes friction between them. Why do you think Rita chooses to stay with Shirley in spite of this?

10. What do you think happens after the end of the novel?

Acknowledgements

Heartfelt thanks to the entire team at Penguin Random House Australia. I'm thrilled that *Shirley* has found a home with you. Special thanks to Beverley Cousins for her belief in the manuscript and insightful editing, and for being so wonderful to work with. Thanks also to Kathryn Knight for taking the manuscript and polishing it to a level I could never have achieved on my own.

Thanks to my agent, the wonderful Haylee Nash, for her help with this project, and also to Natasha Solomun from The Rights Hive for her support.

I am fortunate to belong to a wonderful community of writers: a group of generous and talented individuals, who are always happy to celebrate and commiserate with me on the ups and downs of this writing life. Special mention to my Writer's Camp crew: Amanda Knight, Beck Nicholas, Emily Madden and Rachael Johns. Also, to Jane Cockram, Kirsty Manning, Kylie Ladd, Vanessa Carnevale and all the Bellota gang – long may we share good food, fine wine and raucous laughter! Thanks also to my local writing friends, Nicki Edwards, Ellie O'Neill,

Alli Sinclair, Fiona Lowe and Jennifer Kloester for coffee catch-ups, dinners, drinks and everything in between.

Huge thanks to Sally Hepworth, Kelly Rimmer and Tess Woods, for reading early drafts and for being my people. Also, to Delwyn Jenkins for being such an important part of my life – writing and otherwise.

So many people helped with my research for this book. Thanks to my aunts, Sandra and Pat, for sharing their memories with me, and to Bev Hope for the photos. Thanks also to Andria Richardson, Megan MacInnes and Kerryn Merrett for their information about police and law enforcement. I'm also indebted to Ashleigh Barnes and Cassie Silva for their insights into aged care.

Special thanks to Nina Campbell for her unending support, and also for sharing her local knowledge of Queanbeyan, Mossy Point and beyond. (And for cake!)

Lots of love to my family: David, Charlie, Will and Alex. Thanks for riding the roller-coaster with me.

Most importantly, sincere thanks to everyone who reads this book. I hope you love it.

Lisa Ireland lives with her family in a seaside town on Victoria's Bellarine Peninsula.

After working for many years as a teacher (and a brief stint as a professional organiser – before Marie Kondo made it cool) she is now a full-time writer.

When she's not writing, Lisa can be found running (okay, shuffling), drinking coffee at her favourite cafes or perusing the shelves of her local bookstore.

She loves eating but not cooking, is an Olympic-class procrastinator and (most importantly) minion to a rather large dog.

The Secret Life of Shirley Sullivan is Lisa's sixth novel.